SILENT LUCIDITY

THE INFINITE CITY #1

TIFFANY ROBERTS

SILENT LUCIDITY

He's an alien assassin who has never known a female's touch—until hers.

Abella hasn't allowed four years of slavery to break her spirit, but after numerous failed escape attempts, the chances of making it home to her family seem bleak. That is until she shares a passionate, forbidden dance with a silent stranger. His piercing silvery eyes haunt her with a taste of hope.

Intense, mysterious, and deadly, Tenthil may be the key to Abella's freedom. But as she finds herself increasingly drawn to him, she realizes the truth—Tenthil has no intention of taking her home.

Check author's website for content warnings.

To our readers—we love you.

NOTHIN TO
SEE HERE
TENTHIL
SILENT LUCIDITY

ONE

Arthos, the Infinite City
   Terran Year 2105

EVEN AMIDST THE glow of countless colorful signs, illuminated storefronts, and holographically projected advertisements along the street, Twisted Nethers stood apart. There was something more vibrant about its less-than-subtle signage, something warmer in the pulsing lights along the building's edges, something more imposing about the spotlights on its roof that cut through the gloom to illuminate the metal framework and plating high overhead.

The massive, ever-changing holographic genitalia out front undoubtedly helped it stand out.

Despite the blatant display, the denizens of the Undercity considered Twisted Nethers an exclusive club. It was a place where anyone with enough credits could satisfy their exotic tastes, whether for drinks, drugs, or writhing, naked bodies.

For Tenthil, it was just another stop on a long, blood-soaked path.

He strode toward the club's entrance, weaving through the crowd of diverse beings awaiting admittance. Their features—as varied and colorful as the Undercity signs—blurred together in the shadows cast by the neon lights. He walked as though he belonged here, as though he'd frequented the place for years, as though everyone else should've been honored by his presence.

Many of the aliens waiting in line glanced at Tenthil as he passed. Facial appendages quivered, brows fell low, and mouths opened to voice protest, but the onlookers kept their opinions to themselves when their eyes dipped to the pin on his jacket—a stylized red sun with the white silhouette of an ancient axe at its center.

That pin marked him as part of a street gang, called the Ergoths, that had claimed this sector as their territory years ago. Drok, the owner of Twisted Nethers and Tenthil's current target, had close ties to the gang, though the true nature of his relationship with them was unknown.

The doorman, a burly vorgal with scars crisscrossing the drab green skin of his face, glanced at the pin as Tenthil approached. His mouth, from which jutted a pair of upward-pointing tusks, remained an expressionless flat line as he stepped aside and waved Tenthil in.

The people waiting to enter the club voiced no objections. Though some might've been standing out there for hours, they knew better than to question an Ergoth in this part of the city.

Tenthil walked through the door and entered the dark corridor beyond. His eyes rapidly adjusted to the gloom. The black strips of rounded glass to either side were likely part of a body scanning system, and the pair of guards in front of the door at the end of the hallway held auto-blaster rifles that could fill the air with enough heated plasma bolts to melt the surrounding walls in seconds. There was no cover here were they to open fire.

Just a few more obstacles for Tenthil to overcome when he finally made his move.

He drew in a deep breath as he stepped forward and dissipated his amplified bioelectrical field to prevent it from interfering with the scanners and drawing suspicion from security. Maintaining the disruption field had become second nature over the years, and he felt strange without it in place.

Pulsing bass rumbled through the walls and floors, its vibrations running up through Tenthil's boots and into his bones.

As he came within a few paces of the door, the guard to his right—a pale-scaled groalthuun with four bone nubs sweeping back from the top of his head and glowing green tattoos on his face—held up a hand. Tenthil halted. A faint light shone behind the groalthuun's tinted goggles—likely a readout from the scanners on the walls.

The groalthuun twisted and pressed an unseen button on the wall. A small drawer slid out beneath his hand.

"Put your piece inside," said the groalthuun.

His companion, a craggy-faced bokkan with gray, rock-like skin, remained unmoving, but Tenthil felt the bokkan's eyes—also hidden by goggles—fixed on him. Both guards wore their finely tailored coats open at the collar to display a bit of the combat armor beneath.

"Come on." The groalthuun waved his hand. "Boss appreciates all the business you Ergoths bring in, but the rules ain't changing. No one goes in packing but pre-approved private security."

Moving with deliberate care, Tenthil unfastened his jacket and raised his left arm, revealing the flechette pistol holstered under his armpit. Such weapons were devastating at close range, but they were messy—as the Ergoth Tenthil had taken the pistol and pin from a few hours before might've attested, were the pulverized remains of his head not splattered across an alley wall. It would have been preferable to take the pin through less lethal means, but the Master was unwavering when it came to the tenets of the Order.

No witnesses.

The Ergoth leadership would assume it had been a hit from a rival gang. Many of the criminals in the Undercity and the Bowels carried weapons with flechette ammunition because they were intimidating—few species could survive a blast from one. Even the highest quality combat armor struggled to stop the superheated tristeel darts from close range.

Keeping his movements slow, Tenthil removed the pistol from its holster and laid it in the open drawer.

The groalthuun spread his lips, revealing his wide, flat teeth in what he must've considered a smile. Tenthil's people would've called any creature with such teeth *prey.*

The drawer slid shut, vanishing into the wall without any trace of a gap or a seam.

For most individuals, entering a potentially hostile space while unarmed was a frightening prospect, but Tenthil was unconcerned. He didn't need a weapon to kill; thanks to the Master's training, he was the weapon.

He wasn't here to cause trouble, anyway—at least not tonight. This was a reconnaissance mission. Once he was familiar with the club's layout and Drok's movements within it, Tenthil would formulate and execute a plan of attack.

"Pick it up on the way out," said the bokkan in a deep, rough voice. "It'll be tied to your body scan." His expression hadn't changed, but his stance shifted to subtly direct the barrel of his auto-blaster toward Tenthil.

The guards shifted closer to the walls, revealing a rugged blast door behind them. Whether the rest of Twisted Nethers' security held up to this standard, Drok wanted his patrons to believe they were safe. It wasn't surprising given the wealth of some of the regulars—several of the Undercity's most prominent business people, legitimate and illicit alike, frequented this establishment.

Perhaps this contract would provide Tenthil a challenge. Perhaps it would provide some meaning, however shallow, to his work, which for too long had merely been a matter of following orders. Of being wielded as the Master's blade. Despite spending most of his time outside the temple fulfilling contracts, Tenthil felt caged by his obligations—and that would eventually drive him to madness.

The groalthuun pressed another unseen button, and the blast door rumbled open.

Music swept over Tenthil, loud enough to hurt his ears. Strobing lights and slithering neon text crawls mingled with holographic projections to make it difficult for his eyes to focus. The smells of alcohol, food, and drugs from dozens of worlds, of hundreds of bodies dancing, and of sex, crashed into his nostrils. The air pulsed with vibrations from the music and dancers.

Despite his discomfort, he didn't hesitate to cross the threshold. Once the door had closed behind him, he restored his bioelectric field, finding a hint of comfort in the brief tingling that spread across the surface of his skin.

The interior of Twisted Nethers was larger than he'd anticipated. The place was tiered like a stadium, with two higher levels ringing the main floor. Tenthil stood on the middle level. Several stages along the levels boasted beings of diverse species dancing in varying states of undress. Each stage had its own audience space with tables and chairs, no two of which were quite alike in either furnishings or arrangement.

Straight ahead, a wide set of steps led to the ground level, from which the music originated. It was dominated by a crowded dance floor, but also possessed a wide stage, at least thirty tables, and a huge bar running nearly half the circumference of the space with more than a dozen people behind it, furiously mixing and serving drinks. Projected lights and images rained down from overhead, filling the air with motion and color—naked males and females amidst abstract shapes, all moving, flashing, and changing above the writhing dancers.

Tenthil removed the Ergoth pin from his jacket as he scanned his surroundings. More of Drok's security team were posted throughout the club, but the only ones openly carrying weapons were those stationed at the staircases leading to the upper tier.

He slipped the pin into his jacket pocket and walked around the middle level. He kept his eyes on the dancers as he moved but focused his attention on his peripheral vision to drink in the details of the club's layout and security. Though the music from below was deafening when he was near any of the stairs leading down, it faded completely in the vicinity of the small stages, leaving him to travel through pockets of often drastically different music. There were undoubtedly sound-dampening fields in place to prevent the audio of simultaneous shows from overlapping.

Several corridors and doors branched off the lower and middle levels. Some were marked as lavatories, while the rest declared *STAFF ONLY* in at least a dozen languages beneath bold letters in universal speech.

The upper level extended over the middle far enough that Tenthil could see into it only from the opposite side of the ring. The few beings visible there were clad in rich attire, seated at tables that doubled as dancing platforms. A naked volturian female writhed atop one of the tables, surrounded by seated volturian males who were close enough to her that she must've felt their breath on her bare skin.

Tenthil rounded the tier to stop beneath the volturians. He leaned his arms on the railing, turned his face toward the lower level, and listened.

Countless sounds assaulted him in a chaotic jumble—the music from the nearest stage was the loudest of them, but the din of countless conversations and the thumping bass from the dance floor refused to be overpowered. He moved his head, and the qualities of the sound changed as his ears entered the dead space on the edge of the sound dampening field. It was there that he discovered what he'd sought—the lilting, flowing words of the volturians' native tongue drifting down from above.

Even without his translator implant, he would've understood their complex language; it was one of several the Master had forced him to learn in his youth. The volturian males were arguing over who would have a turn with the female first.

Despite the dampeners, sound traveled well enough from the VIP level for Tenthil to overhear nearby conversations. That could prove valuable; the Master always appreciated his acolytes bringing new secrets when they returned to the temple from their work around the city.

After another visual sweep of the upper level, Tenthil moved on to the three mid-level doors marked as lavatories. All three led into long, high-ceilinged corridors that differed only in the signs on the lavatory doors found along them. Each corridor had a heavy-duty hatch positioned near the center of its ceiling. He paused in the third corridor to study the hatch with more care.

This hatch, like those prior, appeared to be secured with a manual wheel crank. Such mechanisms were common in the Undercity and the Bowels below, but not in establishments like this, where security and modernity were presented as paramount.

The hatches either lacked latches on their other sides or had been fused shut. Possibly both.

Tenthil stepped aside to make space for a passing group of Ergoths. He was glad he'd removed the pin. If he'd been caught posing as a member of their gang, violence would've been unavoidable, and being thrown out of the club for injuring some thugs would only hinder his ability to complete this contract.

Once the Ergoths had entered a lavatory, Tenthil shifted his attention to the walls below the hatch. For the first five meters, they were smooth and wide-set, broken only by random pulses of neon that moved like radiant serpents racing through the dark of the Void. Though invisible to the naked eye when not illuminated, Tenthil recognized the lights for what they were—infinitesimal imperfections of which he could take advantage. Beyond the smooth sections, dozens of exposed pipes and conduits would make the rest of the climb effortless.

Best to check the hatches before I leave tonight, should an opportunity arise.

Leaving one of them unlatched would provide an easy entrance for his next visit, when he'd be a bit less inclined to submit to the weapon-check at the front entrance.

He exited the corridor and returned to the railing overlooking the lower floor, fixing his gaze on the dancers below. This time, he kept his attention on the uppermost edge of his vision. Drok, if present, was most likely behind one of the *STAFF ONLY* doors or up on the third floor.

Tenthil had come to accept the simple truth of his work long ago—no amount of training, planning, or skill could completely cancel out the effects of chance. Even the Void, which touched everything according to the Master, could not overcome the universe's inherent randomness.

Chance was certainly at play when Tenthil lifted his head just as a huge, heavily muscled tralix emerged from the guarded VIP staircase directly across from him. The left prong of the tralix's forehead crest was broken off, and his mottled teal and violet skin was covered with old scars, including a prominent one on his cheek.

He was Tenthil's target. He was Drok.

Drok turned to face the small entourage that had arrived. Four well-dressed, broad-shouldered vorgals flanked a slender, long-necked ertraxxan clad in rich attire. Offering a wide, tusk-filled smile, Drok clasped hands with the ertraxxan. Though the tralix was easily three times the mass of his guest, the ertraxxan maintained a haughty air.

But Tenthil paid little mind to their meeting.

His attention had been caught by the sixth member of the ertraxxan's group—a pale-skinned female with black hair that lightened to blue toward its tips.

He knew her species only because the Master insisted the Order's acolytes study every alien race known to inhabit Arthos, focusing on anatomy to ensure efficient kills. Only the most powerful and influential species—the six races which comprised the Consortium, the city's rulers—had been omitted from those studies.

This female was a terran, a race that only recently begun official migration to Arthos. She was the first of her kind Tenthil had seen outside of holograms.

And she was the most beautiful creature he'd ever seen.

She was tall and slender, wearing clothing that revealed enticing patches of her pale skin, and her hair shimmered in the ever-changing light.

Stepping aside, Drok waved the ertraxxan and his

entourage toward the stairs. The ertraxxan, wearing a displeased frown, lifted his chin and led his people up. Tenthil held his gaze on the terran until she was out of sight; she moved with a subtle swaying of her hips and an unspoken grace in her lithe limbs.

Drok paused to speak with the guards on either side of the steps before following his guests upstairs.

Forcing himself to remain in place, Tenthil looked up at the top tier. The booths along the edge were but a hint of what was hidden above. Private dance chambers and secret meeting rooms were both the most probable and tamest of the possibilities—too tame, perhaps, for a place like Twisted Nethers.

The wealthy of the Infinite City sometimes indulged in dark forms of entertainment.

Chance fell in Tenthil's favor again when the ertraxxan entered the booth to the right of the stairs with the terran and two of his vorgal guards in tow.

Drok joined them soon after, settling onto a seat across from the ertraxxan, who directed the terran onto the table with a flick of his wrist. Drok's gaze locked on the female as she climbed up and began a slow, sensual dance, swaying and undulating her hips, causing her green skirt to part and expose her long legs.

Warmth blossomed in the center of Tenthil's chest and spread outward; the female's hypnotic motions stirred something unfamiliar in his blood, something deep and powerful. A dull, unfamiliar ache coiled low in his belly.

Tenthil glanced down to find himself clasping the railing with knuckles white and claws extended. When he finally eased his grip and lifted his hands, they trembled. Unease sank in his gut like a leaden weight. What was wrong with him? He'd never been so distracted by anyone, by anything.

Rogue thoughts flitted through his mind. How would the

female's skin feel beneath his fingertips? What did she smell like, what did she sound like? Venom flooded the glands above the roof of his mouth, a few drops leaking from his fangs and onto his tongue. Oddly, it lacked its usual bitterness—this was sweet, with a hint of spice.

I have a job to do, he thought. *The Void has accepted Drok's name, and it must also receive his life.*

He barely suppressed a frustrated growl. Shoving away from the railing, he walked around the central level, forcing nonchalance into his steps, forcing himself to peruse the various stage shows as he passed. None of the dancers, whether male or female, clothed or nude, incited the reaction his brief glimpses of the terran had.

Realization struck him—he was no longer in control of himself.

Tenthil should have left the club at that moment. He told himself he remained because of duty, because of his contract, because of his resentment for the Master, but none of that was true.

He remained because he wanted another look at the terran.

Clenching his jaw, he stopped beneath Drok's booth, leaned back against the railing, and watched the dancers on the nearby stage. The guards beside the staircase Drok had used loomed at the edge of Tenthil's vision. Though their eyes were obscured by dark goggles, Tenthil knew they were scanning the crowd for potential threats.

Tenthil relaxed his jaw and tipped back a little farther, pausing when the music from the nearby stage faded and he heard the deep, gravelly voice of a tralix from overhead.

"—can't wait to push it. Think we'll make a killing," said Drok in universal speech.

"Of course we will," the ertraxxan replied in a high, reedy voice. He also spoke universal speech, pronouncing each word with cold precision. "I provide only the highest quality goods."

"I'd almost think you take pride in all this, Cullion."

"I *do*," Cullion said, "and it would comfort me if those with whom I do business show some pride of their own. A bit of poise would do you well, Drok."

"We're making money. What else really matters?"

"Status. Respect. Reputation."

"I got all that. And fear, too—that's more important. People around here know not to mess with me."

"Few appreciate a braggart, Drok. I am not amongst them."

"*This* braggart keeps the gangs in line and the money flowing, all while keeping the heat off you. Need to keep up the illusion that you're legitimate."

Cullion made a frustrated sound—a sort of clicking growl. "I *am* a legit—"

Drok cut off the ertraxxan with a guttural laugh. "Yeah, and I'm running an innocent dance club here. You know the difference between us, Cullion? You were born into what you have. I've had to fight for every fucking credit. Try spending a few years in a fighting pit on Caldorius, and then you can complain to me about this shit."

"I find your language distasteful."

"Yeah, you find everything about me distasteful—except that I turn you profit. Now we going to talk distribution, or what?"

"Once I dismiss my pet, yes."

"I don't mind her."

"You are staring as though you wish to fornicate with her."

"I like watching her. Definitely nicer to look at than you. One of these days, you need to let me at her."

"Just when I assumed you couldn't be fouler. This *thing* is beneath even you, Drok. An animal trained to perform for our entertainment. I would be remiss if I allowed any of my associates, even the most unpalatable, to stoop to such a low."

Drok laughed again, a richer, fuller sound. "For all your fancy words, Cullion, you're a damned fool sometimes. You paid a small fortune for her, and you could earn it back a hundred times over if you'd rent her out from time to time. Hell, half my staff wants to fuck her just to know what it's like. She looks soft. *Real* soft."

Tenthil clenched his jaw. The sweetness on his tongue was replaced by the tang of bitter venom as something dark stirred in his heart.

"I will hear no more of this," Cullion snapped. "If you cannot cease these insults and focus on the important matters at hand, I will—"

"Fine, fine. Send her to the lower stage. My customers appreciate a good show."

"She is *mine*, Drok. Not an attraction in your house of debauchery."

"If I didn't know all ertraxxans were pricks, Cullion, I might believe you had a personality of your own," Drok replied. "Send her to the stage. People will watch her, which means they'll keep buying drinks and drugs. When my business prospers, so does yours."

"Fine. *Go.*"

The conversation ceased, and Tenthil's awareness expanded. A tall, naked cren female with long, pointed ears, two three-centimeter-long tusks protruding from her mouth, and small breasts had taken the nearby stage. She undulated to a quick beat, her motions complemented by bursts of color flashing over her skin. Her music was underscored by thumping bass from the dance floor below, the rhythms just out of sync with one another.

Movement called his attention to the stairs. His eyes flared, and his heart quickened.

He watched as the terran walked down from the upper level, her long legs emerging from beneath her skirt with each step. His gaze dropped to her sandalled feet, to her dainty toes with their short, painted nails, and rose slowly. Golden anklets sparkled around her ankles, and her shapely calves led to toned thighs—hers were the legs of a dancer who had honed her body into a precision instrument. Grace, skill, and confidence permeated her every movement despite the demure downward angle of her chin.

His eyes moved higher still, driven on by the pounding of his heart, which had drowned out the music.

Her midsection was bare above a wide, ornate belt, a delectable span of flesh from the flare of her hips to her chest. The dark blue material covering her breasts bore a metallic glint and was run through with subtle golden accents, matching the belt. A thick necklace, more like a collar than a piece of jewelry, encircled her slender neck. The blue and black of the long hair cascading about her shoulders contrasted her pale skin.

Her face held his attention the longest. There was a familiar symmetry to her features, a configuration common to many of the intelligent beings in the Infinite City, but her face was softer, more refined, and more expressive than those of most creatures he'd encountered.

The slight downturn of her full, pink lips conveyed a sadness so profound that it pierced his chest. Her averted gaze could not hide the emotion sparkling within the frames of her dark lashes.

The terran walked toward the large central staircase leading to the lower level. She didn't look up, though many of the people around her stared while she passed. Oddly, most everyone who noticed her stepped out of her path, a few of them casting worried glances at nearby security guards. Legs moving of their own accord, Tenthil followed her. He felt as though he were floating through the emptiness of the Void, hearing nothing but his own heartbeat, seeing nothing but the terran.

The female continued to the lower floor. Tenthil halted at the top of the stairs as the crowd, even those caught in the deep rhythms of drink, drugs, and song, parted for the terran. No one seemed willing to come within arm's reach of her. Hazy speculations tumbled through Tenthil's mind, but he was too distracted to address them.

Who was this female? Did her kind possess some psychic power that bewitched those around them?

How had merely looking at her triggered these reactions within him?

Keeping her gaze downcast, the terran strode toward the stage. Thanks to the club's special effects, her footfalls left glowing patches on the floor that faded after several seconds; only as those spots faded did the crowd fill in her wake. The conflicting nature of her bold, sure stride and her mournful, downturned expression only intrigued Tenthil further. Those clashing aspects of her shouldn't have fit together.

And he wanted her like he'd wanted nothing else before.

When she reached the steps on the side of the stage, the guards posted there made no move to stop her; they didn't so much as cast her a fleeting glance. She mounted the stage and walked along its length, pausing only to slip off her sandals. Her expression had hardened, leaving only a glimmer of sorrow in her eyes; she now wore the look of a professional preparing for action, of a hunter surveying the killing ground.

Tenthil leaned forward as though that tiny movement

could somehow bring him close enough to smell her, to touch her.

She moved to the center of the stage and turned her back to the crowd. Tenthil barely noticed the hush that had fallen over the place; though the gentle din of conversation continued all around, it was softened by an anticipatory energy thrumming in the air.

Tenthil's legs itched with the urge to move closer, but he held himself in place at the top of the steps. He didn't want to take his eyes off her for even an instant.

The terran turned her head toward the booth from which a four-eyed, violet-skinned valzin controlled the music, and nodded once.

The lights on the stage and dance floor went out abruptly. The ambient glow from the bar and the floors above cast faint highlights on the crowd, but impenetrable darkness dominated the stage. It had become the Void. This was not the first time the Void had devoured Tenthil's desires and snuffed out what small hints of light he'd discovered in the vast, dark universe. Unease reintroduced itself as a boulder-sized lump lodged between his ribs.

Though he couldn't explain why, losing sight of her set him on edge. His muscles tensed, his claws protruded, and his gritted fangs ached. For several moments, everything was quiet and still. The crowd's eagerness suggested this wasn't merely the result of an exotic species taking the stage—they had some idea of what was coming.

She must have performed here before.

Tenthil envied everyone who'd seen her before tonight.

The terran reappeared on the stage, a lone figure cast in violet-blue light. Her back remained toward the crowd. It was only as she lifted her arms to either side that Tenthil noticed the ribbons clasped at her wrists, hips, and near her temples. The first swelling chords of music accompanied her movement.

Her hands rose over her head, slowing their upward momentum. When she swung them down again, the song's first beat played. At the same instant, the ribbons lit up with a neon-green glow. Another drumbeat had her spinning toward the audience. The ribbons left green trails as they flared out with her rotation. Her lips glowed vibrant pink, matching the luminescent pink and purple patterns adorning her face. The patterns were reminiscent of the natural markings common to volturians and sedhi, but these were far more detailed.

As the music picked up speed, so did the terran, her movements flowing in perfect harmony with the sound. The stage remained dark, though her footprints glowed in vivid colors for several seconds after she'd lifted her foot away, creating an ever-changing, surprisingly intricate path around her.

Eyes transfixed upon the terran, Tenthil finally descended. There was a pattern to her dance, barely discernable through the fluid, natural ease of her movements. Just like he'd learned to throw different punches and kicks and to wield various weapons, she must have learned to weave the steps of her dances together, combining basic parts into tantalizing wholes.

Urged forward by a consuming desire he could neither understand nor deny, he wove through the crowd, studying her every move. He needed to stand beside her, to touch her. He needed her scent to wash over him. Nothing else in this place, in this world, in the entire *universe* mattered more. All that existed was this female, dancing amidst the darkness. Dancing for *him*.

A two-meter-wide section jutted into the dance floor from the center of the stage with a guard posted to either side of it. Tenthil worked his way to the left, giving the guards a wide berth. The beat of the music pulsed through him as he tracked the terran's steps.

Tenthil didn't pause to consider his next action; his willpower had succumbed to whatever spell she'd placed upon him. He ticked off the beat in his head as she moved closer him, his muscles instinctively tensing in anticipation. He forced himself to relax.

The terran came within a few meters of the stage's edge and shifted her momentum.

He leapt onto the stage. A collective gasp rose from the crowd, but Tenthil was only distantly aware of the sound—it could have been the sigh of a ventilation system or an effect in the music for all he cared.

Tenthil mimicked her steps, matching her pace as she danced toward the opposite side of the stage.

The female turned and faced him, her eyes widening as she met his gaze. Her skin paled. "What are—"

Without missing a step, he took her hands in his. Heat flared where their skin touched. Electric currents crackled through him, flowing from his fingertips to light every nerve in his body ablaze.

He led her across the stage, and she followed, casting a worried glance toward the crowd. Tenthil pulled her gaze back to him with a gentle squeeze of her hand. Their legs moved in unison, like complementary pieces of a clockwork machine. Even in the dark, her eyes shone a brilliant green, more beautiful than the lush forest of his earliest memories. He lost himself in their impossible depths.

The female smiled.

Her surprise and the sadness that had lurked in her eyes were swept away by a spark of excitement, a joyful gleam, an inner light in defiance of the surrounding darkness. Suddenly, Tenthil was no longer leading.

She released one of his hands and twirled around him, brushing her skirts—and her body—against him. Her scent filled his senses in a rush. Crisp and clean, it reminded him of freshly fallen rain on the plains of his youth, but bore an underlying sweetness that poured fire into Tenthil's blood. An ache pulsed low in his belly, and his cock strained against his pants. That oddly pleasant taste returned to his mouth as venom seeped from his fangs.

Her movements altered; whether it was due to her having a partner or because the music had changed, Tenthil neither knew nor cared. Her body was his guide. She danced around him, and he reacted, reading the hints in her body language to offer an anchoring arm when she dipped, to stabilize and speed her spins, to drop his hands to her hips and lift her off her feet. She raised her legs and swept them to his sides, skimming her bare inner thighs over his clothing. He longed to remove his attire and feel her flesh against his.

Despite her spins and twirls, despite her ceaseless motion, the female's eyes snapped back to Tenthil's time and again, darkening as the dance continued. Soon, the new steps were instinctual to him. Her unspoken desire became his command; he was a slave to her dance, to her body, and he yearned for more, more, *more*.

He dipped her backward and ran his free palm down her abdomen toward her belt, eyes never leaving her face. She laughed, her smile widening. When she came back up, she cupped his jaw between her hands and leaned close, their noses only centimeters apart. Her breath was his, and his was hers. He tightened his hold on the terran and drew her closer.

Tenthil held the female's gaze for another moment, and then lowered his lips and pressed them against hers.

She tensed for an instant, eyes rounding, before her mouth softened and yielded to his kiss. Her hands settled on his shoulders as she closed her eyes, and Tenthil slipped his fingers into her silky hair. His heart pounded against his ribs as fresh venom flowed over his tongue—spicy, woody, saccharine, but bland compared to the tiny sample of her taste he received while their lips were together.

She tasted rich, alluring, and pure, impossibly sweet. She was...

Mine.

Tenthil broke the kiss and drew back from her. She stared up at him with half-lidded eyes, lips parted. He couldn't help but kiss her again more firmly. His muscles tensed as a deep, primal urge to bite her built within him. He swallowed it down; his venom was deadly to most species in Arthos, and he doubted hers would react any differently.

He didn't want to hurt her. He wanted to hold her. To protect her.

His cock pulsed, and a low growl resonated in his chest.

He wanted to—

"Hey! Get your hands off her!"

The world burst back into Tenthil's awareness. The lights were on again, bathing the stage in an intense white glow, and the music had stopped. Powerful silence gripped the club. The crowd was staring at him, many wearing stunned expressions. Two guards were on the stage, quickly approaching Tenthil, but neither had drawn his weapon yet.

A commotion at the main stairs caught Tenthil's attention; Drok, Cullion, and several more guards, including the ertraxxan's bodyguards, were hurrying toward the lower level. The crowd parted again, this time with fearful urgency. Anyone who wasn't quick enough was thrust aside by the burly guards or the massive tralix.

The female shoved away from Tenthil, stepped back, and

dropped to her knees, bowing down to press her forehead and palms to the floor.

Even now, Tenthil longed only to draw her back onto her feet and pull her against him, but the situation was escalating too rapidly. Drok wasn't likely to have him murdered in front of a crowd, but there were a lot of dark alleys and deserted tunnels around the building.

Tenthil had botched his mission, and placed himself in immediate danger, and still his only concern was for the terran.

"What is the meaning of this?" Cullion shouted as his retinue reached the stage.

"I'm sorry, Master," the female replied quickly. "I asked him to join me. We were only dancing."

Tenthil's brow knitted. Why was she taking responsibility for his actions?

Drok pounded a fist on the edge of the stage protrusion. A set of steps rose from the floor.

Cullion did not hesitate to mount them with his bodyguards immediately behind. "That was far more than dancing. His *hands* were on you. His *mouth*. I should have you incinerated just to ensure your cleanliness, you gutter slug!"

The female's fingers curled, her blunt nails scraping the floor, and a shiver wracked her thin frame. Tenthil's legs flexed as instinct demanded he move closer to her, but he dared not approach. Not while she was at risk.

"You all asleep down here, or what?" Drok asked.

The guards who'd been posted at the stage exchanged glances; Tenthil imagined their eyes rounding in alarm behind their goggles.

While everyone's attention was diverted, Tenthil dipped a hand into his pocket, took out the Ergoth pin, and clasped it to his jacket. It was his only chance of deflecting some of the hostility that would undoubtedly be unleashed upon him.

"No, boss. We thought he was part of the show," one of the guards replied.

"Part of the show?" Cullion whirled toward the guard, his thin lips falling into a severe frown. "All of you know this creature"—he jabbed a long, slender finger at the terran—"belongs to *me*. She is *mine*."

Fire flared in Tenthil's chest; the female belonged to *him*, not the ertraxxan.

Cullion stalked toward the terran. He tugged a thin metal line from his pocket and held it up. The free end lashed out on its own, hit the heavy necklace around the female's throat, and connected to it with a click. Looping his end of the line around his hand, Cullion gave it a vicious yank. The terran grunted as she was dragged to her feet.

Tenthil's claws lengthened. He curled his fingers into his palms. Stinging, bitter venom again replaced the strange, sweet flow from his fangs.

The ertraxxan led the female toward the steps. "You will pay dearly for this. Perhaps it is my folly for expecting better from so primitive a creature, but you will learn your place." He brandished his extended finger at Drok. "Should anything like this happen here again, it will be the end of you and your business."

The tralix lifted his huge, blunt-fingered hands, palms out. "A mistake, Cullion. Honest mistake. I'll make sure they all learn their lessons."

Cullion cast a scathing glare at Tenthil. "See to it, Drok. My trust in you will not survive another such blow."

The ertraxxan tugged the terran down the stairs and across the dance floor. She stumbled along behind him, struggling to match his hurried pace. The vorgal bodyguards flanked her.

Tenthil clenched his jaw; it took all his willpower to remain in place and watch her go. Whatever awaited her wasn't good, but it wasn't his fight. He'd done enough damage to his mission already. The contract would be even more difficult to complete after this, and he would undoubtedly be admonished by the Master for it. He hated the dread that thought spawned in his gut.

When Cullion's group reached middle level, the female looked over her shoulder. Her eyes met Tenthil's for an instant; they shimmered with fear, longing, and sorrow.

Tenthil stepped forward.

Drok shifted into his path and slammed a palm into Tenthil's chest. "Where do you think you're going?"

The tralix's blow had been solid, but Tenthil didn't feel any pain. He leaned to the side for a glimpse at the stairs. The terran was gone, along with Cullion and his guards.

"Seems like maybe you don't understand how much shit you're in," Drok said, reclaiming Tenthil's attention. "You got problems, and they're standing right here."

Several of Drok's security guards—six in all, each either a vorgal or a borian—moved closer to Tenthil, three on each side of the tralix. Tenthil gave them no ground.

None of the guards had drawn their weapons; they likely saw no need, given they outnumbered Tenthil seven-to-one, with more security personnel stationed around the club.

"I got all kinds of females in this place." Drok gestured vaguely around him as the valzin began the music again. "Most of them, you can touch or fuck for the right price. But that one? That one's not for touching. I understand the desire to, but she's off-limits. And you...you almost cost me a *lot* of money by being stupid."

Tenthil's foes had moved into a semi-circle, with the two on the end now flanking him. They stood only a couple paces away. Their postures were confident—too confident. But what resistance would they have expected? Even if Tenthil matched the biggest of the guards in height and stature, vorgals and borians had reputations as fierce, skilled warriors, and the tralix was at least a head taller and twice as burly as any of them.

Drok grinned, his dark eyes gleaming beneath the bone crest on his forehead. "There's a nice, quiet room in the back. You're going to walk to it with us all on your own. Then you're going to sit in the chair, and we're going to beat you into a pasty gray pulp. But we're not going to kill you. Hell, I'll even let you come back—at least on nights the ertraxxan isn't coming."

The tralix took a step closer, eliminating the distance between himself and Tenthil. He extended a finger and tapped the pin on Tenthil's chest. "Consider it a favor, okay? You lot are usually well-behaved in here. I'm willing to call all this an unfortunate misunderstanding." Drok raised his hand and brushed the tip of his finger across the scar on Tenthil's cheek. "By the looks of you, you're already used to people making an example out of you. How about one more time?"

Keeping his head tilted back, Tenthil held the tralix's gaze.

Drok's grin faded. "Not much of a talker? Guess we'll have to make you scream, instead."

"Maybe we ought to open up those scars. See how far we can pry his jaw open before it breaks off," one of the guards said.

Drok patted Tenthil's shoulder with a rough palm; though the gesture was gentle, the weight of the arm would've been enough to knock most people down.

"He's a tough one," Drok said, stepping backward. "No more wasting time. Grab him."

The two guards on either side of Tenthil advanced, reaching for him.

The situation was far from ideal, but his cover had been compromised. Even if he were allowed back into the club after tonight, security would always keep a close watch on him, and that wasn't to mention the likely retaliation from the Ergoths when they learned of this incident.

His mind flashed back to the terran, back to the fear and sadness on her face. She didn't have psychic powers, hadn't bewitched him; Tenthil knew that now with unreasonable certainty. He'd connected with her during their too-brief dance. Something had sparked between them—something powerful that had been buried inside of him. But now she was gone, and he might never learn of her fate, might never learn her name.

He latched on to his boiling rage and attacked.

Tenthil thrust a hand to his right, catching the vorgal's wrist and digging his claws into the tough flesh. As the vorgal hissed in pain, Tenthil kicked the left guard in the knee. A cry of pain drowned out the sound of crunching bone.

The other guards were caught in shock as Tenthil tugged the vorgal closer and sank his teeth into his foe's neck, letting his venom flow. The vorgal's pained exclamation intensified. Tenthil pulled the blaster from the vorgal's belt holster and shoved the doomed being aside. The others fumbled to draw their weapons as Tenthil leveled the blaster. He squeezed off three shots, striking two guards in the head and one in the throat before the fourth guard, a dark-haired, broadly-built borian, stepped closer and swung a thrumming energy blade.

Tenthil swayed back from the first swing, dodged a second, and fired the blaster from his hip. A bolt of plasma pierced the borian's thigh. The hiss of sizzling flesh was quickly swallowed by the screams of the crowd and the thumping music.

As the vorgal with the shattered knee staggered forward, raising a blaster in his trembling hand, Tenthil grabbed the borian's arm and wrenched it back. Bones cracked, and the motion swung the energy blade through the advancing vorgal's throat. The vorgal's head tumbled off his shoulders and landed on the stage with a dull *thwap*.

Dropping the blaster, Tenthil tore the energy blade from the borian's grasp and stabbed him through the chest.

Drok released a wordless, enraged cry and charged forward. The stage shuddered under his heavy footfalls.

Tenthil lowered his hand to the gun holstered at the sagging borian's hip as Drok lifted his massive fists over his head. Tenthil leapt away just before Drok slammed his hands down, using his momentum to draw the gun. The stage floor collapsed inward where Drok hit it, producing a deafening crack.

Tenthil stabilized himself on one knee and aimed the gun at Drok. The weapon's short, thick barrel was characteristic of a flechette pistol.

The tralix lifted his gaze to Tenthil, his beady eyes widening. "Who the f—"

Tenthil squeezed the trigger. The flechette pistol roared, spraying fire, and Drok's face disintegrated in a spray of burning blood and mangled flesh.

Turning his attention away from his foe, Tenthil surveyed the club again. The crowd was fleeing, and the congestion caused by hundreds of bodies attempting to press through the single door had created a backlog on the main staircase and the walkway around the middle floor. Several guards were fighting their way toward the stairs.

Drok dropped to his knees with a heavy thud, dark blood running over his teal and violet skin. Tenthil pushed onto his feet, plucked a blaster from one of the fallen guards, and fired two more plasma bolts into each of the beings on the ground. With the flechette pistol in his left hand and the blaster in his right, he hurried to the side of the stage.

Distant shouts came to him over the music, followed by the high-pitched whine of fast-firing blasters. Several plasma bolts struck the walls around him, melting metal and concrete. He wasted no time in thought—he knew of only one potential route of escape.

Tucking the guns into his belt, Tenthil leapt onto one of the massive, wall-mounted speakers beside the stage. The frantic beat of the music pounded into him, louder than ever. It was quick enough to match his racing heart.

He scrambled atop the speaker as plasma bolts whizzed around him, grateful for the guards' poor aim, which was likely worsened by the relatively dim, pulsing lights overhead. Grasping the middle floor railing, he hoisted himself over. Movement flickered at the edge of his peripheral vision.

Landing in a roll, he drew the blaster and fired instinctively. One of the two guards who'd been rushing to intercept him spun aside and fell, an orange hole glowing where the plasma bolt had pierced his groin. The other dove behind an overturned table and fired his auto-blaster blindly around its side.

Fortunately, one of the lavatory corridors stood directly to Tenthil's left. He fired two quick shots at the table and scurried into the corridor, slamming the door shut behind him.

The hall was thankfully deserted. Tenthil returned the blaster to his belt and broke into a run, glancing toward the ceiling. Near the center of the hallway, he leapt, kicking off the right wall to propel himself higher. He bounded off the left wall once he reached it, thrusting himself high enough to grasp the pipes above the smooth portion of the wall. It took seconds to climb to the hatch from there. Bracing his feet on the ductwork nearby, he grasped the wheel and exerted pressure.

Muffled shouts from beyond the closed door echoed down the hallway. Gritting his teeth, Tenthil threw more strength against the hatch. The wheel groaned as it moved, its rotation easing with each turn. He shoved the hatch up the instant the latching arms had released and hauled himself through the opening.

He emerged on a rooftop about ten meters below the metal framework that comprised the Undercity sky. The nearby spotlights cast powerful beams on the metal overhead. The door in the corridor below clanged open, and the shouts grew immediately louder. Muscles tensed, Tenthil gently lowered the hatch, holding his breath until it was fully, silently closed. As he'd guessed, there was no locking mechanism on the top side; it opened and sealed only from within.

After giving the roof a final scan, he hurried toward the next rooftop. His contract was fulfilled, but this matter was far from over. He had badly mishandled the mission and left scores of witnesses. He had only himself to blame, and that was exactly how the Master would see it.

The only positive had been the terran female.

At least he could take solace in the fact that he had a strong lead to seek her out—if her owner, Cullion, was as rich and powerful as his behavior had implied, he would be easy to find.

TWO

Large, rough hands bit into Abella's arm as the vorgal bodyguard dragged her toward the metal box on the back of Cullion's hovercar. She didn't resist when he shoved her into the cage—she couldn't overpower him, and trying to would only earn her a harsher punishment.

She was in deep enough shit as it was.

Abella scooted into the corner, drew her knees to her chest, and wrapped her arms around her legs. A faint hum permeated the cage as the front force field activated. Indistinct lines of energy sealed off the opening as the vorgal coiled the loose end of her leash around his hand. He passed the leash to Cullion when the ertraxxan, chin raised in displeasure, arrived.

"We are ready to depart, sir," one of the other bodyguards said.

Abella had never bothered to learn the bodyguards' names; Cullion paid them far too well for any of them to show her even a sliver of sympathy, if they were even capable of such to begin with.

Cullion yanked on the leash, tugging Abella forward. Her

face hit the thrumming energy bars before she could catch herself. The sting brought immediate tears to her eyes, and she cried out. Flattening her hands on the floor of the cage, she tried to pull her face away, but her owner held the leash taut.

"I do not know which is more insufferable—your continued disobedience, or the tralix's continued incompetence." Cullion leaned closer to her. His small, dark eyes gleamed with reflected light from the energy bars. "You will know agony as never before. I have tolerated much from you and have been merciful in disciplining you until now, but that little act of yours has proven that you are resistant to good sense. I'd hoped you knew better."

Abella glared at him despite her pain. Merciful? Cullion had only shown her mercy unwittingly through his disgust. He considered her an animal, an exotic pet to parade around, and the thought of *anyone* longing for her sexually was obscene to him. That attitude had been the only thing to keep her from being groped—or worse—by Cullion and his associates.

Cullion curled the leash tighter around his hand, forcing more of her skin against the energy field. Abella gritted her teeth but couldn't prevent the pained sounds from escaping her. Though the field wouldn't cause permanent damage or even leave much of a mark, it hurt like hell.

"Remember your place," Cullion said through his teeth before finally loosening his grip.

Abella thrust herself away from the energy field and slammed against the back of the crate. She covered her face with her hand, hoping the slight pressure she applied could assuage the lingering sting.

Cullion attached the end of the leash to the outside of the cage and stepped away. He instructed the driver to return to his estate, and the hovercar rocked gently as he and his bodyguards climbed into the cab.

Animals did not get to ride inside luxury hovercars.

The car doors hissed shut. As the engines revved up—producing a deep, barely perceptible whirring sound—the protective field that cocooned the exterior of the cage shimmered into place.

Abella closed her eyes and let the silence created by the field envelop her. She relaxed her body, sagging against the side of the cage as she turned her thoughts away from what was to come.

Music played in her mind, each note blending into the next to form a soothing melody. The notes soon changed in rhythm and tempo; in her mind's eye, she was back in the club, dancing across the stage. Free. It was only during these quiet, isolated moments that she could imagine herself back on Earth, performing for a loving, appreciative audience who didn't look at her like she was a piece of meat.

But her mind went to *him*—the stranger who'd joined her on stage.

Her fear in the moment she'd first met his gaze had been overwhelming, and it had only intensified when he took her hands. *No one* was permitted to touch her. Her mind had reeled with uncertainty—what would Cullion do to him? To *her*?

But her fears had faded to nothing as she'd stared into those hypnotic, ethereal silver eyes with their slitted pupils. His gaze had held her captive, reducing the entirety of existence to Abella and the stranger; there'd been no stage, no audience, no Cullion, no slave collar around her neck.

Though she didn't know his species and had never seen his like before—and despite his pointed ears, pale gray skin, sharp features, and entrancing eyes—there'd been a familiarity in his face that offered her solace. He looked just human enough to put her at ease. The stranger was handsome, if menacing. A scar at each corner of his mouth, slanting up to his cheekbones, had given a sinister twist to his otherwise stoic expression, yet she'd found it more intriguing than intimidating. Abella was tall for a human woman, but he was nearly a head taller, with broad shoulders and a narrow waist.

And the way he'd *moved*...

Had she not known better, she might've mistaken him for a trained dancer. But something about him—the control he'd exhibited, the speed with which he'd reacted to her steps, the solidness of his hold when he'd lifted her—suggested there was more to him.

He was...*dangerous*.

Abella slid her hand down her face until her fingertips settled on her lips. He'd kissed her. Twice.

She still felt an echo of the warmth of his mouth, of his body against hers, and his tantalizing, masculine scent lingered in her nose like a ghost from the recent past. Her tongue slipped out to slide over her lips, and she savored the hint of spicy sweetness he'd left on them.

It had been the first time she'd danced with anyone since her abduction, and it had been wonderful, exhilarating, freeing. It had felt like...

Being home.

Tears stung her eyes, and she quickly blinked them away.

The stranger hadn't spoken a single word; he'd only stared at her as though she were the only thing in the entire world. She didn't even know his name.

And I'll never see him again.

She'd known what would happen when he'd leapt onto the stage, had known the consequences would be severe, but it hadn't mattered. Every second in his arms had been worth it. Their short dance meant *everything* to her—it was the only time she'd felt like herself, had felt *happy*, since she was brought to the Infinite City four years earlier.

While she was lost in her thoughts, the hovercar had ascended and entered the express tunnels that allowed traffic to move freely through the city. She was aware of other vehicles zipping by, of lights, metal, and concrete blurred by the speed of Cullion's hovercar, but she paid attention to none of it. She only realized they'd reached Cullion's manor when the vehicle came to a halt and the outer protective field dissipated.

Abella dropped her hands to her sides and clenched her fists. The cab doors hissed open.

"Bring my pet to the discipline chamber," Cullion said from outside her field of view.

One of the bodyguards stepped in front of the cage, detached Abella's leash from the exterior, and deactivated the energy field. He tugged on the leash. "Let's go."

Abella gritted her teeth as she unfolded her body and climbed out of the cage. The collar around her neck weighed her down. It was a constant reminder of what she was here—a creature undeserving of respect or dignity.

She'd frequently fought back in the beginning and had attempted several escapes, but each act of opposition had brought more severe punishments, more intense pain. To maintain her sanity, she'd had no choice but to comply with Cullion's orders, but she always kept her eyes open for opportunity.

Though four years of slavery had left her with little hope of reclaiming her freedom, she refused to give up.

The vorgal stepped back to grant her a sliver of space, remaining as close as he could without touching her. Abella kept her eyes downcast as she followed him toward the manor's entrance.

Cullion had spared no expense in the construction of his

home. Like many of the nearby buildings, it stood in defiance of the structures overhead that kept the Undercity in perpetual night—but that defiance was an illusion. Cullion did not rail against the status quo because he was empowered by it.

The manor was a bastion of wealth and luxury that went far beyond what Abella considered tasteful, existing only to stroke its owner's ego.

The manor's architecture was unlike anything she'd ever seen. It faintly resembled the ancient, ornate temples and ruins in southeast Asia back on Earth, but that was comparing apples to oranges. There was nothing subtle or artistic about Cullion's manor or the surrounding homes; they existed to flaunt power and privilege. Everything was trimmed with shining, exotic metals and gems or crafted from carved, polished wood and stone, all of it alien in origin.

Some people might have found the display awe-inspiring and intimidating. Abella thought it was gaudy and excessive. None of it belonged in the Undercity, where everything else was metal, concrete, and vibrant neon.

But wasn't that the point? Beings like Cullion felt they *didn't* belong down here—they were too good for it. They wanted to be in the city above the surface, dwelling in one of the sanctums controlled by the Consortium. That he was unable to enter the sanctums save when invited for business infuriated Cullion like little else.

Abella found quiet glee in that.

Only the alien species comprising the Consortium—a near-mythical group of six races, the members of which Abella had never seen during her time here—were permitted to freely enter and dwell within the sanctums.

The vorgal led her through the large entry doors, which were constructed of thick metal disguised as wood, across the ornate foyer, and into a long, darkly furnished hall. She knew what awaited her at its end.

Her feet felt as though they were made of stone, making every step a struggle. She kept her eyes down, tracing the golden veins webbing the marble-like black floor with her gaze. The décor around her became a blur. She wanted nothing more at that moment than to separate her mind from her body so she wouldn't have to feel anything.

Every tiny hair on Abella's body stood on end as the vorgal led her through the doorway at the end of the hall and to the center of the discipline room. The air within bore a unique chill, and, though she didn't look up, she felt the heavy stares of the guards and servants gathered inside settle upon her. Cages and varied instruments of pain filled her peripheral vision.

"Remove her clothing," Cullion said.

The vorgal guard untethered Abella's leash from the collar and stepped behind her. His hands were dispassionate and rough as he unfastened her belt, letting it fall down her legs and hit the floor with a *thunk*. The delicate fabric of her skirt pooled around her feet along with it. He unhooked the clasps on her top a moment later, forcing it off her arms and dropping it to join her other clothing.

A shiver coursed through her from head to toe, raising goosebumps on her chilled skin. This was humiliating and degrading, yet another attempt to strip her of what dignity she had left, but she clung to her pride with an iron grip.

He will not break me.

"Kneel," Cullion commanded.

She cast a fleeting glance toward the wall, where there was a secret door used to dispose of the pets who didn't survive Cullion's discipline. She'd gone through it once and had followed it into a tunnel outside the manor before she was captured and dragged back inside, kicking and screaming. She'd been so damn close...

Somewhere out there, somewhere in this impossibly large city, there was a United Terran Federation embassy. She'd overhead people talking about it one of the times Cullion had taken her out. There were official representatives from Earth here. All she needed to do was get to them.

One day, she would use that tunnel again. One day, she *would* be free.

Abella lowered herself onto her knees and bent forward. She pressed her forehead to the stone and flattened her palms to either side. The floor was icy against her bare skin, and another shudder crept up her spine. She still felt the guards staring at her, their gazes thick with curiosity, lust, and anticipation, contrasted by Cullion's palpable disgust.

She squeezed her eyes shut, wishing everything around her would disappear, wishing that she'd open her eyes to find herself back home in her bed, having just woken from a vivid but harmless nightmare.

Wishing she could open her eyes and find herself on stage, dancing with that mysterious stranger.

The fabric of Cullion's robes rasped against his legs as his footsteps moved away from Abella. She swallowed thickly when she heard the sound of wood against metal, and her palms dampened with sweat.

"You have disappointed me. Again," Cullion said as he approached Abella from the front and walked around her, like a shark circling its prey. "It was I who rescued you from the scum who abducted you on the backwater planet that spawned your kind. It is I who provides for you, I who shelters you, feeds you, clothes you, pampers you. Everything you have, you owe to *me*. All I ask in return is obedience. Even a creature so unevolved as you should understand that."

An airy whistle was the only warning of the coming blow. Fire flared across her back as the cane struck her with a *crack*—it was one of his favorite implements despite its simplicity. She recoiled, body tensing and fingers curling, but she forced herself to maintain her position.

Abella pressed her lips together to hold in a cry; she refused to give him the satisfaction of hearing it. Pain spread outward in a wave of heat as the point of impact tingled and went numb.

Cullion continued pacing around her. "I will not permit your depravity to tarnish my reputation. You are *mine*, and you will behave accordingly. Were you purposely making a mockery of me tonight?"

Abella kept her lips sealed. She knew this game of his well by now—whatever her answer, it would be wrong. His polished boots halted at the edge of her vision. She drew in a slow, deep breath, willing her trembling to cease.

The silence between blows was always the most frightening part of the whole ordeal.

One of his feet shifted forward, and the cane slice through the air to strike her back twice more. Abella whimpering as the air fled her lungs and tears flooded her eyes. She breathed in and out, quickly and shallowly, and pushed through the agony. Her mind turned toward her years as a dancer, toward the grueling practice sessions and the demanding routines that had left her muscles burning and her feet aching. That pain had made her stronger, better. It had never broken her.

Nothing would break her.

Not this planet. Not her enslavement. And most certainly not Cullion.

"Rather strong-willed tonight, are we?" Cullion stepped back. "That can easily be remedied. You. Fetch the electrolash."

The heavy footsteps of one of the vorgal guards moved away, paused for a moment, and returned, ceasing behind Abella.

"Twenty lashes," Cullion said, walking away from her. "Then take her to the isolation chamber. We will allow her to reflect upon her wrongdoings—and her wounds—for a time."

She finally allowed herself to look toward him, toward his damned polished boots, glaring with more hatred than she would've thought possible to fit in one person's heart.

Cullion stopped a few meters away and turned toward her.

An electric, crackling sound from behind her was followed by the hissing thrum of an activated electrolash.

This wasn't her first time. Unfortunately, knowing what to expect wouldn't diminish the pain.

She pressed her forehead against the cold floor and gritted her teeth as the first lash struck her flesh with a searing sting that locked her muscles. It was followed by another, and another, and another; she quickly lost count. This time, Abella couldn't hold in her cries, couldn't stem the flow of her tears, but she would not beg for mercy. She would never beg him.

I—

Crack.

—am not—

Crack.

—an animal.

Crack.

She twisted her mind to ignore the pain, turning it toward her parents, her two older brothers, her friends. She thought about her late-night dance rehearsals, about the joy and laughter that had accompanied all the hard work.

She thought of the mysterious stranger with the scars on his cheeks and the piercing eyes. He had made her forget it all for a little while, had granted her a brief reprieve from the life she'd been forced into.

Those precious moments spent dancing with him were worth all of this.

THREE

Tenthil guided the hoverbike through increasingly narrow tunnels, moving ever deeper and downward. The colorful neon of the Undercity was far behind him, having been replaced by the yellowish, inconsistent lights of the Bowels, which fell upon dirty, rust-stained metal and concrete.

Though the Undercity wasn't necessarily pleasing to look upon, it always felt lived in, serving as home to countless people of countless species. Its holograms and lights possessed a certain warmth, and every street and alley, however dark or dangerous, was part of a larger web connecting hundreds of millions of people to one another. There was always *someone* nearby—inconvenient for people in Tenthil's line of work, but a small comfort, perhaps, for those who felt alone and isolated in this vast, unforgiving city.

Arthos's nickname—the Infinite City—was fitting in a great many ways.

The Bowels lacked that warmth, even in factories and workshops where massive furnaces and smelters cast orange glows on their surroundings. There'd been no effort made to conceal the ducts, pipes, and conduits feeding power, fuel, and water to the Undercity and the surface beyond. There was nothing to counteract the feeling of being trapped beneath more than a kilometer of metal and machinery.

And yet more people than anyone might've guessed lived down here. They found security in the narrow, labyrinthine passageways, found shelter in out-of-the-way chambers and abandoned facilities. The denizens of the Bowels were survivors scraping by in places no one else wanted to go.

Or at least that had been the case until recently. Over the last decade, Tenthil had noticed increasing activity in the Bowels. It was becoming a popular place for criminals to conduct business.

He slowed the hoverbike as he approached the barricaded entrance of a side tunnel, tugged back on the handlebars, and piloted the vehicle through the narrow opening at the top.

The bike's spotlights provided the only illumination in the dark tunnel, revealing a shallow, mucky stream running along the floor, small piles of debris scattered everywhere, corroded metal support struts, and the occasional scurrying critter. The concrete walls were stained and cracked. He couldn't guess how long ago this tunnel had been built, but the world above had long since forgotten it.

When Tenthil neared the hidden door, he checked behind him for any movement apart from the running water. Satisfied that he was alone, he pulled the bike forward, engaged the brake, and hopped off to press the switch concealed on one of the metal struts.

Despite the age and wear of the tunnel, the hidden blast door—one-meter thick tristeel with a concrete face—rose silently. He returned to the hoverbike and guided it through the opening into another tunnel, this one with curved walls and ceiling. Automatic sensors detected when the vehicle was clear of the entryway and closed the blast door behind him. A gentle rumbling echoed through the corridor as the door touched down and its maglocks engaged.

The overhead lights came on in a chain, leading deeper into the tunnel. Tenthil cranked the throttle and sped forward. He was in no hurry to face what awaited him, but it was best to get it over with. Then he could turn his thoughts back to what truly mattered—the terran dancer.

His lips still tingled with the memory of their kiss. He hadn't planned to do that, to do *any* of it, and he'd never shared a kiss with anyone. What had come over him? All he knew was that his strange mood had not passed; he would find her again.

She was *his*.

I must not allow myself such thoughts in the Master's presence.

When Tenthil reached the interior door, it opened automatically, and he eased the hoverbike into the garage beyond, parking it alongside the other bikes. The collection of vehicles here could rival that of any Undercity elite. The Order of the Void commanded significant resources, and the Master believed in being prepared for all situations. Most any vehicle the acolytes required, from hoverbikes to luxury hovercars to cargo haulers, could be found here or in the larger secondary garage on the far side of the complex.

Tenthil climbed off the bike and walked toward the door leading into the temple. The air here was different than elsewhere in the Infinite City; it seemed cleaner, crisper, and somehow much, much *older*.

The black-robed acolyte beside the door—a horned, charcoal-skinned sedhi whose third eye was obscured by her dark hair—signed to Tenthil as he approached, her fingers moving deftly.

The Master calls.

Tenthil nodded and continued through the door. He'd known the Master would summon him, but that foreknowledge prevented neither the sinking feeling in his gut nor the angry, acidic burning in his chest.

He followed a long, dark hallway into a stone-floored vestibule, where he turned left and stepped through wooden double doors into the cloister. Without pausing, he moved off the walkway and entered the courtyard. There was no open air here, no sky, but constant projections on the ceiling mimicked the slowly changing cosmos as though the temple were floating in deep space, offering fleeting glimmers of distant stars and hints of color from faraway nebulas.

At the center of the yard stood the Well of Secrets—a three-meter-wide pool ringed by figures sculpted out of a strange, dark metal that seemed to swallow light. The figures wore the same robes as the Order's acolytes, with hoods raised and their downturned faces obscured by shadow. The pool between the statues held a black mass of indeterminable depth, the properties of which seemed to change randomly, even as one stared into it. Sometimes it rippled and shimmered like water; sometimes it roiled like viscous sludge; sometimes it resembled thick fog gathered in a ditch. But always it was black, as black as the nothingness between the stars.

Three curved steps led up to the edge of the pool on one side. The Master referred to them as the *stairs to eternity*, and said the well was a direct conduit to the Void. Anything that entered it was devoured, never to be seen again—including people the Master had interrogated. Once their secrets had been extracted, they were brought to the well.

It was only a matter of time before Tenthil pushed too hard and the Master whispered his name to the well. Only a matter of time before Tenthil, body and soul, would be given to feed the Void's insatiable hunger.

He stared into the darkness as he strode past. If he was to become another victim of the Void, another silenced soul, it would not be without a cost to the Order. It would not be without bloodshed.

Though he currently served its will, the Void did not yet own Tenthil.

Wrenching his gaze away from the pool, he crossed the remainder of the courtyard and passed into the nave—a massive, high-ceilinged chamber serving as the Order's primary training space. Dozens of acolytes clad in black, form-fitting combat suits utilized the space now, practicing hand-to-hand combat or the use of various melee weapons. Many of those acolytes sparred with one another under the watch of robed and hooded instructors. Huge, faceless statues loomed along the walls, their heads tilted down toward the acolytes below.

The figures were a reminder—the Master was always watching.

Despite the activity, no one spoke. The only sounds were the quick, crackling hisses of energy blades clashing and the dull *thwaps* of fists, elbows, knees, and feet connecting with bodies. Elsewhere in the temple, acolytes trained with various blasters and firearms, but those chambers were heavily sound-proofed. Even here in the nave, noise was dampened; no sound echoed off the metal and stone of its walls, floor, and ceiling.

Tenthil followed the side wall toward the far end of the nave. A few acolytes glanced at him as he passed. He was still dressed for Twisted Nethers—tall boots, black pants, and a red and violet padded jacket over a white shirt. His clothing befitted an Ergoth gang member, not an acolyte of the Void. Most of those who looked were punished for their distraction by savage blows from their sparring partners and instructors.

When Tenthil reached the end of the room, he rounded the dais from which the Master sometimes surveyed the acolytes' training and stepped through the door behind it. A spiraling staircase led him up to the next floor, where it opened on a long, wide corridor intersected by several perpendicular halls. The space was dark and devoid of adornment save for the statues standing within recesses on either side every seven paces. Though all the sculptures were similarly attired, each had some variation that distinguished it from the others, a unique trait that set it apart.

Sometimes, the statues exhibited subtle changes to their poses—a head might one day be angled down a few more degrees than before, previously curled fingers inexplicably straightened, and the slant of shoulders altered just enough to change a figure's balance.

Tenthil wasn't sure if the changes were real or imagined. He'd been in the temple since childhood, and he'd known nothing of this world when he arrived. This place had been terrifying to him in his youth, and his unease had never quite faded.

He walked through the hallway at a brisk pace, offering no acknowledgement to the silent stone acolytes. His mind needed to be clear when he stood before the Master; it would be his only defense, the only way to protect himself from dire retribution.

The only way to protect the terran.

The Master's chamber was at the end of the hallway. A single acolyte stood outside the entry door, one of only three beings in the Order who'd not undergone the vow of silence—Corelthi. She was a volturian with sharp facial features, blue-gray skin, and glowing orange *qal* marks on her face and neck. Her eyes were the same color as her markings.

She stared at Tenthil as he approached, her lifted chin and lowered brows conveying her sentiments as clearly as though she'd spoken them aloud—which she had several times before.

You do not belong here, and, soon enough, you will be put down like the animal you are.

Corelthi served as the Master's right hand, a deadly assassin in her own right made all the more dangerous by her devotion to the Void and her leader.

Tenthil stopped in front of her. Despite her formidability and her position, he was not afraid of her—his fear was reserved for the being who awaited behind the door.

"Would that you had not come back," Corelthi whispered. "It has been my wish to hunt you down and plunge a blade into your insolent heart for years."

Suddenly more aware of the blaster and flechette pistol tucked into his belt, Tenthil pressed his teeth together, careful to prevent the muscles of his jaw from bunching. The Order had gone to great lengths in their attempts to take his voice, and he'd fought hard to keep it.

But silence seemed the only appropriate response to her.

Corelthi narrowed her eyes and shook her head. "Disciplined only when it suits you. You are not worthy of his favor."

Stepping aside, she tugged the door open.

Tenthil turned his head forward and stepped through the doorway, affording Corelthi no more of his attention.

The Master's chamber was a dark, circular room with its high, pointed ceiling constantly swirling with images like those in the courtyard—occasional glimpses of nebulas and tiny stars amidst the deepest black. The walls were shrouded in thick shadow, impenetrable even to Tenthil's eyes. He was certain hidden doors lurked within that darkness, perhaps even one leading to the Master's personal chambers, but he could not confirm his suspicions.

A cone of light came from the center of the ceiling as though escaping the Void itself, falling directly upon the simple wooden chair in the middle of the room and the gray floor stones around it.

"Sit."

The voice came from everywhere, curving around the room as though it were in command of the laws of acoustics rather than at their mercy. Tenthil knew it well; the Master's voice was the only one he'd heard for years after being brought to the Infinite City as a youngling. It was deep and smooth, but undercut by a barely-perceptible, raspy whisper that gave it an otherworldly quality.

Tenthil strode to the chair and sat. His stomach twisted into knots, but he did not allow the sensation to distract him; he forced his thoughts aside.

The ensuing silence was broken only by the thumping of Tenthil's heart in his own ears. He had endured this often enough to know the game, to understand the Master's propensity for sowing uncertainty and fear.

He heard a whisper of cloth behind him. A moment later, something brushed against his right shoulder, and he glanced down to see the Master's long, gloved fingers curling over his shoulder. In all his time in the Order, Tenthil had never heard a sound when the Master moved. Either the Master was growing careless, or Tenthil's senses were sharper than ever.

"Show me," the Master said.

Tenthil held his memories at bay, focusing only on the present—on the cool air, on the ever-moving darkness overhead, on the chronic ache in his throat, on the strong, spindly fingers gripping his shoulder.

Those fingers squeezed. "You test my patience, Tenthil. Your will is strong, but I will have what I want. Give it to me and save yourself the discomfort."

You already know, Tenthil thought.

"Yes, I do," the Master said, "but I want to see from your

eyes. Truth must be examined from all angles to be understood. I will pass judgment once I have seen your perspective."

The Master portrayed himself as an omniscient figure, an all-knowing being connected to the Void, which itself touched everything. But even Tenthil, who'd spent his earliest years on a primitive planet, raised by a primitive people, knew better. There was no mysticism involved—the Master employed a vast network of spies, hackers, and informants who funneled information to him.

And who constantly kept watch on acolytes while they completed contracts in the field.

The first signs of intrusion came in the form of pressure in the back of Tenthil's mind; it felt like icy fingers were sinking into his brain, sending a chill down his spine. That presence was as compelling as it was cold. The urge to reminisce about his mission awakened in Tenthil's subconscious, but he resisted, having learned years before how to recognize such foreign compulsions.

The pressure in his mind strengthened along with the grip on his shoulder.

Tenthil could resist, but not indefinitely, and the longer he held out the more painful it would be when his defenses finally crumbled.

Squeezing his eyes shut, Tenthil ceased his struggle.

The Master plunged into Tenthil's mind, rifling through thoughts like an Eternal Guard peacekeeper searching a criminal's dwelling. Tenthil did the only thing he could to protect himself—he summoned his memories of the night's events so the Master wouldn't search any further. He began at the slaying of the Ergoth gang member and worked forward. The Master's icy touch slithered over each memory, examining, prodding, and poking.

Tenthil did not omit the human female—the memory gap

would've been too obvious, and the Master's scrutiny would've intensified—but he was careful not to recall his feelings for her save his lingering lust. He wanted to rut her; it was true, even if it was but a sliver of the entire truth.

Once his memories of the evening had ceased, he cleared his mind again, allowing himself no reflection upon any of it. The Master's presence remained in Tenthil's head, cold and alien.

The room was still and silent. Tenthil dared not move, bracing himself for the inevitable pain of the Master seeking to pry out *everything*. His head already throbbed; even the mildest of these intrusions were not without pain.

Finally, the Master broke his silence with a heavy, prolonged sigh. His grip on Tenthil's shoulder tightened for a moment before he lifted his hand away. The pressure of the mental intrusion lessened, but the presence in Tenthil's mind did not withdraw.

The Master walked past the chair and paced in front of Tenthil. His dark, voluminous robes hid the size and shape of his body; he was taller than Tenthil by half a head, at least, with a seemingly wide body but long, thin arms. Tenthil had never seen the Master without his raised hood and black, featureless mask, had never seen the face hidden behind the darkness.

No one knew what the Master looked like. No one knew his real name. No one even knew his species. In an organization founded upon secrets, perhaps the most closely guarded was the Master's identity.

"Do you recall your homeworld?" the Master asked.

Tenthil braced his mind and shook his head. What memories he retained from his earliest years belonged to him, and he refused to share them.

Fortunately, the Master did not probe to determine Tenthil's honesty.

"Your people are a fierce race. Strong, quick, and predatory. Barely more than animals." The Master halted and turned toward Tenthil. "I invested heavily in you. Gave you purpose. Knowledge. Training. I did not pay to have a maddened beast at my command, I paid to have a cunning, methodical killer. Tonight, you disgraced both yourself and the Order. You violated the tenets, shunned my teachings, and spat in my face.

"You lusted after that female like a wild animal, relinquishing all self-control, and your stupidity left hundreds of witnesses to the contract's closing."

Tenthil clenched his teeth and fists as the Master's presence slithered through his mind again. The sensation intensified as it pushed deeper, creating jolts of pain like spikes being driven through his skull. He concentrated on nothingness, on emptiness, and resisted the psychic onslaught.

The Master stepped closer. "You are by far the most skilled of my acolytes. No other would have survived the situation you escaped tonight. For that reason alone, I have been lenient with you. This is the last time."

Crouching slightly, the Master moved his face closer to Tenthil's. "I made you what you are. And I will not hesitate to destroy you. Do you understand?"

Staring at the Master's mask was like staring beyond the edge of the universe. If the Void could exist within a living being, it stood before Tenthil now. A twinge of fear pulsed in Tenthil's chest, but it quickly twisted into something else —anger.

His life was his own. He refused to be cowed by threats from anyone, even the Master.

Swallowing his fury before it boiled to the surface, Tenthil nodded. If the Master sensed Tenthil's anger, he made no indication of it.

The Master straightened and walked past the chair, disappearing from Tenthil's view. "Good. There are many brothels in the Undercity, should you require release. I suggest you visit one before you make another foolish mistake."

The icy, alien presence abruptly withdrew from Tenthil's mind. The stabbing pain resonated in his skull for several seconds before giving way to a throbbing ache. Tenthil drew in a deep breath and forced his clenched fists open as his heartbeat faded from his hearing. The sting of the puncture wounds his claws had opened on his palms added new pain to his growing list.

He didn't look back as he stood up and exited the chamber.

Corelthi was no longer positioned outside the door—a small boon, but one for which Tenthil was nonetheless grateful. He strode through the hallways toward his quarters, denying himself all thoughts. It was not until he was in his room with the door closed and locked that he allowed everything to flood into his conscious mind.

A growl built in his chest, his fingers curled to extend his claws, and his muscles bulged as the fullness of his rage struck him. Bitter venom leaked from his fangs. He longed to attack, to destroy, but he held himself back; the ruckus he would've raised in doing so would not have gone unnoticed by the other acolytes, which meant the Master would quickly learn of it. Tenthil had no desire to give the Master a reason to invade his mind with even greater force.

Slowly, Tenthil's rage diminished, and the tension in his muscles eased. But a fire still burned low in his belly. For the first time since he'd returned from his mission, Tenthil deliberately shifted his thoughts to the terran dancer—to the way her eyes had captivated him, the way she'd moved, the way her body had felt against his. The way she'd *tasted*.

His cock swelled, its ache rivaling the throbbing in his head.

Animalistic lust? If this is mere lust, I am as great a fool as the Master believes.

Tenthil paced back and forth like a caged beast—a comparison more bitter than his venom. He inhaled. He could still smell the female upon him. Groaning, he tugged off his jacket and lifted it to his nose, drawing in the terran's sweet, lingering scent.

He placed the jacket on his bed, pulled the weapons from his belt, and laid them on the chest in which he kept his few worldly possessions. After kicking off his boots, he removed his shirt and pants, tossing them into the corner.

Freedom only slightly eased the strain in his cock.

Snatching up the jacket, he drew in more of the terran's faint scent, which was intoxicating despite its weakness. Her image sharpened in his mind's eye.

Tenthil wrapped his fingers around his shaft and growled. Pleasure like he'd never known filled him, enhanced by a desperate, driving need for release. He stroked his fist down the pronounced ridges of his cock and shuddered. In his memory, the female danced in front of him, eyes locked with his. He slid his calloused hand back up as the music to which they'd moved joined in his recollection, setting the pace for his pumping fist.

What would it be like to have her hand on his shaft, to breathe in her fragrance as she touched him? How would her delicate skin feel beneath his fingertips, how would it respond to his attentions?

Breaths ragged, he shut his eyes and pictured her in the room with him, pictured her slender fingers wrapping around his cock. He imagined her leaning forward without missing a stroke and pressing her lips against his; the phantom sensation of her soft, yielding flesh sculpting to his mouth tingled across his face.

His body tensed, his fist tightened, and his hips jerked

forward as he came with a guttural growl. Pleasure spiraled through him in a rush as the pressure in his cock released, spraying his seed onto the floor in great spurts. He gritted his teeth and pumped faster, harder, until there was nothing left—not even breath in his lungs.

The need raging within him did not ease.

FOUR

The next day, Tenthil was agitated during his morning exercises. He'd dealt with similar frustration in the past. Beneath the Master's watchful gaze, it was best to find quick, productive ways to vent such emotions, as they could not long go unnoticed. He chose to channel his anger in the sparring ring. Whether it was despite his fearsome reputation or because of it, many acolytes seemed eager to prove themselves against Tenthil in hand-to-hand combat.

His first two opponents fell within ten seconds of their bouts commencing, each knocked unconscious. The third was a little more skilled, but that skill wouldn't have been enough, even had Tenthil been calm. After the third match ended with the vorgal acolyte who'd challenged him being carted away to tend his broken leg, Tenthil left the ring in disgust.

What he sought would not be found there.

He prowled the temple halls, restless and angry, for hours. He knew the exact cause of his dark mood, but he refused to think about her. His thoughts were not safe inside the temple.

And yet he found himself in the Hall of Records—a large,

dark chamber filled with data storage cores, holo-projectors, and access terminals—that evening.

This is foolish, he thought as he stalked toward one of the secluded rear terminals. *The Master will know, and he will fulfill his threat.*

Tenthil's legs moved despite his misgivings. He stopped at the terminal, and his fingers flicked through the projected controls, following the directive running just beneath the surface of his conscious mind.

To ensure I can track any loose ends created by my foolishness...

That motivation wasn't true, but his survival hinged on convincing himself it was. When the Master asked why he'd searched for information on Cullion, Tenthil's false reasoning would need to ring true—it had to *become* his truth.

Despite redundant layers of security, encryption, and obfuscation, Tenthil had uncovered a trove of information on Cullion within half an hour. Financial records, business ties and contacts, medical records, daily schedules; little could be hidden from the Master's networks.

Cullion—full name Traxes Cullion Orgathe—was a native of the Infinite City, a tenth-generation ertraxxan importer who'd inherited significant wealth. Numerous investigations had been opened regarding his suspected involvement in the smuggling of illegal goods, but each had been quashed before collecting sufficient evidence for charges to be filed. It seemed Cullion's connections went beyond his senior position in the Union of Intergalactic Cargo Movers and his dealings with criminals like Drok.

No records, legal or otherwise, seemed to exist documenting the ertraxxan's ownership of the terran.

After Tenthil had gathered sufficient information on Cullion, he forced himself to remain at the terminal to investigate other known associates of Drok. He absorbed little of the data; his mind was abuzz with the single most important discovery his search had turned up—the location of Traxes Cullion Orgathe's manor in the Undercity, sector ninety-three, often called the Gilded Sector.

His legs were restless by the time he decided he'd maintained the charade for long enough. His instincts demanded action. He knew where the terran was, and he would find her again.

But his frustration and impatience were not enough to overpower his rationality, at least not yet. The Master would be monitoring Tenthil's movements closer than ever now. As much as Tenthil wanted the female—*his* female—going after her would be his doom. The dead could hold no claim on the living.

Even knowing that, even with his life at risk, logic won by only a hair's breadth.

That night, he stroked himself to climax as he lay in bed, breathing in her scent from his jacket, but his hunger only deepened.

As the days passed, Tenthil sought ways to distract himself, to keep the terran out of his thoughts. A small voice in the back of his mind insisted he already knew what to do, where to go. All his efforts to silence that voice failed; that failure heightened his agitation. His balls ached with the constant need for release, and the terran's smell would randomly return to him, washing over his senses and stiffening his cock. He stole away more frequently to attempt to assuage his body's demands. Each time, he thought of her. Each time, his imagination took things a little further. And each time, despite the temporary easing of physical pressure, his craving for her strengthened.

By the fourth night, he was dreaming of her as he slept. The dreams always began with the dance they'd shared, but grew more wrong with each passing moment, often culminating in shadowy figures tearing Tenthil away from the terran and enveloping him in viscous darkness that slowly broke him down into nothing.

The traces of her scent upon his jacket weakened every day. Before long, he'd only have the memory of her fragrance. That realization triggered an odd panic within him; how could a memory ever be enough?

Seven days after the incident in Twisted Nethers, he still hadn't been assigned a new contract. Many of the other acolytes gave him a wide berth as he strode through the halls. Word of his performance in the sparring ring had spread amongst them, conveyed through brief exchanges in sign language. Tenthil paid no mind them as he passed them.

What were they to him? The Master's love of secrets and silence meant most acolytes, even those who communicated with one another, didn't even know each other's names. They belonged to the Void. Only Corelthi caught Tenthil's attention with her bold, openly disapproving glares. He rarely met her gaze; his frustration was great enough that he couldn't trust himself to maintain restraint in the face of her judgment.

The voice in the back of his mind had grown from a whisper to a roar, but he didn't understand what it truly was until the eighth day. When he woke, the sight of his chamber's walls and door ignited blistering fury in him, spawning a wave of fire that swept up from his gut to fill his chest and crash through his limbs. His fingers tensed, lengthening his claws. He could not bear another night in the temple. His place was elsewhere, and it always had been.

He finally understood what that voice had been all along—not a thought, a desire, or a rage-fueled compulsion, but an instinct. A primal drive embedded deep within him that he could no longer ignore.

Tenthil dressed and donned his combat armor; it was lightweight and flexible enough to offer protection without hindering his speed and maneuverability. Its built-in sheaths allowed him to carry several knives and energy blades in addition to the custom-built blaster on his hip. Such attire was common throughout the Undercity and the Bowels, but only the wealthy and well-funded possessed equipment on par with the Order's.

This was how acolytes equipped themselves when trouble was likely, especially when targets employed private security forces—and Cullion's financial transactions suggested he contracted at least a dozen bodyguards through Starforge, an elite private security organization.

Anticipation thrummed through Tenthil as he walked to the garage. Taking action was a small relief in itself, but his impatience would not subside until he had the terran in his possession. He shouldn't have wasted seven days. He should've acted sooner. His body brimmed with pent-up energy, and his heart beat at an elevated pace. His excitement mingled with his simmering anger to create something new, something dangerous, for which he had no name. One way or another, he would have his female.

He would have her tonight.

Tenthil climbed onto a hoverbike, engaged the engine, and drove toward the exit. The garage was quiet, like every other room in the temple, save for the low, steady hum of antigrav drives.

Something heavy sank in his stomach, and the ever-present ache in his throat intensified. Did the Master already know of Tenthil's intentions? Was there a group of acolytes waiting behind the parked vehicles or on the other side of the garage door, tasked with bringing Tenthil to justice for betraying the Master, for abandoning the Order?

His brows fell low. Whether or not the Master already knew, Tenthil had made his choice, and he would see it through to the end. When the Order came for him, the physical enhancements and skills with which he'd been imbued by the Master would help him exact a heavy toll upon his former comrades.

The blast door slid upward, revealing only the empty, circular tunnel beyond. Once the opening was wide enough, he cranked the throttle, and the hoverbike darted forward. Everything in Tenthil's peripheral vision was reduced to a blur by speed.

Within a minute, he'd emerged from the smaller maintenance passages and was hurtling through the express tunnels, weaving amidst increasingly thick traffic as he ascended toward the Undercity. The bike's protective field blocked the wind and diminished the surrounding noise; a strange urge drove him to deactivate the field.

Roaring air rushed around him, sweeping his hair back and threatening to blow him off the bike, but he tightened his hold against the force.

For an instant, a faded, distant memory rose to the forefront of his mind—he was riding a strange beast beneath an endless, starry sky as it raced across a field of tall, fragrant grass. The wind brushed over his face, tousled his hair...

Tenthil growled. That life had been taken from him forever. He would not allow his female to be taken, too. He reactivated the protective field and pushed his vehicle faster.

Not long after entering the Undercity, he pulled into a narrow, secluded alleyway, and turned off the hoverbike. He pried open the compartment to access the bike's electronic components and ripped out the navigation and tracking system, tossing the parts to the ground. The gap he left in the compartment wasn't pretty, but the bike started when he pressed the ignition; that was all he needed.

He continued his journey, eventually parking a full sector away from his destination. Even with the tracking components removed, he was wary of the Master having some way of locating the vehicle. The day was young, and he had time enough to reach Cullion's manor on foot, but the decision rekindled his impatience. He wanted his female *now*, wanted to renew the strength of her scent in his nostrils, wanted to feel her skin beneath his fingertips and lips. It took a startling amount of willpower to keep himself from climbing onto the bike again and piloting it directly to Cullion's front door.

He navigated the Undercity streets and walkways by memory—years of work had left him familiar with many of its sectors. The streets were filled with beings of all shapes and sizes conversing in countless languages as they shopped, traded, ate, performed, and traveled. Tenthil was aware of them only in that they were potential obstacles between him and his goal; the mere thought of any further delay in obtaining the terran made his chest constrict.

Large, crowded elevators eventually brought him to the next tier—the Gilded Sector. The differences between it and the neighboring sector were stark. Everything here was cleaner and more refined. Fewer people walked the streets, and those who did were well-dressed. The hovercars speeding by overhead were of a higher grade.

Eternal Guard peacekeepers were positioned in plain sight at regular intervals, making their presence clear.

Tenthil knew this area well—he'd completed many contracts here. Though the Eternal Guard was operated by the city's overlords, the Consortium, would-be troublemakers were often deterred from entering such areas by the prevalence of private security personnel employed by wealthy residents and businesses. Such security firms were unconcerned with legal process or moral standing. They were licensed to utilize deadly force to protect the interests and lives of their clients.

But hired guns and sophisticated security equipment had never been a deterrent to Tenthil.

Though his fiery emotions did not ease, his instincts shifted in response to the new challenges presented by his surroundings—he became a hunter stalking the shadows rather than a bloodthirsty, rampaging beast.

Despite the sector's pristine shops, offices, and luxurious homes, it was just as riddled with alleys, maintenance tunnels, and catwalks as any other part of the Undercity. Tenthil used those secluded pathways to his advantage, keeping out of sight as he moved toward Cullion's home. He maintained the faint bioelectrical buzz on his skin that would mask his presence to most electronic devices throughout.

His first glimpse of the manor was from above, when he stopped on a maintenance catwalk which ran across the underside of the sector's ceiling and stared down at his intended destination from fifty meters up.

Cullion's home was emblematic of the people who tended to dwell in these upper-class sectors—it appeared to be constructed of materials that few people could afford, and its exterior lights served only to accent the shining metallic inlays and detailed carvings on its walls. Its dark-tinted windows hid the interior from prying eyes. Cullion wanted the world to know his wealth and to understand it would never be theirs.

A reinforced security wall, adorned to match the manor, enclosed the grounds. The gap between the wall and the building was largest out front, forming an open space fifteen or twenty meters wide. Along the sides of the building, that separation dwindled to only three or four meters. Even those as wealthy as Cullion couldn't afford to leave much space unused.

The sensors, holo recorders, and shock coils atop the outer wall were in plain view. They only enhanced the building's message —*I have it all, and none of it is for you.*

Tenthil counted five guards outside—two at the front door, two patrolling the grounds, and one on the roof. More were undoubtedly stationed inside. The only entrances visible from his vantage point besides the front were a side door and a door on the roof, the latter standing near an empty landing pad.

Normally, he'd only infiltrate such a place after days of surveillance and planning. Patrol patterns, shift changes, staff movements, the target's routine; there were countless variables to take into account. But now, restless twinges coursed along his legs, and his fingers repeatedly flexed and relaxed of their own accord, extending and retracting his claws.

Tenthil didn't have days to watch and plan; he had today. He had one chance.

There could be no failure.

He hurried to the nearest ladder and descended to street level two roads away from Cullion's. No one was nearby when he emerged from the maintenance door, and he plunged into the back alleys to loop around behind his destination. Many of the sector's residents dumped their trash in the rear alleys, out of plain sight, to await collection by sanitation drones. In other sectors, such leavings would've been picked through daily by scavengers desperate for anything they could eat or sell for a few credits. But the residents of the Gilded Sector deemed even their refuse too good for the unwashed masses, and both private security and the peacekeepers cleared out garbage pickers regularly.

Fortunately, that meant such alleys were typically deserted, making them ideal pathways for Tenthil.

He stopped behind Cullion's manor, checked for onlookers, and pressed himself against the rear wall to concentrate. He soon heard what he'd sought—the sound of heavy, booted foot-steps moving toward the front of the manor. Based on what he'd witnessed of the patrols, he had about thirty seconds before the security guard returned.

Drawing in a deep breath, he strengthened his bioelectric field, turned to face the wall, and hauled himself up. The sensor lights atop it flickered for a fraction of a second as he broke their detection field. That was all it took for his body to adapt to and mimic the sensor signal. Briefly, he felt the invisible energy projected around him, stretching along the wall to either side and continuing up to form a dome over the manor.

Tenthil braced his boots atop the wall and leapt across the gap between it and the building. He caught himself within a recess running from ground to roof, glanced around him, and climbed. The sculptures meant to dazzle onlookers provided ample handholds to speed his ascent.

Within moments, he grasped the edge of the roof and lifted his head to peer over it.

The lone rooftop guard paced toward the front of the building, auto-blaster in hand, swinging his gaze from side to side.

With a smooth motion, Tenthil pulled himself onto the roof. He drew a knife as he padded toward the guard, who was another vorgal. Apparently, Cullion preferred the tall, muscular, savage-looking beings for his personal security team. Many species considered vorgals intimidating, especially in hand-to-hand combat.

Just another obstacle in my path.

Tenthil crept up behind the vorgal, reversed his grip on the knife, and wrapped an arm around the guard's head to wrench it backward. Before the vorgal could make a sound, Tenthil extended his other arm past the vorgal's shoulder and jabbed the knife inward. The blade plunged into the center of the vorgal's throat; the species was particularly resistant to having their throats slit due to flexible-but-tough bone-like fibers on the sides of their trachea, an evolutionary remnant from a time when they would battle one another with tusks, seeking to bite vulnerable body parts.

Keeping hold of the vorgal, who was choking on his own blood, Tenthil glanced at the rooftop door. The scanner on the doorframe was the sort that read Consortium-issued ID chips, which were meant to be installed in every being in Arthos. Tenthil didn't have one, and even if he did, it would only trip the alarm if he scanned it here.

All he needed was a chip with the proper clearance—inside a living body.

The vorgal struggled, kicking and grasping blindly with his hands, but Tenthil was unhindered as he dragged his dying captive to the door. He swung the vorgal around to face the scanner. Several thin, indistinct beams projected from the scanner and swept up and down the vorgal's left arm.

With a beep and a click, the magnetic locks disengaged, and the door swung open. Tenthil shoved the vorgal aside, simultaneously twisting the knife and tearing it free. Tenthil caught the door with his boot before it could close, bent to wipe his blade clean on the vorgal's pants, and slipped into the manor. Knife in hand, he walked down the tristeel-grating steps and stopped at the blast door at the base of the landing.

Tenthil pressed his ear against the wall beside the door. He couldn't hear any alarms or panicked voices from the other side —a good sign, but it didn't mean he was clear of danger. Even if his entry hadn't been detected yet, it was only a matter of time before the other guards realized one of their own was down. Things would move quickly once that happened.

He tapped a knuckle against the control panel. The door receded into its frame, opening on a hallway adorned with stone sculptures, columns inlaid with gold, and dark, patterned carpeting. Tenthil stalked forward, shifting the knife into his left hand to drop his right hand to his blaster. His ears twitched and his nostrils flared. The place was quiet, but a variety of smells filled the air. One of them, though faint, belonged to the terran female—he had no doubt of it. His blood heated as he drew in a deep breath and focused on her scent.

She'd been here. She *was* here; he knew it instinctively, though logic dictated he couldn't possibly be sure.

When he reached a smaller hallway branching off the main one, he paused and sniffed the air again. The scent was subtly stronger there, so he turned and followed the new path. The corridor's modest décor suggested it was meant to keep servants out of sight.

Tenthil's conscious thoughts gradually retreated to the back of his mind, leaving only his immediate sensory perception and the driving need to locate his female.

He passed several closed doors, following that scent onward. The terran was somewhere deeper inside the manor, caged like an animal, kept as a trophy for this arrogant ertraxxan to show off as he chose. The flames already raging in Tenthil's chest intensified, spreading heat through his body.

He rounded a corner and nearly collided with another vorgal guard, this one stationed in front of an elevator.

The surprised vorgal turned toward Tenthil, his gaping mouth displaying jutting tusks. Before the guard had completed his turn, Tenthil lunged forward and pushed up off the floor, throwing his weight behind his elbow as he slammed it into the guard's chin. The vorgal's head snapped back and struck the wall. Tenthil grasped the back of the vorgal's skull, holding it steady, and thrust his knife into the underside of his foe's jaw. Blood flowed over Tenthil's gloved hand and dripped onto the floor. He tugged his weapon free just as a door opened a few paces down the hall.

Two more guards hurried into the hallway—a broad-shouldered, scaled ilthurii and a dark-skinned volturian with glowing silver face markings.

The volturian tapped the comm unit on his chest. "Intruder on the upper—"

Tenthil drew his blaster and fired before the volturian could finish. A plasma bolt zipped through the volturian's throat and disappeared into the wall behind him, leaving a hole ringed in glowing orange. The dead vorgal, who Tenthil had released to draw his gun, collapsed to the floor.

Tenthil angled the blaster toward the ilthurii, but the scaled warrior was quick, charging forward before a second shot could be fired. Tenthil swayed aside, flattening himself against the wall.

The ilthurii's feet caught on the vorgal. He twisted and fell, raking his claws across the belly of Tenthil's armor as he passed. Angling his shoulder downward, the ilthurii threw himself into a roll.

Tenthil fired three plasma bolts into the ilthurii. The scaled warrior tumbled into the wall and went still.

The odors of freshly spilled blood and sizzling flesh filled the air, but they were not enough to mask the terran's scent, which was only more pronounced now that adrenaline had amplified Tenthil's senses.

Raising his blaster, he checked the room from which the guards had emerged. It was full of holo screens displaying surveillance feeds from all around the manor and its grounds. Each feed was designated by source location. Tenthil swept his gaze over all of them, pausing only when he saw *her*. Second floor, zoo chamber one. She wasn't alone—three females of other species were in her room.

More guards moved through the other feeds, four of whom were coming up the rear staircase with rifles at the ready. It would be difficult to avoid their blaster fire in these narrow halls. Several more were entering what appeared to be Cullion's study, where the ertraxxan, looking even more agitated than usual, sat behind a large wooden desk.

Tenthil leaned forward and manipulated the control console, changing the nearest holo to a three-dimensional map of the manor. A flashing yellow beacon pulsed in the third-floor hallway just outside the surveillance room, where he'd killed the guards. The security alert warned *INTRUDER, SHOTS FIRED*, but it seemed no external alarm had been sounded. The Starforge guards must've intended to deal with the problem themselves.

Within a few moments, Tenthil had committed the map to memory. He had only one goal here. All this was pointless if he didn't get the terran.

He fired his blaster into the control consoles. The equipment sparked and smoked as it shorted out, and the screens flickered off. Without wasting another second, he reentered the hallway and hurried toward the front staircase, away from the ascending guards.

Several male voices sounded from somewhere behind him, muted too much for it to have merely been the result of distance—there were likely sound dampeners positioned throughout the manor to maintain what people like Cullion called *dignified silence*.

Tenthil opened the stairwell door and slipped inside, keeping his blaster up as he walked down the stairs. When he reached the second-floor landing, he opened the door, checked his angles in both directions along the hallway beyond, and stepped through. He moved cautiously despite his impatience; the sound dampeners would quiet his enemies' movements as much as they would his own.

He inhaled. The female's scent was stronger here than it had been upstairs.

She was close.

Summoning the manor's layout in his mind's eye, Tenthil hurried through the corridors, heading back toward the rear of the building. Somehow, he'd encountered no one by the time he turned into a wide hallway with plush carpeting and colorful cloths and tapestries on the walls. Sculptures of naked females from half a dozen species stood along the sides. Each statue was somehow majestic yet meek, powerful yet subservient. Perhaps it was the commonality in their stances—though each exhibited a certain confidence in their postures, all had their chins down-turned and eyes averted.

They reminded Tenthil of the way his terran had carried herself at Twisted Nethers.

The terran's scent strengthened with each of Tenthil's steps, drawing him along steadily faster. The hallway ended in a large, circular antechamber ringed by elaborately carved wooden doors, with several long, low couches at its center.

The zoo—where Cullion kept his pets.

Striding forward, Tenthil approached the central door. It was larger than the rest, its white, gold-accented face in sharp contrast to the blacks, browns and dark reds of the other doors. This was the chamber housing Cullion's favorite pet. Too bad for Cullion that his ownership was invalid; Tenthil had the only legitimate claim on the terran.

He glanced over his shoulder; there was no movement from down the hallway, no muffled voices. Whatever time remained before the guards discovered his current location needed to be used as efficiently as possible.

Tenthil opened the terran's door.

Her intoxicating scent enveloped him, and all he could do was close his eyes and breathe, relishing the dizzying power of her fragrance. The brief delay was nearly too much to bear; his cock strained within the confines of his pants, and a ravenous, maddened growl threatened to rise from his chest.

Clenching his jaw, he shook off the spell. He could lose himself in it later.

He opened the door wider and slipped through.

Tenthil studied the room as he eased the door shut behind him. Given the décor in the antechamber, the furnishings here weren't a surprise. Gauzy panels of colored cloth hung from ceiling to floor, warping the perceived shape and size of the room. Several sets of holographic orbs provided light, revolving and twirling overhead in a ceaseless dance that made the metallic accents and billowing cloths all around shimmer.

Several couches and seats, covered with pillows of varying colors, sat in the open space between Tenthil and the far wall, which had two doors. A glance was all it took to tell this was a place of luxury, a place for a pampered pet.

The three unfamiliar females were seated on the couches around the terran, whose back was turned toward Tenthil. His female was fully clothed now, displaying little of her pale skin. The other females chatted quietly as they tended to her—her cosmetics, nails, and hair—but she did not join the conversation.

The female volturian glanced toward him, and her eyes widened. She released a high-pitched shriek, yanking the brush through the terran's hair as she scrambled up and over the back of the couch.

"Ouch! What the hell?" The terran—*his* terran—flinched, and her hand flew up to grasp her scalp. She rose from the upholstered stool she'd been seated upon.

The other two females turned their heads toward him. With fear shining in their eyes, they leapt off the couches and retreated to the farthest wall, joining the volturian.

The terran stiffened. She slowly slid her hand down her hair until her fingers touched the brush tangled in it. Grasping the handle, she tugged the brush out of her hair and spun to face him, brandishing the object as though it were a deadly weapon. The gesture, though futile, was oddly endearing to him.

She had a brave heart, and he admired her courage.

Despite her body being concealed by her clothing, he immediately recognized the difference in her—she was thinner than before, paler.

He clenched his jaw against a flare of rage.

Returning his knife to its sheath, Tenthil stepped deeper into the room.

With her brow creased and lips pressed into a tight line, she swept her gaze over him. Her eyes rounded and lit up with sudden recognition when they met his.

"*You,*" she breathed.

FIVE

The world around Abella fell away; her reality unraveled, thread by thread. It was *him*—the scarred stranger—here in this room, right in front of her.

And that wasn't possible.

She'd dreamed of him every night and imagined him every day since their dance. Recalling those moments with the stranger had been her only solace during her punishment, and now he was *here*. But there was something different about him, something...*primal*.

His features seemed sharper, the scars on his cheeks stood out in stronger contrast to his pale gray skin, and his eyes, formerly bright silver, were now black pools, twin abysses that would devour her if she stared too long.

She lowered her gaze, trailing it over his dark armor and the knives strapped to his chest and belt.

He was covered in blood. She found that more unsettling than the gun in his hand or his arsenal of blades, because the blood meant he'd *used* those weapons, perhaps only seconds before entering her room.

That realization, paired with the intensity of his stare, sent a shiver up Abella's spine.

She took several unsteady steps backward, stopping only when her calves bumped the couch behind her. "What do you want?"

The stranger lifted his empty hand and pointed at her.

"Me?" Her eyes widened as she glanced at his gun. "Look, I don't know what I did... If...If you got into some trouble back at Twisted Nethers, I'm sorry, but I *really* don't think you should use that on me. It won't fix anything."

In her peripheral vision, she saw Belanna, Moya, and Tenel—the females Cullion tasked with her care, as though she were incapable of bathing herself or brushing her own hair— clinging to one another as they inched along the wall toward the exit.

The stranger raised the gun slightly. Abella's heart leapt into her throat, and she might have released a strained whimper. His eyes flicked to the weapon, and when they returned to hers, he shook his head. Continuing his slow advance, he slid the gun into the holster on his hip and held his hand out as though he expected her to run forward and take it.

The other women raced to the door. The stranger was either oblivious to them or simply didn't care. The door clicked open, and they disappeared into the chamber beyond.

Leaving Abella was alone with the stranger.

Her eyebrows fell. "You...you want me to go with you?"

He nodded once.

Abella's breath left her in a rush. She swept her gaze over his towering frame again, and a thrill swept through her. She lowered her trembling arm and her pathetic *weapon*. After her time in the isolation chamber, during which she'd received little food and water, even holding up a hairbrush for more than a few seconds was too much exertion. Her battered back ached, her muscles were stiff, and her skin felt stretched thin over her narrow frame.

The discomfort and exhaustion she'd forgotten in the throes of fear came back to her now, but she wasn't so tired that she'd pass up an opportunity to seize her freedom.

"You're going to help me escape? You're going to free me?" she asked.

Another nod. The black in his eyes receded, revealing slivers of his silver irises. He stepped closer, leaving barely half a meter between them, and raised his hand toward her face as though he meant to touch her. He stopped it abruptly, turning his palm to stare down at it. Dark blood clung to his glove and the tips of the claws protruding through the material. The his mouth dipped in a slight frown.

Abella swallowed thickly. "You're not going to hurt me, right?"

She knew she couldn't stop him if he wanted to, but she'd endured so much pain, and she wasn't interested in experiencing any more.

His brow furrowed. Curling his bloody fingers into a loose fist, he shook his head. Something in his face—perhaps the light in his eyes—made Abella believe him.

"Are you going to help get me home?" she asked, her stomach clenching with a foolish surge of hope like she'd not felt in years.

His pointed ears twitched, and he snapped his head to the side. A few moments passed before she heard what had caught his attention—voices from the hallway beyond her door, Cullion's the loudest amongst them. And they were increasing in volume.

"You need to hide!" she said, moving around him and advancing a few steps.

He turned to face her, his eyes once again black voids. His

nostrils flared, and his upper lip curled, revealing his savage fangs.

The expression sparked unexpected heat in her core and made her sex clench.

What the hell? Definitely not the time!

Especially as those voices were drawing closer.

"Really, you need to hide. They'll kill you if they find you in here." She pointed behind him, toward her bedchamber. "Go in there. I'll let you know once it's clear."

For a moment, she swore he'd advance on her again. Her body strained toward him, toward the memory of his touch, of his warmth. But he turned away and darted to her bedroom instead, opening the door and entering without making a sound.

She inhaled shakily and planted her feet beneath her. This was the sort of opportunity she'd sought for four years—and this time, it could work. This time, she stood a chance of reclaiming her freedom. She wouldn't spoil that chance by succumbing to lustful impulses.

"Do you need to be reminded who is the employer and who is the employee?" Cullion said as he strode into Abella's room with two bodyguards ahead of him and two more behind.

"No, sir," replied the foremost guard, a large, tan-skinned borian, "but you pay us to keep you safe. That means we need to get you to the hovercar out front and off the premises until we've cleared the building."

"I will not leave my most valuable pet behind while an intruder prowls my home." Cullion leveled his furious gaze on Abella as he approached her.

She bowed her head, averted her eyes, and clasped her hands in front of her midsection.

"Where is he?" Cullion demanded.

"Gone," Abella said.

"You expect me to believe he just *left*?" Cullion caught her cheeks between his long fingers, digging his fingertips into her flesh, and forced her face toward his. He glared down at her, his long neck bending forward. "Do not mistake me for a fool, you ungrateful wretch. The others said he came in here for *you*."

Abella squeezed her hands together as his fingernails bit into her cheeks. No matter her reply, Cullion wouldn't believe her. "He didn't say anything while he was here."

It wasn't a lie. The stranger had never spoken a word to her.

The fury in Cullion's eyes intensified. He didn't look away from her when he barked a command to his guards. "Search these quarters."

Cold dread flooded Abella.

The borian cleared his throat. "Sir, we need to evac—"

Cullion spun toward the borian, silencing him with a glower. "I will not be forced out of my own home by street filth! Find him and kill him, or you will have to explain to your superiors that you are personally responsible for the termination of my contract with Starforge."

No. Please. Please don't find him.

The words repeated over and over in her head. The silent stranger was her only hope, her only chance to be free, to leave this place, this planet, and get home.

But how could the stranger evade Cullion's security? There was nowhere to hide, only one way out, and he was outnumbered.

The other bodyguards—three vorgals—walked forward with their gunstocks against their shoulders, checking behind the couches, cushions, and gauzy, hanging cloths. The borian remained near Cullion, who forced Abella to her knees with a dismissive shove.

She gritted her teeth against the jolt in her legs and the twinge in her back.

Cullion slipped his fingers into her hair, seized a fistful of it, and pinned her head to his robed leg, allowing her neither to bend down into her normal submissive position nor straighten her back.

With her heart thundering in her chest, she watched the guards from the corners of her eyes.

The vorgals stopped in front of the bathroom door. One of them kicked it open with a crash, clearing the way for his companions to enter the room. The scene reminded her of the police movies she used to watch with her dad when she lived at home—his dental career hadn't offered much excitement, so he'd garnered vicarious thrills through action movies.

The memory made her chest constrict. Her disappearance must've crushed him. Was he okay? Were her mother and brothers okay? Were they still looking for her, or had they given up and assumed her dead?

"Clear," one of the guards called from within the bathroom. They reentered the main room, and all three relocated to the bedroom door.

Abella tensed. Her tongue suddenly felt like it was made of sandpaper, and her breaths were too shallow to fill her lungs. Cullion's grip on her hair tightened.

The bedroom door was opened a crack, but the room beyond was dark. The vorgals took their positions on either side of the doorway. One reached forward, flattened his palm against the wood, and pushed the door open. Soft light spilled into the bedchamber, creating a weak patch of illumination.

Abella's breath caught in her throat when two of the vorgals entered the bedroom. Her speeding heartbeat drowned out all other sounds.

With a choked grunt, one of the vorgals inside the room stumbled backward. Abella lost sight of the pair. The high, punchy sound of their guns firing punctuated their alarmed shouts, and the room lit up with the strobing glow cast by their weapons. All too soon, the room fell silent and dark.

Cullion growled and thrust Abella aside. She caught herself on her hands and pushed back onto her knees to stare at the open doorway.

The borian had positioned himself in front of Cullion and stood with his rifle aimed toward the bedroom.

"Gorok? Vreg?" called the vorgal who hadn't entered the bedroom; his back was pressed against the wall beside the doorway.

The only answer he received came in the form of three blaster shots. Abella jumped as plasma bolts burst through the wall behind the vorgal. Two caught him in the legs, and he fell toward the opening with a pained snarl.

The stranger was suddenly in the doorway. He caught the falling vorgal from behind, looping an arm around his neck, and hefted him up, using him as a shield. He peered over the vorgal's shoulder with one black eye—not at his foes, but at *Abella.* Her breath quickened, and, shamefully, a rush of heat spread low in her belly. His stare was so bestial, so possessive, that she was more a slave to the stranger in that moment than she'd ever been to Cullion.

"Shoot him!" Cullion shouted.

"I'm not going to shoot my own man," the borian replied.

"I pay you. Your lives belong to me!" When the borian continued to hesitate, Cullion snarled, "Shoot him *now!*"

Releasing a frustrated shout, the borian fired his weapon. The bolts hit the wide-eyed vorgal in the chest; he was dead before he had the chance to make a sound.

Despite the horrific scene unfolding before her, it was the stranger who held Abella's attention. Moving faster than she thought possible for anyone—whether human or alien—he leapt aside a nanosecond before the gunfire struck the vorgal. A metallic flicker was the only indication of his wrist moving.

An instant later, the borian hissed in pain and dropped his rifle. The grip of a knife protruded from his forearm.

The stranger charged forward in another blaze of speed, leaping over a couch to slam his knee into the borian's chest. The borian crashed down onto his back, and the stranger landed atop him, pressing the barrel of his blaster to the guard's chin.

A wiry arm wrapped around Abella's throat and tugged her up and backward. She bumped into Cullion's chest, and he tightened his hold on her. She struggled against his grasp, fighting through the pain of another spasm in her back, but Cullion held her firmly.

A single blaster shot went off. The stranger rose and turned his head toward Abella, but now he was looking past her, fixing those impossibly black eyes on Cullion.

"Stay back," Cullion spat, body trembling. "Money, power, influence—whatever you want, I can give it to you. Just back away!"

The stranger paused and dropped his blaster into its holster. His fingers curled, and his claws lengthened.

Cullion tensed. "*You.* From Twisted Nethers. You are the one who murdered Drok. The one who dared to touch my pet." His voice lowered, turning into something closer to a growl. "All this for an *animal?* For this wretched, disobedient creature? If she is truly what you are after, I *will* kill her. It is my right as her owner."

The stranger took a step closer. Cullion staggered back, dragging Abella with him and strengthening his grasp. She grunted and clenched her jaw, nostrils flaring as her airflow was cut off.

Hell no. Not now, not like this. Not when freedom is so close.

A fire ignited in her chest. She would not be brought low. She would not die at the hands of this foul being who'd demeaned and abused her for the last four years. She would not die here, and she refused to spend another second as his *pet*. She wouldn't let all her suffering be for nothing.

Fury like Abella had never felt swept through her. She bared her teeth, raised her hands, and bent her fingers like talons, raking them across his face. He started with a gasp, his hold on her loosening enough for her to turn and press her attack. She screamed, releasing all her pain, anger, and grief as she scratched at his flesh.

He extended his arms to shield his face from her strikes, but Abella was faster. She thrust her hands past his defenses and gripped the sides of his head, jamming her thumbs into his cruel, beady eyes. He yelled and swatted her arms away, but not before one of her nails punctured his eye.

Cullion shrieked. One of his flailing arms struck Abella's head; it was a glancing blow, but it gave him an opportunity to grab a fistful of her hair. He raised his other hand to join the first, and, using his greater weight, swung her around and forced her backward.

Her head struck the wall before her body did. Her vision blurred, and the room spun around her.

Still shrieking, Cullion tugged her away from the wall and slammed her against it again. Abella's vision went black for an instant. Her knees buckled, but he held her up by her hair, adding a fresh sting to her mounting pain. Blue blood oozed from Cullion's eye, trickling over his pronounced cheek bone to stain his bared teeth. She grasped his forearms, desperate to break his hold, but she couldn't find the strength.

Darkness flowed in at the edges of her vision.

No. Not here. Not now. Not him.

The stranger appeared behind Cullion. Abella's blurred vision blended light and shadow to turn him into a dark, avenging specter. He reached over Cullion's shoulders, clamped his hands on the ertraxxan's head, and wrenched it to the side.

The skin of Cullion's neck tore, spilling more blood, as the stranger twisted the ertraxxan's head around until it faced backward. The series of wet, jarring cracks that accompanied the motion were some of the most horrifying—yet satisfying—sounds Abella had ever heard.

Cullion's hands, suddenly limp, fell away from her hair. The alien who'd owned Abella for four years, who'd kept her as his performing monkey, collapsed.

Finally free.

It was her last thought before the darkness claimed her.

SIX

Tenthil stepped over the dead ertraxxan and bent forward, slipping his hands under the sagging terran's arms to catch her before she fell. Her head lolled. Frowning, he swept her hair back from her face and examined her for injuries. Cullion's blue blood had spattered her face and chest and covered her hand, but as far as Tenthil could tell, she wasn't bleeding herself. She did, however, have a lump on the back of her head, and her complexion was pallid.

He clenched his teeth against a fresh wave of rage. He should've moved quicker, but he hadn't wanted to risk harming her. Though he admired the fight she'd put up, she'd made it difficult for Tenthil to get in a clean blow during her struggle with Cullion.

Crouching, Tenthil laid the unconscious female over his left shoulder and looped his arm around her middle. He turned his face toward her, inhaled her heady scent, and nuzzled his cheek against her side.

He grappled for control as his muscles stiffened and his cock throbbed anew. His body didn't seem to care that this was not the time. There were more Starforge personnel on the premises, and the Eternal Guard had likely been alerted by now. He needed to get her out of this place and tend her wounds.

Only when she was safe and healed could he give in to his primal desires.

Tenthil drew his blaster with his right hand, checked its charge, and stepped over the corpses to enter the bedroom. He dialed the weapon's power to maximum; it emitted a high hum as its core heated. Turning his body sideways to shield the terran, he extended his arm and aimed the blaster at the recessed wall behind the wide, low bed. He suspected it was a window that had been covered at some point.

There wasn't time to waste hoping he was correct.

He turned his face away and squeezed the trigger. The blaster's whine intensified to an undulating buzz. A second later, a massive burst of plasma erupted from the barrel. The room shook with a deafening boom, and rubble, smoke, and dust filled the air.

Tenthil waved the blaster to clear away some of the acrid fumes. The slowly dissipating smoke revealed a two-meter-wide hole over the debris-laden bed, its edges glowing orange. The alleyway behind the manor was visible through the opening. He holstered the blaster; it was hot enough that he felt it through both the shielded holster and his pants.

Gently, he slid the human off his shoulder and gathered her in his arms, clutching her against his chest. He ran forward, hopped onto the bed, and leapt through the hole.

His boot touched down atop the wall; he used that point of contact to thrust himself back toward the manor, landing in a crouch on the ground between the building and the barrier. He shifted the female over his shoulder again as he rose and drew his blaster. Working with one hand, he ejected the smoking power cell and slid a new one into place. A flick of his thumb closed the cell compartment.

Tenthil dialed the output down to normal as he jogged along the three-meter-wide path. He needed to leave the sector as quickly as possible, and he knew of only one vehicle nearby.

Turning at the outside corner, he hurried down the side of the manor toward its front yard. Only as he neared the next corner did he stop to carefully lower the terran, tucking her in the shadowed base of a recess in the wall. Once she was sitting —unresponsive but breathing—he rounded the corner.

Two vorgal guards stood beside the hovercar, their attention directed toward the manor's front entrance.

"Report team two," said one of the guards. He was silent for several seconds; his expression falling, before he turned away and spat out a series of curses in his native tongue.

"What does he mean they're all dead?" the other guard demanded, looking at his companion.

Their distraction was the opening Tenthil needed. Keeping low, he crept forward, reaching the hovercar on the side opposite the guards. A few more steps brought him around to face them. He fired rapidly into the nearest guard's back. Several of the plasma bolts pierced the first guard and hit the second. They both released abrupted, choked cries and fell.

Tenthil tugged open the rear door and was rounding the vehicle to return to the terran when he paused. There was a cage built onto the back of the car. Any creature inside would be on full display, like an animal in a mobile zoo.

His stomach sank when he realized its purpose. He hurried back to the female and frowned down at her.

Had she been forced to ride in that cage, exposed for the world to see? Had she served as a living ornament for the wealthy ertraxxan's vehicle? He swallowed his anger; it would do no good now. Cullion was dead.

Tenthil lifted her over his shoulder again. Her closeness renewed his awareness of her scent, and it took a surprising amount of willpower to ignore it.

We must *reach safety.*

He brought her to the car, checking behind him frequently over the short trip, and laid her across the back seat. He had no doubt that Cullion had reclined in comfort in the luxuriously furnished cab while the terran had been stuffed in the cage out back. Fresh rage flowed through Tenthil's body, but he did not give it control. He gently shut the door and climbed into the driver's seat.

Dipping a hand into one of the pouches on his belt, he removed a tiny disc the size of his fingertip and pressed it onto the control panel. With an electric crackle, the device activated. The hovercar's display flashed an error, warning that the navigation network could not be accessed; the jammer was functional. The hovercar would be untraceable for three hours.

That was more than enough time.

He pulled back on the controls, guiding the hovercar upward, and angled it toward the nearest express tunnel. Without a backward glance, he engaged the throttle and sped away from Cullion's manor.

Even without the navigation equipment running, Tenthil knew the way back to his hoverbike; he followed an out-of-the-way, meandering route, watching for pursuit throughout. He landed the hovercar a kilometer away from the bike.

The terran's weight was slight, but carrying her through the sometimes cramped maintenance tunnels and catwalks he traveled to avoid prying eyes proved challenging. He had no desire to harm her further, meaning he was often forced to slow his pace.

As time and distance separated him from Cullion's manor, a rational voice reemerged in the back of his mind, reminding him that there would be consequences for what he'd done. He cast it aside; his needs, at that moment, were simple—a safe location and equipment to tend to his terran. Everything else could wait a while longer.

When he reached the hoverbike, he turned the female toward him and sat her in front of him, leaning her against his chest. He hooked an arm around her torso to secure her in place and grasped the controls with one hand. She'd been unconscious for almost an hour now. He knew enough about terran anatomy to kill one efficiently, but he wasn't certain of their limits, tolerances, and normal functions. Was this typical, or was it a bad sign? How easily did they suffer internal damage?

How durable were they?

Her head settled against his shoulder as they darted through another express tunnel, and he rested his cheek on her hair. It was soft, smooth, and fragrant, adding a floral note to her scent. If her closeness alone hadn't been enough, her smell pushed him over the edge. His body demanded her, cock pulsing and balls aching. To have her here, in his hold, and be unable to *do* anything was maddening.

Growling, he twisted the throttle, making the hoverbike lurch forward with a fresh burst of speed.

Despite his concern for the terran's wellbeing, he drove two full sectors in the wrong direction before finally diverting to one of the many Order-operated safehouses scattered throughout the city. The severity of the bump on her head wouldn't matter if they were blasted out of the air by a Starforge clean-up crew.

After guiding the vehicle into the small garage and sealing the entry door, Tenthil climbed off the bike and lifted the human into his arms. He glanced at the surveillance screen positioned beside the stairwell entrance. The feeds monitored all sides of the large building, watching for activity, but everything was currently clear. Tenthil carried the terran through the interior door and into the living space.

Like most of the Order's safehouses, the furnishings were sparse but functional. Food storage and preparation shared a room with the bed. A door in the corner led into a lavatory with a narrow shower stall. Another door—designed to blend seamlessly with the wall—opened on a chamber containing weapons, ammunition, equipment, and a terminal to access the Order's network.

He laid his terran on the bed and paused, briefly debating whether to scour the room for surveillance equipment and deactivate it. He opted not to; disabled feeds would rouse immediate suspicions back at the temple, drawing the Master's attention to him that much faster. He could shroud himself from the cameras. That would have to be enough for now.

Tenthil turned away from the female to remove his armor, boots, gloves, and combat suit, setting it all aside for later cleaning. Dressed only in his undershorts, he walked back to the bed and stared down at her.

It was the first quiet moment he had to truly look upon her, to examine her face in pure light and absorb its details. Her skin was pale, nearly translucent, offering hints of thin, blue veins at her temples and on her delicate eyelids. He placed a hand upon the bed next to her shoulder and bent closer. Thick, dark lashes rested upon her cheeks, and shapely brows arched over her eyes, leading to a straight, pert nose.

Tenthil moved a hand to her face and lifted several strands of hair that had fallen over it, rubbing it between his fingertips. Many species in Arthos had hair, but hers was unlike any he'd encountered. Though it was straight and thick like his, it was softer, and possessed a subtle sheen. He trailed his fingers down the strands, which shifted from black to vibrant blue. His knuckles brushed the smooth skin of her neck, sending a wave of heat up his arm.

His gaze dropped to her mouth. Sweet venom flowed over his tongue as he recalled the feel of those pink lips against his. Soft, inviting, yielding. He swallowed thickly and lowered his mouth toward hers only to halt when he caught scent of blood—Cullion's blood. Clenching his teeth against his desire, against the throbbing in his groin, against his need to touch her, Tenthil drew back.

He grasped her blood-stained shirt by the collar, punctured the fabric with his claws, and split the material from her throat to belly. He sucked in a sharp breath, and his eyes widened.

She was bare beneath.

His heart pounded. Despite the blue blood that had seeped through her clothing to smear her pale flesh, she was the most beautiful creature he'd ever seen. Before her, he'd never felt such desire, had never fallen victim to his body's cravings, had never abandoned self-control like he wanted to in her presence. Everything within him yearned for this female—for her touch, her scent, her *taste*.

He lowered a hand to her breast and brushed the pad of his thumb over her pink nipple, which hardened immediately. It was only then he realized his hands were trembling—not because the high of battle had finally faded, but because of his overwhelming, unfathomable *need*.

Never in his life had his hands been unsteady—it was unacceptable for what he was, for what he did.

Tenthil snatched his hand away from her, breaking that contact, and released a shuddering breath.

Fuck.

Straightening, he thrust his clawed fingers into his hair, tugging it back hard enough to produce sharp pain on his scalp, and growled. He backpedaled and forced himself to turn away from the terran.

What is wrong with me?

The question tumbled through his head, repeating itself, but he focused past it; at that moment, the answer was unimportant. His world had been one of shadows, violence, and death for almost as long as he could remember, and he'd learned long ago that thinking too far ahead could easily cause more trouble than it solved. Tenthil worked best when he tackled one issue at a time.

He needed to check her for wounds and tend to them as best he could—that was the priority now.

He couldn't afford to stop and imagine how different his life could be with her in it.

Clenching his jaw, he hurried into the lavatory, where he scrubbed the blood off his claws, fingertips, and face. Then he returned to the bedside. He ignored the ache in his groin as he took careful hold of her, worked her arms out of her sleeves, and rolled her onto her side to pull away her shredded shirt. He stilled when his gaze settled on her back.

Dark, thin bruises crisscrossed her back, each surrounded by irritated red skin indicative of mild burns.

He knew the marks for what they were—wounds from an electrolash. The Master had used one on Tenthil before in hopes of curtailing his tendency toward insubordination. His own back tingled with the memory of the pain.

The fury that had prompted him to action earlier rekindled, replacing the oddly sweet venom in his mouth with the bitter. His claws lengthened as his muscles tensed. He should have taken his time with Cullion, should have made the bastard suffer for hours, for *days*, before granting him the release of death.

A low growl rose from his chest as he grasped her collar on

both sides and pulled. The ornamented metal bit into his fingers, but he ignored the pain. With a groan, the latch broke, and the sides of the collar bent outward. He tossed the neck-band aside.

The faint scarring around her neck—barely perceptible against her pale skin—further fueled his now-impotent rage. But with no immediate threat to her, his instinct turned in another direction—he wanted, *needed*, to draw her close and comfort her, to nurse her wounds, to make her know everything would be all right. That there was nothing more to fear.

She was *his*. And he would protect her from anyone, *anything*, until his dying breath.

SEVEN

Abella's head throbbed. The pain pulsed from her temples to encompass her entire skull, amplified by every beat of her heart. She'd never had a headache this severe, not even after she'd overindulged at her first college party.

Groaning, she pulled her knees toward her chest to curl into a ball, but she stopped when she remembered the wounds on her back. Over the last week, any movement that stretched her back had agitated the angry bruises inflicted by the electro-lash, leaving her in agony. Yet there was no tightness now, no discomfort—not even a twinge. All she felt was the caress of a cool, soft sheet against the bare skin of her back.

Bare skin?

Abella frowned, lifted her head, and opened her eyes, blinking against the light until her vision cleared. A wholly unfamiliar room greeted her. It was a little larger than her bedchamber, and its practicality, lack of decoration, and mini-mal, utilitarian furnishings stood in harsh contrast to the gaudiness of Cullion's manor. The walls and ceiling were the same dull gray. Several rectangular panels overhead cast the room in a dull white light.

This place was like the studio apartment of a man who was never home, the kind of man who slept and ate only because those things were necessary to fuel his body.

Brows low, Abella sat up. The movement brought on a wave of dizziness; she winced and pressed a hand to her head. The blanket fell to her lap, baring her breasts, and her frown deepened.

Where the hell was she?

And where the hell were her clothes? She never slept naked.

The click of a latch called her attention to the door across from the foot of the bed. She looked up, and her breath caught in her throat. *He* stood in the doorway, wearing only a pair of black pants, his damp silver hair hanging about his shoulders.

Everything returned to her in a rush—she remembered being released from the isolation chamber, remembered being bathed, remembered the servants preparing her for an audience with Cullion. That was when this scarred stranger had entered her room. She remembered...blood.

Cullion's blood.

The air fled her lungs as she stared at the stranger, who stared right back at her. His eyes dipped, reminding her of her nudity.

Cheeks flushing, she gathered the blanket and clutched it over her chest. His gaze returned to hers, pupils swallowing a little more of his silver irises, and even though her breasts were no longer on display, her nipples hardened as though he'd physically stroked them.

She tightened her grip on the blanket. "Is Cullion...really dead?"

The stranger nodded. Her heart fluttered as he stepped closer.

"It's over?" she asked. "I'm free?"

He moved closer still, his toned muscles rippling beneath his pale gray skin, his eyes intense.

"Um, my name is Abella. What's yours?"

The stranger paused at the foot of the bed. For a moment, she thought he'd finally reply to her, that she'd finally hear his voice. Instead, he placed his hands on the bed, climbed atop it, and crawled toward her.

Her breath quickened, and she scooted back, keeping a tight hold on the blanket. "W-What are you doing?"

He moved with the surety and grace of a stalking panther, shrinking the distance between them until he was close enough for her to feel his heat, to feel his weight pull the bedding taut over her thighs. He leaned over Abella, caging her between his arms, and dipped his head to press his lips against her neck. He drew in a slow, deep breath. A growl rumbled from him, and his claws flexed on the bedding.

The shocking feel of his warm breath and lips on her skin sent a thrill straight to Abella's core. The sensation was so powerful, so frightening, that she panicked. She placed her hands against his chest and pushed; he was startlingly solid and heavy.

A look of surprise crossed his face as he tumbled over the edge of the bed, landing on the floor with a loud thump. Abella scrambled off the other side of the bed, dragging the blanket along to keep herself covered, and backed away.

The stranger rose slowly and turned to face her. His expression was unreadable.

She had a sense that he'd crawled over her with deliberate slowness. She'd seen how quickly he could move back in the manor and had no doubt he could've crossed the bed and banded his arms around her before she'd even gained her feet if he'd wanted to.

"Did you steal me from Cullion just to make me *your* slave?" she asked, glaring at him. "Because I won't be. I will not spend even one more day as someone's property."

The fire in his eyes never flickered, never dwindled. It burned for *her*. The corner of his mouth tilted up.

"Did you hear me?" Abella demanded, anger overcoming her good sense—she had no leverage in this situation, no power, no leeway to dictate the terms of their relationship. "I won't be your slave or your whore!"

The stranger's gaze lingered on her before he turned and walked to the kitchenette in the far corner. He opened a cabinet, took out a tray, and placed it inside a microwave-like device. He pressed a few buttons, and a progress bar appeared on the display.

Abella's anger intensified. It was terrible enough to realize she'd been kidnapped for a second time rather than rescued, but to be ignored and so casually dismissed on top of that was infuriating.

The only things that had changed were the face of her owner and the appearance of her cage.

From the corner of her eye, she spotted another door, this one on the wall against which the bed was positioned. She slowly moved toward it while the stranger's back was turned. When she was within reach of the door, she leapt for it, curling her hand around the handle and turning it.

But the handle didn't budge. Growling, Abella threw her weight behind it, the cords of her neck standing out as she strained against the uncooperative latch. Only after her face was heated with exertion did she notice the small control panel on the door frame, displaying a set of alien symbols.

There'd been a translator implanted in her head when she

was brought to Arthos, granting her understanding of every language she'd heard during her time here, no matter how strange it sounded to her ears. But the translator did not extend to written language.

Not that it would've helped her in this situation—there was undoubtedly a code to unlock the door.

Something beeped in the kitchen. She turned her head to see the stranger approaching her with a steaming tray balanced on his hand. The aroma of hot food struck her, making her mouth water and her stomach growl.

The stranger met her gaze and pointed to the bed with his free hand.

Abella shook her head. "No."

He dipped his chin in a shallow nod. She'd never realized how powerful so small a gesture could be—he wasn't offering her a choice.

"I said *no*."

The stranger narrowed his eyes. Abella braced herself as he stepped forward, but he moved past her without making physical contact. He stopped at the foot of the bed, laid the tray atop it, and faced her again.

Abella turned toward him. "No. How many times do I need to say it? I want to go. Outside. Back to my people."

He advanced on her.

"Stay away from me!" Abella raised her hands—as though *she* would be able to fend him off—and stepped back. She bumped into a solid surface and started, glancing back to find the door behind her.

She'd never realized how quickly a person could come to hate an inanimate object.

When she looked forward, the stranger was already there.

Slipping one arm behind her back and the other beneath her knees, he swept her off her feet before she could react. He drew her against his chest; his heat enveloped her, radiating into her, despite the blanket pinned between their bodies. She struggled as he carried her toward the bed, but her resistance was fruitless—his hold, though not painful, was as strong as steel. He wasn't going to let her go, not until *he* was ready to.

The frustrated tears welling in her eyes only made Abella angrier. She hadn't allowed Cullion to break her, and she sure as hell wouldn't let this stranger do so either. She was tired, weak, her head hurt like a motherfucker, and all she wanted was to finally go home, but she was *not* broken.

She punched his shoulder as she sniffled. "I said *no*. I won't be your slave. I won't let y-you..."

The stranger stopped and gently sat her on the edge of the bed. She swept the blanket around her sides to cover herself as he released his hold and eased back, dropping into a crouch to meet her gaze. His pupils had reverted to slits again, granting her full view of the mercurial silver of his irises. There was something feline about his eyes that enhanced his air of mystery and danger.

"Tenthil," he said, his voice a harsh whisper.

Abella blinked, and a tear trekked down her cheek. "What?"

He lifted a hand and tapped his claws against his chest. "Tenthil."

"Your name?"

Tenthil nodded. His lips twitched, but she couldn't tell if they'd been shifting toward a smile or a frown before they reverted to a neutral line. He pointed to the food again.

She dropped her attention to the tray, glancing up at Tenthil uncertainly. "That's...for me?"

With another nod, he took the edge of the tray between the pads of his forefinger and thumb and dragged it closer to her.

"It will help." He raised a hand to the back of his head, indicating the same spot as the lump on her head.

The way he spoke reminded her of when she'd had laryngitis as a child, and her voice had stopped working. Was speaking as painful for him as it sounded? Perhaps he hadn't been ignoring her, after all. Maybe it was just difficult and physically uncomfortable for him to speak.

Did that mean he *was* going to help her? All she needed was a little glimmer of hope, a tiny spark, and she could get through this.

Abella tucked the sides of the blanket beneath her armpits, picked up the tray, and placed it on her lap. The food was unlike anything she'd eaten in the last four years—she suspected she'd been fed scraps from Cullion's meals all along but could know for sure. This stuff looked like canned dog food, but it smelled all right, and she was hungry enough after her time in the isolation chamber that she didn't much care about appearances.

Hesitantly, she picked up the pronged spoon from its shallow indentation, scooped up a chunk of food, and brought it to her lips. She met Tenthil's eyes as she slipped it into her mouth.

The texture was reminiscent of thick beef stew, and the flavor existed in that gray area between not bad and not good. But she at it swiftly, one bite after another, wolfing it down like she'd never eaten before. It wasn't until she'd scraped the tray clean and was raising it to her face to lick the remaining juices that she realized Tenthil had watched her, unmoving, the entire time.

Cheeks warming, she lowered the tray. "Thank you."

Tenthil nodded and took the tray from her, the pads of his fingers brushing against her knuckles for an instant.

She pulled her hands back, reminded of her nudity beneath the blanket. "Do you have any clothes I can wear?"

He carried the tray into the kitchen, dropped it into what was either a trash compactor or a washer of some sort, and turned his head toward Abella. His gaze dipped, and his pupils dilated. As black overwhelmed the silver of his irises, Abella realized his eyes weren't *empty* when they darkened like that.

They were full of hunger—and not for food.

Self-consciously, Abella tugged the blanket a little higher, covering as much of her chest as possible. When he only continued to stare, she narrowed her eyes and cleared her throat.

He lifted his chin, meeting her gaze again. His pupils slowly contracted. Offering her another nod, he walked across the room, stopping to the left of the bathroom door. Her brow furrowed as he raised a hand and tapped a spot on the empty wall.

A meter-wide section of the wall shifted a few centimeters backward before sliding aside and disappearing. Tenthil's body blocked most of the room beyond from her view, but she caught a glimpse of guns racked one of its walls.

He stepped through the opening, ducked out of sight for several seconds, and reemerged with a set of black clothes draped over his hand. He tossed them onto the bed beside her and set a matching pair of boots on the floor nearby.

Abella picked up the top garment and held it out in front of her. It was a long-sleeved black shirt, and appeared to be the right size for her. The material had a slightly rough texture on its outside and stretched a little when she tugged on it.

She returned her gaze to Tenthil. "How...did you survive all that? At Cullion's, I mean."

"They weren't very good," he said in his low, gritty voice.

Abella's brows lower. Not that good? Cullion had never

directly shared information about his dealings with her, but she'd overheard him brag about his security being the best money could buy on several occasions.

"Who are you?" she asked, glancing into the room behind him. "*What* are you?"

"Tenthil." The ghost of a smile crossed his lips as he gestured toward the clothing. "Need to go soon. Get ready."

Abella straightened. "Go? Go where? Are you taking me—"

But Tenthil had already turned away and walked back into the secret room, making no indication that he'd heard her. She had a feeling he wouldn't have told her much more anyway.

Despite her frustration and uncertainty, a tiny spark of hope lit within her. They were leaving. Though Tenthil had touched her—kissed her—without her permission, he'd done nothing to harm her. He'd fed her *and* clothed her. He didn't seem keen on giving her answers, but she didn't think he'd hurt her.

Things could be worse.

That thought reminded her of the wounds on her back— wounds that had been causing her immense discomfort before Tenthil had come for her.

She rose, scooped up the clothing he'd left on the bed, and moved to the center of the room, seeking a mirror or any surface reflective enough to grant her a glimpse of her back. There were none in plain sight. Frowning, she turned her head and attempted to check her back directly. When that didn't work, she settled for bending an arm backward and running her hand across her lower back. She encountered only smooth skin.

Her frown deepened as she twisted her torso side to side and bent forward, stretching her back. She felt no pain, no twinges, not even a hint of tight, healing skin. The damage inflicted by the electrolash was gone. Facing forward and standing straight, she looked over her arms and peeked beneath the blanket. There was no trace of the blue blood that had splattered her skin earlier.

She glanced at the secret room. Tenthil had cleaned her and tended her wounds while she was unconscious. That explained why she was naked. Heat suffused her; she'd been trying to cover herself this entire time, and he'd already seen *everything*.

And he apparently liked what he'd seen.

Cheeks flaming, she turned her back toward the secret room and released the blanket, which whispered down her body to pool around her feet. It was in that moment that she realized something else was missing—her collar. She pressed a hand to her throat, and though the weight of the collar was gone, a heaviness settled on her chest. Relieved tears once more stung her eyes.

I'm finally free of him.

She hurriedly dressed. Even though she wasn't entirely aware of her current circumstances, she knew they were better than before.

At least now she had a chance of getting home.

TENTHIL PAUSED as he opened one of the cabinet doors inside the equipment room and turned to look back into the living space.

Abella stood with her back toward him. His eyes roamed up her long, lithe legs, lingered on her rounded backside, and followed the graceful curve of her spine up to the blue tips of her long hair. She bent forward to pull on her pants, granting him a fleeting glimpse of her sex.

His body responded instantly, balls tightening and cock

stiffening. He gritted his teeth and curled his hands into fists. The prick of his claws breaking his skin didn't distract Tenthil from the sight before him. He wanted nothing more than to walk up behind her, take her hips between his hands, bury his shaft in her heat, and rut her until he'd spent every bit of strength in his body.

But he knew even that wouldn't be enough. His hunger for her was fathomless.

Straightening, Abella tugged the pants up over her hips. Tenthil turned his head away quickly. He released a shaky breath and squeezed his eyes shut for a moment.

I am acting like an animal.

This was the second time he'd lost himself in a haze of lust within the last fifteen minutes. Had she not shoved him off the bed when he pressed his lips to her neck earlier, he would have succumbed to his desires, would have obeyed his instincts and marked her with his fangs. That was unacceptable. He might have stumbled through his clouded judgment to make it this far, but he needed to think clearly if he intended to keep her safe.

Prioritize.

They needed supplies. Cullion had many connections, and it was possible some of them would seek retribution for his death, if only because he'd been one of the elite. That meant possible involvement from the Eternal Guard and Starforge. More worrisome than both—and far more dangerous—was the Order. The Master and his assassins posed the true threat.

Tenthil took the top half of a battle suit out of the locker and tugged it on, sealing it down the front. He fastened his belt over it, pulled on a pair of boots, and immediately set about supplying himself. He stuffed power cells, a spare blaster, blades, a few situational tools, spare clothing, a pair of thin-but-tough cloaks, food, and medical supplies into a durable backpack, grateful that most of it was extremely compact.

As he was emptying a small lockbox of untraceable credit chips, a familiar voice turned Tenthil's blood to ice.

"In a hurry?" the Master asked.

Tenthil turned slowly, dropping his hand to his blaster.

A holographic projection of the Master stood in the center of the equipment room, life-sized but faded. "Show yourself, Tenthil."

Tenthil clenched his jaw, maintaining his amped-up bioelectrical field to keep himself from showing up on the surveillance feeds.

"I know you're there." The Master tilted his head. "Just as I know the terran female is there. *Abella.*"

Hearing her name spoken by that voice, the voice he hated more than any other, poured fire into Tenthil's veins. His sudden realization that the Master had likely seen her naked only fanned the flames.

As though summoned, Abella peered around the edge of the door, long hair dangling below her tilted head. Her eyes widened.

The Master turned toward her. "Curious creatures, these terrans—or *humans,* as they sometimes call themselves. Still rare enough to be valuable."

She gasped and ducked out of the doorway.

The Master's low, dark chuckle made Tenthil's skin crawl. He released his bioelectric field as the Master faced him again.

"There was no contract on Traxes Cullion Orgathe," the Master said. "You killed him and ten members of his security team without any order to do so. And you stole his property."

Tenthil stared into the darkness beneath the Master's hood as the black-robed being stepped closer and raised a long-fingered hand. The holographic digits brushed through Tenthil's shoulder. He barely suppressed a shudder.

"The Eternal Guard has begun a formal inquiry into Cullion's death," said the Master, lowering his hand, "and Starforge Security is likely to launch their own investigation. That is not to mention the backlash amongst Cullion's numerous business partners, many of whom wield great influence. Though none are a threat to my Order, even you will understand that this situation will be a blight on our reputation should they discover the truth."

The Master walked through Tenthil, whose skin prickled with mingling fear and rage as he turned to follow the projection's movement.

"I am disappointed, Tenthil. All that potential wasted. All that talent and skill, all the time and money invested, all for nothing. The exceptional physical attributes of your species cannot make up for your inherently feral nature. You have left me no choice."

Tenthil's eyes rounded in sudden realization. He forced his bioelectric field back up, slung the bag of supplies over his shoulders, and darted out of the equipment room.

The Master chuckled. "I have whispered your name into the Well of Secrets, Tenthil. The time has come to admit my mistake, correct it, and continue forward. Make it easier on all of us—do not resist."

Abella stood with her back flattened against the wall beside the doorway. Fear gleamed in her eyes. "Tenthil, who is th—"

He dipped his shoulder, pressing it against her middle as he lifted her off her feet and dove toward the far side of the bed. Though the sound was muted, he heard an undulating buzz from the garage. He buried the claws of his free hand in the bed as he bounced off it and rolled onto the floor, landing with his body over Abella's and hauling the mattress over them.

Abella screamed as an explosion shook the room and debris pattered atop the mattress. She grasped his combat suit and buried her face against his neck.

The sound and stench of burning fabric suggested the mattress was on fire. Tenthil tugged his blaster free and aimed it under the bed. The boots of the acolytes who'd stepped through the breach were reduced to shadowy apparitions in the smoke, but that was all the target he needed.

He fired. Grunts of pain accompanied the thumping of falling bodies.

Tenthil broke Abella's hold and pushed himself to his feet, shoving the mattress aside. He swung the blaster toward the gaping, smoldering hole where the front door had stood a moment before. The overhead lights flickered off; small fires burning on the floor, mattress, and bed cast an orange glow on the room.

Angling the blaster down, he squeezed off five more bolts into the writhing acolytes on the floor, ceasing their movements. The slowly dissipating dust revealed only two bodies. Tenthil knew there were more assassins outside; the Master wasn't foolish enough to believe two would be adequate to close this contract.

A small device flew through the opening. Tenthil perceived only a small cylinder, no bigger than his thumb, before instinct kicked in. Turning his face away, he squeezed his eyes shut.

The device hit the floor with a delicate *clink*, followed immediately by a deafening bang. The flash of light it emitted was powerful enough for Tenthil to see through his eyelids even while facing the opposite direction.

His ears rang in the total absence of sound, but when he opened his eyes, his vision was unaffected. He turned back toward the breach and charged forward just as another acolyte entered.

Tenthil leapt over the bed and slammed his knee into the side of the acolyte's head, his momentum driving them both to the ground in the kitchen. Tenthil rolled aside, landing a half a meter away with his back against the wall. The acolyte scrambled unsteadily to his knees and swung his arm around to aim his blaster.

Shoving himself away from the wall, Tenthil kicked the acolyte's hand. The blaster flew out of the acolyte's grip and clattered across the room.

Two more black-clad assassins rushed in. Tenthil leveled his blaster, but the acolyte on the floor lunged at him before he could fire. He drove his elbow down on the acolyte's spine twice, denting the backplate of his foe's armor.

The newcomers raised their blasters and aimed them at Tenthil.

Growling, Tenthil hammered the butt of his blaster into the back of the still-struggling acolyte's head, grabbed hold of his foe's armor, and hauled the acolyte's body up to shield himself just as the other two opened fire.

The acolyte shook as plasma bolts struck his armor, and he released a pained groan—the sound was still distant to Tenthil's recovering ears—when the protection finally gave way. Even the best armor couldn't withstand sustained fire in the same place without time to cool. The acolyte's mouth opened in an agonized, silent scream. It would only be a matter of seconds before the bolts penetrated him completely. Tenthil already felt the heat, smelled the burning flesh.

Someone screamed—Abella, her voice muted by the temporary damage to his hearing.

More blaster shots sounded, but they originated from another part of the room.

Abella.

Tenthil risked a glance around his meat shield to see the

remaining pair of assassins taking fire from behind; they were turning toward the source.

Abella!

He roared, leapt to his feet—lifting the dead acolyte with him—and charged the assassins.

Caught between two enemies, the assassins froze for an instant. Tenthil threw the body at the one to the left and tackled the other, forcing the vorgal—the same one whose leg he'd broken earlier that week—back-first into the growing fire on the floor.

Tenthil slashed his claws across the vorgal's face over and over in rapid succession, shredding flesh and rending muscle. Dark blood spattered his hands and arms and hissed as it fell into the flames.

From his peripheral vision, Tenthil saw the other assassin shove the corpse aside and struggle to his feet. Tenthil turned, prepared to leap at his final foe, but a bolt of glowing plasma struck the assassin just beneath his left ear and burst out the right side of his head, leaving a mess of charred flesh behind.

The assassin stumbled aside and fell to the floor.

Tenthil snapped his attention to Abella. She stood on the far side of the bed with a blaster clutched in both hands, her eyes so wide and terrified that he feared they were about to pop out of her head. Arms trembling, she met his gaze.

He nodded and waved her over as he stood up. She hurried toward him, eyes on the floor as she stepped around blood, debris, bodies, and fire.

"What's happening?" she asked. "Who are they? W-what do they want?"

Based on the volume of her voice, Abella's hearing was still recovering, just like his.

Tenthil jabbed a thumb toward his chest. Bending forward, he swiftly unbuckled one of the acolytes' gun belts. He turned to Abella, and without releasing his blaster, reached around her to fasten the belt about her waist.

Once the belt was in place, he took her free hand with his and stepped toward the exit. The still-cooling edges of the ruined doorway glowed red orange.

He checked to both sides before stepping through into the garage. There were no other acolytes in sight. The bay door was open, and an unmanned hovercar idled just outside, blocking in Tenthil's hoverbike.

Can't use either vehicle, anyway. The Master is tracking their whereabouts.

Realization struck him like a slap to the face; the Order's vehicles were not the only thing the Master tracked.

He tracked its acolytes, as well.

Spawn of a skeks.

The tracker had been implanted in Tenthil so long ago that he'd forgotten about it. He'd have to take care of it quickly.

"Tenthil, look," Abella said.

He followed her pointing finger to the surveillance screen on the garage wall. Several individuals dressed in dark attire were entering the building through the ground-level doors, which were about a hundred meters away—the Order maintained only a small portion of this otherwise derelict building.

Releasing her hand, Tenthil opened the pouches on her belt one-by-one until he found what he'd hoped to locate. He removed the palm-sized, five-centimeter-thick disc from its case and ran to the stairwell entrance, from which the next team of assassins would soon emerge. He crouched and placed the disc low on the wall half a meter away from the door, pressed the control to arm the device and seal it in place, and hurried back to Abella.

"What was that?" she asked.

"Proximity mine." His throat burned a little more with each word. "Trust me?"

"About the mine?"

He shook his head and slipped his blaster into its holster. Watching him with a furrowed brow, Abella holstered her weapon. When Tenthil took her hand and tugged her close, she didn't resist, though her confused expression lingered.

"About *what*, Tenthil?"

He flicked his gaze toward the bay door. It opened on a relatively narrow alley...four stories below.

She followed his eyes with her own and shook her head, pressing her hands against his chest to shove away from him. "Oh, no. *No*. Please tell me you just want to take the hovercar."

Tenthil wrapped his arms around her and lifted her against him, front to front, hiking her thighs around his waist and cupping the back of her head to force her mouth against his shoulder. He ran forward. Her struggles ceased as her entire body tensed. His body muffled her scream as she wrapped her arms around him and clung desperately.

He leapt off the edge of the opening, aiming for the building across the alley. Extending his right leg, he caught the wall with his boot. Momentum bunched the muscles of his leg. He sprung off, repeating the process against the other building, ricocheting back and forth until they reached the ground.

Abella was trembling when he released her, but it wasn't merely due to fear—anger gleamed in her eyes. He settled his hand over her mouth, silencing any forthcoming reprimand.

"Need to go," he rasped. "*Now*."

Brows angling over the bridge of her nose, she snapped her head away from his touch and glared at him. "Fine."

He took her hand and led her down the alley. They needed to cover some distance before he removed the tracker, and they didn't have time to waste.

"At least give me some warning next time before you—"

Abella's words were cut off by an explosion from the safe-house. Rubble rained onto the spot where Tenthil had touched down only moments before. She turned to look back, but he tugged her along.

The time for looking back had passed for both of them.

EIGHT

Abella's leg muscles burned as she and Tenthil ran, and her ribs felt like they would collapse inward with every labored breath. Tenthil kept his arm around her shoulders, holding her securely against his side, making an already strenuous activity more challenging. No matter how many times she tried to pull away from him, Tenthil neither released his hold on her nor slowed his pace.

Their path weaved through countless dark alleyways and passages, its twists and turns well beyond Abella's ability to track. Her body told her she'd been running for days, but her rational mind, though muted by her pain, insisted it couldn't have been more than fifteen minutes. The punishment she'd endured over the week had left her endurance severely limited.

When her knees wobbled, threatening to give out, she decided she was done. She dug her heels into the ground and shoved against Tenthil's side. "*Enough.*"

Tenthil stopped but did not ease his hold. "Need to keep moving."

Wheezing, Abella bent forward as much as his grasp allowed. "I can't...keep going."

Tenthil crouched, wrapped an arm around her legs, and hefted her over his shoulder.

"What are you doing?" she screeched as her world tilted upside down. She flattened her palms against his back to push herself up. "Oh, I'm going to hurl."

But he was already running even faster than before. He darted across a quiet street and entered another dank, dirty alley that looked just like all the rest. Though the city had seemed far more intriguing from that damned cage on the back of Cullion's hovercar, she preferred being on the ground despite the filth.

She would've preferred it even more were she walking on her own two legs to a destination of her choice.

Fortunately, Tenthil didn't carry her very far—the alley ended at a railed walkway that ran perpendicular to it, beyond which was a huge tunnel. Vehicles of all sorts sped by through the tunnel, their engines silent but for low hums she felt more than heard.

Tenthil bent down and set Abella on her feet. He twisted to look back.

Abella's stomach lurched, and she spun away from him, doubled over, and covered her mouth as she gagged.

Don't puke, don't puke. Please don't puke.

She took in a series of deep breaths, forcing the nausea back. Once she was reasonably certain she wouldn't vomit, she straightened and turned to face him again.

One of his hands was positioned at the base of his skull, holding his hair aside, and his head was tilted to the right. He lifted his other hand, which held a knife. Without hesitating, he pressed the tip of the blade against the back of his neck and sank it into his skin. Crimson blood welled around the tip.

Abella's brow creased. "What are you *doing?*"

Her jaw fell as he pressed the blade deeper and wiggled it. Blood trickled down his neck in a rivulet.

The only change in his face was a slight bulging of his jaw muscles.

She heard the knife scrape against something hard, and a shiver ran down her spine. Her stomach flipped and clenched.

He twisted the knife slightly and tilted his head to a harsher angle. Now his expression did change; his eyebrows fell low, and his pupils dilated, swallowing his eyes.

"Tenthil! Stop it!"

He grunted and wrenched down on the knife grip, producing another scraping sound.

Something was hooked on the tip of the blade as he tore it out of his skin. Shifting his hold on the knife to free his forefinger and thumb, he pinched the crimson-smeared object and pulled.

The object, which looked like a small bone with a glob of mangled, bloody flesh attached to it, made a wet, sucking sound as it came out. She heard the sound clearly despite him releasing a guttural growl at the same moment.

Everything she'd seen, everything she'd done, rushed back in a merciless torrent, combining with Tenthil's self-mutilation to finally push Abella past her limit.

She spun away, clutched the nearby railing, and emptied her stomach onto the concrete walkway. Disgustingly, the food she'd eaten looked the same coming out as it had going in.

Averting her gaze from the mess she'd made, Abella settled her hands on her thighs and breathed for a few seconds. Once her stomach eased, she spat some of the foul taste from her mouth, wiped her lips with her sleeve, and glanced at Tenthil over her shoulder. "What did you just do?"

He drew his arm back and threw the bloody object over the

railing. Abella turned her head to follow its trajectory, but the visual chaos of moving vehicles caused her to lose sight of it almost immediately; its path seemed to cross with that of a huge garbage hauler that sped by an instant later, though she couldn't be sure.

Abella straightened and turned toward Tenthil.

Using a piece of cloth, he cleaned his fingers, knife, and neck. "Was being tracked."

"That was a tracker?" she asked. "And you just...cut it out of your neck? You could have killed yourself! What if you cut an artery, or damaged your spinal cord?" The sucking sound of the object coming free replayed in her mind; she shuddered, stomach churning anew. "You're crazy."

He shrugged as he folded the cloth. Fresh blood oozed from his neck wound, flowing down to disappear beneath his shirt. Moving at a leisurely pace, he pulled a small bandage from a pouch on his belt, removed it from its packaging, and placed it over the wound.

"That's it?" Abella stepped closer, frowning. "You're just slapping a band-aid on it and calling it good?"

The bandage glowed faintly for a moment, and when the light faded, it seemed to meld into his skin. The wound vanished. There was advanced tech on Earth, especially for medicine, but the level of technology on display in this city was on a whole new level. She would've slowed down to appreciate how amazing it was if the delay wasn't likely to get her killed.

Tenthil looked at her, his face back to its typical unreadable expression. "We need to go."

Abella's gaze fell to the scars on his cheeks. If tech here was capable of healing wounds as quickly and completely as she'd just witnessed, why did Tenthil have such prominent scars? Cullion had left countless marks on her over the years, but he'd always erased them eventually, or else her back would've been comprised primarily of scar tissue.

"Who were those people?" she asked. "Who was that masked man in the room? Why are they after you?"

Tenthil look back in the direction they'd come from before taking her hand and tugging her closer. "Later."

Abella yanked her arm back. "No. If they're trying to kill *you*, what'll stop them from killing me too?"

"Me," he growled, maintaining his hold on her hand. He leaned closer. "They will do you no harm."

"You can't know that."

"Five."

"What?"

"We killed five," he replied. "Will kill them all if needed."

The promise in his harsh words sent a chill through her. "Who are they, Tenthil?"

"Need to go, Abella."

"Then go without me." She tugged on her hand again. "I'm just slowing you down anyway."

He bared his teeth, revealing sharp fangs—his canines came in pairs, enhancing the menace of the expression. "You are coming. *Now.*"

He pulled on her arm again, and though she knew she couldn't overcome his strength, Abella fought him.

"Let me go!" She bent at the waist, leaning her backside away from him to use her weight as an anchor.

Without displaying any sign of effort, he tugged her closer.

Abella dropped her hand to her hip and drew the gun holstered there, pressing its barrel against his abdomen. Her hand trembled as she adjusted her grip on the weapon. "I said let me go, Tenthil."

His body stilled, and his eyes dipped to the gun before meeting her gaze. His face betrayed nothing of his thoughts or feelings. The only thing Abella could be sure of was his utter lack of fear.

She'd never been a violent person, had never even been in a fight. Her involvement in the battle at the safehouse had been triggered by adrenaline and panic. But *this*, threatening Tenthil with a gun, made her feel almost as sick as watching him mutilate himself.

Yet what choice did she have? She wanted to go home, and whether he promised to keep her safe or not, he was currently holding her against her will.

"I was just freed from one captor," she said. "I will not let myself be taken again. Please, just let me go."

He held her gaze for what felt like an eternity. Her heartbeat grew louder with every passing moment.

"No," he finally said, instilling that short, simple word with crushing finality.

"Don't make me shoot you."

"Later."

"What? I...I have a gun pressed against your stomach. Do you not understand that, or—"

"Abella, we need to go *now*. They are near, and if they find us, they will kill you too."

Each of his words was raspier than the last, each sounded more pained.

She yanked against his iron grip. "Then release me and go!"

Faster than her eyes could perceive, he caught the barrel of the blaster in his fist and wrenched it aside. She gasped as the weapon—her one bit of leverage—twisted out of her hold. He slipped his other arm around her, pressed a hand to the small of her back, and forced her body against his.

"I did all this for *you*," he said, eyes instantly black, fangs bared. "Tracked Cullion to get *you*. Killed them all to have *you.*" He lowered his face closer to hers and tightened his hold so her body was flush with his. "I will *not* let you go."

Abella stared up at him with rounded eyes and parted lips. The logical part of her mind told her this was *not* okay—his motivations only made this whole episode more disturbing, and she was right to be afraid of him. Yet, another part of her was turned on by his vehemence, by the way his eyes and arms locked her in place. As much as she wanted to pull away, she had an urge to press closer and absorb more of his heat.

Just as she was forming a response, Tenthil wrapped an arm beneath her ass and lifted her onto his shoulder.

Not again!

Anger swept through her, and she punched his back, succeeding only in making her hand ache. "Damnit, Tenthil!"

She was tired of being hauled around, tired of her wishes being ignored. She'd had her fill of such treatment over the last four years, and Tenthil's continuation of it was infuriating.

But again, what choice do I have? Wander an alien city, lost and alone, until whoever is chasing us murders me...or stick with the devil I know?

At least Tenthil wasn't trying to kill her.

His words echoed in her mind.

I did all this for you.

Why would he risk his life to obtain her? What was so special about her?

And what did he intend to do now that he had her?

TENTHIL LIMITED himself to a brisk walk as he led Abella across the skyway bridging the abandoned factories. Whether motivated by anger, fear, exhaustion, or some combination of the three, she hadn't spoken a word since shortly after he'd removed his tracker. Her silence was unsettling, but he admired her perseverance all the same.

Though clearly exhausted, she'd made the two-kilometer walk from maintenance tunnel where they'd abandoned their stolen hovercar without complaint.

He glanced out one of the skyway's long, narrow windows. Most of the surrounding factories and warehouses were dark, desiccated husks, forgotten by the city above and left to slowly rot. Detritus littered the area. Everything here in the Bowels had a worn look, the result of decades—if not centuries—of neglect.

Surveillance was limited in places like this, making them sanctuaries for fugitives and the homeless, for people desperate for refuge.

Tenthil and Abella were both homeless and on the run. Where better for them to hide until they determined their way forward?

He held his blaster at the ready as they entered the next building. In the Bowels, *abandoned* had taken on a new meaning, and was no longer synonymous with *uninhabited*. Tenthil slowed his pace, and Abella kept close to him, her footfalls thankfully quiet. Few of the interior lights were functional, but Tenthil's eyes adapted to the gloom.

The interior of the building was just as messy as its exterior. Old food wrappers, musty blankets, and broken heating coils were scattered in the dust, signs that people had sheltered here at some point after its abandonment.

But Tenthil didn't plan to hunker in a dark corner with a filthy blanket over his shoulders; he had a specific destination in mind. He'd chased a mark into this building years ago—an ilthurii gang boss who'd run afoul of some powerful individuals —and had found his target hiding in a secured room nestled deep within these silent halls.

"Is this place...safe?" Abella asked.

Her voice jarred him from his thoughts. She'd been quiet for so long that he'd thrown all his focus into keeping alert for danger and visualizing the route of that long-ago hunt. He glanced at her over his shoulder.

Abella's features were drawn with worry, dark circles hugged the undersides of her eyes, and her already light skin looked even paler than normal. Tenthil frowned; he was uncertain of the limitations of her species, and he was likely pushing her too hard.

"Safe enough," he replied.

Her deepening frown suggested his answer hadn't been reassuring.

She is not trained for this life, he reminded himself. He'd spent so long in the Order that he often forgot his experiences were not typical.

After fifteen minutes of searching—just as his frustration had built enough for him to consider turning around and leaving—he discovered the door he'd sought. The dirt on the floor in front of it was undisturbed; it hadn't been opened for some time. He stopped at the door and released Abella's hand to draw a small, egg-shaped device with an old-fashioned touch screen on its face. His masterkey.

He raised the masterkey to the door's wall-mounted control panel and activated it. A tiny wire extended from the tool's narrower end and latched onto the panel. The key began its program. Fortunately, he'd used the same masterkey to open this door the first time he'd come, and it still had the decrypted access codes stored in its database.

The masterkey's screen flashed green, and the door slid open, disturbing the nearby dust to create a cloud in the air. Tenthil waved the dust away as the lights inside the room flickered on. After returning the masterkey to his belt pouch, he took hold of Abella's hand and led her across the threshold.

The room could only have been considered clean in comparison to the rest of the building—there were no vermin droppings on the floor, and the dust was minimal, but the wear of time had dulled everything.

A large, banged-up desk had been pushed against the far wall, its narrower sides wedged between the tall, dilapidated shelving units that ran along the same wall in both directions. The computer terminal built into the top of the desk was dark and cracked. A sagging couch rested against the left wall, its upholstery tattered and frame buckling in the center. A pallet fashioned of blankets and couch cushions lay in the right corner. The sliding door toward the back, which led into a lavatory of questionable functionality, was stuck two-thirds open at a slanting angle.

Tenthil glanced down at the dark stain at the center of the floor.

He'd removed the ilthurii's body after his contract's completion but hadn't bothered cleaning the blood. The Eternal Guard rarely ventured into the Bowels, and they weren't likely to take interest in the murder of a known criminal, even had they found this evidence.

Twisting around, he pressed the interior panel button, and the entrance door rumbled shut. It sealed with a metallic clang that likely echoed through the whole building, alerting anyone and anything inside that this door had just been used.

"Thank God," Abella said as she released his hand and walked toward the couch.

Tenthil's hand twitched; he barely resisted the urge to reach for her again.

She collapsed upon the only remaining cushion on the couch and drew her legs up, curling into a ball. She closed her eyes, inhaled deeply—her nose wrinkling endearingly as though she'd caught scent of something foul—and released the breath in a heavy, relieved sigh.

Tenthil's gaze lingered on her, roving over the battle suit and the way it molded to her legs and ass. He forced his eyes away.

Priorities. Food, water, rest. Then plan.

He slipped off his backpack, set it on the desk, and opened it to rummage through its contents. Fortunately, he'd thought to grab a few of the rations that had been stored in the safehouse. He tore one open and sorted through its individually packaged contents as he walked toward Abella.

"Eat," he said, the word like molten metal rising from his ragged throat.

She didn't respond, didn't move.

"Abella?" Her name seemed to be the one thing he could say without pain, and he didn't think he would ever tire of hearing it.

He stopped in front of the couch and stared down at Abella, studying her relaxed features and the slow, steady rise and fall of her chest as she breathed. He brushed the back of a claw over her cheek, caught a strand of her dark hair, and tucked it behind her ear. Tilting his head, he traced the top of her ear with the same claw.

Arousal stirred in his belly; it had never truly faded since the moment he'd first seen her, despite the events of the last week. Abella had triggered something powerful within Tenthil. He didn't understand it, didn't have a name for it, but he knew it could not be reversed. He craved this little terran—*his* little terran.

Tenthil returned to the desk and leaned against it as he ate. The meal was bland. Like most food the Order supplied its acolytes, it was meant for nutrition, not enjoyment. He folded the empty packages and stuffed them into the outer bag when he was done, placing the garbage on the desk's surface. After brushing his hands off, he walked to the bedding in the corner and sorted through it, separating pillows and cushions from ratty blankets. He selected the few in the best condition and brought them to the couch.

He dropped the bedding on the floor, keeping only the nicest blanket in his hands, and leaned forward to cover Abella, but paused before doing so. The blanket's fabric bore many smells, most of them subtle but unpleasant. Instinct drove him to raise the blanket and rub it over his cheek and at the corner of his mouth, where venom seeped from his fangs, adding his scent to the mix, marking it—marking *her*—as his. He draped it over her carefully before turning to arrange a makeshift pallet for himself on the floor in front of her.

He couldn't help but feel foolish for succumbing to the instinct as he lay down on his side and rested his head on his arm.

Closing his eyes, he focused on the sound of her breathing and on her scent, letting the latter overpower the other smells in the air until it was all he perceived. His weariness made itself known, pressing in at the edges of his consciousness. He made no effort to resist; he drifted to sleep within moments.

His dreams were shadowy, indistinct, and instilled with an ominous energy, but they dissipated, leaving only a sense of unease in their wake, when nearby movement woke him. He slitted his eyes open and watched as Abella carefully stepped over him. Her bare feet were silent on the floor, and even her smallest motions conveyed the controlled grace of a skilled dancer. It wasn't until she was a few paces away that he noticed her boots dangling from her left hand.

His internal clock told him it hadn't been more than an hour since he'd fallen asleep. Had she woken so soon by chance, or had she fooled him? He smiled; either way, she was a spirited female, and that only strengthened his desire for her.

Abella stopped at the desk, gently set her boots atop it, and glanced back at him. Tenthil kept his body still and his eyes slitted, hoping the poor lighting would mask his wakefulness. After a moment, she turned her head forward and opened the backpack.

She withdrew the extra blaster—the one he had taken from her was still tucked away in his belt—and slipped it into the holster on her hip. She opened the bag wider and peered inside. Her tongue slipped out and wet her pink lips; despite everything, it only made him yearn to taste her again.

After closing the bag, she lifted it off the desk, swung it behind her back, and stared at Tenthil as she slowly looped the straps over her shoulders. She picked up her footwear and crept to the door, only pausing when she stood immediately in front of it.

Tenthil guessed this wasn't the first time she'd attempted an escape.

She shifted her attention to the control button beside the door and lifted her left hand. It was there she hesitated; she knew the door was loud, knew it would wake him, and was likely building her nerve for the inevitable chase.

He couldn't allow this to go any further. Rolling onto his front, he flattened his hands on the floor and pushed himself up, silently getting his feet beneath him. He stalked toward her. Even now, he couldn't help admiring her lithe figure, her dark hair, her smooth skin.

Tenthil came to a stop immediately behind Abella. Her attention remained on the button. She drew in a deep breath and moved her hand forward.

He caught her wrist before her finger could touch the button. She gasped, body tensing as he spun her around to face her. She dropped her boots and reached for the blaster. The weapon was already halfway out of its holster when Tenthil dropped his hand over hers, halting her motion.

She lacked training, but she possessed natural speed and instincts that could be honed into something dangerous, given the opportunity. She was the sort of being in which the Master might have chosen to *invest*.

He pried the blaster from her grip and tossed it aside. Before she could pull away, Tenthil released her hand to loop his arm around her waist and pull her close. She bared her teeth and struggled as he wrestled the backpack off her shoulders and let it fall at their feet.

"Let go of me!" Abella kicked his shin and grabbed a fistful of his hair, yanking on it.

Tenthil snarled and grasped her wrist, pressing his thumb against the tendons between the bones of her forearm. She cried out and loosened her hold on his hair. The pang of guilt that struck his chest wasn't strong enough to overpower the excitement sparked by her resistance, and he shoved it away. He spun her around again so her back was against his chest.

She screamed. The high-pitched sound was filled with fury, frustration, pain, and a hint of fear.

He banded an arm around her torso, trapping her arms against her sides, and clamped his other hand over her mouth.

Abella thrashed against him, clearly unwilling to cease her resistance despite its futility.

He said her name. She responded by using what little freedom her arm had to punch him in the groin.

Tenthil grunted; the pain coalesced low in his belly, but his entire body tensed for a moment, tightening his hold on her rather than easing it.

Growling, he lifted her off her feet and stepped forward, forcing her against the door with his body. He caught both her wrists, raised them over her head, and pinned her hands to the door. When she tried to kick again, he caught her leg between his knees and twisted his hips away from her, moving her primary target out of reach.

"Fuck you!" she spat. "You're just like him! Just let me go. I just...I j-just w-want to go."

He pressed his cheek to her hair, positioning his mouth near her ear. "Go where?"

"Home," she cried softly. "I want to go h-home." She sniffled and sucked in an unsteady breath. "Someone out there can help me, someone—"

"*No one* out there will help you. They will buy you, sell you, hurt you, *kill* you. Anything but help."

"There are other humans out there! A terran embassy. I heard people talking about it in one of the clubs Cullion took me to. The embassy would help me. You can take me to them. *Please.*"

Tenthil clenched his jaw, nostrils flaring. "No."

"Why?" Her voice shattered, breaking under her anguish, and her body trembled. "Why are you doing this?"

Tenthil pressed himself more firmly against her, as though that could ease her pain—even though he was its current cause. He brushed his nose over her hair, drawing in her scent. "Only I can protect you. We are hunted."

"But if it's an embassy, they—"

"You are *mine*," he growled. The thought of anyone taking her from him ignited that uncontrollable fire inside Tenthil, making his fingers itch with the urge to lengthen his claws and shed blood.

"I'm not yours."

"You are." He brushed his lips over the soft skin of her neck, making sure to keep the sweet venom from overflowing his mouth. His balls ached not because of her blow but due to desire. The drive to claim her, to mate with her, grew with each passing second, reaching new heights of urgency. He shifted his hips forward, pressing his pelvis against her back and coaxing a soft gasp from her parted lips. "You are mine, Abella, and I must keep you safe. I *will*."

"I'm not a belonging, not a thing, not a *pet*." Despite the defiance in Abella's words, her voice was small, and her body eased.

"You are still mine."

He released her wrists and slid his palms down her arms, wishing they were gliding over her bare skin instead of the combat suit. Gritting his teeth against his need, he placed his hands on her hips and guided her away from the door. She walked to the couch with his guidance, though she lacked her usual grace and confidence. He tightened his grip and stilled her when she moved to climb back onto the sofa.

She looked back at him with wet, tired, narrowed eyes. "What?"

With the toe of his boot, he spread the blankets on the floor, widening his pallet. He drew her down with him as he lay on his side. Wrapping his arms around her, he tucked her body against his, back to front, and pressed his face into her hair. He inhaled deeply, and something in his chest rumbled contently. Despite her stiffness, she fit against him perfectly.

She squirmed, and a shudder wracked him as her backside rubbed his hardened shaft. She sucked in a sharp breath and tensed.

"Sleep, Abella," he said as softly as he could. However much he yearned to take her, they needed rest.

Priorities. Rest, food, a plan to move forward...

But part of him insisted Abella was his *only* priority.

NINE

Abella woke with sore, puffy eyes, a painfully full bladder, and a rather large, incredibly hard cock pressed against her ass. She'd been well aware of it when Tenthil had shoved her up against the door before they'd gone to sleep, and she'd remained aware of it when he lay down behind her. It was difficult to ignore.

Despite her anger, dismay, and sadness, her body had reacted to him. The press of his shaft, his closeness, the security of his embrace, the possessive way he buried his face in her hair, and his soft, warm breath on her ear—all of it had affected her deeply.

Though she'd lain awake for some time after they settled down, her sleep had been the most restful she'd had in four years. It frustrated her to no end. She should've been *furious*, should've been fighting him, should've been planning another escape.

She shouldn't have been getting aroused because he smelled *so* damn good.

I'm pathetic. Weak.

And horny as fucking hell.

It's not my fault. I haven't had sex in nearly five years, so it's only natural... Isn't it?

Why wouldn't her body react when an attractive male looked at her, touched her, and held her the way Tenthil did?

"You're awake," Tenthil said, his raspy voice sending thrilling tingles across her skin that gathered in a spot she'd rather not have thought about.

His hand, which rested low on her stomach—close to the spot she was trying to ignore—flexed, and he pulled her closer to nuzzle his face against her neck. His lips parted as his mouth caressed the sensitive skin of her throat, skimming up until it settled beneath her ear, over her pounding pulse. He licked her. The hot, wet flick of his tongue lit the fuse leading straight to her core. Her sex clenched, and it took everything within Abella to keep from making a sound and pressing her ass back against his cock.

Thankfully, her stomach chose that moment to profess its hunger, rumbling long and loud against his hand.

Tenthil stilled, lifting his head. His hair brushed over her neck and cheek. Abella had never been so grateful for an interruption in her life.

She'd been mere seconds away from letting him go further, from begging him to slide his hand lower to stroke her aching clit.

"I need to pee," she said quickly, pulling away from him and sitting up.

He released his hold on her without a fight and scooted back as he also sat up, affording her some precious space.

Using the edge of the broken-down sofa as support, Abella stood. She ignored the throbbing between her legs and cast a quick glance around the room. "Um...where do I..."

Tenthil pointed at a partially open door in the back. Based

on its angle, it wasn't going to close without being wrestled back onto its tracks. She hurried over to it and peered inside.

A light beyond the doorway flickered on, likely triggered by her movement, to reveal a dirty, cluttered bathroom. Like every bathroom she'd seen in this city, it contained several strange fixtures she couldn't identify. She didn't waste any time trying to imagine the alien appendages they were meant to accommodate.

She looked over her shoulder. Tenthil had risen and now stared at her silently. His hair was mussed, his eyes hooded, and his cock's shape was prominent through his pants. Abella swallowed thickly. Even the scars on his cheeks enhanced his sexiness, adding a wicked mystique to his appearance.

"Does this door close?" she asked.

He shrugged and shook his head at the same time, turning his palms upward.

"You're no help," she muttered, turning back to the bathroom. She stepped inside, wrinkling her nose as she tip-toed through the mess.

She found what appeared to be a toilet in the back corner—a tankless oval bowl jutting from the wall. Were it not positioned so low, she might've mistaken it for a sink with a missing faucet. Leaning forward, she peered into the bowl, bracing herself for the discovery of some new, grotesque horror.

Surprisingly, the bowl was empty—and oddly clean, especially compared to its surroundings.

Abella turned her back to the bowl and positioned herself in front of it. "You'd better not peek!"

To her startlement, she heard Tenthil's soft footsteps retreat from near the doorway. She hadn't heard him approach the bathroom.

Her cheeks warmed. "Oh my God."

Four years without the luxury of privacy should have killed

any modesty or shame Abella once possessed—she'd constantly been washed and dressed by attendants to meet Cullion's standards, and he'd always had her stripped naked in front of the guards when she was disciplined. Nudity had become a common state of being. Outwardly, she'd maintained her dignity and pride, but now that she thought about it, she realized she'd always been ashamed beneath the surface. She'd always felt violated.

With Tenthil...it was different. She didn't feel shame—at least not like before. Part of her wanted him to see her, wanted his eyes on her body, drinking in her form like he'd just crossed a desert and she was a cool, refreshing stream.

But not while I'm peeing.

She kept her gaze on the bathroom entrance as she shoved down her pants and precariously sat down. Her relief was immediate and immense.

After she finished, the bowl flushed on its own. Abella started; the sound hadn't been loud, but it had been unexpected. Automatic flushing was old tech, even back on Earth, but it didn't seem like anything should've been functional in this place.

She twisted to look over her shoulder but couldn't find any switches or sensors—nor could she find anything with which to clean herself.

Just as she was about to stand up, cold water blasted her crotch.

She screamed, leapt off the bowl, and turned to face it. Water continued spraying from the front edge for another second.

At the edge of her vision, Tenthil's form appeared in the doorway.

Abella's eye's widened, and she quickly dropped her hands to cover herself. "I'm fine!"

She cringed at the water trickling down her legs.

His shadow lingered for a moment, as though he were considering whether to enter anyway, before he retreated.

"Damn thing crotch shot me," she said, glaring at the bowl as she tugged up her pants.

She moved to the sink and looked at herself in the cloudy, cracked mirror. Her hair was a tangled mess, her eyes were red from exhaustion and tears, and she'd lost weight. Raising a hand, she touched one of her slightly sunken cheeks and frowned.

She'd worried about her weight so much back home, always stressing about keeping off the extra few pounds that would've somehow made her unfit compared to the other dancers. Now, she'd kill to have a double cheeseburger with all the fixings, fries, and a giant chocolate milkshake.

Tenthil doesn't seem to mind.

Abella felt her body flush. She glanced at the doorway, but he was nowhere in sight.

What am I going to do about him?

His claim on her was no different than Cullion's had been, and yet...something about the way Tenthil said *mine* was wholly unlike the way her former master had asserted his ownership. Tenthil's claim meant something more. He didn't seem to see her as a thing to own, as a pet, but rather as...

Well, I guess I don't know what he sees me as.

She did know that every time he said she was his it did funny things to her, made her feel like she'd never felt before. She should've resented him for keeping her, but instead she was *lustful*—and that scared the hell out of her.

She'd been ready to risk everything, to brave an unknown city full of alien beings, on a one-in-a-billion chance that she'd make it to the human embassy, and they'd send her home. After four years as Cullion's slave, she refused to live another day as someone's belonging. Death was preferable to that.

No matter what Tenthil made her feel, she couldn't accept his claim. Her lust was nothing more than a biological reaction from sex-starved body.

She genuinely believed he meant her no harm—at least no physical harm. But he was holding Abella against her will, and he refused to bring her to the people who could help her get home.

Her question from earlier repeated in her mind.

Why me?

Why was he putting himself through all this for her? Wanting to fuck her was the only evident motivation, but that seemed too shallow. It would have been much easier, much more sensible, for him to have gone to one of the city's many brothels to have sex with women far more experienced and exotic than Abella.

A sharp, jealous pang struck her chest.

Abella gasped and pressed a hand over her heart. He was a stranger! Why would the thought of Tenthil with other women produce such a strong reaction within her? So what if part of her wanted him too? She couldn't let lust cloud her judgment, couldn't let it make her complacent.

Whether she liked it or not, Tenthil was all she had in this city, and he'd proved that he was willing to fight for her. She'd often been dragged along by Cullion as he met with some of the most intimidating beings she'd ever seen, and she had no doubt Tenthil was more dangerous than all of them.

Tenthil leaned into the doorway, his brow furrowed as his silver eyes fell upon her.

"I'm fine," she repeated. She turned back to the sink and pressed the button near the faucet. Water flowed from the spout. It swirled in the basin, washing away the grime inside as it drained.

Cupping her hands beneath the water, she splashed her face a couple times, scrubbed away the sweat and dirt from the last day, and cleaned her teeth as best she could with her finger. When she straightened, she used her wet fingers to comb through her hair, tugging apart the knots and tangles.

Yesterday, she'd been a pampered pet—bathed and groomed, dressed in flattering outfits befitting a dancer, living in quarters at least three times the size of her college dorm room —and she'd despised every bit of it. Now a hot shower sounded like the pinnacle of luxury.

From the corner of her eye, she saw Tenthil turn and side-step through the narrow doorway.

"What are you doing?" she asked without looking away from the mirror.

He stopped beside her. She turned toward him, reflexively stepping back. He gently caught her wrists and guided her hands out of her hair. Abella was too confused to resist.

Tenthil released his hold on her arms, stepped behind her, and raised his hands to her hair, giving her a glimpse of his wicked black claws. Continuing to move with surprising care, he combed his claws through her hair, easing the tangles, grazing her scalp so lightly that his touch produced only plea-sure rather than pain. Her eyes drifted shut of their own accord as she gave in to his soothing ministrations, relaxing so much that she swayed toward him with each stroke of his claws.

I should tell him to stop.

A soft moan escaped her, and she tilted her head back.

I should really tell him to stop.

But it feels so damn good...

Tenthil stepped closer—so close she should feel his body heat through their clothes. Her skin prickled in awareness, and her breath quickened as he ran the tips of his claws along the outside of her arms, eliciting tingles and warmth that swirled through her to coalesce low in her belly.

He inhaled deeply, and a growl rumbled in his chest. "Your scent has changed."

My scent...?

Abella tensed, eyes widening.

No. No way.

Could he really smell her *arousal?*

She slipped out of his arms and spun to face him. Black dominated his eyes. No one had ever looked at her the way he did, with such intense longing, with such insatiable hunger. It only made her sex wetter.

Despite how much she wanted his touch, despite how much she *craved* it, Abella thrust aside her desire. "If I'm going to be with you"—her eyes widened—"I mean, stick with you! If I'm going to *stick* with you, you need to answer my questions."

Tenthil blinked and tilted his head. His nostrils flared, and his pupils shrank down to normal. He held her gaze for a moment before turning and walking out of the bathroom.

"Eat," he said over his shoulder.

Abella stared after him, mouth agape. Did he seriously just walk out on her without even acknowledging what she'd said?

She made her way back to the doorway and slipped through. Tenthil was standing beside the desk, upon which he'd placed the backpack.

Abella marched toward him. "I'm tired of you ignoring what I want. I deserve to know what is—"

She froze as her eyes fell upon a large, dark stain in the middle of the floor. How hadn't she noticed it before?

Because I was tired as hell from running for my life, and it's dim in here.

"Is that blood? Was someone *killed* here?" she asked quietly.

Tenthil glanced at the stain. He lifted his gaze to her a moment later, offering the ration package in his hand. "Yes. Now eat."

"And...are you the one that killed them?"

He nodded.

Abella's brows drew together. "How can you be so...so detached about death?"

She'd taken a life for the first time in that safehouse and felt ill every time she thought about it.

"Part of the job." He dipped his chin toward the ration.

She drew back. "Job? You..." Suddenly, it all made sense. "You're one of *them*, aren't you?"

He stepped forward, grasped her wrist, and pressed the package onto her palm. "You eat. I will speak."

Her fingers numbly closed around the ration. "Okay."

Tenthil released his hold on both Abella and the package and took a step backward.

Abella stared at him for a moment. With a final glance at the bloodstain, she pressed her lips into a tight line, walked to the couch, and seated herself on the edge of its remaining cushion. She looked up at Tenthil again. When his eyes dipped to the food, she sighed, shoved her fingers into the opening, and pulled out one of the smaller packages. She tore it open and ate without looking at it.

The food didn't have much flavor, but at this point, she didn't care. It would fill her belly, and finally getting some answers from Tenthil was far more important than enjoying a meal.

As she chewed, he turned and paced away from her, directing his gaze toward the floor. He stalked back and forth like a caged animal; Abella couldn't guess at what was going through his mind, but it seemed serious.

After she'd taken a couple more bites, he finally stopped. He stood with his fists clenched at his sides and did not look at her when he spoke.

"They were acolytes of the Order of the Void. I am one. *Was.*"

"And what does that mean? What's this order's purpose, besides...death?" she asked.

"Secrets. Collecting them, holding them. But mostly death." He angled his head downward, and his hair fell to block his face from her view. "We are assassins. The best."

"You're an *assassin?*" The food she'd just swallowed felt like a rock in her gut. "Were you...supposed to kill me? Is that why they're after you? After us?"

He lifted his chin, brushed his hair aside, and met her gaze, his silver eyes ablaze. He shook his head. "Because I killed Cullion. Because of how I killed Drok. I disobeyed, caused too much trouble. Exposed the Order to witnesses."

Abella lowered the package, her brows falling. "Why?"

Somehow, the fire in his eyes intensified. "I needed you."

Her heart skipped a beat. "What?"

"Needed you," he repeated, approaching her. "From the moment I saw you, I needed you, Abella."

On the night they'd danced, she'd seen the yearning in his eyes, had *felt* it, had responded to it. She'd reveled in it—and she had wanted him, too.

Tenthil stopped before Abella and sank to his knees. He leaned toward her, placing his hands on her hips. Her breath caught at the prick of his claws. Rather than scare her, they only heightened her awareness, making her wonder how they'd feel gliding across her skin.

"So all of this...is because of me?" she asked.

"For you. Not because of you." He tightened his hands and pulled her closer, wedging himself between her knees. "You haunted my thoughts while we were apart. You danced in my dreams. You are mine, Abella, as much as I am yours."

His words made her heart quicken; his nearness made her sex pulse. "All from one dance?"

Tenthil caught her free hand and drew it toward him, flattening her palm against his chest. "I feel it inside. I recognize it in your scent. You are my mate."

Oh God. His mate?

"B-But we're from two different species," she said, drawing back.

The look on his face—those silver eyes intent, slowly being devoured by the black of his pupils; those lips pressed together in a firm, unwavering line—was his answer. It didn't matter. He didn't care.

"Tenthil, we just met."

His expression didn't waver.

"I'm going to the embassy," she pressed. "I'm going *home*."

His eyes held hers for a few more seconds before he rose, withdrawing his hands from her. "Eat."

"Tenthil?"

He turned his back on her and walked toward the desk.

"I am going home, Tenthil! I have a family there, friends, a life. I have a home."

Pressing a hand atop the desk, Tenthil bowed his head. His posture tensed. She heard him release a slow breath before he shifted his attention to the nearby backpack. He collected the few supplies that had been removed from it, returning them all to the bag save one—the blaster she'd been carrying when she tried to sneak out. Though he settled his hand atop it and slid it toward the backpack, he stopped himself.

"Eat. We need to leave." Without looking at her, he slid the blaster to the corner of the desk nearest Abella, turning it so the grip was toward her. He lifted his hand away.

Abella gritted her teeth. Tenthil knew she wouldn't use the gun on him. She'd had her chance—several chances—and hadn't taken a shot. She couldn't stomach the thought of hurting him, not even if it meant her freedom.

She wouldn't have thought twice with Cullion. She would have pulled the trigger over and over, blasting the son of a bitch to pieces.

But not Tenthil.

"Damn you," she said, glaring at him. She turned atop the sofa cushion so he was no longer in front of her and forced her attention to her food.

TEN

Tenthil kept his arm around Abella's shoulders as the small maintenance elevator rumbled to a halt. He drew her a little closer when the door rose, opening on a long alley spotted with puddles of unidentifiable composition. They stepped off the elevator together. Abella matched his pace, though she remained tense, and the hand she held against his side seemed perpetually on the verge of pushing him away.

She hadn't spoken to him since before they'd left the abandoned factory in the Bowels. Hours of travel through tunnels, across catwalks, and up staircases and elevators—often with their bodies pressed together—hadn't produced a single comment from her. He wanted to believe it was because she'd accepted her situation, but he feared the opposite was true.

There was no sense in delving into it now. He had a plan, and that took priority. As long as he and Abella were in Arthos, they were in danger. They could work through their interpersonal issues once they were off-world.

Unfortunately, leaving the Infinite City was a complicated

process for people like them—people who'd been smuggled here and sold as slaves.

When they emerged from the alley, it was like stepping into a different universe. The dimly lit, rundown, industrial aesthetic of the Bowels was absent here in the Undercity, replaced by bright neon lights, holograms, and sleeker architecture.

He followed the general flow of foot traffic along the street, mapping out the sector in his mind's eye. Being in the Undercity meant exposure to more surveillance, but it was possible to get lost in the crowds.

They just needed to move quickly and carefully.

Tenthil glanced at Abella. She kept her face turned away from him, her gaze roaming in every direction but his; it seemed too deliberate to be an accident.

I should have told her more.

But part of him reeled at the little he'd shared with her. The memories of his earliest youth, of his people and his planet, of the stories they told one another, were distant and faded. He'd been raised by the Order, where secrets were paramount. Only the Master and the Void were privy to secrets. It was not for one such as Tenthil to share information, for any reason, with anyone but the Master. His duty was to kill on command.

And to allow the Master to pluck any desired knowledge from his mind.

That is no longer my life. It was never what I wanted, never what I chose. Now, I have made a choice. A better choice...

He wanted Abella to know. He wanted to unburden himself, to shed the weight of the secrets he carried by sharing them with someone he trusted. Who better than her? Who better than his mate?

Tenthil frowned down at her. He recognized his selfishness

in this. He wanted her, needed her, and everything he shared with her only made her more of a target to the Order. His instinct was to protect her, but he'd been the one who put her in danger. He was the reason the Master knew her face, her name.

And yet Tenthil could not let her go.

His chest constricted, and he longed for little more at that moment than to dip his chin and press his lips to her hair, to breathe in her scent and forget the rest of the universe. Her presence soothed him; he could not remember ever sleeping so soundly as he had while she was in his arms. Whatever demons usually haunted him hadn't dared visit while she was near.

He released a heavy breath. He could not afford such distractions while they were traveling through the Undercity. Tenthil's bioelectric field would shield them from most electronic surveillance, but the Master had access to countless spies throughout the city, below and above. Anyone on this street could have connections leading back to the Order through a tangled web of informants, whether they knew it or not.

His gaze settled on a pair of Eternal Guard peacekeepers standing on a street corner, clad in their signature golden armor with vibrant teal markings at the shoulders and chest. Though their attire stood out from the crowd, the passersby paid little attention to them—the peacekeepers' presence was intended more to deter crime and put citizens at ease than enforce the law.

Tenthil glanced at Abella. Her attention was fixed on the peacekeepers. He guided her into a turn, moving away from the guards and onto a larger, busier street. Her head turned to keep them in view until she and Tenthil were swallowed by the thickening crowd.

The din of conversation increased in volume, backed by overlapping music from countless shops and vendor booths.

Tenthil returned his attention to his terran despite his need for alertness; her continued silence was in harsh contrast to their surroundings, making it even harder to ignore.

She was still looking away from him, maintaining her stiff posture. Her message was clear—she would rather have been anywhere but tucked against his side. Something heavy sank in his gut. Her place was with him, and his was with her. He still didn't understand *why*, but he knew it was true, and he longed for her to accept it too.

His discomfort only grew as they walked, and soon her silence was all he could focus upon.

Silence was not the natural state of life. Even after decades in the Order, Tenthil understood that. His earliest memories were full of sound—wind sighing through long grass; whooping calls of the hunters returning with fresh meat; stories and songs shared around crackling fires. The gentle rasp of his mother's palm atop his hair.

He clenched his jaw against a sudden tightness in his throat. Abella had spoken often during their time together, sometimes just to herself, and he hadn't realized how much he'd already come to appreciate the sound of her voice until she chose to deny him the pleasure of it. This...this was too much like his life in the temple. Silence was what he wanted to leave behind.

"Abella," he said, his raspy voice so small and insignificant in a world flooded with rich, vibrant sounds.

Her jaw muscle ticked. She kept her face turned away, with her chin raised in defiance and her eyes forward.

Tenthil's frown deepened, and his eyebrows lowered. He repeated her name louder.

She turned her head a little farther away.

Holding his breath to keep from growling, he altered their

course wildly, cutting across the street and through the other pedestrians to enter a dark alley.

He shifted Abella to stand before him, caught her chin between his fingers, and angled her face toward his. "Abella!"

She fought his hold, attempting to pull her face away. Her lips were pressed into a tight, flat line, and her glaring eyes were focused on the nearby alley wall.

"Speak," he said.

Somehow, she closed her lips together even tighter, creating patches of pale skin around her mouth as the blood was forced away from her lips.

Tenthil could not suppress a growl now—it rumbled up from his chest, tore along his throat like hot gravel, and escaped through bared fangs. "I will not be ignored."

She swung her fiery gaze to meet his. "Doesn't feel good, does it?"

It took a moment for her words to sink in, for him to understand. *This is what I have been doing to her.*

He couldn't argue her point, but it was only as she held his gaze that something within him shifted and snuffed out the agitated fire in his gut.

It didn't matter whether it had been the result of his upbringing, his training, or his personality—he'd done this to her. This was how he'd made her feel by refusing to answer her questions. She would not like the answers, but if he wanted her trust, he needed to be honest. He needed to be open.

Could he do that? Was he capable of it, after so many years of the Master's influence?

"It doesn't," he said through his teeth.

"Good. Now you understand one of the many reasons why I'm pissed at you."

He drew back slightly, eyes narrowing.

She grasped his wrist and tugged it down, breaking his hold on her chin. "If I need to elaborate, you're pretty damn oblivious to your own behavior."

Tenthil was aware of his actions, even those motivated purely by instinct; everything he'd done since breaking into Cullion's manor had been for her. "I'm protecting you."

"You're keeping me captive, Tenthil."

"*Protecting* you. From yourself."

This time, she drew back, and her brows fell. "Excuse me?"

"You don't know Arthos. Don't know the people. It is dangerous."

"I don't see what's dangerous about bringing me to my own people."

"This is a city of infinite secrets, Abella." He brushed the backs of his fingers over her hair. "I will tell you more. But not here."

She stared at him silently for a moment, jaw ticking again, and nodded.

He extended his left arm and gestured for Abella to come closer. Her frown deepened, but she stepped forward and nestled herself against his side. Tenthil settled his arm over her shoulders.

"Can you at least tell me why we have to walk everywhere like this?" she asked as they turned and moved back to the street.

"To shield you from cameras," he replied.

"What do you mean? You're big, but you're not *that* big."

The answer was yet another secret the Master never wanted revealed, but the Master's wishes no longer mattered to Tenthil.

"I can alter my bioelectrical field. Obscure myself from recordings."

"Is that like...some kind of cyborg thing or something?"

He scanned the crowd as they walked, careful to keep their pace steady and casual despite his urge to get to their next destination as quickly as possible. "No. Bioengineering."

"Okay... I'm not dumb, but I went to a performing arts school for dancing. Science and technology weren't exactly my areas of interest. Are you saying you were made in a tube or something?"

Tenthil drew in a deep breath through his nose. Her scent was on the air, strengthened by her nearness, but there were hundreds more smells all around, and now it was the smell of cooking food that caught his attention. He altered their course again, angling toward one of the many food vendors set up along the sides of the street. It had been a long while since they'd eaten, and he needed to provide for his mate, preferably something more than the bland, pre-packaged meals they'd been living on.

"No. I was born," he replied. "But I was...*changed*, as a child. I look like one of my kind, but I am different inside."

"Why would you do that to yourself?"

"I didn't."

He felt her slight resistance as her steps faltered, and he slowed to accommodate her.

"Someone else did?" she asked. "Why?"

"To make me what I am." Tenthil brought them to a stop at the end of the short line for one of the vendors. Aromatic meats and vegetables roasted and fried in the booth, which was oper-ated by two tall, four-armed dacrethians. Tenthil kept his arm around Abella, holding her close.

It was dangerous to draw such comfort from her nearness, to find such joy in her warmth, to become so attached to her in so short a time, but he was helpless when it came to Abella.

"Was it...that man?" she asked. "The one from the hologram?"

Tenthil's hold on her tightened involuntarily. He nodded.

She frowned and reached up to brush the tips of her fingers over the scar on his cheek. "Did he do this too?"

Tenthil's chest constricted. He clenched his jaw and nodded again. Her touch had no right feeling that good, not there. Her fingers lingered, lightly stroking the scar tissue. When he glanced down at her, there was a sorrowful, troubled gleam in her eyes.

Abella lowered her hand. "Why would he do that?"

The person in front of them completed her order and moved aside. Tenthil stepped up to the window, grateful for the interruption. He pointed to the food he wanted on the flickering holo-menu and paid the female dacrethian who was taking the orders, using one of the untraceable credit chips from the safehouse. Then he walked Abella to the next window to await their food.

He felt Abella's expectant gaze upon him, but he couldn't bring himself to say more—not here, not now. She must've seen it on his face when their eyes met, because she nodded slightly and turned to watch the dacrethians cook.

When their food was served up, he handed the first container to her and took the second in his free hand. They continued walking along the street, following his mental map toward one of the few places in the city that wasn't under the Master's constant vigil.

Abella brought the container to her nose and sniffed the steam rising from it. She groaned low and deep; sound went right to Tenthil's cock.

"This smells *so* good," she said

"Eat." Tenthil raised his container and tore off a bite of meat. He'd rarely had the pleasure of a hot meal—had rarely taken pleasure in food at all—and this tasted better than anything he'd ever had.

Apart from Abella; her taste would forever be his favorite.

He watched her while he chewed. She devoured the food, occasionally bumping his abdomen with her elbow as she took successive bites. She ate like she'd been starving.

She was thinner when I took her from Cullion's than she was at the club.

Had the circumstances been less chaotic, he would've taken more time to consider her state when he'd saved her. Abella had been slim to begin with; for there to have been a noticeable difference in her weight after only seven days meant she'd gone hungry during his period of hesitance and indecision.

Guilt burned in his chest like acid. Her suffering was his failing.

Never again.

She licked her fingers. "So, where are we going?"

He swallowed another bite of food and ran his tongue over his fangs, which were coated in sweet venom—as they were almost constantly while she was near.

"A safe place to sleep," he replied. The burning pain in his throat was worse now than ever; he'd spoken more in the last two days than in the twenty-five years prior.

Abella's eyes flicked up to meet his. "Wasn't the last place safe enough?"

He dipped his chin. "Safer. But more resources here."

"Will they...find us?"

"Not if we are careful." He tightened his arm around her. "I'll keep you safe, Abella."

TENTHIL SLIPPED the masterkey into his belt pouch and preceded Abella through the open door with his blaster at the ready. She kept close behind him, one hand on his shoulder, as he swept the apartment. Fortunately, it was still empty. This was one of only a handful of locations he'd been able to recall that wouldn't be on the Order's list of obvious places to search.

The place was similar in size to the safehouse where they'd been attacked; here, the larger entry room was a combination living space and kitchen, while the bed had its own room in the back with an adjoined lavatory. While the safehouse had minimal, purely functional furnishings, this place felt like someone actually lived here, with random trinkets scattered about and a few pieces of holographic art on display.

That was because someone *had* lived here. At least until a few months ago.

After closing and locking the door, he turned to Abella, who stood in the center of the main room studying their new surroundings. The apartment was by no means luxurious, but it would suit their needs. The automated cleaning bot had apparently done its job keeping the place neat despite the permanent absence of the apartment's resident.

"How long are we going to stay here?" Abella asked, looking at him over her shoulder.

"As long as necessary."

She nodded and faced forward again, raising her hands to remove her cloak. She stepped deeper into the room and draped the cloak over the back of a chair in the kitchen. "Is this another safehouse?"

Tenthil walked to the other chair and shrugged off his cloak, folding it in half over his arm before setting it down. "No. Belonged to a target."

She stilled for a moment, then shook her head as she muttered, "Guess sleeping in a dead guy's apartment is still better than Cullion's place." She frowned and looked back at him. "How many people have you killed?"

He held her gaze but offered no answer; he didn't have one.

"Stupid question, huh? I don't think I even want to know." She ran her fingers through her hair and bit her lower lip. "Can you at least tell me if you enjoy it?"

"Only once."

"Once?"

Tenthil nodded, moved to the sink, and brushed the back of his hand over the fixture. Steaming water flowed from the faucet. "Cullion."

"Oh."

"Don't feel much, otherwise." He shut off the sink and turned to face Abella. Her eyes were locked on him, her head tilted slightly, but he couldn't read her expression, couldn't guess at her thoughts. He gestured toward the bedroom. "There's a shower in back."

Abella's eyes rounded, her lips parted, and her brows rose. "A shower? Really?"

He nodded, unable to keep the corner of his mouth from tilting up. "Go."

Her black and blue hair fanned around her shoulders as she spun away from him and darted through the bedroom door.

A few moments later, the water in the lavatory came on, followed by Abella's voice. "Oh, my God, yes!"

Tenthil's chest swelled. That so simple a thing as a hot shower could elicit such joy in her was a wonder—and he had been the catalyst for her joy. Knowing he'd brought her some happiness, no matter how small and fleeting, brought Tenthil a sense of satisfaction he'd never experienced. He walked to the bedroom doorway and leaned against the inside of the frame, crossing his arms over his chest and closing his eyes.

Deep within his oldest, dimmest memories were a few exchanges between his parents, quiet moments that had, until now, seemed inconsequential to him. He remembered his mother giving his father a new satchel she had stitched together with hide and sinew, one with little patterns pressed into its flap, remembered the contentment on his father's face—and the pride on his mother's. Or when his father had brought home a large bundle of tiny blue flowers after a long hunt and handed them to Tenthil's mother, knowing they were the kind she used to make her favorite dye. They'd looked at one another as though they saw no one else in the world.

Tenthil understood something new now, something he'd not realized before and never would have realized without Abella—he could derive joy from his mate's pleasure. Making her happy made *him* happy...and that was not an emotion with which he was very familiar.

He opened his eyes at the sound of her footsteps. She appeared in the lavatory doorway, caught his gaze, grinned, and closed the door.

Tenthil's heart skipped a beat; this was the first smile he'd seen from her since they'd danced in Twisted Nethers, and he'd forgotten how radiant and infectious it was. Its warmth pierced his chest and spread throughout his body. He couldn't help but grin himself.

Perhaps I have a chance of making her happy after all.

A new sound drifted to him from the lavatory despite the muffling effect of the closed door—the gentle rustling of fabric. It was followed by a change in the tone of the falling water. Abella had stepped into the shower stall.

She released a long, low moan. The pleasure in her voice shifted the direction of Tenthil's thoughts.

Was that how she would sound when he mated with her? He had seen her naked body while she was unconscious in the safehouse, but he'd somehow managed to keep focused on treating her wounds. Now, he could not help but imagine the water cascading over her bare skin, dripping from the tips of her small, pink nipples, and trickling over her mound and toned thighs.

He grunted against the ache in his erect cock, dropping a hand to grasp it through his pants. How long had it been since his last release? Time had lost meaning in Abella's company; days had passed, perhaps. Not that his hand would provide much relief. Anything he did for himself would be hollow, meaningless, unfulfilling. The treatment of a symptom rather than the cause.

He needed *her*.

Forcing his hand away, he walked into the bedroom, took off the backpack, and set it beside him as he sat on the edge of the bed. Once he'd removed his boots and set them aside, he tugged his shirt off over his head, tossing it next to the backpack. The caress of cool air against his skin did nothing to ease the desire burning in his veins. He curled his hands into fists and rested them atop his thighs, bowing his head.

I can focus past this. I am in control of myself.

Another sound came from beyond the lavatory door—music. His mate was *singing*.

Tenthil raised his head to stare at the door, his ears twitching as the song dipped low and soft—so soft that he had difficulty hearing it. Without meaning to, he stood up and drifted to the lavatory, his mind clouded in a haze created by the allure of his mate's sweet voice.

He leaned forward, pressing a hand and an ear to the door. Her voice steadily increased in volume as she continued singing. Despite his translator granting him knowledge of each individual word, he couldn't quite understand their meaning when strung together in song, but he didn't care—because she was singing, and it was beautiful, especially after her long period of silence.

Her song changed several times as he listened over fifteen or twenty minutes, each bearing its own tune, rhythm, and lyrics, but her voice remained constant; she sounded carefree. Happy.

This is how I want her to sound always.

Even when she turned the water off, Tenthil could not bring himself to move away from the door. Her words gave way to pleasant humming, as pure and entrancing as her singing had been. He curled his fingers against the door; he would never allow the Master to silence her. He would never allow anything in this world—or any other—to take her from him.

The click of the interior handle was his only warning before the door opened, granting him a split second to straighten. Abella gasped and froze in the doorway, one hand still on the handle, staring up at him in surprise.

Tenthil's swept his gaze over her. Her pale skin bore a healthy, pink flush, and her dark hair hung wet around her shoulders, its tips beaded with water droplets. She was clad only in a towel, which was wrapped around her torso; it revealed the tops of her breasts and ended mid-thigh to show-case her long legs.

That single glance was more than enough to rekindle Tenthil's desire. It roared to life inside him, a firestorm that suffused his entire body.

"Were you, um, standing outside the door this whole time?" Abella asked, tucking a strand of hair behind her ear.

He took a step forward, eliminating the space between them. Abella did not retreat; she simply tilted her head back to keep her eyes locked with his. The warm, humid air inside the lavatory only strengthened her scent, which enveloped him and added a lustful note to the haze lingering in his mind.

Tenthil lifted a hand and brushed the back of his finger over her cheek. A shuddering breath escaped her. He trailed his finger lower, following the delicate curve of her jaw, tracing the graceful line of her neck, flowing over the gentle swell of her breasts. She shivered, her chest straining against the towel. His eyes followed his touch. He was spellbound by her body's responses, enthralled by her scent, enraptured by her feel.

He met her gaze. Desire burned in the depths of her eyes.

His body tensed, and he clenched his teeth. Instinct roared within him to take her, to mount her, to rut her, to make her *his*.

"Tenthil..."

Though she spoke only his name, her voice said infinitely more, brimming with her every secret.

In a rush of movement, he curved his hands around Abella's ass, grasped the backs of her thighs, and lifted her off the floor. She wrapped her legs around his waist and plunged her fingers into his hair. Her blunt nails grazed his scalp. In three quick strides, he carried her across the lavatory and pressed her back against the wall, his mouth slanting over hers to claim her lips in a savage kiss.

She whimpered, but it wasn't a sound of fear. It was a sound of need as she returned his kiss with a ferocity to match his own.

Her tongue flicked past his lips and stroked his tongue. Tenthil started in surprise only to groan as her sweetness filled his mouth. An inferno rose within him, threatening to engulf him completely, but it didn't stop him from deepening the kiss, from demanding more.

Clutching her closer, he ground his cock against the juncture of her thighs. She tightened her grip on his hair and moaned, undulating her pelvis. Intense pleasure swept through him. His claws lengthened, and he snarled against her mouth as shudders wracked his body. Her heat pulsed into him through his pants, and the scent of her desire, thick and arousing, flooded his senses, pairing with her taste to instill him with bestial energy.

"Abella," he growled, holding back nothing.

ELEVEN

Abella burned with desire. Tenthil's fingers were like branding irons on her thighs and ass, scalding her, igniting a fire in her belly. Every scrape of his callused palms, every prick of his claws, and every tiny move of his fingers sent a spark of excitement through her and made her sex clench in need. She tightened her legs, digging her heels into his lower back as she shamelessly rocked against the hard length of his cock.

She panted against his mouth as pleasure built within her. And *oh, God*, his mouth was sublime! She nipped and sucked at his lips and stroked her tongue against his. A woody sweetness burst across her taste buds, reminiscent of cinnamon, and she tilted her head to kiss him deeper, harder, unable to get enough of his flavor. Even the scrape of his fangs against her lip wasn't enough to deter her from this—from him.

Tenthil thrust against her. His cock, separated from Abella only by the fabric of his pants, rubbed against her clit, creating delightful friction. Her towel fell loose to drape over his arms and dangle around her hips; she used the opportunity to press her breasts to his chest, which vibrated with a deep, satisfied growl that stimulated her budded nipples.

She didn't care about her nudity—she needed him closer, needed to feel his hot skin against hers, needed him *inside* her.

The thought of him pushing into her, stretching her, filling her, sent a pulsing, electric thrill to Abella's core and set her alight from within. The pressure inside her built higher and higher with every fierce snap of his hips until it finally burst.

Throwing her arms around Tenthil, Abella tore her mouth away from his and succumbed to the ecstasy. A guttural cry ripped from her throat. She was beyond speech, beyond thought. Her body seized as pleasure swept through her, lighting up her every nerve with delicious torment, flooding her with liquid heat. Her nails bit into Tenthil's back.

His thrusts became more powerful, more urgent, and his breath rasped against her neck. He brushed his lips across the sensitive skin of her throat, and Abella tilted her head back to allow him access.

Tenthil tightened his grip on her thighs, pressing the tips of his claws into her flesh, as his body stiffened. He opened his mouth against her neck.

Sharp pain broke through the fog of Abella's lust. For a panicked moment, Abella stilled, uncertain of what to do.

Tenthil had sunk his teeth into the flesh between her neck and shoulder.

But all her thoughts and fears were swept away by a tidal wave of intensified pleasure that left only mind-shattering exhilaration in its wake.

She screamed and clutched at him as she reached another peak, miles above anything she'd known possible. Tingling, tantalizing heat spread from the point of his bite and sizzled through her veins. It was like he was touching every part of her, like he was *inside* her, like they were one with each other. It was amazing. It was agonizing.

It was utter bliss.

Tenthil released a bestial growl. His hips jerked forward, and he pulled her closer to grind against her sex. She felt his shaft swell and pulsate through his pants, felt fresh heat as he came.

Breathless, Abella maintained her hold on his shoulders as Tenthil shuddered around her, until finally, he withdrew his fangs.

He bit me.

He removed a hand from her thigh and pressed his forearm against the wall, bracing himself. His broad shoulders and powerful chest heaved with his ragged breaths. He brushed his nose over her neck, beneath her ear, and into her hair before inhaling deeply.

He bit me.

Heated euphoria still flowed through her, the result of whatever he'd injected her with.

Despite that, reality slammed into Abella. She was naked, pressed against a wall, and in the arms of an alien. She'd just been intimate with an alien. She'd nearly had *sex* with the alien who was holding her captive.

And he'd *bitten* her.

Abella lowered her legs, slid her hands down to his chest, and shoved. He staggered backward a few steps. His brow furrowed over his impossibly black eyes.

She caught herself against the wall, snatched up the sides of her towel, and wrapped them around her torso. Raising a hand, she pressed her fingers to the spot between her neck and shoulder where he'd pierced her skin. The wounds were two pairs of raised bumps, tender to the touch, and there were traces of blood and a clear, unknown liquid on her fingertips when she pulled them away and looked down.

She glared at Tenthil. "You bit me!"

He blinked and dragged a hand over his face, shaking his head. Slowly, the black of his pupils receded. His eyes widened when he looked at her shoulder, and he stepped forward.

Abella thrust a palm toward him. "No."

He halted, raking his concerned gaze over her. "Abella—"

She shook her head and sidestepped along the wall toward the bathroom door, unable to ignore the wetness between her thighs as she moved. "Look, we were both caught up in the moment, and it's been a really, *really* long time for me"—*so damn long*—"and it just happened. Shouldn't have, but it did. Let's just, um...move on, okay? I'll even forgive you for biting me."

What is there to forgive? It felt so good.

Even now, as she retreated from him, she wanted nothing more than to jump back into his arms and do it all over again—to do more, to have him inside her. She wanted to feel him moving in and out of her, wanted his hands and mouth all over her body, wanted him to make her climax again and again.

What the hell is wrong with me? He bit me! And who knows what freaky alien stuff he injected me with. I shouldn't be thinking of having sex with him!

Abella took in his scars, his lean, powerful, sexy-as-sin body, and the outline of his cock, which stood out clearly through his pants. Her sex clenched; apparently, her body wasn't on the same page as her mind.

He can smell my desire.

Her breath caught in her throat, and she snapped her gaze up to his. Hunger had rekindled in his eyes, and his pupils were expanding. He took a step closer.

Oh, fuck. I need to get out of here.

"Shower's yours! Enjoy!" Abella darted through the doorway and slammed the door shut behind her. She leaned against it, clutching the towel to her heaving chest, and squeezed her eyes shut.

Shit! Shit! Shit!

What was she going to do? She'd never been with a man who elicited even a fraction of the response from her that Tenthil had, and no one had ever looked at her with even a sliver of the passion that blazed in his eyes. However much she wanted to resist, she was undeniably, inexplicably drawn to him.

He's my captor. He's no better than Cullion...

But he *was*. Apart from the bite, which had been pleasurable, he'd never harmed her. He'd treated her as though she were the most precious thing in his life, not because he wanted to show off an exotic pet, but because he cared.

No. She couldn't afford to develop...feelings for him. Couldn't allow herself to care.

But she did. And she wanted him.

"It's just sex," she whispered.

But it wouldn't just be sex. It never was for Abella. She'd never been one to have casual sex; she had to feel something, had to feel like she mattered. If she were to go all the way with Tenthil, something inside her would shift irreversibly, and he would consume her.

She would become his.

What kind of life could she have with him? He was a *killer*. She'd seen him take lives without hesitation, and he'd admitted to being an assassin in a matter-of-fact tone. He seemed to have no remorse for what he'd done.

But he said he didn't enjoy it. Doesn't that count for something?

If she stayed with him, they would constantly be on the run, forever hunted by shadowy forces.

Abella missed her home, missed her family, and she finally had a real chance to get back to them. She needed to seize the opportunity. She couldn't let herself get distracted, couldn't let lust cloud her mind. She couldn't let her heart warm toward Tenthil any more than it already had.

The shower came on, its sound muffled but unmistakable through the door at her back. She breathed a sigh of relief; he wasn't coming after her.

Abella's eyes fell on the backpack atop the bed.

He's not coming after me.

She turned around and stared at the bathroom door, softly placing her palms against it. Part of her expected it to burst open any moment. After a few seconds, she backed away, one hesitant step at a time. The tone of the water changed; he'd stepped into the shower.

Now was her chance.

She crept to the bed and opened the backpack, sorting through its contents until she found the extra clothing Tenthil had packed. With her heart pounding and her eyes flicking repeatedly toward the bathroom, she dropped the towel and dress quickly. Her gear was in there with him; hopefully, that would make him think she didn't plan on going anywhere. She looped his belt around her waist, brushing her fingertips over the blaster as she drew in a shaky breath.

Abella tiptoed to her boots—she'd kicked them off when she first entered the bedroom—and stepped into them. Exiting the bedroom, she gently closed the door behind her before hurrying to the chair to pick up her cloak and whip it over her shoulders.

So long as she kept her hood up, her head down, and didn't call attention to herself, she could find one of the Eternal Guard peacekeepers stationed throughout the city. She'd seen them on several occasions while caged on the back of Cullion's hovercar and had spotted a few while traveling here with Tenthil. They'd know where the human embassy was. They would help her.

Soon, she'd be on her way home.

As she reached the door, Abella hesitated and glanced back at the bedroom.

She'd asked Tenthil repeatedly to take her to the embassy, to help her find her way home, and he'd refused to answer. Tenthil had secrets—likely more than she could imagine—but he struck her as guarded, not dishonest. He'd avoided answering because he had no intention of bringing Abella to her people.

He thought he was protecting her, but he was taking away her choice in the process. He was ignoring her wishes. He was acting like her owner, not her defender.

If I don't go now, I might never have another chance. I can't be a slave again. I can't.

Eyebrows lowered, Abella faced forward, lifted her hood, and pressed the button the wall. The door slid open. Without another look back, she crossed the threshold.

She paused as the door closed behind her, sweeping her eyes back and forth. The apartment's entrance was in a long, dimly lit corridor. Tenthil had led her through several such passages after they'd left the street, winding deeper and deeper into the chaotic mass of buildings that comprised so much of the Undercity. As confusing as these corridors were—especially when so many of them looked the same—she would find her way out to the street again.

And once she was there, she'd get help.

Setting a brisk pace, Abella retraced the path Tenthil had taken to the apartment to the best of her recollection.

It felt strange not being tucked against his side with his arm around her shoulders as she walked. That feeling compounded with a growing sense of isolation as she hurried through the deserted corridors, climbed several sets of stairs, and passed numerous closed doors.

She'd heard people call Arthos the *Infinite City* more times than she could count and guessed there were hundreds of millions—if not *billions*—of people living here. How could any part of it feel so empty?

After a while, dread pooled in her gut, and she suddenly didn't feel so alone. Keeping her head tilted down, she glanced back.

Four figures, dressed in the same black attire as the assassins from the safehouse, were following only ten or fifteen meters behind her.

Abella's blood turned to ice. Facing forward, she dropped her hand to the blaster at her hip and quickened her steps, taking several random turns in the hopes of losing her pursuers. Her pounding heartbeat filled her ears, and her breath burned her throat. When she looked over her shoulder again, the dark figures were only closer.

No. No, no, no no!

Tenthil had been so careful in making sure they hadn't been followed. How had the assassins found her?

Have they found Tenthil as well?

Fear slithered through Abella and wrapped its cold tendrils around her heart. He'd been in the shower when she left, with no one to warn him of the danger.

Tears stung her eyes as she broke into a run. Despite the immensity of her fear, it was overpowered by her regret. All she'd wanted for four years was to be free, to go home, but what price was she willing to pay to get there? Was she prepared to sacrifice the life of the man who'd saved her from Cullion if it meant seeing Earth again?

She pressed her fingers over the bite mark hidden under her shirt. It wasn't like she had a choice now; she'd led the assassins through so many twists and turns that she didn't even know how to get back to the apartment.

Tenthil knows how to take care of himself. I've seen him fight. He'll be...he'll be fine.

But the thought offered her no comfort; she'd left him vulnerable. She'd left him without a word.

She rounded another corner, and some of her hope was suddenly restored—only five or ten meters ahead, the corridor opened onto a main street, where a multitude of aliens of various shapes and sizes were going about their business. The dim, oppressive passageways through which she'd fled gave way to the vibrant, kaleidoscopic holograms of the Undercity.

She'd never been so happy to see advertisements.

Abella didn't dare look back as she sprinted the remaining distance to the street; she felt her pursuers' closeness, and even the briefest backward glance would slow her too much. She plunged into the crowd, muttering apologies when she bumped into the aliens on its fringes, and slowed to a quick walk. Rapid, ragged breaths burned her lungs and throat as she fell in with the general flow of foot traffic.

She scanned the crowd, looking for gold-clad members of the Eternal Guard. This was the safest place until she found help—Tenthil said these assassins were all about secrets. They wouldn't act with so many witnesses present.

Would they?

Maintaining her forward momentum, she twisted to check behind her. Though they'd fanned out, she quickly spotted all four of the cloaked figures following her; they wove through the crowd effortlessly, steadily closing the distance separating them from Abella.

She faced forward and hurried along until her frantic gaze

finally settled upon a peacekeeper. Heart fluttering, she charged toward him through the throng, ignoring the snide remarks and threats tossed at her, shrugging off an angry shove and an elbow to her side. When she finally burst out of the press of bodies, she stumbled forward. She caught the peace-keeper's arm to hold herself upright.

"Please," Abella rasped, tilting her head back to look up at the peacekeeper's face. He was a borian, his features both harsh and refined, and stood over two meters tall. His species had always reminded her of elves from fantasy books and movies—if those elves were broad-shouldered, towering barbarian warriors. "I need help."

The peacekeeper frowned down at her. His sharp brows were angled low over his straight, aristocratic nose. "It is a criminal offense to lay hands upon a member of the Eternal Guard."

Abella glanced at her hands, released her hold on him, and took a small step back before meeting his gaze again. "I need your help, please. I was kidnapped and sold, and I'm just trying to get back home, and now I'm being followed by assassins."

The peacekeeper raised his armored forearm and pressed a finger to the wrist guard. A tiny orb rose from the armor and hovered in the air between Abella and the borian, tiny beams of soft light pulsing from its underside.

"Stand still so I can scan your identification chip," he said.

"I-I don't have one."

The borian's frown deepened. He lifted his finger off the wrist guard, and the orb disappeared into the armor. After lowering his arms and settling a hand on the grip of his holstered blaster, he looked past her.

The peacekeeper's eyes widened for an instant. He made a soft grumble and tilted his head to the side. "Come with me."

Relief flooded her. "Oh, thank you."

She moved closer to the peacekeeper's side. When she

glanced behind her, there was no sign of the assassins in the crowd. Had they gone? Had the mere presence of the Eternal Guard deterred them?

Abella walked alongside the borian, having to take almost two steps to account for every one of his long strides. She received a few curious glances from the people around them, but that was most likely because she was accompanying a peacekeeper—without her raised hood obscuring her human features, there would likely have been more stares. There always were.

"There's a human embassy in the city, right?" she asked.

The borian glanced down at her. "Is that what you are?"

Abella frowned. "You've never seen a human? Um, maybe you know us as terrans?"

"So...you're a terran with no identification chip who was kidnapped and is being chased by assassins? Am I missing anything?"

"No... That's it." She flexed her fingers and wiped her sweaty palms on her pants. "You can take me to the terran embassy, right?"

"Don't worry. We'll get all this resolved for you."

His avoidance of her questions opened a crack in Abella's sense of relief, allowing a lick of unease to flow through. That crack split wider when he led her onto a quiet side street where the crowds she'd seen throughout most of the Undercity were absent.

"Is the embassy around here or is it on the surface?" she asked. "Isn't there a more...public route?"

He didn't look at her when he replied. "This is the way. I'll get you where you need to go."

Despite seeming to have seen the assassins when he looked up, the peacekeeper was making no effort to survey his surroundings; he was acting as though they were in no danger whatsoever.

Abella stopped when he turned into one of the dark, narrow alleys branching off the street.

The borian proceeded a few more steps before he halted and twisted to face her. "Come on."

She shook her head. "I don't know what you're trying to do, but—"

"Helping," the peacekeeper said firmly.

Abella took a step back. "I...think I'll find someone else."

A solid, strong hand clamped over her right shoulder. Abella's heart leapt into her throat as she glanced back to see a female ilthurii standing behind her. The ilthurii's reptilian snout protruded from beneath the hood of a black cloak identical to Abella's. Three other black-garbed assassins stepped into her peripheral vision, one on the right and two on the left, all wearing combat armor like Tenthil had worn before they were run out of the safehouse.

"Whatever happens in your organization is your business," the peacekeeper said, calling Abella's attention back to him as he lifted his empty palms and walked out of the alley. "I didn't see anything."

Abella stared at the guard, dumbfounded. "You're *helping* them?"

"I'm helping myself," he replied, turning his back to her. "You have no ID, you're not my problem. Not going to die for you."

Abella's shock disintegrated in the heat of her anger. "You asshole!" She jerked her arm forward, attempting to dislodge the ilthurii's hold.

The assassin tightened her grip, claws pricking Abella's flesh through her shirt, and dragged Abella's shoulder back.

Wincing, Abella returned her attention to her assailants.

Fear churned in the pit of her belly, but she wouldn't let it win —she wouldn't let them win. She wouldn't give up without a fight.

Using the momentum of the ilthurii's pull to speed her movement, Abella spun toward the assassin, dropped her hand, and drew her blaster. She fired the instant its barrel was pointed at the ilthurii.

The ilthurii's slitted pupils expanded in shock, and she bared her pointed teeth. Her hand fell away from Abella's shoulder. She stumbled a few steps to the side before her legs gave out and she collapsed. Smoke drifted from a glowing impact hole in her hip.

The scent of burning flesh stung Abella's nose.

Abella took a two-handed grip of her blaster and raised it toward the other assassins, but her enemies were too close. The nearest assassin darted forward and kicked the weapon from her grasp. Before she could even register what had happened, an arm slipped around her neck from behind, yanking her backward.

With a choking grunt, Abella clutched the iron-strong forearm with both hands and swung her legs up, kicking the assassin in front of her with both feet. The blow caught him in the chest, and he staggered backward.

Just as he recovered his balance, a gray-skinned hand fell on his shoulder and spun him around. The assassin jerked, made a wet, gurgling sound, and fell to the ground.

Tenthil stood on the other side of the body, holding a knife in his blood-soaked hand. His feral black eyes met Abella's gaze.

TWELVE

Rage roared through Tenthil's veins, but he was too lost in a battle haze to determine its exact sources. All that mattered was the danger to his mate.

One assassin dead, one seriously wounded, two still in the fight. The vorgal acolyte had Abella in a choke hold, while his only standing companion, a stone-skinned bokkan, had turned toward Tenthil, brandishing a meter-long energy blade in each hand.

The odds meant nothing while Abella was threatened. Tenthil had overcome far worse with less motivation.

The bokkan charged, his energy blades creating arcs of blurred light as he swung them.

Tenthil drew his blaster—from the belt Abella had been wearing not long ago—and fired rapidly from his hip, backpedaling to avoid the swinging blades. Several of the bolts dissipated against the bokkan's armor, hissing with flashes of orange and red, but several more struck unarmored parts of the acolyte's body.

One of the energy blades flew from the bokkan's nerveless

fingers after a plasma bolt struck the underside of his arm. Tenthil swayed to the side. The whirring, crackling blade zipped through the air centimeters from his face, and electricity tingled across his skin.

The bokkan recovered with surprising speed despite his injuries and swung his other blade toward Tenthil's side.

Abella screamed his name, but her voice was cut off by a choked grunt.

Tenthil reversed his hold on his knife and stabbed downward. The blade punched through the bokkan's hard skin with a crack; at the same instant, the bokkan's energy blade struck Tenthil's side. He grunted at the searing pain, but his own strike halted the blow before it went any deeper. Keeping his blaster low, Tenthil angled the barrel upward and fired two shots into the underside of the bokkan's chin.

The plasma bolts burst out the top of the acolyte's head. Deep cracks spread across the gray skin surrounding the wounds. The energy blade dropped to the ground, sizzled against the concrete, and sputtered out.

Tugging his knife free, Tenthil shoved the bokkan aside and shifted his attention to Abella and the remaining acolyte. The black-garbed vorgal had dragged her several meters down the street, unaffected by her struggles.

Tenthil charged forward.

The vorgal's eyes widened when they fell upon Tenthil. He reached down and drew a knife from his belt, lifting it toward Abella's head.

Though already impossibly hot, Tenthil's fury intensified. Before the vorgal could get his blade near Abella's face, Tenthil straightened his arm and fired his blaster. The weapon made its high, punchy sound, and the plasma bolt zipped past her head, singeing a few strands of her hair, to strike the vorgal between the eyes.

Abella cried out in startlement. The vorgal's arms dropped, his dagger clattered to the ground, and he sagged forward. She twisted aside, escaping his collapsing bulk.

Tenthil slowed and turned his blaster toward the ilthurii, who was on her belly, dragging her limp legs and tail behind her as she crawled down the street. He shot her twice in the head before dropping his weapons into their holsters and rushing to Abella's side.

He caught her arm in his hand, forcing her to turn and face him. Her fear-filled eyes were wide when they met his, and she was trembling. He grasped her shoulders and steadied her as he swept his gaze over her body from head to toe.

"Are you hurt?" he asked. At a glance, the only damage she'd suffered was some redness around her neck and a bit of burned hair, but not all wounds were readily apparent.

"N-No." She looked down at his side. "But I saw you—"

"I'm fine." He released his hold on her. His pain was distant, and the energy blade had cauterized the wound, so he wasn't bleeding. It would require some attention to heal properly, but there was no time for that now.

These were acolytes from the Order, and not only had they targeted Abella, they'd attempted to take her *alive*.

"Tenthil, you're not fine," Abella said. "I...I saw him cut you!"

He stepped aside, slid off his backpack, and crouched over the vorgal. He transferred the dead acolyte's ammunition and supplies into the bag and tugged the blaster from the vorgal's holster before rising and striding to the ilthurii's corpse to repeat the process. Only when he was about to move to the next body did he notice the device attached to the ilthurii's wrist armor. After slinging the backpack over his shoulders, he lifted the acolyte's limp arm and touched the control on the wrist device.

A holographic screen appeared, displaying a map of the surrounding area. There were five markers on the map—four green and one red. Tenthil's brows fell as he flicked his gaze across the dead acolytes. Their positions corresponded with the green markers on the map.

He met Abella's gaze. "Step back."

Abella frowned. "What?"

"Just do it!"

She flinched, caught her lower lip between her teeth, and took several backward steps.

The red marker moved to reflect her new position.

He snarled a curse and slammed the ilthurii's hand down before rising. He'd removed his tracker, so they'd found a way to track Abella instead—undoubtedly through a device Cullion had implanted in her.

Tenthil raked his fingers through his hair, tugging it back from his face. He turned slowly to take in the scene. Four dead acolytes in and around the alley's entrance, and a dead peacekeeper fifteen meters down the street who Tenthil had killed before rushing to Abella's aid.

The body count was high enough to bring attention even without counting the peacekeeper amongst the dead, and the Master was tracking Abella on top of that. The Infinite City held enemies at every turn.

Tenthil stalked toward Abella.

She retreated, holding her hands up as though warding him off, until her back bumped a wall. The fear in her expression struck Tenthil like a blow; she was afraid of *him*.

Abella's eyes glistened with unshed tears. "I'm sorry! I know it was stupid, but—"

Tenthil stopped directly in front of Abella and pressed a finger over her lips, silencing her. He bared his teeth and narrowed his eyes. "The people of this city are *not* your friends.

They will buy and sell you if it benefits them even a little. *No one* is going to help you, Abella. No one but *me*. Do you understand?"

Her breath quickened as she held his gaze, tears leaking from the corners of her eyes. She nodded.

Adjusting his hold on the vorgal's blaster, he dropped it into the holster on her hip. His throat felt like it had been shredded and lit on fire. "Need to go."

Without waiting for her to respond, he put his arm around her shoulders, pulled her against his side, and walked into the nearby alleyway.

"Are there more of them?" she asked quietly.

"Always."

She looked up at him. "I'm sorry. I know I screwed up, but I had to try."

Tenthil couldn't recall ever experiencing anything like the maelstrom of emotion within him. He'd plummeted from a sexual high—a peak of intimacy he'd never shared with anyone —to sinking disappointment when he heard her leave the apartment. That disappointment had quickly given way to anger and fear as he'd tailed her through the streets.

He hadn't been sure how the acolytes had found her, but they hadn't been subtle about following her.

I screwed up was an understatement. He wanted to rage at her for leaving. He also wanted to hold her, to comfort her, to run his hands over her body and know she was okay.

But he wouldn't be able to provide comfort for either her or himself. Not for a while, anyway.

"There is a tracker in you," he said.

"What?"

Tenthil guided her into an intersecting alley and ducked into one of the recesses along its length, positioning Abella with her back against the wall. He turned to face her. The pipes and ductwork running into the building nearby hummed and clanked steadily.

"There is a tracking device implanted inside your body, Abella."

Her brow furrowed, and she frowned. "No. I'd feel it, wouldn't I? I would know."

He raised his hands and pressed the pads of his fingers to the back of her neck.

Abella's muscles tensed. She flattened her hands on his chest. "What are you doing?"

"Relax," he growled. He felt for anything abnormal beneath her skin; the device would be tiny, but there were only a few places in which they were typically installed.

If they were lucky, they had a few minutes before the bodies were discovered—but he didn't plan to put their lives in the fickle hands of chance.

"Don't growl at me," she said.

Tenthil leaned closer to her, tilting his chin down. "I'd be yelling if I could, Abella. *Relax.*"

Her hands tensed, exerting pressure against him briefly before she finally relaxed. He resumed his examination, prodding around the base of her skull and the top of her spine. Abella's breaths were quick and warm against his throat. Despite everything, he felt the stirrings of arousal in his blood, and his cock throbbed. His body's reaction only reminded him that he'd not yet fully claimed her, making him angrier.

Something small, solid, and loose beneath her skin caught his attention, thankfully distracting him from his agitation. He moved his thumb over the spot in a little circle. The object rocked beneath his touch.

Tenthil lowered his hands and stepped back from her. He drew his knife, plucked a sanitizing wipe from his small cache of medical supplies, and used it to clean the blood off the blade. "Turn around."

Her eyes rounded, and she flattened herself against the wall behind her. "What are you doing?"

"It has to come out."

"You're going to cut me open?" Fear crept back into her eyes.

"Turn around," he repeated. Nausea added itself to the growing list of things he was feeling; the thought of doing her harm made him ill, but it *had* to be done. He couldn't keep her safe while she was being tracked. Even Tenthil had limits. Ceaseless attacks from Order assassins would wear him down before long, and then Abella would be defenseless.

Her lower lip trembled, but she turned, giving him her back.

"Hair up," he said.

She gathered her hair, holding it atop her head, leaned forward, and tipped her forehead against the wall. "I can do this," she whispered. "I took Cullion's punishment for years. I can do this."

Tenthil stepped forward and raised his hands to her neck. Gentle prodding with his fingers relocated the object beneath her skin, and he settled the point of the blade beneath it.

He drew in a disturbingly shaky breath and rasped, "The pain will pass."

He sank the knife into her skin. Red blood welled from the wound, and Abella gasped, muscles tensing. She hissed as he pressed the blade deeper. In his mind's eye, he tried to recall the detailed holograms of terran anatomy he'd been forced to study, and he was suddenly fearful all over again—what if *he* did significant harm to her? What if he was making a mistake?

Clenching his jaw, he continued his work. Abella cried out when the blade lightly scraped bone. Tenthil's nostrils flared;

her scent was strong, but it was overlaid by the smell of her blood. The combination did strange things to him—he wanted to tend to her wound, rut her, and protect her all at once. He fought back his tumultuous instincts as best he could.

Gently, he angled the blade and used it like a lever to pry the object out. It emerged from the cut a moment later, a tiny, crimson-stained tristeel orb with a bundle of hair thin tendrils on one side. Keeping the knife in place, he pinched the orb between the claws of forefinger and thumb and pulled. The wires went taut for a moment, clinging to their internal anchor points, before breaking free.

Abella released a muffled cry, and her body sagged as her knees buckled. Tenthil withdrew the knife and slid a leg forward, pinning her to the wall with his hip before she fell farther. Fresh blood flowed from her wound.

"Almost done," he said as soothingly as his broken voice allowed. He tossed the tracker aside, adjusted his hold on the knife, and plucked a bandage from his belt. Using both hands, he settled the bandage over her wound.

It activated quickly, closing the cut as it faded into her skin.

Tenthil covered the hand she had fisted in her hair with his own, loosening her hold and guiding it down. He wiped the blade of his knife clean on his pants and sheathed it before combing the fingers of his free hand through her tangled hair, smoothing it back down.

"Can you stand?" he asked.

Abella nodded, straightening her legs. She sniffled, raised an arm to wipe her eyes, and turned to face him when he shifted backward.

He cupped her cheek with one hand and tipped his forehead against hers. He just wanted to hold her against him and never let go, wanted to let the city around them, the *universe*, fall away into nothingness, leaving only the two of them.

"We need to go," he said softly.

"Okay."

Slipping his arm around her shoulders once again, he drew her against his uninjured side and continued along the alley. He gradually increased their pace, easing her toward greater speed, mindful of both her needs and the danger they were in.

Luck was the only reason he hadn't lost her, and he had no intention of relying upon it again.

TENTHIL TURNED his head to glance behind them as he stopped at the entry door. The journey back into the Bowels had been a long one. His muscles ached, and his wounded ribs throbbed, but he hadn't stopped. Abella had remained at his side throughout, silent but for occasional sniffles and sobs. Though hearing those sounds crushed Tenthil's heart, he couldn't tend to her until they were somewhere safe.

Satisfied they were alone, he lifted the small, disc-shaped chip in his hand and held it up to the reader beside the door. After a moment, the door beeped and slid open. Tenthil guided Abella inside and finally released her. She stepped away from him slowly, as though in a daze.

The room had a faint, musty smell, but it was surprisingly well-kept for a place in the Bowels. The furniture was simple but clean—a wide bed, a table with four chairs, a footlocker, and a desk with a lone console to access the plexus, Arthos's integrated collection of computer networks. Two doors led out of the bedroom, one into a small kitchen and the other into a lavatory.

He'd not thought to come to one of these places—discreet safehouses scattered throughout the Bowels which could only be rented through hidden, automated terminals—because he'd never had to use one. This was the sort of place where he'd found a few of his marks over the years, the sort of place to which prey fled. A desperate shelter for targets of the Order.

And now I am a target of the Order.

From experience, he knew these safehouses were entirely off the record; the terminals accepted only credits that weren't linked to accounts and kept no documentation regarding their patrons. Finding people holed up in such places was not impossible, but it was difficult, and Tenthil had already set a pattern the Order might not have expected him to break—he'd been staying in locations previously used by targets he'd eliminated.

Tenthil could only hope he and Abella would have some time to breathe here.

He turned, slid the heavy-duty deadbolts into place, tossed his backpack and cloak onto the floor, and walked to Abella. Grasping her shoulders, he spun her to face him. For a few moments, she stared up at him, her glistening eyes, red from her tears, wary. Tenthil wasn't sure of everything he felt in that moment—there were too many feelings to ever sort out—but a sense of relief was foremost.

He took her in his arms and drew her against his chest, lowering his cheek to her hair. Smoothing a hand up and down her back, he willed away the tension threatening to curl his fingers and extend his claws.

Her shoulders shook as she cried against his chest, letting out full, raw sobs. It was as though she'd held on to these tears for years, as though she'd been unwilling to release her pain and loss. Her fingers clutched at his waist, pressing into the flesh above his hip bones.

"Why didn't you just take me to the humans?" she asked between cries.

The pain and despair in her voice sank into Tenthil's gut like the twisting blade of a knife.

"They cannot protect you from the Order," he said. "Only I can."

"You don't know that!"

He rubbed his cheek against her hair, inhaling her scent, which had changed subtly since they'd come together in the lavatory earlier. He swore he detected a hint of himself in her smell; he shrugged it off as a matter of him holding her while they traveled over the last several hours.

Gently, he ran his claws through her hair. "You are mine, Abella."

She shook her head and pulled back, lifting her face to look up at him. "No, I'm not. The choice is *mine*, Tenthil. Mine. You can't just...own me."

"Neither of us has a choice in this."

"What do you mean? We always have a choice."

"I don't. Not when it comes to you."

Her brows lowered. "I don't understand."

Tenthil looked down, searching for the right words. He'd spent most of his life prying secrets from others, and yet he still found it difficult to reveal his own, even to her.

"Something in me recognizes you." He met her gaze again. "Something in me knows that you are mine. That I am yours. I cannot ignore it, cannot deny it. It is the deepest, most primal part of me."

"Are you...are you talking about soulmates?"

Soulmates. He'd never heard the term before, but it sounded right.

"Yes."

Her eyes searched his. "You think I'm your soulmate?"

"I *know*."

Abella looked away, giving him a fleeting glimpse of the flush that had risen on her cheeks. "That kind of thing isn't real. People want to believe in it, want to believe there's a true love out there for them, but...it's just not real. You don't know me, Tenthil. What you feel is lust."

"You think lust alone could have driven me to do what I have done?" Every word was like a hot coal in his throat, but he couldn't stop, couldn't bear more silence. He caught her chin between his fingers and forced her to look at him. "I have made war on all I knew to have you. I have risked *everything* to have you and will continue to do so until the Void swallows me for eternity."

Fresh tears gathered in her eyes, shimmering as they caught the overhead light, and spilled down her cheeks. Her fingers tightened on his waist until, finally, she slid her arms around him and rested her head upon his chest.

Something warmed inside Tenthil. He wrapped his arms around her and held her close, once more settling his cheek atop her hair and drawing in her scent.

"I had a life before this," she said softly. "A family, friends, a home."

"So did I."

"You did? Before you were..."

"Changed." He clenched and relaxed his jaw. For most of his life, he'd carefully guarded his memories of his home world, knowing the Master would take them if they rose too close to the surface. They'd faded significantly over time, so much so that he knew many were lost to him forever, and it pained him that he could not remember more of what he was, of the place from which he'd come.

"I lived with my people when I was young," he said. "Was five or six years old when slavers came, packed my tribe into ships, and brought me here. I had a mother. A father. Brothers and a sister. I had a tribe."

"Oh, my God. And you never saw them again? None of them?" she asked.

He shook his head. "Some of them were on the ship, but...I cannot remember clearly anymore. We were all sold to different owners. The Master bought me...to make me into what I am."

"I'm so sorry." She turned her head and pressed a kiss to his chest before resting her forehead against it. She laughed humorlessly. "All this time I was crying about going home, not realizing everything you've suffered and endured... My experiences seem mild in comparison."

Tenthil slid a hand up her back to her neck, gently brushing the pads of his fingers across the spot he'd bandaged after removing the tracker. She shivered and held him a little tighter.

"My pain does not invalidate yours," he said softly. "You were taken, too. Our experiences are the same."

Abella tilted her head back to look up at him. Lifting her hands, she lightly traced the scars on his cheeks with her fingertips. "Will you tell me how you got these?"

He covered her hands with his own, meaning to guide them away, but stopped himself. The scars were part of him, and he was Abella's. "The Vow of Silence. It is a ritual the Master performs so acolytes may prove their devotion to the Order and its secrets. It involves the removal of organs necessary for speech, so it varies between species. All are required to take it save the Master and his favored second. I refused."

"And these were your punishment?"

Tenthil shook his head. "No. These are the result of one of their failed attempts to force my vow."

"*One* of their failed attempts?"

"The first time, they poured a concoction down my throat meant to destroy my vocal cords." The memory made it just a little more painful to speak. "I sent two of the acolytes involved to the infirmary. The next night, they tried again. I was ready that time. The second group of acolytes were in recovery for more than a week. The final time, the Master sent a group of five acolytes into my room while I slept to cut out my tongue."

Abella expelled a soft breath. She stared up at him with eyes wide, brow creased, and lips parted.

He moved her hands down so only the tips of her forefingers touched his scars and guided them both outward from his mouth. "This is as far as they got. I killed two of them with the knife they brought in. After that, the Master decided it best to allow me what remained of my voice, and I vowed *he* would never hear it again."

Her fingers curled around his. "Talking hurts as much as it sounds like, doesn't it?"

Tenthil nodded. "Worth it with you."

Abella's cheeks reddened further. She pulled her hands free and lowered them to his sides. Tenthil stiffened when her nails brushed over his wound and sent a jolt of fresh, electric pain across his torso.

She drew back. "You *are* hurt!"

He leaned to the side and shifted his arm to look down at the damage. The scorched gash on his ribs was clearly visible through his torn shirt. Reaching down, he pressed his fingers to the flesh above the wound and pulled it tight. He hissed through his teeth at the fresh agony.

"Low priority," he said.

"It's not low priority now." She took his hand and led him into the lavatory. "Take off your shirt."

He offered her no resistance. With many of his earlier distractions gone, Tenthil's awareness of the injury—and the pain it caused him—had only increased. He unfastened his shirt and shrugged it off his shoulders, letting it fall to the floor. Even the small amount of twisting he had to do to divest himself of the garment produced another flare of pain.

Abella silently trailed her gaze over his torso, and desire

kindled in her eyes before they settled on his wound. Just seeing the heat in her gaze was almost enough to make him forget his pain. He'd not nearly had enough of her.

Tenthil forced his hand into his main pouch and took out the medtool from within. It was cylindrical, with a forty-five-degree curve on one side that ended with a metallic disc. The disc had a central circle with eight blue lines radiating from its center. There was a simple switch near the opposite end of the handle, just in front of a tiny projector port. The whole thing was only ten centimeters from one end to the other.

Abella covered the device with her hand. "Let me clean your wound first."

"Might as well shower," he said, unable to pry his gaze from their hands. Her skin was so soft, so warm, so enticing. Even wounded, he didn't think he could control himself if she touched him again. His blood was still too hot, his emotions too raw. "You should get some rest."

"Oh." She withdrew her hand.

The disappointment he saw in her expression before she turned her face away hit him hard, but no matter how much he wanted her, she wasn't ready for him yet. She wanted the choice. Tenthil would make sure he was the *only* choice worth making. That meant respecting her desires as best he could, even if he had to deny his own.

He eased closer, cupping her cheek to make her look at him again. "Promise you will be here when I am done."

She loosely wrapped her fingers around his wrist and nodded. "I promise. I won't run again."

For a moment, he stared at her, lost in her beauty, caught in her magnetic pull. He was helpless when it came to Abella. Tenthil was not happy that his need for her was causing her distress, but he could not set it aside—and though she fought it, she seemed to feel a pull toward him, as well.

He brushed his thumb over her cheek and lowered his hand. "Go. Rest."

She hesitated, her gaze flicking to his wound, before she finally nodded and exited the lavatory.

Tenthil gently closed the door. His yearning to be at her side flared—he needed to have her within sight so he *knew*, without a doubt, that she was safe, she was here, she was *his*—but he shoved it aside.

Priorities. Clean myself, treat my wound.

There was so much he wanted to say to her, but he wasn't sure how. She woke things within Tenthil for which he had no name.

Soulmates.

What they shared now, what they would share in the future, could not be fully conveyed with words. It was about action, about *doing*. And he would do everything he could to make sure she was irrevocably his and eternally safe.

THIRTEEN

Abella's eyelids fluttered open as she slowly woke. The room was dim; the meager lights in the corners provided just enough illumination to cast everything in shades of gray.

Even four years in the Infinite City hadn't helped her overcome the disorientation of never knowing whether it was night or day. There was no sun, no moon, no sky at all below the surface, just the distant, diffused glow of lights set in the metal plates and framework that was always overhead, shining like lonely stars amidst vast darkness.

She'd been forced to match Cullion's schedule—when he'd been awake, it was her daytime; when he'd slept, it was her night. But now the passage of time was disjointed. She found it impossible to track, and it wasn't merely because she and Tenthil were spending most of their time running for their lives.

A soft, warm breath tickled her scalp, and Abella smiled. She lay tucked against Tenthil's side with her head beneath his chin, her hand on his slowly rising and falling chest, and her leg over his thigh. He had one arm around her, holding her close.

His clawed fingers flexed slightly in response to her every little movement.

Abella traced small circles over his bare chest, marveling at the feel of his strong, steady heartbeat beneath her palm. The weak lighting made his gray skin appear brighter, especially compared to hers.

For a moment, she let everything fall away—the deadly assassins chasing them, the city full of people willing to sell her out, the years of enslavement, and the family waiting for her at home—and found herself at peace. A contentment she'd not felt in a long, long while settled over her.

If she'd met Tenthil under different circumstances, how could she have resisted him?

She could admit that his appearance was perhaps a bit uncanny—at times, he looked downright scary—but the very traits that made him intimidating were those which she found dangerously attractive. He looked at her as though she were his everything.

And he could be mine.

His words from the day before resonated in her mind.

Something in me recognizes you. Something in me knows that you are mine. That I am yours. I cannot ignore it, cannot deny it. It is the deepest, most primal part of me.

Abella flattened her hand over his chest and closed her eyes, focusing on the rhythm of his heart.

What if she were to give it all up? What if she were to forget about going home and have a life with Tenthil instead?

It was a frightening thought...but also a compelling one. She had been ripped away from all she'd known and thrust into a new world, a world of enslavement, humiliation, and pain. Tenthil represented the possibility of claiming this world as her own, of experiencing it as a person instead of a belonging.

But what would their shared life be like? Would they always be on the run? Would they always be hunted?

Could she just...let go of her old life? Her family had likely moved on, but did they long for closure they'd never received? Had they already mourned for her?

She wasn't sure if she could forsake her dream of returning home to embrace a life in the shadows alongside Tenthil. Though she was drawn to him, she hardly knew him.

Soulmates.

Would she regret it if she didn't stay with him?

He was a stranger, a dangerous alien, and yet something about being with him felt right, felt *real*.

Maybe she'd taken Tenthil's words to heart. Maybe she'd allowed him to stir up some old, romantic notions and longings she'd thought forever lost, but...

"There's still time to sleep," Tenthil said softly.

Abella started and opened her eyes. Nothing in his breathing or heartbeat had changed to indicate he was awake. "Is there?"

An affirmative hum rumbled in his chest, vibrating into her hand and up her arm to send little tingles through her. His rough and distorted voice, combined with his heat and his solid embrace, reignited the ever-present desire lurking in her core. And now that he was awake...

She inhaled deeply, taking in his clean, masculine scent, and brushed her nose against the base of his throat. His hand on her spine stiffened, his claws slightly pricking her skin where her shirt had ridden up to expose her lower back.

Suddenly, she wasn't tired at all.

Abella slid her hand down, tracing the musculature of his abdomen, until it reached the edge of the blanket resting over his pelvis.

"Abella?" he asked in a hoarse whisper.

"Hmm?" She lightly ran her fingers back and forth along the blanket's edge; the low position of the fabric suggested his shirt wasn't the only article of clothing he'd forgone after his shower.

His stomach trembled, and his breath quickened. He grasped a fistful of the bedding with his free hand as his fingers flexed against her back, intensifying the scrape of his claws just enough to send another thrill through Abella. A bulge rose in the blanket only centimeters away from her fingers.

She pushed herself up, and when Tenthil moved to rise with her, Abella pressed her hand against his chest and shoved him back down. Their eyes met; his pupils were ringed by only the thinnest silver bands.

"Stay," she commanded.

Confusion creased his brow, and his lips parted to reveal the tips of his fangs, but he remained in place as she brushed her fingers over his lower lip and the scars at the corners of his mouth.

"Stay," she repeated, running her hand down his torso. When she reencountered the covers, she pushed them farther down. She turned her head to follow the path of her hand with her gaze until, finally, her eyes settled upon his erect cock.

At a glance, his shaft appeared like a human's, but its alien features became apparent as Abella's eyes further adjusted to the dim lighting. A series of overlapping ridges ran along its underside, and three rows of small nodules swept back from its broad head to its base on the top. His sack rested beneath, totally hairless—just like the rest of his body apart from his head.

Though she'd seen plenty of alien cocks since Cullion had begun showing her off like an exotic pet in Twisted Nethers, she hadn't known what to expect with Tenthil, couldn't have guessed what he'd look like. But the sight of Tenthil's throbbing erection sent a rush of heat through Abella. Her sex clenched in need; she could imagine the pleasure those nodules and ridges would create inside her.

A bead of moisture gathered at the tip of his cock. Her mouth watered. Humans had a salty taste; would Tenthil? Or would his seed bear a hint of sweet cinnamon, like his kisses?

Abella crawled down the bed, nudging his legs until he spread them and made room for her to kneel between his thighs. A spicy aroma filled her senses. She breathed it in deeply; it was coming from him. Supporting herself with one hand on the bed, she wrapped her fingers around his shaft.

He sucked in a sharp breath and tensed, raising his knees and grasping the bedding beside him. Abella glanced up to see his fangs bared and his wide eyes fully black. The sight of him, so affected by such a simple touch, triggered a flood of slick, wet heat between her legs. Her sex pulsed as she tightened her grip on him.

"Abella?" His raspy voice was thick with passion and uncertainty.

She knew then that his tension wasn't solely the result of pleasure. He was nervous.

Abella swiped her thumb over the tip of his cock, spreading the beaded moisture, and slid her fist down his length, relishing the feel of every nodule and ridge along the way. His gaze darted from her face to her hand and back again as a shudder wracked his body.

"Yes, Tenthil?" She slowly moved her hand back up.

His eyelids fluttered, his head tipped back, and he let out a low groan.

A smile spread across her lips. She pumped her hand a few more times, enthralled by his responses to her touch and unable to tear her eyes away from his face. He was...*beautiful*. She knew it was strange to describe a man that way, especially Tenthil, but in that moment, he was. All the worry, pain, and coldness had vanished from his face, giving her a glimpse of the man behind those scars.

A glimpse of a man whose choices had been stolen from him.

Abella looked down to see his cock seeping from its tip. Without a second thought, she lowered her head and took him into her mouth. His flavor—like that of his kiss, but richer—burst upon her tongue. She moaned, swallowing more of him.

Tenthil's legs stiffened, and the bed dipped as he sat up suddenly. There were brief ripping sounds to either side of Abella, as though cloth were being torn, but she paid no attention.

He whispered her name; it was a question, a caress, a prayer.

She'd never considered herself particularly good at giving blow jobs, but with Tenthil, she felt empowered—he reacted to her every movement, no matter how miniscule, as though she'd pushed him beyond the pinnacle of ecstasy.

Abella closed her eyes. He was large, but not so large that she couldn't take him deep. She used her fist on the bottom half of his shaft, pumping in time with the motions of her mouth. Her tongue and lips glided over his ridges and nodules, and her sex clenched as she imagined what they would feel like against her sensitive inner walls.

His fingers brushed hesitantly over her hair, his claws combing through the strands, before he settled his palm atop her head. The delicacy of his touch belied the tension in his body; he was being careful, holding himself back.

But she didn't want him to hold himself back.

She slid her lips off his cock and looked up into his half-lidded eyes before lowering her head again to slowly run her tongue along the underside of his shaft. His eyelids dipped, and he shuddered. Without hesitation, she took him into her mouth again, holding his gaze as she sucked and licked, moving her head up and down, over and over. She squeezed her thighs together against the ache of her own desire.

Tenthil's breathing grew harsher. The muscles of his jaw bulged as he threw his head back, and a strained growl rose from his throat. His hips bucked, and Abella felt his struggle to contain himself through the increased strain of his muscles. His fight did not last long; Tenthil's growl gave way to a brief, deep, bestial snarl as his cock swelled in her hand.

His heat poured into her mouth, and Abella closed her eyes, swallowing as much of him as she could. His hand tightened in her hair, and his claws grazed her scalp, but she didn't care. She moaned as she licked his length, prolonging his pleasure, unwilling to let any of his seed go to waste.

When at last his tremors subsided, Abella released him and raised her head, smiling.

Chest heaving, Tenthil lifted his head to meet her gaze. His black eyes gleamed with tiny reflections of the dim corner lights; to Abella's surprise, the hunger in his gaze was undiminished. His lips parted, and his tongue slipped out, running over the tips of his right upper fangs to collect the drops of liquid that had gathered upon them. He stared at her for several seconds. Anticipation sped her heart.

Before she could react, he pounced.

TENTHIL CAUGHT Abella's shoulders in his hands as he sprung forward, pushing her aside and onto her back before coming down atop her. He pinned her in place with his body and dropped his mouth over hers, taking freely of her taste, of her breath. Her flavor was tinged with hints of his own. A shudder coursed up his spine as he recalled the heat of her mouth around his shaft.

He wanted more of her heat. *Needed* a different heat.

Heart thundering, he moved his hands to her wrists and forced her arms over her head. He tore his mouth from hers to sample her skin with his lips and tongue. She tilted her head back with a soft moan as his lips trailed down her throat, and she spread her legs wide, allowing him to settle between them.

The barrier between her body and his—her clothing—created sweet friction, but he needed to feel *her*, only her, with nothing separating them. Crossing her arms at the wrists and holding them in place with one hand, he brushed his other hand down her forearm, over her elbow, and past her bicep and shoulder to the collar of her shirt. He slipped his fingers beneath the garment and curled them, extending his claws. The fabric shredded. Taking a handful, he tore the shirt in half down the front, exposing her soft breasts and hard, pink nipples.

"Tenthil," she breathed.

Raising his head, Tenthil looked down at Abella. Her dark hair was spread around her head like a dual-colored halo, her gleaming green eyes were half-lidded, and rapid breaths flowed between her delicate, parted lips.

Mine.

He gave the thought no voice—he was beyond that now. There was only one way to ensure she knew, to make her understand once and for all that she was his.

Shifting back on his knees, he lowered his mouth over her breast and sucked her nipple between his lips. She released a ragged sigh and arched her back. He sucked harder, eliciting a cry from Abella, and lightly grazed his fangs over the tender flesh of her breasts. Her hips jerked; Tenthil growled as her pelvis stroked the underside of his cock.

The heady aroma of her arousal flowed into his nose, and his shaft, impossibly, hardened further. It was her scent, but it was more; it was the answer to his desire, the answer to his need. It was the most primal signal of *her* need. The deepest, most instinctual part of Tenthil would not allow him to go another moment without claiming his mate.

Tenthil released his hold on Abella's wrists and dropped his hands to her hips. Gripping the waistband of her pants, he yanked them down her legs as he crawled backward, dragging her toward him until she laughed and raised her backside to assist him.

She propped herself up on her elbows, grinning at him as he worked her pants off her feet. "In a rush?"

Growling, he threw the pants against the wall, dropped onto hands and knees, and prowled toward her.

Abella held out a hand, bracing her palm on his shoulder and locking her elbow. Tenthil halted, curled his claws into the blanket, and met her gaze. The haze of his lust left him unable to guess why she'd stopped him. He wasn't even sure why he'd obeyed, when the throbbing in his cock was so strong it pained him.

"Is this your first time, Tenthil?" she asked softly.

He drew in a fresh breath; the air was laden with her desire. His eyelids drooped, and he nodded.

Smiling, she lowered her hand and spread her knees, opening herself to him. His eyes cut right to her sex, where her folds opened like the petals of a flower, pink and glistening.

"Then do as you like with me," she said.

Without wasting a single moment in thought, Tenthil dropped his head between her thighs, his pulsing shaft, now pinned between his pelvis and the bed, temporarily ignored.

He swept his tongue over her folds and lapped up her essence. Abella gasped, and her fingers delved into his hair.

Tenthil pulled back, pausing only long enough to savor her sweetness on his tongue and lick her moisture from his lips before he returned his mouth to her sex. He drank from her ravenously, learning every bit of her by feel, gauging her every reaction by the sounds she made and the way her body moved.

She fell back against the bedding, panting, until the tip of his tongue flicked to the top of her sex and slid over a small, hardened nub. Her hips jerked, and she released a sharp gasp.

Tenthil glanced up her body and between her pert breasts to see her head tilted back, allowing him only a glimpse of her face—eyes closed, cheeks flushed, and lips parted. Her chest heaved with her rapid breaths. He wrapped his arms around her thighs and held them open as he licked the spot again.

She dug her nails into his scalp. "Yes! Right there, Tenthil."

Abella's pleasure sparked a new, prideful fire in his chest, making his desire burn hotter. He quickened his tongue, sweeping it ruthlessly over and over against the nub that brought her so much delight. She writhed beneath him, grinding her sex against his mouth, and her sweet cries permeated the room. He would never be able to bear silence again after hearing such a sound.

She released his hair, and her hand fell to grasp the covers.

Tenthil tightened his hold on her, unwilling to let her escape. He latched his lips onto that nub and sucked. Abella gasped, squeezing her eyes shut as her body tensed and her back arched off the bed. Her scent strengthened, and a rush of liquid heat flowed from her. He relinquished his hold on that sensitive little bud to lap at her sex, drinking every drop of delicious nectar her body offered, and slipped his tongue into her sex to take straight from the source. Her inners walls clenched and quivered.

Licking his lips, Tenthil pushed himself up on his arms and grunted at the ache in his cock. He took hold of her hips and pulled her limp body toward him, guiding her legs around his waist. Her eyes, hooded and dark with desire, met his. Without a word, he moved over her and pressed the tip of his cock to her entrance. He bared his teeth with a low growl and plunged into her depths.

Abella cried out, digging her heels into his lower back as she tilted her head back.

For a moment, Tenthil held himself still. Blissful heat embraced his cock. Her flesh was smooth and soft, but tight, *so* tight. The feel of her mouth and hand on his shaft had been sublime, but this was on an entirely new level; it was other-worldly, divine.

It was beyond his ability to put into words.

Tenthil lowered his head and pressed his face against her neck. Flexing his hips, he pushed himself deeper into her until he was fully sheathed by her sex. A groan escaped him.

Abella's arms slid around his sides to embrace him. Turning her head, she rubbed her cheek against his hair.

A fresh torrent of venom dripped from his fangs, its sweetness nothing compared to hers. Muscles tense, he bunched wads of the blanket in his fists and pushed himself up, easing his hips back. The slide of her inner walls around his shaft made him shudder in ecstasy; he'd never felt anything so exquisite. As the rim of his cock's head neared her entrance, he pushed forward again.

The change in direction altered the glide of flesh against flesh, creating powerful new sensations. He swallowed a mouthful of venom and stared into her eyes as he continued moving at a slow, steady pace. The pressure building inside him made his muscles tremble.

She panted beneath him, lifting her hips to meet his every

thrust. Each time their pelvises came together, their force increased infinitesimally, heightening the already overwhelming pleasure by an equal degree. Her eyelids drooped, but she held his gaze. She slid her hands up, over his arms and shoulders, to slip her hands into his hair again.

"Tenthil," she whispered, her hold on him tightening as she moaned.

His senses overloaded. The feel of their coupling, the scent of her arousal, the taste lingering on his tongue, the sight of her blissful expression, the sound of his name on her lips; it all came together to become something new, something mind-shatteringly potent.

This is mine. She *is mine.*

Mine.

For an instant, his chest swelled, and all his muscles bulged with a burst of untold strength. He couldn't breathe, couldn't hear his heart beating. Then his head dropped, and his fangs, as though guided by an outside force, sank into the same spot between her neck and shoulder that they had before. That sweet venom pumped into her as his hips pistoned wildly, introducing a new, frantic pace to their joining. Her body welcomed him, her inner walls clamping around his shaft and pulling it ever deeper.

Ragged, bestial breaths tore from his burning lungs, each closer to a guttural grunt than the last. The metallic tang of her blood crossed his tongue; it urged him on harder, faster.

She was his, and she would know it. The whole city would know it.

Abella tensed around him. She dropped her hands and buried her nails in his shoulders, releasing a choked cry as her sex tightened, its inner muscles fluttering maddeningly around his cock. Hot nectar poured from her, bolstering the scent in the air and amplifying his ever-growing need. Her moans escalated in pitch and volume with each of his thrusts.

He pushed harder and faster still; he needed to leave his mark on her, inside and out, needed to brand her as his and his alone. He needed to show her this was what she wanted—what she *needed*—as well.

His sack tightened, and something in the pit of his stomach lurched. For an instant, his limbs threatened to give out, and a sound rose from his chest and caught in his throat. The immense pressure within Tenthil threatened to tear him to pieces, and it would leave nothing of him when it was done. During that moment—an eternity in his mind—he teetered on the edge of a precipice both familiar and unknown, a point from which there was no return. A point from which he never wanted to return.

Tenthil lifted his mouth from her neck and exploded with a roar from the deepest part of his soul. His mind fragmented, and its pieces careened across the universe, finding Abella everywhere. His seed filled her, and her body demanded more, more, more. He complied, bucking his hips despite all his muscles locking at once.

He growled what must've been her name—it was the only word he knew, the only word that mattered.

He wasn't sure how much time passed as his racing heart calmed and his breathing eased. Abella's breath, sweet and warm, fanned over his sweat-dampened chest. He turned his face into her hair and inhaled. Their mingling scents forced a swift wave of possessiveness through him.

Abella gently stroked his shoulders and back with her hands, her touch as soothing as it was arousing. He flexed his hips, burying himself deeper inside her, and she moaned, squeezing her thighs around him. He didn't want to leave this spot. For this little while, they could be as one. It was a feeling he'd never experienced, had never imagined possible, and a small part of him feared he would never have it again once this ended.

He slid his fingers into her hair, tilting her face toward his to meet her tired but sated gaze. "You are mine, Abella," he rasped. "Forever."

Before she could reply, he pressed his lips over hers, pouring all the fire raging within him into the kiss.

FOURTEEN

Tenthil stared up at the ceiling as he trailed the tips of his claws up and down Abella's back, following the graceful line of her spine. She lay atop him, resting her cheek on his chest, and her warmth flowed into him freely. Like so many of his experiences with her, this was new. He'd never been held with affection, had never been comfortable enough with anyone—much less felt the urge—to lie with them, defenses lowered. Silence had stretched between them, but he found this silence comforting. It was companionable, natural, a suitable response to what they'd shared; though many words could be said about it, none were necessary.

Abella stirred, sliding her hand along his shoulder. "Abella isn't my full name."

He tilted his head to glance down at the top of her hair. Her confession intrigued him not because it was another secret to hoard, but because she was choosing to share with him. This was a secret given, not a secret taken.

"What is your full name?"

"Isabella. Well, technically Isabella Diane Mitchell." She

curled her fingers around his shoulder and brushed her thumb back and forth across his skin. "When I was born, my parents said one of my older brothers had trouble saying my name. *Abella* was the best he could manage. It just kind of stuck, and that's what everyone's called me since then. Well, unless I did something bad, then my mom would use my full name so I *knew* I was in trouble."

Her wistful tone made it clear that she missed her family. Tenthil's mind flashed back briefly to his own childhood, so far away and clouded by time. He couldn't remember if he'd missed his family; he'd been taken too long ago. "Which do you prefer?"

"I'm fine with Abella. It's who I've always been."

He nodded and returned his gaze to the ceiling. Though he'd never been to this safehouse before coming with Abella, it was already more a home to him than the temple had ever been. "The Master gave me my name."

Abella raised her head and looked at him. Her hair fell around her head in disarray, its soft, dangling strands tickling his chest.

Tenthil swallowed, throat suddenly tight. He'd never reflected much upon his feelings about his past. The anger he felt whenever his mind turned toward what had been taken from him, toward the life he'd lost by no fault of his own, had been enough.

But thanks to Abella, he now understood that so much more ran beneath that anger.

"I remember little of my people," he said, the lump in his throat thickening, "but I know males were not granted names until they proved themselves capable hunters. I was too young to have done so when I was taken."

"And Tenthil was the name he chose for you?" Abella asked.

"He said it was the name the Void whispered to him."

She frowned. "The Void?"

He nodded. He'd told her enough already to earn himself a place at the bottom of the Well of Secrets; why stop now? "It is the entity to which the Order is dedicated. The nothingness between the stars. It is said to touch everything, to know every-thing...to be the ultimate keeper of secrets."

"So...some kind of god, or a higher power. Do you believe in it?"

"When I was young." He pressed his hand a little more firmly on her back, massaging the muscle beneath it. "But I have seen the true powers in the universe. I know where his secrets come from, and it is not the Void. He is arrogant or mad. Both."

Abella moved her hand to his face, lightly tracing one of his scars with her thumb. "I think you've proven yourself a capable hunter by now, don't you? What name would you pick for yourself?"

He shifted his gaze to stare into her entrancing green eyes.

I can be whoever I choose.

Despite his rebellious nature, despite his resistance to the system into which he'd been thrust, that notion had never occurred to him. *He* could define himself.

He settled a hand on her cheek. "Tenthil. It became my own once it came from your lips."

Her face reddened, and she ducked her head down. He could feel her smile against his chest. "Tenthil it is then."

Silence stretched between them again, and Tenthil closed his eyes, content to hold her close, to feel her body against his.

"What else do you remember from your home?" Abella asked.

He released a long, slow breath. "Not much. More people like me. Grass stretching on and on, broken only by a river and a nearby forest. The trees had green and violet leaves. I remember...singing. Dancing. But not like yours."

"What kind of dancing was it?"

"Wild," he replied with a chuckle as the fragmented, unfocused memories flitted through his mind. "People chanted and banged on drums, faster and faster, and the beat was so loud, so strong, that everyone was compelled to move to it. And that's what they did. Just...moved however they felt the song told them."

Abella lifted her head, and Tenthil opened his eyes to see her smiling down at him.

"I think that's the first time I heard you laugh," she said.

He chuckled again; it felt *good*. "Me too."

Something softened in her eyes. "We have dances on Earth like what you described. I can almost imagine it."

"Can everyone from your world dance like you?"

"There are lots of people who dance better than me. But no...only those who put years of practice into it can dance like I do." She tilted her head, plucked up a strand of his hair, and twirled it around her finger. "I've loved dancing ever since I was little. My mom was a *ballet* dancer, so I used to watch her all the time, fascinated by the way she moved. She retired early after having kids and started teaching classes. As soon as I could walk, I was dancing with her, always eager to learn more."

Abella grinned. "My dad used to come home after work and see us practicing, and he'd pick me up and twirl me around and around and around. I was his little *ballerina*. After high school, I went to a performing arts school, hoping to eventually become a professional dancer. I was on my way back from a rehearsal the night I was taken."

Though she spoke in universal speech, a few of her words—like *ballerina*—were in her native tongue, and his translator offered no satisfactory understanding of them. Fortunately, her story gave him enough information to infer her general meaning. Dancing was her life. It was what she'd chosen, what she loved.

The first time he'd ever chased something for himself, something he desired, had been when he'd followed Abella down to the dance floor in Twisted Nethers.

"What is it like to have a family?" he asked. His own memories were so distant, his own experiences so different, that he couldn't imagine it.

Her smile—which had fallen when she spoke of her kidnapping—returned, though it was not as wide or bright as it had been. "Like you're never alone. It doesn't matter if you've gone hours, days, or months without seeing each other, you know they're always there. They uplift you, care for you, encourage you, and even if you don't always get along, you know you still love each other."

Tenthil's jaw clenched. That was what he denied her by refusing to take her to the terran embassy. That was what his mate had longed for since she was taken, what she'd yearned for above all else. His emotions, his thoughts, and his instincts were at war with each other. He wanted her, needed her, could not let go of her, but he also wanted her to be happy. He wanted to fulfill her every desire. He wanted to take away her sadness and pain.

But he could not go to the terran embassy. If he gave her what she wanted—if he gave her *that*—he would lose her.

Abella cupped his cheek. "What's wrong, Tenthil?"

"I'm not what you chose," he said, forcing the words up from his ragged throat, "but I want to be all that to you."

Tears welled in her eyes as she searched his face. There was conflict within them—longing, sadness, uncertainty, even a hint of affection, all in a chaotic swirl. Her lips parted as though she meant to speak, but she closed them and leaned forward to brush them across his instead.

He wrapped his arms around her and slipped a hand into her dark hair, holding her closer and deepening the kiss. She opened to him, and their tongues met as they tasted one another.

Warmth kindled in his chest and spread through his body, coalescing into a flame deep in his belly. His cock pulsed and slowly hardened as his awareness of her—of her scent, taste, and feel—heightened.

Breaking the kiss, Abella opened her eyes and met his gaze. She slid down his chest, spreading her thighs to either side of him as she sat up and positioned her sex against the tip of his shaft. Slowly, so slowly, she lowered herself, taking him into her tight, wet heat.

Tenthil gritted his teeth and placed his hands on her hips, hissing at the sensation of her enveloping him.

She rose up on her knees and sank back down upon him just as slowly, over and over again. Her lashes fluttered, but she kept her eyes on his. What her movements lacked in speed and intensity they made up for in deliberate sensuality. With each thrust so prolonged, the resulting pleasure was amplified by a building sense of anticipation.

He lowered his gaze to the point where their bodies were connected. Flexing his fingers, he released a growl. The sight of his cock, glistening with her nectar, sliding in and out of her sex intensified his desire beyond anything in the known universe. It was the rawest evidence of what he knew in his heart—she was *his*.

Her thighs trembled, and a series of soft moans escaped her. She moved her hands to her chest, cupping her breasts as she continued her slow rise and fall, and her pace faltered as her breath quickened.

"Tenthil," she pleaded, her eyes dark with desire. "Love me."

Love.

Tenthil understood what it meant only indirectly—the Master loved secrets, loved the Void; some of the acolytes seemed to love their work; Abella loved dancing and her family. Perhaps his parents had loved each other. But what did he really know of love other than that he longed for it from Abella? Could the jumble of emotions he felt toward her be love?

He knew that he'd risked everything to have her, that he'd risk far more to keep her, that he'd make the choice to go to her again and again regardless of the consequences.

This was different than claiming a mate; this was deeper, on an even more primal level.

Love.

That was a true connection between souls, wasn't it? Not all the races in the Infinite City talked about it, but enough did for Tenthil to have heard.

He sat up, guiding her legs around his sides. Abella wrapped her arms around his neck as he rested his forehead against hers. He stared into her eyes, and she stared back. This moment was more than fucking, more than a claiming. It was a joining at the highest level. She hadn't voiced what she wanted, but she was showing him with her expression, with her eyes, with her body.

And he wanted it too. Wanted to know there was one person in all the universe he was closer to than anyone, that there was one person for whom he'd do anything, one person who would do anything for him.

He slid his hands to her ass and rocked her back and forth on his cock, continuing the slow, deliberate pace she had set, and watched her face as their mutual pleasure grew. He increased the speed only when the pressure in him bordered on pain.

Instinct bade him claim her with his bite, but he held back, kissing her instead. Her wicked little tongue slid along his fangs to sample the venom flowing from them. When he felt the first stirrings of her climax, he rocked her harder, faster, and deeper, pushing her over the edge. The quivering of her tight sex dragged him along with her, plunging him into a chasm of ecstasy as his seed spilled into her.

Breaking the kiss, she screamed his name, and he roared hers as they came undone in each other's arms.

FIFTEEN

Abella ate from one of the packages of bland food as she watched Tenthil clean and reload the blasters. She focused on the play of tendons beneath his skin when his fingers moved, on the definition lines as the muscles of his forearms flexed and relaxed, on the way his claws extended when he curled his fingers.

She'd felt those hands, those claws, all over her body.

A shiver raced through her, and she squeezed her thighs together to alleviate the sudden pulsing of her sex. If not for the soreness between her legs, she'd have stripped her clothes off just to feel his hands upon her again, to feel his lips brush over her skin, to experience the delicious friction of each ridge and nodule as his cock stroked inside her.

Hell, she was tempted to regardless of her soreness.

Abella's gaze roamed to his face. His brow was creased in thought, and his cheek scars stood out starkly against his pale gray skin.

He was beautiful.

He's my captor...

But he's also my savior.

Her heart sped as his earlier words echoed in her head.

I am not what you chose, but I want to be all that to you.

Abella forced herself to look away from Tenthil. He was so...*lonely*. He'd given up everything, had turned against everyone he knew, for *her*. She was all he wanted. And in his eyes, she was already his.

She raised her hand and touched the puncture wounds at the tender spot between her neck and shoulder. They didn't really hurt; whatever venom he'd injected into her had not only heightened her pleasure but had acted as a healing agent, sealing the wounds much faster than was natural.

Despite the accelerated healing, the marks were likely to scar; she found the thought of it oddly appealing.

Sometimes, it was easy to forget Tenthil wasn't human, that he'd been raised in an entirely different culture. The Order had shaped him, but whatever upbringing he'd had before that, with his own people, was far removed from Abella's experiences. From what he'd told her, his species lived in hunter-gatherer tribes that would've been more at home on Earth ten thousand years ago than here in this claustrophobic city of technology.

The rules and values with which Abella had been instilled didn't necessarily apply to Tenthil.

For all his intelligence and skill, Tenthil was still a member of that primitive, bestial race. The blood of an instinct-driven animal flowed beneath the veneer of training and education the Order had provided him. That instinct had pushed him to stake his claim upon her—a claim she couldn't bring herself to reject.

What did that say about *her*?

She knew the rules, knew what was right and what was wrong. She didn't have to accept his claim because of what he was or what he'd done for her. And yet...she did accept it. Tenthil wasn't the one who'd taken her from home, wasn't the one who'd enslaved and humiliated her, wasn't the one who'd hurt her repeatedly over the last four years.

He'd *saved* her.

Would it be so bad to be his mate, to claim him as hers?

Abella stilled.

I had sex with him.

The realization of what she'd done suddenly struck her. She had sex with an *alien*.

Fuck!

She'd had sex with an alien *multiple times*, and not once before now had she considered any of the potential consequences. Her birth control implant had expired two years ago.

Could Tenthil impregnate her? They were from two different species, so there was no way she could conceive his child...right?

Abella dropped her free hand to her belly.

Though the notion of carrying a half-alien child should've scared the hell out of her, she found herself surprisingly calm. She wouldn't lie to herself—it was scary, but not for the reasons she would've expected. Their child would have been the most protected little thing in the entire universe thanks to Tenthil, but what kind of life would that child know? Constantly on the run, constantly under threat of death, never having peace...

What the hell is wrong with me? I should be thinking about getting home!

Had she given in so easily? Had she given up?

She slowly turned her gaze back to Tenthil. Was it wrong to want him, too? Why couldn't she go home *and* have Tenthil?

Would he want to go with her?

He lifted one of the blasters off the table and slid a fresh power cell into it. When he closed the compartment, the weapon made a soft click. As he laid the blaster on the table, he met her gaze and tilted his head. "You okay?"

"Huh?" she asked, mentally shaking herself. "Yeah, I'm fine. Why?"

He dipped his chin, glancing at the hand she held over her stomach.

Abella looked down and yanked her hand away as though it'd been burned. "It's nothing." She nodded toward the weapons. "Are we...expecting company?"

His gaze lingered on her middle for a moment longer. "Always."

"They'll never stop, will they?"

"When we are dead," he replied, his frown at odds with his upturned scars, "or when *he* is."

"Do you intend to go after him?"

Tenthil's silver eyes shifted to the weapons on the table. She'd seen him use them, had seen him take down larger beings with only a knife, and she didn't doubt he was just as deadly with his bare hands.

Several seconds passed without an answer from him.

"Are you afraid, Tenthil?" she asked as gently as she could.

Tenthil sighed and averted his eyes. "I wasn't, before. Even when I was young, I understood that my relationship with the Master would end with one of us dead by the other's hand. Death never frightened me. But he knows who you are, Abella, and that...that is terrifying."

Abella's heart clenched, and something in her belly coiled tight. How could she remain unaffected when he said such things?

Setting aside the remainder of her food, she rose and walked to him. He tilted his head back as she neared, and when she was standing immediately before him, she cupped his cheeks between her hands and ran her thumbs over his scars.

"He can't have me," she said.

Tenthil wrapped his arms around her and pulled her close. "Never."

Abella slid her hands up and combed her fingers through his hair as he rested his head against her stomach. Her belly fluttered. "What are we going to do?"

"Supposed to be a forger in Undercity who can fool Consortium ID systems. We're going to find him and get identification chips made." He drew back and looked up into her eyes. "Then we will be able to clear the checkpoints and get off this planet."

Though she couldn't shake the memory of the borian peacekeeper who'd refused to aid her, Abella asked, "Why don't we just go to a checkpoint? Wouldn't they help us?"

Lifting his arms, he took her hands in his, squeezed them gently, and guided them down. "You may make it. Your people have an embassy here, and you've only acted in self-defense. But me..."

He has no one.

"If you don't have a chip, how could they know who you were? What you've done?" she asked.

"They wouldn't. Not immediately. But they would detain me and start looking. I am careful, Abella, but I have worked for the Order for many years."

"So they'd eventually find something, and it wouldn't be good. And the Master is searching for you too."

"His web is wide and tangled," Tenthil said, his voice hoarser with each word. "He has many contacts and connections in the Eternal Guard. He'd ensure I was dead before I revealed any of his secrets."

Abella opened her mouth, meaning to ask if he'd take her home, if he'd go with her, but she stopped herself. She'd wait until they were closer to having a means of escape. She'd wait until she knew if what they shared was more than lust or a passing infatuation.

She was already almost certain it *was* more. Far more.

"Why didn't we get IDs when we came here?" she asked instead.

"We were brought here illegally. When someone comes here legally for the first time, they go through a Consortium checkpoint and are given three things—a universal translator implant, a mutative compound that allows their biology to adapt to conditions their race would not normally survive, and an identification chip that registers them within the Consortium systems.

"The organizations that traffic alien beings into Arthos usually administer the first two because they are necessary...but if people like us get an ID chip, it gives us a tool to get help. To escape. Property doesn't have an identity. Pets aren't people." By the last few words, his voice was so raw that it was little more than a raspy release of air.

Abella pressed her lips together as a flash of anger swept through her. That was what she'd been, what Tenthil had been —property. Pets. Creatures forced to do the bidding of their masters, punished harshly whenever they disobeyed.

With a sigh, she pulled her hands from Tenthil's and knelt before him, leaning forward to press her lips to his throat.

"No more talking." She kissed his neck again.

He placed his hands on her shoulders and guided her back just enough to lower his face and slant his mouth over hers. She'd never thought it possible for such a simple action to hold such meaning, but those few seconds with their lips touching spoke volumes of what he felt—he was here, he cared, he appreciated her, and he'd do anything and everything for her.

And Abella swore to herself that she would do anything and everything for him.

A small part of her mind whispered that this was too fast, that she shouldn't have allowed herself to grow so attached to him so quickly; it couldn't have been much longer than a day ago that she'd left him behind in her attempt to find her way back to her people.

She quieted that voice. Fear had driven her away from him.

Mortals could not dictate the speed of life, and the last few days had felt more like years. What she and Tenthil had been through could bring anyone together. As though the shared trauma of their respective kidnappings wasn't enough, the violence and fear they'd endured together had forged a tight bond between them—and that bond was solidified by his genuine caring about her.

Soulmates.

She hadn't believed in such a thing since her youth, back when she used to read fairytales and romances and had spent her time daydreaming. Life had a knack for eventually killing all the magic and wonder it promised during a person's childhood. But now?

Abella slipped her arms around Tenthil and held him closer.

Now she desperately hoped that soulmates were real.

SIXTEEN

Tenthil raised a hand to adjust the hood of his new coat and shift the mask covering the lower half of his face into a more comfortable position. His other arm remained around Abella, keeping her against his side as they walked so he could project his bioelectric disruption field around her.

Their first stop after leaving the safehouse that morning had been to purchase new clothing. They should have done so much sooner. Traveling Arthos dressed in Order clothing wasn't the best way to avoid the notice of the Master's spies.

Tenthil's new clothes brought his mind back to the night he'd first encountered Abella. His current attire was similar to the gang clothing he'd worn, though this was a bit less colorful. His black hooded jacket was accented in several places by strips of silvery metal and lines of glowing blue. It was long enough to keep his gun belt hidden, but not so long as to hinder his movement.

Abella's attire was the same style, though she'd opted for lighter colors and pink accents rather than blue. Tenthil wished she didn't have to keep her hair pulled back and hidden beneath her hood; he wanted to see the contrast between the pink light on her clothes and the blue-black of her hair. But just as his scars made him easily identifiable, the combination of her two-toned hair and distinctly human features would make her stand out.

The shred of anonymity provided by their change of garments hadn't much eased Tenthil's concerns; he kept alert as they walked, discreetly seeking the criminal contacts he'd used during his time in the Order. He would've been able to move faster alone, but he wouldn't chance leaving Abella on her own. She'd been lucky so far in her encounters with the Order, but she would've been captured had he not intervened last time.

Obtaining information on the forger proved difficult, and Tenthil's worn, ragged voice was little help. Fortunately, Abella took over when Tenthil's words became too weak to understand. Despite having never dealt with such elements directly, her time following Cullion around as he met with various unsavory characters had instilled her with discretion and confidence that went a long way with the often uncooperative and evasive informants.

They'd eventually been directed here, Nyssa Vye, the Under Market, a border sector between the Undercity and the Bowels. Its flashy neon lights clashed with exposed pipes and ductwork and set the countless puddles—each comprised of unidentifiable runoff and leakage from those pipes—ablaze with vibrant color. This was a place where the infinite worlds represented in the city collided, the place where anything could be obtained.

This was the black market where smugglers and thieves peddled their wares.

The Eternal Guard largely kept away from the sector,

entering only to address extremely serious matters—always in force. So long as the city's overlords received their portion of the profits, they seemed little concerned with operations that technically violated their laws.

The people on these streets were more diverse than perhaps anywhere else in the Undercity. Species of all sorts, hailing from all corners of the universe, milled about. Most were likely here for a taste of some exotic food from their home-world, purveyed by one of the many street vendors, or to obtain exotic clothing or jewelry that wasn't sold in higher sectors.

All manners of body adornment and enhancement were on display—hair colored in a multitude of hues; piercings of various body parts, including horns, tusks, and teeth; tattoos in more patterns and styles than Tenthil could count, some glow-ing, some *moving*; clothing of wildly varying fashion and mater-ial; cybernetic limbs and implants. The latter were particularly prevalent with the rough-looking groups who lingered on the edges of the crowd, often near unmarked doors. Many of them were members of various gangs. This was one of the few sectors where no single gang claimed dominance, and a loose agree-ment prevented violence between the groups. Many more were hired thugs guarding the entrances to businesses—not the shops selling exotic food or clothing, but the brothels, smuggling rings, unregistered cybertech surgeons, drug dealers, and forgers.

Tenthil glanced down at Abella to find her studying their surroundings with unmasked wonder. She'd seen the Under-city before, but she'd likely never seen it like *this*. Under different circumstances, he'd have taken her all around Arthos, would have shown her everything there was to see, even if it took a thousand lifetimes, but the city wasn't safe for them.

And it probably never would be.

He led her down a side street toward the alleyway entrance to which they'd been directed. The crowd was thinner here, as it always was off the main stretches. He used his free arm to sweep back the side of his coat, exposing his holstered blaster.

Sometimes, such a display was enough to deter would-be troublemakers.

It did not, however, deter the prostitutes who stood at various intervals along the street. They unashamedly displayed their *wares* to Tenthil as he passed, beckoning him closer. At least two dozen species were represented amongst them—some male, some female, some falling into neither category, and at least a couple who seemed to fit both.

Abella glared at them, and a small growl rumbled in her throat. "He's taken."

Tenthil couldn't hold back a small smile, but something powerful stirred inside him all the same—she'd claimed him. She'd claimed him as her own, as *taken* by her.

When several of the prostitutes—females included—shifted their focus to Abella and made the same offers, she turned her face away and nestled closer to Tenthil. "I'm taken too."

Though he knew his claim on her was not under any true threat, his smile fell. He was glad for the mask in that moment, if only because it hid his bared teeth from her. She was *his*. His instincts would tolerate no competition.

Unfortunately, even in a city as massive and chaotic as Arthos, it would be frowned upon to murder other males who looked upon his mate covetously.

He shifted his gaze to the alley that was their destination. It was marked by a holographic sign a few meters from its entrance—an advertisement for a nearby restaurant specializing in various roasted larva and worms. The sign's three-dimensional projections left little to the imagination; Abella turned her head to the side, covered her mouth with a hand, and gagged.

But it was the three beings standing at the alley's entrance who caught his attention, not the vibrant sign. Two cren, each taller than Tenthil, with dark skin and tusks as long as his thumb, leaned against the walls. A burly, furred azhera stood between them. The three were engaged in a quiet conversation. Though none of them wore uniforms or visible combat armor, the blasters on their hips were high-quality.

It was best not to have obvious guards posted for places like this—it would only make people wonder what they were guarding. A group of random thugs standing around an alleyway, while still visible, was far less suspicious.

Tenthil dipped his head closer to Abella's. "If you must shoot, aim for the head."

She straightened, eyes wide, as she looked at the guards. "Do...you think I will have to?"

"Always a chance."

He lifted his head and continued his approach, releasing his bioelectrical disruption field so as not to rouse suspicion on the surveillance systems the forger undoubtedly had in place nearby.

The guards noticed his intent from several meters away; the cren fixed their gazes on him, their irises—one set yellow, the other green—vibrant against their black sclerae. But it was the azhera who stepped forward, blocking Tenthil and Abella's path.

The azhera met Tenthil's gaze, flared his nostrils, and released a low growl barely audible over the sounds from the street. His bestial face twisted into a snarl, pupils expanding. "Alley's closed. Walk on."

"Here on business," Tenthil rasped; the words were like broken glass in his throat. The azhera's scent set him on edge. Though they looked nothing alike, Tenthil had a sense that his people and the azhera were more similar than appearances suggested.

The azhera smelled like a predator. Few species in this city possessed such scents.

"Walk. On." The azhera bared his fangs, fur rising in agitation, and the two cren pushed off the walls they'd been leaning against to loom behind him.

"We're here to see Alkorin," Abella said, "to arrange a naming ceremony."

Shifting his attention to Abella, the azhera narrowed his green eyes, leaned forward, and sniffed the air. A growl sounded deep in Tenthil's chest; he drew Abella back and turned his body to position himself in front of her.

The azhera exhaled heavily through his nose. "She wears your scent, hunter."

"She is mine," Tenthil replied. A primal part of him wanted to attack the azhera to prove his dominance, to establish an order. To make it clear that Abella was *his*.

Lips peeling back in a snarl, the azhera shook his head and stepped aside. His fur slowly settled, but his pupils remained dilated. "Third door on the right. Mind yourselves. He doesn't care for trouble."

Tenthil nodded and drew Abella more firmly against his side. He walked past the azhera and between the two cren, who said nothing as they fell into place behind him, lingering a few paces back. Tenthil felt their stares on his back as he led his mate down the narrow alley.

Though he kept his eyes forward, watching for the door the azhera had indicated, Tenthil focused on his hearing. The cren made no attempt to quiet their footsteps, which were the dominant sound in the alley.

He released a ragged breath when they reached the door. The entry was plain, unmarked, even a bit rundown, but Tenthil had expected nothing different. Lifting a hand, he pressed the button on the inside of the doorframe.

A few seconds later, the door's maglocks released with a resonating, metallic *thunk*.

The cren halted, lingering nearby with gazes fixed upon Tenthil and his mate.

Tenthil reached down, grasped the handle, and looked at Abella. "Stay close."

She nodded and leaned against him a little more as he pushed the door open.

A long, dimly lit hall stretched beyond the doorway, partially blocked from Tenthil's view by another cren, this one larger than the other two, with electric blue eyes that would've been at home on many of the holographic projections throughout the Undercity. Tenthil instinctively shifted to walk in front of Abella and shield her from the new threat.

Her fingers brushed against his back, letting him know she was there, urging him to remain calm.

The cren's expression didn't change save for a slight twitch of his long, pointed ears. He turned and extended his arm, pointing to the stairs at the end of the hall.

Tenthil clenched his jaw, released a slow, quiet breath through his nostrils, and nodded. The tight space would've set him on edge even before he'd betrayed the Order, but now his senses were on full alert. Danger lurked around every corner and behind every door. The Order could strike anywhere, anytime.

He led Abella past the cren, down the hall, and up three flights of stairs. The last flight opened on a wide landing with a single blast door, its metal etched with intricate isometric patterns from top to bottom. The pair of vorgal guards standing to either side of the entry looked as big and sturdy as the door itself. There was no more pretense here; they were equipped with undisguised, high-grade combat armor and auto-blasters.

The vorgal on the left dipped his gaze toward Tenthil's waist. "You carrying?"

Tenthil came to a stop a few paces away from them. "Everyone is around here."

"Boss doesn't care," the vorgal said. "Just likes me to remind customers that he's covered by four autocannons in there. You go for your piece, you leave as a bag of ashes."

"Understood."

The vorgal raised a hand and turned the inside of his wrist toward his mouth. "Let them in."

The etched door lifted off the floor silently and disappeared into the wall above, revealing a large room lit by red and purple wall panels. Tenthil walked forward with Abella slowly, ignoring the restlessness in his fingers that urged him to draw his weapon. He wasn't used to trusting anyone but Abella. This forger's reputation didn't assuage Tenthil's misgivings; reputations often lost meaning when people found themselves at odds with the Master.

As they entered the chamber, the door slid shut behind them, leaving only that moody, violet-red light. Several long, low couches ran to either side of the entrance, and large, clear-glassed water tanks filled with strange, bioluminescent creatures adorned the walls between the light panels.

The carpet was dark save for a two-meter-wide strip leading from the entrance to the far side of the room, which bore the same isometric pattern etched on the outside face of the door. The colors came together well, the reds and purples strengthened by their contrast to the black of the floor and the furniture.

"Well, this place is a few steps up from Cullion's," Abella muttered. "Maybe a whole flight of stairs up."

Tenthil agreed, though he saw it as a needless display of wealth, regardless. He shifted his gaze toward the far end of the room, where several wide steps led to a raised platform atop which rested a long worktable, several computer terminals, and at least three dozen holographically projected screens and control panels. It was also where the forger was standing.

Alkorin remained behind the table, facing Tenthil and Abella as they approached. He was a sedhi, with sharp, angular facial features, long, curving black horns extending from his temples, and three faintly glowing yellow eyes surrounded by black scerla—one of which was positioned vertically in the center of his forehead. That third eye was turned toward Tenthil and Abella while the other two were intent upon whatever work he was doing atop the table.

Tenthil came to a stop a few meters from the steps and waited until the forger finally lifted his face toward them.

The sedhi spread his arms to either side and smiled. He was clad only in a loose, silken red robe with billowing sleeves that hung loose about his shoulders and bared the toned muscles of his gray-skinned torso. Glowing yellow *qal* markings flowed from his upper chest toward his shoulders and neck, reaching all the way to his face, where they nearly circled his left eye. Long, jet black hair, swept to one side, hung past his shoulders.

"New customers. Always a delight," he said in universal speech as he lowered his arms. "Who, may I ask, referred you to me?"

"No one," Tenthil replied.

The forger's smile tipped up at one corner. "Good. An individual of discretion. I've little time or interest to work with anyone lacking it."

Abella eased out from behind Tenthil and cocked her head, staring intently at the sedhi. "What's it like having three eyes?"

The forger's third eye opened a little wider, and its slitted pupil dilated and contracted. His lips parted as he laughed, displaying his fangs. He walked slowly around the table, his long, thick tail swishing in the air behind him, and descended the steps.

"Normal, at least from my perspective." The forger narrowed his eyes. "Tell me, what are you?"

The interest and intensity in the sedhi's gaze was unsettling. Tenthil's chest tightened, and a burst of heat flowed into his muscles, threatening to thrust him into a battle state.

Tenthil extended his arm and swept Abella behind him. "A client. We need clean chips."

"And so you came looking for Alkorin the Forger," the sedhi said.

"That's you, isn't it?"

The sedhi shifted his arms behind his back and circled Tenthil slowly, likely seeking a better angle from which to see Abella, but Tenthil moved along with him to block her from the forger's view as much as possible.

"It is one of several aliases I've used. As good as any, I suppose." The sedhi's eyes were fixated on Abella as he casually continued circling. "*Alk* is close enough to the truth, if you wish. Far more interesting than all that, however, is this female."

Taking in a deep breath, Tenthil curled his hands into fists. It was the only way to keep himself from drawing a weapon.

"I'm his," Abella said. "And there really isn't anything interesting about me."

Alk raised a hand—both the sedhi's hands were cybernetic, cased in a dark metal run through with glowing yellow lines that matched his *qal*—and pointed toward Abella's head. "Lower your hood for me, would you?"

Tenthil growled, bared his teeth, and took a step forward. The sedhi shifted his hand to direct all his fingers at Tenthil, who barely registered the sound of machines moving in his fury. The autocannons at each of the room's corners dropped into attack position.

"Tenthil, no!" Abella wrapped her arms around him from behind, leaning her face close to his ear. "It's okay. I'm yours, remember?"

Her touch, her voice, broke through the enraged haze in Tenthil's mind.

We need this forger if we want a chance to live, he reminded himself.

The sedhi hadn't moved; he stared at Tenthil and Abella with a strange mixture of fascination and amusement in his expression. He flicked the fingers of his raised hand aside nonchalantly. The autocannons reverted to neutral positions, their barrels angling slightly upward.

"The security system is a bit...*sensitive* to my prompts," Alk said, holding Tenthil's gaze. "Of course, should we come to an arrangement, I will need to know what she is and run a full-body scan to complete the chip. The operation, of course, would be *purely* professional."

Alk's smile was anything but reassuring—it was a challenge, a subtle shove, a bit of posturing.

This is his home. His sanctuary. His fortress. He thinks he's safe here, thinks he's untouchable.

Keeping one arm around Tenthil, Abella tugged her hood down. "I'm human. Err, a terran."

Tenthil clenched his jaw, but he made no move to stop her. He had to acknowledge that, despite his greater experience with the Infinite City and its diverse species, Abella was better at talking to people. Situations like this—and with the azhera outside—were some of the few in which Tenthil's instincts were not necessarily of benefit.

He'd never experienced this before; his common sense had

been overridden by anger or bitterness from time to time, but his instincts had always been reliable in every situation.

"Human," Alk repeated, almost purring the word. "I was curious when terrans first came to Arthos a couple years ago, but you are the first I've met." The pupil of his third eye expanded and shrank again.

Abella chuckled. "Yeah, well, like I said, nothing interesting. I mean, when you're around all these other people with fur, fangs, claws, horns, tails, and"— she swept an arm toward Alk—"*three* eyes, a plain ole human is nothing to get excited about."

Tenthil turned his head toward her, brows falling low. Was that truly what she thought, or was she simply playing a part? He couldn't tell, but the idea that she saw herself as plain, uninteresting, or boring upset him in a subtle yet powerful fashion. It could be perceived as unhappiness, and he would not allow his mate to be unhappy.

"It's all a matter of perspective, isn't it?" Alk blinked, his central eye lagging the other two by half a second. "Perhaps where you come from, I am exotic. But here, it is you—"

Abella held her hand up, palm out. "Let me stop you right there. I had a...let's just say, a *really* bad experience recently, and I would rather not talk about how *exotic* I am. Okay? I just want some normalcy. Some freedom. That's the only reason we're here."

Alk's smile softened, and he gestured toward the nearby couches. "Then please, let us discuss business."

Abella returned his smile. "Thank you."

A firestorm raged within Tenthil, and the only logical thought process he could manage for several moments was a calculation of whether he'd be able to close the distance between himself and the sedhi before Alk manually aimed and fired the autocannons. He was relatively certain he could. It wouldn't have been easy or safe, but he'd dealt with similar automated weaponry before, and he'd never encountered one with a targeting system that could overcome his bioelectric disruption field. He could engage his field in a millisecond.

It might have been worth it just for the look on Alk's face before Tenthil killed him.

Abella looked up at Tenthil, and her smile wavered. She slipped her hand into his and wove their fingers together.

I am yours, her eyes said.

The gesture was enough to force him back from the edge, though it did not quench the fires burning in him. He allowed Abella to lead him to the nearby couch, where he sat down beside her and looped his left arm around her shoulders, leaving his right hand free in case he needed his blaster. Part of him still hoped for a good reason to draw it.

Alkorin sat down across from them, spreading his arms along the back of the couch and crossing one leg over his other thigh. The sedhi's legs were cybernetic as well, made from the same dark metal as his hands, bearing the same sleek design and faintly glowing yellow lines.

"Shall we leap to it?" Alk asked. "Are either of you currently registered in the Consortium's identification database?"

"No," Abella said.

"So, we will need two fresh chips. One for a terran, the other for a...?"

"Khetun," Tenthil replied.

"I'm not sure I am familiar with any such species, and I make a point to keep myself *very* well-informed of the peoples listed in the Consortium registry."

Tenthil released a sharp breath through his nostrils; *khetun* was what his people had called themselves. What they should've been called here and anywhere else. But they were a race who had not even progressed beyond living in mud-daubed huts and cured-hide tents. They had no say in a place like this. "Zenturi."

"*Zenturi*," Alk narrowed his eyes and looked toward the ceiling, and his tail—which lay across the cushion to his left—slowly undulated over the fabric. "Ah, I recall now. Popular in the underground arena circuits. I'm embarrassed by my own forgetfulness on that. It's an unregistered species, illegally imported."

Something didn't ring true in Alk's words.

"That a problem?" Tenthil asked.

"That would depend on how we approach it, my dear little zenturi."

Tenthil tensed, but Abella squeezed his hand before he could lean forward and growl. He'd seen enough interactions between people like Alk—criminals of varying specialization and standing—that he should've recognized this for what it was. Shows of weakness were perceived as vulnerability and were considered fair grounds for attack. Shows of strength, whether of position, influence, or body, established superiority and sometimes gave pause to would-be attackers.

This was a game. A dangerous game, undoubtedly, but Tenthil had always played with the highest possible stakes. He'd killed people a hundred times wealthier and more powerful than this sedhi.

"If you're not skilled enough, we'll seek elsewhere," Tenthil said, pushing himself up.

For the first time since Tenthil and Abella had met him, Alk showed something other than smugness—a flash of anger crossed his face, turning the pupil of his third eye into an almost imperceptibly narrow line and brightening the glowing marks on his skin.

"You will find *no one* in this city more skilled than me," Alk said through clenched teeth, leaning forward and jabbing a finger toward Tenthil. "And you will find no one else in this line of work who treats the privacy of their clients with the respect and care I offer. If you want to pay a hack to implant chips that will get both of you arrested by the Eternal Guard, or who will sell your new identities to anyone who offers a few credits, so be it. But I will not be insult—"

"Neither will I," Tenthil said, meeting the sedhi's gaze. He eased down onto the couch. "You are the best at what you do. I respect that. I'm the best at what I do. Respect me in turn."

Alk clenched his jaw before taking in a deep breath. "And what is it you do, zenturi?"

"Kill people like you."

Abella tensed, her blunt fingernails biting into the back of Tenthil's hand. She turned her wide eyes toward the sedhi. "Let's...just calm down. We're here to do business, right?"

Alk didn't look away from Tenthil. "Remove your hood and mask."

Tenthil pulled back his hood with one hand and tore the mask off his face with the other, dropping the latter onto the couch beside him.

The sedhi's stare persisted before his eyes rounded, and he straightened. "You're the one who attacked Drok a couple weeks ago. Right in the middle of his own club."

Tenthil nodded once. He kept his attention on the edges of his vision, from which he could see two of the four autocannons mounted on the ceiling. Had he pushed the forger too far? Had he overstepped the unspoken boundaries of this verbal game?

Abella leaned forward and said calmly, "We're not looking for any trouble, Alkorin. We came to you because you're the best, because you have a reputation for discretion, and because we had faith that you'd be able to help us. Tenthil and I have both been used as slaves. We have people after us, and there's nowhere safe for us in this city. All we want is our freedom—and that means getting off this planet. Neither of us ever asked to be brought here."

Alk lifted one of his hands. Tenthil tensed, ready to draw his gun and shove Abella away from the inevitable autocannon blasts, but the sedhi only ran his metal fingers through his dark hair, pulling it back between his horns.

"This is my business, not a charity," Alk said. "But...we can all pretend we're good friends while we sort this out, and I may even be inclined to *slightly* reduce my usual rates in your case. Once we're done, you go on your way, and we all forget you were ever here and continue on with our lives."

Tenthil nodded again.

"I never disclose the names of my clients or the details of my business with them," the sedhi continued, "but I can assure you that Drok was no friend of mine. News of his murder sent shock waves throughout the Undercity because of its audacity, nothing more. I find that keeping up to date with such occurrences allows me to better protect the interests of my clients.

"That said, I don't want to know anything more about your situation. I don't want to know who's after you, I don't want to know what trouble you're in—unless it pertains directly to the identification chips you need."

"Good," Tenthil said.

Abella's tension eased, and she leaned against Tenthil. "Thank you."

"I do it for the credits, not the thanks." Alk sat back, though his previously leisurely position had taken on an undeniable stiffness now. The sedhi was likely rattled, but that didn't mean he would be docile.

"How much?" asked Tenthil.

"Thirty thousand."

"No."

Alk's dark brows angled downward over the bridge of his nose. He lifted his arms off the back of the couch, palms toward the ceiling. "Your situation isn't exactly simple, is it?"

"Make us the chips and we leave. Simple."

"I thought we were approaching this from a stance of mutual respect, zenturi." Alk shook his head. "You need to pass through a checkpoint to leave the planet. That's fine, my IDs can manage it. But she is part of a race that only has a few thousand registrants in a city of tens of billions, and *you* are part of a race that isn't in the registry at all. That makes my work extremely difficult, because anything I produce will need to stand up to even greater scrutiny than normal. If you're one in a billion, the Consortium doesn't care. But one of a kind? *That* would draw their attention."

"Fifteen," Tenthil said, forcing his face to remain neutral; the sinking feeling in his gut was becoming too familiar as of late.

"Thirty is already low."

Tenthil only stared at the sedhi.

"Give me the human, and I'll make yours free of charge," Alk said, his third eye shifting to glance at Abella.

Abella gasped and threw herself on top of Tenthil in the same instant that he surged forward. It was only some vague instinct that halted his momentum—even in the depths of his rage, he could not allow himself to do her harm. Still, his muscles bulged, his claws shredded the couch cushion beneath him, and he snarled through bared teeth.

Abella glared at the sedhi. "Are you serious? You're basically asking to be ripped to shreds! I'm not his plaything or his property. I'm his *mate*."

Hearing Abella reaffirm it once again, hearing her own their connection, was like a splash of cold water on Tenthil's face, cooling him off enough to clear a bit of the rage fog from his mind. He slipped his arms around her and shifted her aside. He would not allow her between himself and the sedhi. It was his place to shield *her* from harm, not the other way around.

Alk's eyes were wide, and he was pressed so far back against the couch that it seemed the frame was likely to snap, but he kept his seat. Whether it was arrogance, stupidity, or fear that had held him there, Tenthil neither knew nor cared.

The sedhi's tongue slipped out and ran over his lips. "Twenty-five for both. That's the best I can do."

There was a gleam of something else in Alk's eyes, something Tenthil would never have expected to see in such a situation—curiosity.

"You can make them both free and I'll let you live," Tenthil said, for once relishing the burning sensation in his throat as he spoke.

"I'm not keen on the idea of dying, zenturi, but as I said, this is not a charity."

"Twenty."

"Even if you manage to kill me, you two won't make it out of this room alive. Is that what you want for the terran?"

Tenthil tipped the corner of his mouth up in a lopsided smile; it was the only outward display he permitted of the pain and worry he felt at the thought of losing Abella. "You'd be too dead to care."

Abella placed her hand over Tenthil's and looked at him. "Twenty-five. He's not our enemy. Let's not make him one."

Clenching his teeth, Tenthil turned his head to meet her gaze. The worried light in her eyes and the concerned crease between her eyebrows nearly undid him. "Fine."

Alk groaned, lifting a hand to massage his forehead. "Twenty, all right? I'll do the damned job for twenty. Bring me half to get started, the rest when we implant. Now, if you wouldn't mind, I *do* have other work to attend to."

Tenthil wasted no time in getting to his feet, keeping an arm around Abella to bring her with him. He walked with her toward the door.

Grinning, she twisted to look behind them and offered the sedhi an enthusiastic wave.

He wasn't sure if she was being friendly or condescending, but when Alk only released another groan in response, Tenthil couldn't help the swell of pride and satisfaction in his chest.

SEVENTEEN

Tenthil sank into a low crouch, placing one hand on the metal beneath him. The shadows he'd positioned himself in were a welcome comfort, especially paired with his natural disruption field, but he refused to lower his guard.

He ran his gaze over his surroundings. From his perch atop their current safehouse, he could see the entirety of the chamber in which that safehouse stood, including the other units nearby—he guessed they'd originally been intended as storage units. Dirt and trash had built up on the ground, obscuring much of the concrete and metal. There were even some pale, sickly plants growing in a few places.

The chamber was perhaps twenty meters high and a hundred meters across at its largest point. The walls slanted toward the center, where the only light—a huge, yellow-orange circle that sometimes flickered—was situated. Its illumination was broken by prominent pipes and large, squared-off bulges in the concrete and metal, casting irregular shadows on the buildings and the debris-strewn ground.

There'd been no sign of movement over the last ten minutes

apart from a lone sewer skrudge; the half-meter-long vermin had dug something out from beneath a rusted metal sheet and scurried into a crack in the wall.

Tenthil's eyes shifted frequently toward the entry tunnel, which was lit by dim, failing lights. There were at least two other routes by which the chamber could be exited—ladders leading up from several of the storage units to the catwalks overhead, and a smaller access tunnel on the ground level, hidden behind a tristeel door that only looked like it wouldn't open.

As he rose from his crouch, he unintentionally turned his mind to Abella. Pride warmed his chest, and a small smile spread across his lips. She'd done well today, better than he would've expected—better, even, than the best he could've hoped for from himself.

Frustration sparked in his gut to clash with that sense of pride. She wouldn't have had to step in if not for Tenthil's mistakes. He'd allowed his instincts to get in the way of his purpose, and his need to protect Abella had placed her in *greater* danger. Their only goal had been to obtain the ID chips, and his need to assert dominance over anyone who challenged his claim on Abella had almost plunged their mission into chaos and bloodshed.

Were the forger not an honorable individual—at least on the surface—Tenthil and Abella would never have left that place alive, and only Tenthil would've been to blame.

Abella, on the other hand, had proven herself clever, attentive, and adept at reading people and situations. She'd carried herself with poise and confidence through circumstances that would've rattled many other individuals. If he hadn't known better, Tenthil would never have guessed that her only experience in Arthos had been as a slave.

He walked to the edge of the roof and leapt across the two-meter gap separating their safehouse from the adjacent unit. Setting a casual pace, he searched for potential listening devices or surveillance equipment; fortunately, the search turned up nothing.

He reflected upon his growing adoration and admiration of Abella as he silently traveled from unit to unit, continuing his search. His attention repeatedly returned to the safehouse door, which, at a glance, was indistinguishable from the entrances of the other units.

Even if his initial urge to claim her had been driven by lust —which he didn't believe—his feelings for her had deepened significantly over their time together.

Abella was brave, spirited, and determined, but she was also gentle, graceful, and compassionate. She was Tenthil's first real taste of many of those traits, and he was addicted to them as he was to her scent, taste, and feel. That a person such as her could exist went against everything Tenthil had known in the Order. Compassion and selflessness were weaknesses. That she could be strong *and* caring simultaneously shouldn't have been possible.

And yet there she was. Proof that what he'd been taught by the Master hadn't been the accumulated secrets of the Void, or a path to enlightenment, or how to serve a higher calling. All they'd taught him was how to kill.

Abella was teaching him how to *live*.

She was the only reason they'd been able to get information on the forger's location from the informants. She was the only reason they'd made a deal with Alkorin.

That deal meant another shift in priorities; they had a source for the IDs, and now they needed funds. The credits Tenthil had taken from the Order safehouse were enough to keep him and Abella fed and sheltered for a few weeks, but they wouldn't cover even a quarter of one of the ID chips.

The Order had access to vast amounts of liquid currency, but attempting to access any of it was far too risky. That path was closed off. He needed a means of obtaining a large sum of unlinked credits in a very short while.

Unfortunately, Tenthil's training hadn't involved lessons on obtaining money quickly. The Order had always provided his housing, food, and allowances—undoubtedly through funds that he and his fellow acolytes had brought in by fulfilling contracts. And dwelling on the credits he'd earned for the Order wouldn't do anything but make him angry.

Growling to himself, he completed his circuit of the storage units and jumped down to the ground.

The Infinite City was massive, and some people claimed the Bowels were larger than the Undercity and the city on the surface combined; even the Order's expert hunters wouldn't be able to find Tenthil and Abella right away. He had a little time to plan.

A little time to tend to the needs of his mate.

Nonetheless, he checked over his shoulder as he approached the safehouse entrance. He doubted he'd ever feel fully safe, fully secure, no matter how long he lived, but he was grateful for his alertness now. It was one of the few things that could guard his mate from harm.

He opened the door and paused. Music pulsed from within the room, muffled by the sound dampening field that likely spanned the walls and doorway. Tenthil stepped across the threshold, and the music struck him full-force—drums pounding in a wild, savage rhythm, loud enough for him to feel the bass of each beat down to his bones, but not nearly loud enough to be deafening.

Abella looked at him and grinned from her place beside the desk, upon which the console's projection displayed a series of moving bars that pulsed in time with various pieces of the music. She wore one of the outfits they'd purchased before meeting with the forger. She'd thrust it at him before he had a chance to examine the garment, but he recognized its colors. It was a formfitting, long-sleeved black dress with swirling violet and green designs, its hem stopping mid-thigh. Her blue-black hair hung loose around her shoulders and down her back.

His gaze moved up her long legs and over the curves of her hips and breasts, and desire swept through him. It didn't matter that he'd claimed her body, that he'd marked her with his fangs, his venom, touch, and scent; he wanted her again, and again, and again. His hunger for her would never be sated.

Abella rushed to his side, pushed the door closed, grabbed his hand, and tugged him farther into the room.

"Does this sound familiar to you?" she asked, raising her voice over the music.

With Abella's hand touching his, it was difficult to focus on anything other than her, but Tenthil closed his eyes and made himself hear the music, made himself *feel* it. Little by little, memories emerged. The sound of different drums from long ago and far away played in his head, keeping a quick, steady beat that sometimes built into a frenzy.

This music was not the same—and in his heart, he knew nothing ever could be—but it was reminiscent of the drums of his youth. It had similar energy, even if the sound was different. And, like that memory-music, there was something about this that demanded *movement*, something that burrowed into his mind and set off something deep and almost instinctual.

Opening his eyes, he smiled and nodded.

Her grin widened as she released his hand. She backed up a step, bent her knees, and began stomping her bare feet and pumping her hips and chest to the beat of the music. She swung her arms back and forth and stepped side to side to complement her other movements.

Her eyes never left his. "What about this?"

He watched her intently, marveling at the ease with which she'd fallen into the beat and the effortless way she moved with the music.

He shook his head and strained to raise his voice over the music. "It is yours. It is *you*. More special than anything from before."

Abella paused, a shy look briefly crossing her features before she closed the distance between them and kissed him. It was a quick kiss, but it was no less powerful than any they'd previously shared, and it stoked the ever-burning fire within him.

She moved her mouth toward his ear to whisper, "Dance with me."

Pulling away, she returned to her prior position and resumed her dance, closing her eyes and throwing her entire body into it. Every part of her moved to the pounding drums. She undulated and spun, flipping her hair, and Tenthil was as transfixed as he'd been the first time he'd seen her.

He drew in a deep breath, drinking in the sweetness of her scent, and stepped forward to join her, giving himself over to the music—and to his mate.

ABELLA'S HEART thumped in time with the music; the drumbeat flowed through her, and she became one with it, moving her body as though she were possessed. Dance was the one thing that had kept her sane through her years as Cullion's pet, the one thing that kept her going. Though he'd often ordered her to dance, she'd never once danced for him or any of his associates—she'd done it for herself. She'd done it to claim those fleeting moments during which she was swept away from everything by the music.

Now, she danced for Tenthil.

She opened her eyes and raised her head. Tenthil stepped close, placed his hands on her hips, and spun her to face away from him as he drew her against him. Abella gasped. Her backside met his pelvis, and he slid his hands down to her thighs, gyrating against her in time with the music.

Abella settled her hands over his, and he guided her arms up, bringing her wrists around the back of his head. He trailed his fingers down her forearms, over her elbows, and along her sides, stopping them at her waist. Abella shivered as lust surged through her. She leaned back while his hands trekked upward again, over her stomach, to brush the undersides of her breasts.

She trembled in the wake of his touch, her already hot blood heating further as tingles raced across her skin.

When she tipped her head back against his shoulder, he lowered his face and captured her mouth with his own. His sweet, cinnamon taste burst across her tongue; it was an aphrodisiac that she couldn't get enough of. Their motions no longer matched the music, but they didn't need to—Tenthil and Abella had fallen into their own rhythm, a rhythm dictated by pounding hearts and ragged breaths, by electric jolts arcing through her body to coalesce at her core.

He deepened the kiss, his tongue moving in time with his rocking groin. Arousal slickened her inner thighs. Tenthil inhaled, tensed, and growled, grazing the fabric of her dress with his claws.

Abella grasped his hair and pulled her head back slightly, breaking the kiss. She opened her eyes to stare up at him. The sight of his gleaming black gaze sent fresh ripples of excitement through her; she knew what that darkness meant, knew he was on the verge of giving himself over to instinct.

"Fuck me, Tenthil," Abella whispered. "Take me however you want."

Moving forward in a rush, he wrapped an arm around her, lifted her off her feet, and carried her with him. In two strides, he had them at the wall. She had just enough time to get her arms in front of her and flatten her palms against the wall before he shoved her against it. His mouth pressed to her ear.

"Stay," he rasped.

Tenthil released her for the space of a few heartbeats. During that time, she heard his ragged breaths, the jingle of his belt unbuckling, the whisper of his clothes coming off, the thump of his boots being tossed aside. She remained in place, her anticipation and arousal growing with each little sound as slick gathered between her thighs.

When he pressed his body against her back, she felt only the heat of his skin and the solidness of his muscles through her clothing. His hands dropped to her waist and quickly slid lower to catch the hem of her dress. He yanked it up, baring her ass, and grasped her hips. Kicking her feet apart, he spread her legs wider and tilted her pelvis back. Without warning, he plunged his cock into her sex.

Abella gasped, squeezing her eyes shut. He filled her, stretched her, hurt her, and made her feel *so* damned good; she could only beg for more.

And Tenthil gave it to her. He drew back and thrust into her again and again, pounding her against the wall, taking her in a frenzy. There were no words, only the blistering pleasure of his cock slamming in and out, his ridges and nodules stroking her inner walls, creating a maelstrom of sensation inside Abella.

She scraped her nails against the wall as his claws dug into her hips. The bit of pain his hold produced only added to her mounting pleasure.

Abella lifted her hips and pushed back to meet his thrusts. He snarled and drove into her harder, faster. He was a beast—brutal, animalistic, feral—and she was his mate.

She was *his*.

Tipping her forehead against the wall, Abella came with a choked cry. There was no forewarning; it burst through her with all the intensity of his ravenous black eyes, with all the savagery of their joining. He didn't slow despite her knees buckling. He simply held her in place, pinned against the wall, as her toes curled, and her sex convulsed around his shaft. Her mind was swept away on a surging tide of ecstasy.

When the quivering of her sex eased, Tenthil pulled back and withdrew from her. She immediately felt *empty*, and a desperate whimper rose from her throat.

He bunched the fabric of her dress in his hands, pulled it off over her head, and spun her around to face him. Abella stared into those black eyes; they brimmed with passion, with affection, with *hunger*.

Tenthil dropped his hands to her ass and lifted her off the floor, drawing her body against his. She instinctively threw her arms around his neck and wrapped her legs around his waist as he lowered her onto his cock. Her moan was lost amidst the continued pounding of the drums. He kissed her hard. She tasted his sweet venom and greedily swept her tongue along his fangs for more.

Keeping her secure in his hold, he carried her to the bed and climbed onto his knees. A moment later, she was falling, her back landing on the soft blanket. Tenthil broke the kiss and leaned over her, caging her with his powerful arms to either side of her head and stopping his face only centimeters from hers. Throughout, his thick, throbbing cock had remained inside her.

He jerked his hips forward, and Abella's lips parted to release a sharp breath at the force. She smoothed her hands down to his chest, where she flattened her palms to feel the thumping of his heart. She focused on his heartbeat, on his guttural sounds, on every ridge on his cock as it moved in and out of her. Warmth blossomed within her as she neared the edge of oblivion once more.

His eyes bore down into her, possessive and fierce, and the curtain of his silver hair closed out the rest of existence, creating a space only for Tenthil and Abella.

In that moment, she knew, without a doubt, that he was hers. Her mate. She was the entirety of his world. He would do anything for her, everything for her, just to keep her as his own, to keep her safe. How could she consider giving this up? How could she give up this chance at happiness, especially after all he'd sacrificed, after all he'd risked for her?

How could she give him up?

She couldn't. She knew that now. Even if she returned to Earth, she wouldn't be happy without him. He'd already taken a piece of her heart. It was only a matter of time before he had it all. With every wicked curl of his lips, every darkening of his eyes, every touch of his hand, she knew the inevitability of her surrender. She would be his completely. It was the only possible outcome.

Tenthil growled and shifted his hips, thrusting into her at a different angle. Sparks flashed across her vision and danced behind her eyelids when she squeezed them shut against the fresh torrent of pleasure. His body tensed, and his warm breath swept over her skin as he pressed his mouth to her neck.

He didn't slow his thrusts, didn't waver in his rhythm as he pierced her flesh with his fangs.

"Tenthil," she breathed before words became too much for her lust-hazed mind to produce.

She wrapped her arms around him and let ecstasy, amplified by his warm venom, carry her away.

Everything around them—the room, the city, the whole universe—ceased to exist, leaving only the two of them, only their connection. Abella cried out; Tenthil threw back his head and snarled. His cock expanded and his heat poured into her as he bucked his hips, somehow forcing himself deeper. She dug her heels into his lower back to bring him closer still, unable to get enough.

When they finally settled but for the occasional shudders that passed between them, Tenthil pressed his face to her neck and kissed the flesh where he'd bitten her—the same place he'd bitten her the other times they'd made love. He didn't move, and she didn't want him to. Abella relished the feel of him buried inside her. She stroked his back, running her palms over the wide expanse of flesh and muscle, tracing every scar she encountered.

A strong wave of protectiveness swept through her. Tenthil had suffered so much—too much. She didn't want him to suffer anymore and wished she could take away the pain he'd already endured, wished she could alleviate the agony he carried in his soul. If he'd been able to grow on his own, without the influence of the Order, what sort of man would he have become?

What sort of man could he be alongside her?

She had no answers to those questions. The path ahead was long and dangerous, and Abella was certain only of one thing.

Tenthil was hers—*hers*—and she would *never* let him go.

TENTHIL LAY ON HIS SIDE, arms around Abella with her back against his chest. He wasn't sure how long they'd reclined together after making love, save that it had been long enough for the music to cease automatically. Time hadn't mattered in the aftermath of their joining. The only important thing was that he had her here with him—her warmth, her softness, her scent.

Releasing his hold on Abella, he propped himself up on an elbow and looked down at her, running a hand over her pale skin. His blood froze. Dark, finger-shaped bruises marred her hips, and crusted blood clung to several shallow scratches on her thighs.

It was only then that the lingering haze of his passion cleared from his mind and he realized how far he'd gone, how much control he'd relinquished.

His heart thundered. "Sorry, Abella. I'm sorry..."

Abella turned her head to look at him and took his hand, which she pulled around to her front. She ran her fingertip along the edge of one of his claws.

"Don't be, Tenthil. I'm not."

The lightness of her tone did little to console him. The evidence was clear—he'd gone too far, had been too rough. He'd done harm to *many* people throughout his life, but he'd never wanted her to be part of that list, never wanted to see her blood on his hands. *Never*.

"I hurt you." He barely managed the words, his voice shattering like glass against stone.

"You did." Abella kissed his palm and placed his hand to her hip. "You hurt me here"—she lowered his hand to her thighs—"here"—she guided his hand between her parted thighs to cup her sex—"and here. And it felt *good*, Tenthil. So good."

Her heat radiated into his hand, and her essence slickened his fingers, which had pressed into her slit. He brushed the pad of his finger against the little bud that brought her so much pleasure and suddenly wished that he possessed her short, blunt nails so he could touch her more intimately, could caress her delicate folds, could stroke her inner depths with his fingers alone.

She inhaled sharply, laughed, and rolled over to face him.

"Not all pain is bad." She trailed a finger over his bare chest. "Some can be quite pleasurable."

"The bruises. The blood."

"Will disappear over time." Her smile widened. "And besides, I like them."

Tenthil's brows fell; his mind went to his facial scars, the most prominent marks he possessed. Though he'd come to appreciate them for the defiance they represented, he could not imagine *liking* them. "*Like* them?"

"Because they were made by you in a moment of passion. Because you were with me, inside me, letting go. You didn't do it out of spite or malice." She ran her hand down his arm. "Do you like it when I scratch your back as you make love to me?"

Faint but exhilarating tingles danced over his skin in response to her touch. He nodded.

"It hurts, but it also feels good, right?"

"Yes. But it's nothing compared to this."

"To what?"

He placed his hand lightly over her bruises. "This."

"They don't really hurt, Tenthil. And if they did, it'd only remind me of you and how much pleasure you gave me. Think of it like...another mark you put on me. Another claim." She covered his hand with one of hers and guided it up to the bite wounds between her neck and shoulder. They were already scabbed over, though it couldn't have been more than a couple hours since their joining.

Tenthil frowned. Each time he'd bitten her, it had been the result of overwhelming instinct—he'd never once made the conscious decision to do so. Something within him said it was what he should do, said it was the way to solidify his claim, to mark her as his, to make her feel *good.*

He finally eased himself down onto the mattress, drawing

her against him. She slipped one of her legs between his and draped an arm across his chest.

"I'm fine, Tenthil." Abella kissed his cheek, right over his scar.

Once she'd pulled back, he brushed his lips against hers. He wanted to experience moments like this for the rest of his life—and he wanted that life to be a long one. Perhaps he didn't deserve happiness, didn't deserve her, but he intended to seize both, nonetheless.

That meant overcoming a few not-insignificant obstacles first.

"Need to find a way to get the credits," he said.

It killed him a little inside when her smile faded.

"How many credits do we have?" she asked.

"Little over fifteen hundred."

She cringed. "So we're not even close."

Tenthil shook his head. "But we're not beaten yet. Just need to find a big payoff. Can probably find a contract. Might take a few days, but—"

"No. I don't want you to do that."

"Longer we take, closer they get, Abella." He settled a hand on her cheek and caressed her cheekbone with the pad of his thumb. "We need to work as quickly as possible."

A little crease formed between her brows as she stared into his eyes. "All the killing you've done since you took me from Cullion's was to keep me safe, Tenthil. It was necessary, and I know a lot of them weren't good people. But if you take a random contract to kill a random person who has nothing to do with any of this... I don't know, maybe it's naïve of me to think so by this point, but it would be *wrong*. You escaped the Order. You're making your own choices now. You don't have to be like them anymore."

He recognized the truth of her words, but his instincts still ran strong—protect her at all costs. No life mattered more than hers, not even his own. If he had to kill a random stranger, an innocent, he would, just to ensure Abella's safety. Right now, leaving the planet was the only way to keep her safe. That meant earning the credits they needed as fast as possible by whatever means necessary.

"It is all I know," he said.

"I know," Abella sighed. She tightened her arm around him and lowered her gaze. The crease between her brows lingered.

She was quiet for a time, and Tenthil was content to simply lie with her, to feel her skin against him, to absorb her warmth.

Abella suddenly tensed and raised her head. "What if... I think I know where we can get the credits."

Tenthil furrowed his brow; something in her tone suggested he wouldn't like what she was about to suggest. "Where?"

"Cullion's."

"Wouldn't his assets have been claimed by now?"

"I don't know much about the way finances and inheritances work here, but I heard enough from him to understand that they're complicated. It'll probably take months for anyone to legally get their hands on his money, probably longer because he had no next of kin. But we're not going after that stuff. He had credits stashed in a few places around his house. Places no one else knew about."

Tenthil's mind raced through possibilities. Cullion had been wealthy and well-connected—both through legitimate and illegal avenues—and had flaunted his fortune everywhere he went. News of his death would have spread rapidly. That meant scavengers, opportunists eager to pounce on the chance of pilfering a vacant manor.

"With your bioelectric-thingy we could sneak in undetected. I think there's a secret way in we can use, and I can show you where he stashed the credits he got through shady deals," Abella said. "I was usually beneath his notice, a pet more than a person, so he didn't care if I was around while he conducted business so long as I kept my mouth shut. Bastard thought I was too simple-minded to understand anything that was going on apart from when he told me to dance."

"There are likely guards posted," Tenthil said. "His connections would want his assets protected until they can divide them appropriately. I'd be taking you directly into danger."

"Tenthil, we've been in danger since the moment you took me. Sometimes you have to face the danger head-on if you want to eventually get past it, and I refuse to sit around while you put yourself at risk. Anyway, Cullion always went on about how the bodyguards he employed were the best in the business, and how many of them did you take down by yourself?"

He tilted his head. "Thought you didn't want any more death."

"I don't. We're not going there to kill anyone, and we'll do our best not to...but I'm not going to stop you from defending our lives."

Tenthil stared into her eyes, searching them—though he wasn't sure for what. Perhaps a sign that she was joking? "Isn't it the last place you want to go?"

"It's just a place. The person who hurt me is gone...because of you." She pressed a kiss to his lips. "This is the only way I can think of for us to get those credits. Unless you have a better idea?"

He ran his tongue over his lips, picking up a hint of her taste upon them, and drew in a deep breath. Her scent—tinged with the perfume of her arousal—flooded his awareness. His cock stirred, and sweet venom trickled from his fangs.

Abella's plan was better than anything he might've come up with, and he had to accept the fact that anything they did would endanger them both, even if it was merely because he'd be forced to leave her alone while he worked. But having a plan didn't mean they had to rush off to it. There was some time... and they were still in bed, naked.

"Only one other idea," he said.

Abella raised her eyebrows. "What is it?"

Tenthil propped himself up on an arm, placing his other hand on her shoulder. He pushed her onto her back and shifted himself over her, letting their bodies touch, skin to skin, heat to heat. Lowering his head, he kissed her lips, then her chin, her neck, her collarbone, working slowly down her body.

"Oh..." Abella breathed.

He kissed her flat stomach and the bruises on her hips. She shivered and caught her lower lip between her teeth when his chin brushed over her pelvis. Without breaking eye contact with her, Tenthil spread her thighs, dropped his mouth to her sex, and slid his tongue between her folds to tease her clit.

Abella gasped, and her head fell back. She moved her hands to his head, twining her fingers in his hair, and pressed his face down, wordlessly asking for more.

Tenthil obliged.

"Oh, I really love this plan," she rasped.

EIGHTEEN

Tenthil slowed the hovercar as it entered the airspace over the Gilded Sector's residential area. "There."

Abella leaned closer, placing her hand on his thigh to brace herself, and looked at Cullion's manor through the driver's side window. Her hair fell over his sleeve. He longed to feel the delicate strands brush against his bare skin.

Priorities, he reminded himself. *We have a job.*

"I didn't think seeing that place again would bother me, but..." She frowned. "The sight of it makes everything I experienced there come rushing back to me. Silly as it is, it feels like if we go inside, he's going to be there, waiting for me."

Tenthil dropped his hand to cover hers, giving it a squeeze. "He's dead. Gone forever."

Abella looked at him and smiled.

He guided the hovercar through a wide, looping as he studied the manor. The exterior lights were on, and there was a vehicle parked out front—a bulky, armored transport, the sort favored by many private security firms. The logo painted on its front marked it as property of Tegris Security, one of Starforge's competitors.

At the back of the building, the hole he'd blasted in Abella's former quarters had been patched by a flat white material that stood out starkly against the surrounding adornments. He fought back the memories of that night; there was no time for flashbacks. He needed to focus.

The lack of visible guards outside roused Tenthil's suspicions. Tegris wanted their presence known—hence the clearly-marked transport out front—and would have warm bodies on site if they'd been hired to protect the manor. Where were they?

Narrowing his eyes, Tenthil scanned the manor and its grounds.

"Looks about the same as always," Abella said softly. "Though this is my first time seeing it from *inside* a car."

Tenthil gritted his teeth. "Wish he were alive so I could kill him again."

Abella brushed her fingers along the side of his jaw. "Like you said, he's gone. And I don't think I ever thanked you for everything you've done for me."

He turned his face toward her, met her gaze, and smiled. "You are with me. That is all I need."

She returned the smile and slipped her fingers into his hair, leaning forward to press her lips against his. Tenthil fought back his urge for more as he kissed her back.

We are here for a purpose.

Abella pulled back and chuckled. "After."

He groaned and shifted on his seat, hoping to relieve the sudden, throbbing ache in his groin. "Yes. *After*."

As Tenthil returned his attention to the manor, a brief, metallic flash caught his eye. Brows falling low, he leaned closer to the window and squinted. Even with his sharp vision, it took him a few seconds to spot the object that had produced the flash—a small surveillance drone hovering over Cullion's property. A quick scan of the nearby airspace revealed two more.

Were they supplemental to the existing surveillance equipment, or had the system not been repaired since Tenthil blasted the control room to pieces?

He piloted the hovercar to street level and landed it in an alleyway a few hundred meters from the manor. After cutting the engine, he gently tapped the signal jammer disc he'd attached to the control panel. "This has about an hour and a half left. Need to get in and out, quickly and quietly."

"Okay." Abella peered past him. "If we don't run into too much trouble, it shouldn't take long. I know exactly where his hiding places are."

"Keep in contact with me at all times. Don't know what surveillance is inside." He swallowed and drew in a heavy breath; he hated that his next words would echo what he'd heard time and again from the Master. "We can leave no evidence. No witnesses."

"I know," she said quietly.

Tenthil grasped her chin between his forefinger and thumb, forced her to meet his gaze, and kissed her. It was the only way he knew to tell her he was there, to assure her they would be all right, to swear he would keep her safe. He withdrew only when some of her tension eased, and somehow—despite allowing his tongue to emerge and lick her taste from his lips—he kept himself from tearing her clothes off and taking her right there.

They exited the vehicle and walked through dimly lit alleyways toward Cullion's manor with Abella tucked against Tenthil's side. The area was quiet, and they saw no other living beings. There was only trash, all of it stacked in the shadows to await collection like it was an embarrassing secret.

Tenthil slowed their pace when they entered the alley

behind the manor. He glanced upward as they neared the outer wall, spotting one of the hovering drones; it was difficult to discern against the dark, distant Undercity ceiling even from this close. Abella's stride faltered. This was a vulnerability he'd rarely glimpsed from her. He knew she'd suffered here, but she hadn't often shown how much it affected her.

"You are okay," he whispered, running his palm up and down her arm. "I'm here."

She nodded and pressed closer to him. "Should be somewhere along here. A hatch, or something. I saw the ladder from below one of the times I tried to escape, but they caught me before I made it any farther."

He nodded. Though his instinct was to keep his attention directed up, toward the most immediate threat, he turned his gaze down. The ground was a combination of concrete and metal sheets blended together somehow into a surprisingly even surface. It was less of a patchwork than in other sectors, but still exemplified the random way the Infinite City had been constructed—outside the sanctums, there'd been no unifying plan for most of Arthos.

That blending of materials served to make the hidden opening more discreet; when he first saw the faint, parallel seams, he nearly dismissed it as a quirk of the construction, but a slight tilting of his head revealed the perpendicular lines that met the others to form a rectangular outline. He crouched over it. Abella's thigh pressed against his as she sank down along with him.

Tenthil ran his palm over the hatch slowly, seeking a control mechanism or a compartment to open. The metal surface was gritty with accumulated dirt.

"Is that it?" Abella asked in a low voice.

Replying with only an indifferent grunt, Tenthil continued his search until his hand brushed over a rougher spot where the texture was created not by the dirt, but the metal itself. He wiped away some of the grime and ran a finger over the spot, leaning closer to study it.

A light flicked on at the touch of his finger. He pulled his hand back and instinctively twisted to block Abella's body with his own as the light coalesced into a small, holographic keypad.

"Think it is," he muttered as he reached into his pouch to retrieve his masterkey. After setting the tool in place on the hatch and activating it, he turned his head, checking in both directions along the alley, and glanced up. Fortunately, the estate's outer wall sheltered them from the nearest drone. Even if it couldn't capture Tenthil and Abella on its sensors, it would have likely detected the motion of the hatch opening were it in a direct line of sight.

The masterkey flashed green. The hatch beneath Tenthil rumbled and released a soft hiss. He snatched up the masterkey and moved backward, pulling Abella with him, as the hatch sank a few centimeters and slid sideways into the ground.

Soft, yellowish light emanated from the opening, revealing a ladder leading down.

Tenthil leaned forward, bracing himself with one hand on the edge of the opening. The ladder descended to a metal-grating catwalk which ran along the side of an access tunnel. Apart from the gentle sound of flowing air, the tunnel was silent.

"Climb on my back," he said.

Abella looked at him questioningly for a few moments, her brows drawn together as she bit the inside of her bottom lip. Without fully breaking physical contact, she stepped behind him, slipped her arms around his neck, and pressed her body against his back. Tenthil reached back and hooked his fingers around behind her knees, lifting her off her feet. She wrapped her legs around his middle at his guidance and locked them together at the ankle.

Her weight was slight, but he could not ignore her body.

Not now, you fool.

He moved forward and lowered his boot onto the top rung. Releasing his hold on Abella's legs, he grasped the sides of the open hatch and continued down as quickly and smoothly as he could. Her arms and legs tightened around him despite his care. Part of him felt an indescribable satisfaction at the way she clung to him; it felt good to be needed by someone, to be depended upon, to be *trusted*.

It felt even better to have someone he needed, someone he depended upon, someone *he* trusted.

When his boots touched down on the catwalk, he moved his hands to Abella's legs and patted them gently. She unlocked and lowered her legs, kissed him just beneath his ear, and released her arms from around his neck to slide down his back. Her boots hit the grating with a pair of soft clanks. She quickly nestled herself against his side.

The hatch overhead slid closed when Tenthil pressed the button on the nearby wall. He slipped an arm around Abella's shoulders, turned, and surveyed their new surroundings.

The hexagonal tunnel was at least fifteen meters high by fifteen wide. It had likely been constructed for maintenance use. A meter-wide catwalk ran down either side, and inset lights above and below provided the weak illumination. The floor of the tunnel had a narrow metal grating running down its center, likely to collect the rivulets of unknown liquid trickling down the walls in a few places.

Had he not known better, Tenthil might have thought they'd descended into the Bowels.

There were two doors on the nearby wall, separated from each other by only a few meters. Both had the look of heavy-duty blast doors, though the second was large enough to fit most medium-sized hovercars through. Tenthil had no doubt it hid some sort of vehicle.

If Abella had made it here during an escape attempt, she'd come painfully close to freedom—not that the tracker Cullion had implanted in her would've allowed her to stay free for long.

Expression grim, Abella pointed to the smaller door. "That's where I came out right before they caught me."

They walked to the door she'd indicated, and Tenthil took out the masterkey again. The access panel on this door was the same as the one on the manor's roof—it read ID chips rather than requiring an input code or some sort of keycard.

If this tunnel had been built as part of the city's intended infrastructure, access through the alleyway hatch was controlled by maintenance codes—if city workers even used this space for official business anymore. It was far more probable that the sector's wealthy residents kept it open as a means of traveling to and from their homes in secret.

Tenthil set the masterkey to work. Such locks often took a long time to break, if they could be broken at all.

Abella shivered against him. "This is how...how they removed the bodies."

Tenthil frowned, making the skin around his scars pull taut. "Bodies?"

"Sometimes Cullion would get...carried away with his punishments."

Nostrils flaring with a heavy exhalation, Tenthil nodded. He'd seen the evidence in the marks on Abella's body when he'd rescued her from this place. Though he'd long since lost count of how many people he'd killed, Tenthil could at least say one thing about himself with certainty—he'd never gone out of his way to make any of his victims suffer.

Perhaps it was only a small, ultimately meaningless distinction, but it was all he had.

The masterkey's small display flashed green, and the door's maglocks released with a metallic *thump*. The door opened on a hallway with metal floors. To the left stood another door, likely leading into the garage. Depressed grooves lined the floor on both sides—more runoff drains, undoubtedly. The short corridor ended on a set of double sliding doors less than ten meters away.

Tenthil collected the masterkey, pausing for a moment to study it on his open palm. He'd expected a much longer wait; was it possible that the system controlling the locks had also been damaged during his prior visit?

He couldn't quite shake the suspicion that this was a trap, though logic said it was merely a matter of the would-be inheritors of Cullion's assets refusing to perform any repairs on the manor until the legal matters regarding their inheritance had been cleared up.

When Tenthil stepped forward, Abella moved with him, her stride in sync with his. The door to the access tunnel closed behind them.

Her tension had not eased; in some ways, he understood her trepidation, but he could never fully know what she'd experienced, could never fully understand how it had affected her. All he could do was eventually figure out how to take that pain away from her.

"Where do we need to go?" Tenthil asked as he pressed the button beside the double doors.

"He had a few stashes throughout the house," she replied, "but the biggest was always in his bedroom. Third floor, toward the back. Right over my...over the chamber he kept me in."

The double doors slid apart silently, opening on a small elevator with another set of identical doors directly ahead. Just like the corridor in which they stood, the elevator was devoid of the overwrought ornateness permeating the rest of Cullion's estate. Its rundown floor and walls were covered in faded stains.

He had to discreetly dispose of the evidence. Even though they were his property, he knew there'd be uncomfortable questions asked if he wasn't careful. Even he couldn't have bribed his way out of alien trafficking and murder charges had all this been exposed.

Abella could've been one of the nameless slaves dragged through this tunnel if Tenthil hadn't acted when he had. Her blood might have contributed to the stains on the floor.

They entered the elevator together, and Tenthil glanced down at the controls. The only thing on the touch display was an arrow pointing up. He reached for it but stopped his hand before making contact.

"Ready?" he asked.

Abella dropped her right hand between their bodies, grasped the blaster at her hip, and nodded. "Yeah."

Tenthil tapped the arrow.

The doors slid shut behind them with a faint *whoosh*. Only a barely noticeable hum and a slight sinking sensation in Tenthil's gut indicated the elevator was moving. Within a few seconds, the doors in front of them opened.

Dropping a hand to his blaster, Tenthil led Abella off the elevator. The room they entered was lit by pure white overhead lights, and everything within was pristine, shining as though it had been polished only moments before. It reminded him of a surgical room, with an adjustable table in the center—but the gutters running along the underside of the table, which emptied over a floor drain, suggested a sinister purpose.

He lifted his gaze. Large hooks dangled from chains in the corner, attached to the ceiling by automated pulleys. Along a section of one wall, half a dozen long, black bags hung on a rail. Tenthil didn't need to open the cabinets to guess the sorts of tools stored within them.

Wasting not another moment, he hurried across the room and through the only other door into a dark room.

Cages lined the walls, and numerous implements of torture were on display. Tenthil glanced down at Abella. She stood with her head turned toward him and her nose buried against his chest. She stared ahead with one wide, determined eye, but her face had paled, and her lips were pressed tightly together.

Even the strongest of us have weaknesses.

The room's confused smell assailed him. It wasn't a single scent, but an amalgamation, with blood and metal being the foremost components. His chest constricted; part of the blood-odor was familiar. He focused on it and was forced to clench his teeth against the wave of revulsion and rage that crashed through him when he realized what it was—Abella's blood.

"It's okay, Tenthil," she said softly, tightening her arm around his waist. "It's over. I'm with you now."

Shouldn't I be comforting her?

"Never again," Tenthil vowed, tugging her closer. He closed the door, glancing behind to see that it blended seamlessly with the wall, as though it had never existed.

More secrets.

The Master would've delighted in learning of them, though this chamber wouldn't have roused much suspicion, even in the social circles to which Cullion belonged. The wealthy enjoyed many of their kinks without shame or limitation, thanks to their standings.

Allowing himself no further time to contemplate this torture chamber—and having no desire to imagine Abella on her knees here, being whipped and beaten without mercy—he walked with her to the door at the center of the far wall. Her movements were stiff, but she didn't lag.

However much he wanted to be done with this, she must've wanted it a thousand times more.

They emerged at the end of a long, dark hallway—dark due as much to the décor as the lack of light. He shut the as door as quietly as possible without releasing his hold on Abella before continuing forward.

The sound of voices from far down the hall halted Tenthil after only a few steps. He darted aside, taking cover with Abella behind one of the sculptures arranged along the hallway, and peered in the direction from which the voices had come.

A pair of armored guards walked across the opening at the end of the hallway, their shoulder-mounted lights casting luminous blue-white cones in front of them. Their heavy footfalls echoed on the polished stone floor.

Abella tensed against Tenthil, and he swore he could almost feel her pounding pulse through their clothing.

The guards moved out of sight.

She pressed her lips close to his ear and whispered, "Second door on the left leads to a servant's corridor. There are stairs there that go all the way up and let out near Cullion's room."

Tenthil nodded. He waited a moment longer before creeping out from behind the statue. Abella matched his slow, careful steps as they approached the door she'd indicated, but even their caution was not enough to fully silence their passage —the stone floor and walls amplified each nearly silent footstep. He kept a hand on his blaster as they moved.

Somehow, they reached the door without being heard. Tenthil kept his eyes on the open space at the far end of the hallway while Abella opened the door, producing faint clicks as she grasped the handle and the latch released.

She slipped through the opening first, tugging Tenthil along behind her. He released hold of his weapon only long enough to close the door once he'd cleared it, teeth clenched against the inevitable sound of it latching.

Despite the darkness, the narrow hallway was familiar to Tenthil—it was almost identical to the one in which he'd killed the guards and destroyed the surveillance equipment the night he'd saved her.

They hadn't gone far when Abella turned and crept through another doorway to a staircase. The steps to the right led upward, while the left set led down.

"This will take us to a hallway upstairs, just a few meters from Cullion's chamber," Abella said.

Tenthil kept his left arm around Abella's shoulders as they ascended. Fortunately, the stairs were carpeted, padding the sound of their movement. They turned at the landing and moved up the next flight. Tenthil froze near the top, staring at the door that led to the second floor; faint light was visible in the tiny gap at its base, and an instant later he heard soft footsteps over the carpet on the other side. A shadow passed the sliver of light, trailing darkness in its wake.

Though the footsteps had been too muted to tell for sure, Tenthil guessed it had been another pair of guards who had walked past the door. There were likely more in the transport out front; many security forces used such vehicles as mobile surveillance centers. It was safe to assume they were dealing with at least six guards on the premises.

He counted fifteen seconds before he resumed their upward trek. When they reached the third-floor door, he paused, pressed his ear against it, and listened.

The only sounds he picked up were those of his own heartbeat and Abella's soft breaths. Leaning back, he carefully cracked the door open and peered into the hallway. It was dark and still—a fitting atmosphere, given the death Tenthil had delivered in this corridor before.

Slipping through the doorway, he and Abella turned right and walked toward the rear of the manor. Soon, they entered a larger hallway with high ceilings and Cullion's preferred overbearing adornment; this was the antithesis of the secret tunnel below.

Abella pointed to the large wooden door at the end of the hall. Despite the dimness, the metallic accents inlaid amidst the door's intricate carvings gleamed with reflected light.

A faint sound from somewhere behind them made Tenthil's ear twitch as he reached the door. He turned his head to listen; it took a moment before he realized that he was hearing the quiet jingling of equipment as someone walked.

Blue-white light spilled into the far end of the hallway from one of the side corridors.

He turned his attention back to the door, but Abella had already taken hold of the handle. She pushed it open and darted inside, pulling him along.

Tenthil released Abella once he was inside the room and spun to face the door, taking the handle in one hand and flattening the other higher up on its surface. Holding his breath, he eased the door closed, releasing the handle only after it was in place.

The latch clicked; the sound was thunderous in the silence.

Tenthil turned his head toward Abella, catching her worried gaze.

"Are they coming?" she asked quietly.

"Hide," he whispered before pressing his ear to the door.

Muffled voices drifted to him from somewhere down the hallway—apparently, the sound dampeners Tenthil had sworn were in effect when he'd first come here were no longer active. Footsteps sounded in the hall, drawing steadily closer.

He turned his gaze to the room. It was a huge chamber, with a wide, four-poster bed directly ahead. The posts were in constant, steady motion, spinning around an invisible axis and occasionally breaking into shards to rearrange themselves into new, matching shapes. To the left and right, low steps led up to raised portions of the room, one of which was furnished for lounging while the other, obscured behind a partially drawn privacy curtain, sported mirrors and wardrobes. The carpet was soft and intricately patterned, and everything was draped in luxurious fabrics of more varieties than Tenthil had thought possible. In the center of the room were two crescent-shaped couches arranged in a broken circle with a low, round table between them. The diffused light from the windows in the lounge area only deepened the shadows dominating the room.

Abella ducked behind the privacy curtain, vanishing into the darkness.

Tenthil dashed across the room and joined Abella behind the curtain, crouching beside her amidst the thick folds of fabric. She caught his free hand after he drew his knife. He turned his head and listened.

Only a few heartbeats passed before the door latch clicked, and a blue-white light swept into the room, flicking through the dressing room. The guards' boots whispered over the carpet, and their gear made the faint jingling that had originally alerted Tenthil to their presence. The play of moving shadows and light told of the guards' slow search of the room.

"There's nothing here," one of the guards said.

"There never is," the other replied, "but we have to check anyway. We make good on this contract and it only makes us look even better than Starforge, you know?"

"Yeah. Best thing for us that they fucked up as bad as they did. I heard there's still a lot of money being thrown at this contract."

One of the lights turned toward the dressing area. The circle it cast on the wall swayed and grew as a guard's muted footsteps drew nearer. Abella released Tenthil's hand, and he raised his knife, preparing to strike.

The guard grasped the edge of the curtain and dragged it toward Tenthil and Abella.

Tenthil hooked his left arm around Abella's waist and stood up, sidestepping with the moving curtain. The folds of fabric bunched around them like a flimsy cloth cocoon. Within a few seconds, Abella was pressed against the wall with Tenthil against her, chest to chest, his arms to either side of her body.

He forced his breathing to remain slow and silent as the sliver of space between the wall and the swaying edge of the curtain lit up with the guard's light. For an instant, the darkness surrounding them receded, and half of Abella's face was illuminated by reflected light, revealing one rounded green eye.

The light abruptly moved away.

"Third floor disturbance all clear," said the nearest guard. His quiet footsteps moved toward the door. "Now we can head back down and let Jharon and Krag take over second patrol. Bout time we had a chance to sit on our asses in the transport for a while."

"These patrols are pointless. We have the perimeter under constant surveillance. Nobody's getting in here without us knowing," the other guard said.

"Those Starforge fuckers probably thought the same thing."

"Whatever. Let's get out of here. I'm starving."

The door opened and closed. Abella released a soft *whoosh* of air, and her head fell forward to rest against his chest.

"That was close," she whispered.

Tenthil slipped his knife into its sheath and cupped the back of her head with his other hand, smoothing his fingers over her hair. "Almost done."

When he could no longer hear the guards' movement and voices through the door, Tenthil counted to thirty; only afterward did he brush aside the curtain and push away from the wall. He lingered at the edge of the steps leading back down into the main area.

"We should have a few minutes while they change shifts. Let's move quickly," he said.

Abella walked past him and descended the steps. She extended her arms around waist height as she moved toward the bed—her vision in poor light apparently wasn't as keen as Tenthil's—but seemed familiar enough with the room to avoid the obstacles in her path. Her footfalls were silent as she navigated the shadows between the furniture. Tenthil followed close behind her.

When they reached the bed, she placed a hand atop it and walked to the headboard, which was made of the same slate gray material as the moving posts. Tenthil wasn't sure if it was metal, stone, or some strange combination of the two. The headboard was divided into panels depicting scenes of some ancient story, the stylized figures within them lacking any semblance of realism.

"I need some light," she whispered.

Tenthil dipped a hand to his belt and removed a hardlight projector from one of the pouches. He placed the small, disc-shaped device on the back of his left hand. It sealed itself in place on his glove. With his right hand, he pressed the activation button on the edge of the disc.

An orb of light coalesced in the air about ten centimeters over the projector. He moved the fingers of his left hand to manipulate the orb, shaping it into a cone and directing its beam toward the bed.

"Over here," Abella said.

Tenthil shifted the light to the place she'd indicated as she leaned forward and pushed aside the long, concave pillows gathered around the headboard, revealing the sculpted paneling beneath.

She placed both hands on the borders between the panels and trailed her fingers over the decorative carvings. "Somewhere along here..."

Keeping his arm steady, Tenthil twisted to look toward the door. The room was quiet enough for him to hear the gentle scrape of her fingers over the wood. Thankfully, there were still no sounds from beyond the door. He'd been aware of the risks before he and Abella had come here, but their close call a few moments earlier had reminded him what was at stake—her life was in danger every second they spent in this house.

A blazing need to whisk her away from this place raged within him, existing on a primal, instinctual level, but he held it back. Despite the risks, this was a necessary step on their journey to true freedom.

There was a soft click from the headboard.

"Got you," Abella said.

Tenthil turned back toward her to see one of the panels sticking a few centimeters out from the headboard. At her gentle touch, the panel slid straight up.

His pride and admiration for her swelled to new heights. She'd lived in this house as a prisoner, as a piece of property, for years. She'd been beaten, spoken down to, and forced to perform at the whim of a cruel and arrogant spawn of a skeks. Yet throughout her time here—and despite her suffering—she'd held on to hope. Abella had not allowed Cullion to break her spirit. She'd remained observant. She'd discovered and retained her former master's secrets, and Tenthil had no doubt she would have harnessed her attentiveness and tenacity for future escape attempts had he not rescued her.

She had held on to herself after she was taken from her

home. What had Tenthil held on to apart from a defiant streak? He'd become what the Master had wanted him to be, had been shaped into an instrument of death.

Abella would forever be more than he deserved; he was fortunate beyond words to have a mate so beautiful, talented, and strong.

He angled the light into the now open compartment.

Abella reached into the opening and plucked up one of the many credit chips piled inside. "These are what we need, right?"

Though Tenthil understood the importance of money, the function of it, he had never been motivated by it. The Master and Corelthi had always handled the Order of the Void's earnings and expenditures, granting acolytes allowances only to purchase goods and materials necessary to complete contracts, and his people—as far as he could recall—hadn't used currency of any sort. But seeing so many credit chips, knowing some of the business Cullion had been involved in, moved something within Tenthil.

There was likely enough here for him to provide luxury and comfort to Abella for the remainder of their years, for them to enjoy a life of wealth and leisure. A life in which she'd never want for anything. Something about that notion was appealing

And something about it was revolting; using Cullion's ill-gotten riches to pamper Abella seemed somehow perverted, creating a sinking feeling in Tenthil's gut.

"Yes," he said. "Take whatever you can carry."

Together, they emptied the compartment, stuffing credit chips into belt pouches and pockets, arranging the chips as best they could to avoid any rattling or clanking. When they were done, Abella carefully shifted the panel down and closed it.

Tenthil returned the pillows to their original positions and switched off the hardlight projector. He removed the device and returned it to his belt pouch before taking Abella's hand in his. He led her toward the door, keeping ample distance between their legs and the furniture to ensure she didn't trip.

"Just have to retrace our steps, right?" she asked.

He nodded and released her hand to place his arm over her shoulders, drawing her against him. Ideally, their exit would be fast and simple, but in his experience, things rarely went as planned. He pressed his ear to the door and listened. The silence on the other side persisted.

Tenthil opened the door, and he and Abella crept into the hallway, keeping close to the wall as they returned to the servant's corridor. He neither heard nor saw signs of any guards during their descent to the first level. When they reached the door leading back into the darkly decorated main hall, Tenthil opened it a crack.

Several voices echoed from down the hall, made indistinct by distance and distortion. Tenthil crouched low and peered through the gap. The large front doors stood at the farthest end of the hall, visible despite the sculptures and decorations in Tenthil's line of sight. One of the doors was open, allowing the muted light from outside to spill in, and four armored Tegris guards stood in front of it in a loose semi-circle. Their body language and voices suggested a casual conversation.

He dropped his gaze to the floor; the polished, gold-veined stone reflected the light from outside for a long distance, but the strongest of the reflections ended a couple meters away from the door into the servant's corridor.

Time was limited. Once the jammer failed and the stolen hovercar's tracking systems were reenabled, the Eternal Guard would come looking. Leaving the vehicle behind was an option, but it was a sloppy one. An abandoned, stolen vehicle would rouse suspicions in a sector like this, especially if Tenthil and Abella's trespassing was discovered.

Could they afford to wait the guards out, or was the conversation distracting enough to allow a quick, unnoticed escape?

His nostrils flared with a heavy exhalation.

We need to get out of here. Need to get to safety. I need to get my mate out of danger.

He leaned back and eased the door closed only enough to eliminate the gap. "Going to cross together. Need to stay low, move quick and quiet."

Tenthil turned his face toward Abella. She remained tucked against his side, and the darkness of the servant's corridor reduced her features to an indistinct patch of shadow just a bit paler than the rest.

She nodded.

They stood up together. For a moment, Tenthil kept his arm still save to tighten his grip on the door's handle.

Supposed to be careful, not stupid. Protect her from danger, not put her in even more than she's already in.

But we need *to leave...*

He thrust aside his conflicting thoughts. He'd been taught careful planning and preparation during his time in the Order, and he understood the value of methodical, thought-out approaches, at least in theory; in practice, he'd always been better served by *acting*. By trusting his instincts.

And his instincts said to *go*.

Opening the door, he entered the hall with Abella at his side. They hunched down and crept along the wall toward the cage-filled room. He gritted his teeth. Their boots were quiet, but not silent, and he could only hope the statues would obscure himself and Abella enough to prevent the guards from noticing them.

His back was burning by the time they reached the door, set ablaze by the knowledge that four heavily armed guards had a clear line of fire toward himself and his mate.

He opened the door. The sound of its latch releasing echoed down the hallway.

"What was that?" one of the guards said.

"Hey! Stop!" another shouted.

Boots clattered over the floor, quickly approaching.

Tenthil shoved Abella through the door ahead of him. He slammed it shut once he was inside the room and stepped aside, drawing his blaster. "Go hide."

Abella grabbed his arm with one hand. "Come on. We need to move."

"I'll stop them."

She bolstered her hold with her other hand, tugging him toward the secret door. "They didn't have surveillance on the entrance below," she said hurriedly. "We just need to have the door closed before they get in here."

Though her words had been rushed, adding a thicker accent to her universal speech, he understood completely. If Tegris had known about the tunnel entrance, there would've been either a drone or a guard positioned there.

He nodded, and they sprinted across the room together. The shouts and footsteps in the hall increased in volume.

Abella pressed a spot near the base of the wall with her boot, and the hidden door swung open. She dashed through the doorway, keeping a hand on his arm. Tenthil twisted to look behind him as he followed her. Still holding his blaster, he grasped the interior handle with two fingers and tugged the door shut.

The cage room's entry door burst open in the same instant the hidden door closed.

Abella's fingers dug into Tenthil's arm as they ran to the elevator. He wasted no time before pressing the down arrow on the control panel once they were inside. The double doors *whooshed* closed, and the elevator made its quiet descent.

She was running again as soon as the elevator opened enough to allow her through; Tenthil had to turn sideways to avoid slamming into the moving doors. They were on the catwalk in the access tunnel seconds later. Abella hurried to the ladder and reached for one of the rungs.

Tenthil caught her arm. "There should be other hatches. We will use one closer to the vehicle."

He tried to ignore the thunderous pounding of his heart, the tightness in his chest, and the red tinge of rage at the edges of his consciousness demanding he go back and kill the men who'd chased them.

All those things faded away when Abella turned her face toward his.

Her cheeks were flushed, her pink lips parted with quick breaths, but when she smiled, she looked more beautiful than ever before—an excited light gleamed in her eyes. She leaned forward and pressed a quick kiss to his lips. Before Tenthil could respond, they were running along the catwalk, hand-in-hand.

NINETEEN

We did it!

Abella could barely contain her elation as she and Tenthil navigated the side streets and alleyways on their way back to Alkorin's place. She'd thought she had moved on from her time at Cullion's, that she could no longer be affected by it, but all the pain and trauma had flooded back to her the moment she saw the place. Stepping into the discipline chamber had been one of the most frightening things she'd ever done, somehow made worse because she knew it was irrational. The people who'd hurt her were gone.

But she'd overcome her anxiety, had overcome her fear. She and Tenthil had accomplished their goal, and now they were going to obtain the means to leave the planet.

They'd made it.

The azhera and the pair of troll-like cren guarding the forger's alleyway entrance let Tenthil and Abella pass without issue. She walked down the alley alongside him in excited silence, and that excitement didn't fade as they entered the building, passed the lone cren, and proceeded up the stairs.

Each step up toward Alkorin's chamber felt like another step toward freedom. *True* freedom.

At the foot of the final flight of stairs, Abella caught Tenthil's hand and pulled him to a stop. He turned to look at her, furrowing his brow. His slitted pupils expanded and contracted.

"No matter what he says, remember that I am yours," Abella said. "Don't let him get a rise out of you."

His frown—which he'd worn since they neared the alleyway with the roasted-worm sign out front—deepened. "No promises."

Smiling, Abella reached up to brush a strand of his hair back, tucking it behind his pointed ear. Her fingers lingered, tracing the tip of his upper earlobe. "I know you have some pretty...*strong* instincts, but just know that I'm not going anywhere. I'm with you, Tenthil, and nothing is going to change that."

He settled his palm over her cheek and trailed the pads of his fingers over her cheekbone. The feel of his gloves made her long for the gentle scrape of his callouses.

"I know," he said.

Abella took his hand and brought it to her lips. "Remember, we have some...unfinished business. After." She kissed the pad of his finger through his glove before playfully nipping it.

Tenthil dipped his face closer to hers, inhaled, and released a low growl. "We do. Let's be quick about this."

Abella pecked a quick kiss on his lips and drew away. She looked up at the elaborate door at the top of the landing. The two vorgals standing guard on either side both stared down at them, one of whom wore a smirk. To Abella, their species was reminiscent of orcs from the fantasy movies popular at the beginning of the last century, though vorgals were more appealing in appearance.

Tenthil stepped past her and led the way up the stairs. He seemed to purposefully keep his hands away from his weapons, but his posture was stiff, and his fingers were curled into tight fists.

"Are you sure it's the forger you're looking for?" one of the vorgals asked. "Or do you just need a room?"

"I'd pay credits to watch," the smirking one replied, sweeping his gaze over Abella.

Abella eased forward, slipping her arm around Tenthil as he tensed, and smiled. "We'll be getting a room *after* we've spoken to Alkorin, and there isn't enough money on this or any other world for you to have even the tiniest peek."

Tenthil's tension didn't diminish. He held his gaze on the guards, and in a low, dangerous voice, said, "Plenty of time to kill both of you beforehand."

The vorgal's smirk stretched into a grin, and a wild light sparked in his eyes. He tipped his head slightly aside, drawing Abella's attention to the scars on the side of his skull. "Wouldn't be the first to try."

"But I would be the last. Eyes off my mate and step aside."

Letting his blaster rifle fall to hang by its strap, the scarred vorgal spread his arms to the sides. "I got nothing fucking better to do right now."

"I don't think Alkorin would take too kindly to his staff fighting paying clients," Abella said.

"Back off, Thargen," the other vorgal growled. He lifted his wrist to his mouth. "Open it up."

The etched door behind him opened.

"Always spoiling my fun." Thargen grunted and returned to his place beside the doorway.

"Can't have fun if you're fucking dead." The other vorgal stepped back and jerked his chin toward the next room. "Go on in."

Slipping an arm around Abella to hold her closer, Tenthil walked with her through the open door.

Alkorin's chamber was just as she remembered, though her appreciation of it was increased having just left Cullion's. The moody lighting and coherent, minimalist design of this place was an expression of wealth in direct opposition to the opulence of Cullion's manor. The forger, if nothing else, had decent taste and at least some understanding of subtlety.

The blast door closed behind Abella and Tenthil, and they stepped deeper into the room.

"Welcome back," Alk said, calling Abella's attention to one of the long couches.

The forger was reclining against an armrest, with one leg bent and his arm settled atop his knee. His robe was open to reveal the sculpted muscles of his torso and the glowing yellow marks on his chest and neck. He smiled, his intense, shining eyes focused solely on Abella.

"You don't look very busy," she said.

"When I received word you were on your way in, I decided to make myself presentable."

She swept her hand to indicate his state of dress—or lack thereof. "*This* is presentable? Doesn't look like you're waiting to conduct business to me. Looks more like you're waiting to be serviced."

Tenthil growled.

Alk's smile broadened into a grin. "Simply waiting to *serve*."

"Great. In that case..." Abella opened one of the pouches on her belt, scooped out a handful of credit chips, and held them toward Alkorin. "We're ready for those ID Chips."

The forger's three eyes rounded for a moment before he swung his legs down, settling his feet on the floor, and stood up. He walked toward them; Tenthil kept himself between Alk and

Abella until she finally shrugged out of his hold and stepped forward.

"Abella," Tenthil rasped.

"It's okay, Tenthil," she said.

"You're a brave little thing." Alk stopped about a meter away, thick tail swaying lazily behind him.

"Not so much. I think I just know you won't hurt us. You're one of the good ones."

"Am I?" Alk's eyes narrowed, the central one a little more than the other two. "I'm the head of a criminal enterprise, employing armed guards who would kill at a flick of my wrist. Is that the sort of individual humans usually find worthy of trust?"

Abella glanced back at Tenthil. He'd killed more people than she could even begin to imagine, but he wasn't *bad*. Misguided, desensitized to death, but never cruel.

She looked back to the forger and shrugged. "Not all bad guys are *bad* guys."

Alkorin tilted his head to the side, and a few strands of his long, dark hair fell over one of his eyes. "Are all terrans like you, or are you unique among your kind?"

"The chips," Tenthil said.

Alkorin sighed, shook his head, and extended a hand. The credit chips clinked on his metal palm as Abella dropped them onto it.

"This should be more than enough for both of the ID chips." Abella lowered her arm. "We'd just *really* like to get out of here as soon as possible."

Alk's brows fell, and his smile faded. He plucked up one of the credit chips and slid the pad of his thumb over its surface. A tiny hologram projected from the top of the chip. Though she couldn't read any of the many written languages common throughout the city, she'd seen the characters in the hologram often enough at Cullion's to know they were numbers.

"This single chip more than pays for what you require," Alk said, releasing the button. The hologram disappeared. "We had an agreement. Why give me more, after those negotiations?"

There was suspicion on his face now, and the change was so drastic that it jarred Abella's thoughts.

"Twenty thousand. Half to start, half when done. It does not put me at ease that you've given me several times more than the amount we agreed upon." Alk dropped the chip back onto his open palm and closed his fingers around the credits, stepping backward. His gaze flicked to Tenthil. "Trust is a thing earned. I have not earned your trust. I've done nothing to warrant this"—he raised his fist—"so *why?*"

"Because I believe your word," Abella said. "And...you're kind of our last hope here."

"You have your reputation for a reason," Tenthil added.

"You've a reputation of your own," said Alk, "and it doesn't leave me inclined to take you at your word."

Tenthil released a frustrated breath. "If I had been contracted—"

Abella turned to Tenthil and placed a hand on his arm. When he snapped his mouth shut and met her eyes, she shook her head. She waited until he eased before looking back at Alkorin.

"You said you didn't want the details of the trouble we're in, and I understand that," she said, "so I'll review the basics. There are very dangerous people out to kill us. Getting off this planet is our *only* chance to live. And we cannot do that without IDs. Coming to you was already a massive risk to us. We just want you to know that we are serious. You are the only one who can help us." She glanced at his closed hand. "Maybe use the extra for the next human who comes needing help. I know I can't be the only one who was taken."

Alk's gaze remained fixated on Abella, so intense that she could almost feel it piercing her. Suspicion lingered in his eyes, but there was something else there, something deeper—*desire*. His third eye shifted toward Tenthil, followed by the other two a moment later. "You won't reconsider my prior offer?"

Tenthil stepped forward, his stride slow and measured and yet somehow fluid. He stopped directly in front of Alk and angled his chin down, holding the forger's gaze. "Ask again."

Despite his outward stillness, the air around him was thick with cold, seething fury; Abella could *feel* him bristling.

Abella moved to Tenthil's side and slipped an arm around him.

"Tenthil is my mate," she said firmly.

Alkorin lifted his hands—one still closed around the credit chips—and bowed his head. He backed away a few steps before he turned and straightened, dipping his hand into his pocket. The chips clinked as he released them.

"I will need full body scans to begin compiling profiles," Alk said as he walked toward the far end of the room. He climbed the low stairs up to the work area and gestured toward a circular platform on the floor against the right wall, which had a glowing white surface.

"One at a time, please." He turned toward Abella and Tenthil, though his attention was focused on one of the holographic screens before he looked up. "Your clothing, of course, will need to come off. To ensure the most accurate scans possible."

Abella sensed Tenthil's intention to charge. She threw her other arm around him, locking her hands together, and braced her legs wide, planting her heels in the carpet before he'd managed a full step. Heat poured off his body. His muscles tensed and trembled; she wasn't sure if it was because of his fury, his restraint, or both.

"Tenthil," Abella said.

He didn't look at her.

"*Tenthil.*"

With fangs bared, Tenthil finally turned his face toward her. His eyes were fully black.

Abella reached up and cupped his cheeks with both hands. "You need to calm down. We *need* to do this so we can get those IDs, so you have to try to tone back your instincts...or leave."

His nostrils flared, and he shook his head. She knew what he was saying no to—leaving. She didn't want him to go either.

"Then let's get this done so we can go somewhere private and I can get naked for *you*, okay?"

He remained tense, his inner conflict plain in his furrowed brow and lingering scowl.

"Contrary to earlier appearances, I *do* have other things to do," Alk called.

Abella brushed her thumbs over the scars on Tenthil's cheeks and searched his eyes. "We can get through this."

When Tenthil finally nodded, a wave of relief swept through Abella. She dropped her hands to her sides, walked to the platform, and mounted the steps, stopping when she stood before the scanner.

"So, I just...take my clothes off and step on?" she asked over her shoulder.

"Yes." Alk offered her a smile. "But *you* can feel free to take your time."

Abella rolled her eyes and shook her head. She had to give the alien credit. He was charming, attractive, and persistent, but he wasn't Tenthil.

She inhaled deeply and reached for the hem of her shirt,

but apprehension halted her hands. How many times had Cullion forced her to strip before punishing her? How many times had she been bathed and dressed by the servants attending her? She'd never had a choice on those occasions, and it felt like she didn't have one now. This was a completely different situation, a totally new set of circumstances, but part of her felt the same way she had with Cullion—small, powerless, subhuman.

Abella turned her head and sought Tenthil. He'd mounted the platform as well, though he hadn't followed her to the scanner. His posture expressed his continuing agitation, but at least his scowl had softened to a displeased frown. He held her gaze for a moment before walking to Alkorin. Tenthil stopped immediately in front of the forger, who looked up from his screen and recoiled slightly.

With surprising calm, Tenthil shifted his body to block Alkorin from Abella's view—meaning he was blocking her from Alk's view, as well.

Her heart nearly burst with affection and appreciation.

"I need to see when she's on—" Alkorin began.

"She'll tell you when," Tenthil said.

Abella smiled and stripped quickly, piling her belt and clothing atop her boots beside the scanner. She shivered as she dropped her attention to the scanner's white floor and stepped onto it.

"I'm ready," she called, keeping her arms at her sides despite the urge to cross them over her breasts. She felt too vulnerable like this.

"All right," Alk said.

The platform beneath Abella hummed gently. White light rose from the scanner's base, encasing her in its glow and obscuring the rest of the room from her view. Despite the intensity of the illumination, it oddly didn't hurt her eyes—but the strangest part of the experience was that she didn't *feel* anything even though she was cocooned in white.

"I'll see her on the screen once the scan is complete, you realize," Alkorin said.

"Fine. But you will never look upon her directly, or you'll have to find three new cybernetic optics," Tenthil replied.

"Why do you need nude scans of my whole body, anyway?" Abella asked.

"It's Consortium procedure," said Alkorin. "They are quite detailed in their documentation of everyone who receives an ID chip. I have to make sure the profile I build for you contains all the pertinent information so as not to rouse suspicions when you attempt to use it."

Despite being shielded by the light, Abella still fought the desire to cover herself. "Guess they don't care much about privacy here, do they?"

Alkorin scoffed. "This is a city of billions. Hundreds of thousands die here every day, and not always peacefully. These scans are used for identification both before and after death, and the Consortium mandates fresh scans every ten cycles. Doesn't do them much good if all they know about your body is that you were wearing black leather on your last scan—especially if all that's left of you is a forearm or an ankle. Just to keep everything running smoothly for the Eternal Guard, they need to keep their identification database updated. That means right down to your bones, organs, blood...your genetic makeup."

The white light intensified, growing so bright she was forced to squeeze her eyes shut against it. For the first time, she *felt* the light, felt it on her skin, felt it *inside* her.

Just as quickly as it had come, the sensation vanished.

Abella opened her eyes, blinking away the dark spots drifting across her vision. Tenthil remained in place, blocking her from Alkorin.

"Done," Alk said. "And let me say—"

"Nothing," growled Tenthil. "Get dressed, Abella."

Cheeks flaming, Abella stepped down from the platform, turned away from Tenthil and Alkorin, and hurriedly dressed. She pulled her hair out from beneath the collar of her shirt. "Done."

Abella turned toward the males to find Tenthil approaching her, the muscles of his jaw ticking as he moved. She stepped aside to allow him access to the scanner. He paused in front of her and extended an arm, brushing his palm over her cheek and slipping his fingers into her hair, guiding it back behind her ear. Only thin rings of silver surrounded his dilated pupils, and the fire gleaming in his eyes was undeniable. He didn't speak a single word, but he didn't need to; his feelings were evident.

Abella covered his hand with her own. "Yes, I *am* yours. Now hurry up so I can show you how much I mean it when we get back."

For the first time since they'd returned to Alkorin's place, a faint smile touched Tenthil's lips. He lowered his hand and set about removing his clothing. If he had any inhibitions, he made no indication of them. Abella stepped back to watch, letting her eyes roam up and down his body as more and more of it was revealed; for that little while, she forgot where they were and what they were doing. All she could focus on was the breadth of his shoulders, his sculpted ridges of muscle, and the length of his stiffening cock.

She squeezed her thighs together, but it did nothing to alleviate the sudden, heated ache between her legs.

Tenthil's nostrils flared, and one corner of his mouth lifted higher, giving her a brief glimpse of his fangs. "After," he rasped before turning and stepping onto the scanner platform.

After, indeed.

How could she wait? She was addicted to his touch, his kisses, his *taste*. She wanted all of him, all the time.

Alk cleared his throat. "The two of you will save any such activities for *after* you've left my place of business. Unless... you'd be open to another partner?"

"Not gonna happen, Alkorin," Abella singsonged as she glanced at him. "Focus on the scan."

"Things are better in threes." His third eye closed briefly.

Was that the sedhi version of a sly wink?

Tenthil growled and spun around as though he were about to leap off the scanner. Eyes suddenly wide, Alk hurriedly manipulated the controls. The white light enveloped Tenthil, leaving only a vague, shadowy outline of him. Somehow, even his indistinct form looked furious.

Abella laughed and shook her head. "I think you'll just have to find yourself your own human, Alk. This one is taken."

Alkorin lifted a hand to his face, brushed his metal fingertips across his chin, and hummed thoughtfully. "Perhaps I will."

Though Abella's laughter faded, her spirits didn't fall. Perhaps she should've been upset by Alk's constant flirtation, but she couldn't bring herself to be. She and Tenthil were almost there, and Alkorin was instrumental in them having a life together. The forger's attitude struck her as little more than posturing. He knew just as well as she did—she was Tenthil's, and nothing he could say or do would change that.

She stood by her initial judgment of Alkorin—he was a decent person at heart, even if he'd done some bad things.

"Done," Alk said.

The light from the scanner receded into the base, and Tenthil stepped off it, any sign of humor or calm he'd previously displayed having been replaced by fresh rage.

"Hurry and dress," Alkorin said. "You two have that look in

your eyes, and I'll not tolerate you mating here. I've only just had the couches cleaned, and I'd rather not soil them beyond the damage you've already done. That is, unless I have the pleasure of being involved in the festivities. Be gone."

Tenthil made no move for his clothing; all his attention remained on Alkorin. "The chips."

"Take time. With the amount of fabrication I'll have to do, it should be about four days. Come back then."

"Fabrication?" Abella asked. "Aren't the chips just tiny little implants?"

"Not physical fabrication," Alk replied, leaning a hand on the control panel as he turned to face her. "I have to build histories for both of you that will fool the system, including likely places your chips might have been scanned without your knowledge and detailed medical records. I have to code *his* genetic profile in such a way that it doesn't trigger any alarms as a previously unregistered species. Then I have to take all that information and sneak it *into* the system—into *two* systems, so you'll have emigration data from your home planet that won't rouse suspicion. It's delicate work, but it's necessary if you want this to succeed."

Abella nodded. "We'll be back in four days then."

Tenthil grunted and bent to gather his clothes, tugging them on piece by piece. He picked up his belt last of all and glared at Alkorin while he drew it around his hips and buckled it into place.

Abella covered her mouth to hide her widening grin.

After a few more moments of pointed glaring, Tenthil put his arm around Abella's shoulders and guided her toward the steps.

"Can't wait to see you again either, zenturi," Alk called with a laugh.

TWENTY

Tenthil forced himself to take deep breaths as the door closed behind him. The air in the alleyway was cooler than that within the forger's building, but it did little to reduce the inferno blazing inside him. Alkorin had made repeated blatant advances toward Abella despite knowing she was Tenthil's mate.

It had nearly been enough to drive Tenthil to violence. After his first encounter with the sedhi forger, he'd thought Alkorin had been attempting to assert dominance in a primal, unsubtle fashion. Tenthil had wondered if the sedhi was motivated by instincts similar to his own. But this...

This had been, at best, insulting. Abella's trust in Alkorin was the only thing that had spared the sedhi significant pain.

He clenched his jaw, tightened his hold on Abella slightly, and walked toward the alley's exit at a deliberately slow pace. That he was so easily provoked by Alkorin only increased Tenthil's anger. He was capable of far more discipline, far more control, than he'd exhibited as of late.

Control and discipline will only serve me now when they can keep Abella safe.

"Tenthil."

Abella's voice broke through his tumultuous thoughts. He stopped and turned his head just as she placed her hand on the back of his neck, drawing him down to press her lips to his. Tenthil's brows shot up in surprise, but quickly fell as his eyelids drifted shut.

She kissed him hard, teasing his mouth open with her tongue. He tugged her against him as her tongue slipped into his mouth to slide along his tongue and fangs. A shudder swept through her, and more of that sweet mating venom flowed into his mouth. When she deepened the kiss, Tenthil lost all sense of awareness, lost hold of his fury.

There was only Abella—his mate, his everything—and her delicious taste.

After one last nip on his lower lip, Abella broke the kiss and drew her head back. Her eyes met his. "I love you."

She'd spoken quickly, breathlessly, but her words were no less impactful than if she'd shouted them. They pierced his chest, and a new heat spread outward from his heart, so far removed from the fires of his anger that its existence seemed impossible.

Abella slid her hand into his hair and clutched the strands between her fingers, producing a tantalizing sting on his scalp. "It's probably crazy—*I'm* probably crazy—but I know what I feel, and what I feel for you is real. And I wanted you to know just in case...in case anything..."

Tenthil framed her face between his hands and covered her lips with his thumbs, silencing her. He shook his head; he would not allow anything to happen. Wouldn't even entertain the possibility. He ran his gaze over her features as he stroked her kiss-swollen lips.

He had wanted Abella from the moment he'd first seen her. His want had quickly grown into a need, into an *obsession*, and had pushed him to do things that violated everything he'd been taught, making him an immediate target for the Order.

Abella was his mate. He'd do anything for her, endure any amount of pain to keep her from harm. There was nothing he cared about more than Abella.

When she'd asked him to love her days before, he had only truly understood the request in physical terms—he felt a deep, undeniable affection toward her, but he hadn't even known if he was capable of love.

So much had changed in the short time since. It was only putting a name to what he already felt for her, defining his emotions with a deceptively simple term, but he understood now how important it was.

He'd always believed that actions were more important than words, that they were all that truly mattered, but he knew different now. Words could be a sort of action of their own, and sometimes...

Sometimes, some things needed to be said aloud.

"Love you too," he rasped.

Her lips lightly brushed his thumbs as they spread into a wide smile, revealing her flat, white teeth. "Really? You do? Like, not just in an instinctual—"

Tenthil shifted his thumbs aside and silenced her with a kiss, pouring everything he might have said into it. Abella moaned and pressed closer. The scrape of her nails over his scalp elicited a pleased rumble from his chest.

After.

That quickly, he needed *after* to come *now*.

He pulled back and met her half-lidded gaze. "Need you. Need to go."

"Mhmm," she replied.

She nestled against his side when he slipped his arm over her shoulders. They turned and walked toward the exit of the alley at a hurried pace.

The alley guards stepped aside without comment when Tenthil and Abella neared; Tenthil felt the azhera's weighted gaze on him as he led his mate past, felt that stirring of instinctual protectiveness, that need to assert dominance, but he had something much more powerful on his mind now.

Abella.

He needed her, yes—needed her to the point that he ached with it—but the joy that had sparkled in her eyes today had ignited something new within him. They were so close to achieving their goal. So close to leaving this place behind and starting a new life somewhere else. And she *loved* him. That was more than a claim on him, more meaningful, more powerful.

This wasn't the first time he'd allowed himself the luxury of hope, but he'd mainly pushed forward through stubbornness and willpower up until now. It had been better not to think about the overwhelming odds they faced. And, though he hadn't doubted that they'd make a future together, he'd not dared to imagine it. But now, for the first time, he had some understanding of how that future might be like, of how it would feel to truly be with her.

They emerged onto the side street and followed it to the main street, where they fell into the flow of the crowd. Despite the alien bodies surrounding them, Tenthil remained focused on Abella. He could feel the steady beat of her heart through their clothing, and his skin tingled beneath the hand she'd placed on his side. The drive to mate with her, to place his claim on her anew, to pump that sweet venom into her veins, was immense, and he would not be able to deny it for long.

There were places nearby where they could rent a room

without an ID scan; was it worth the risk to go to one of them, or could he withstand the discomfort and consuming desire until they made it back to the safehouse in the Bowels?

Am I actually considering risking my mate's safety in favor of sex?

With that thought, Tenthil realized his mistake—he'd allowed himself to become distracted.

That realization came too late.

Had he been paying even a modicum of attention, Tenthil would've noticed the tralix far sooner, but his distraction had him looking up only a moment before the huge being plowed into him and Abella. Despite Tenthil's enhanced strength, the tralix's weight and momentum were too great; he'd been afforded no time to brace himself for the impact. Abella was knocked out of Tenthil's hold, and he stumbled aside, catching his balance only after coming down hard on one knee. The tralix grunted and came to an abrupt halt.

Tenthil shoved up to his feet and turned toward Abella, but he was met by the wall of mottled blue and green flesh that was the tralix.

"Watch where you're walking, you little skrudge!" the tralix boomed.

Tenthil moved to step around the burly being. He needed to know if Abella was all right; she was a piece of delicate blown glass compared to the rough-hewn boulder that was the tralix. But the tralix blocked Tenthil's path.

"Talking to you, worm." The tralix thrust a thick, blunt-tipped finger into Tenthil's shoulder, producing a distant pulse of pain.

Rage reignited deep inside Tenthil, a low, smoldering flame that only needed a little fanning to become a firestorm. He shifted his direction to go around the tralix's other side. Abella was his only concern at that moment. He was aware that the crowd around himself and the tralix had thinned, and he knew instinctually what was happening—they wanted to see a tralix tear someone apart—but he couldn't waste time with that.

"Abella," Tenthil called.

"You look at *me* when I'm talking to you," the tralix growled. He stepped forward, simultaneously jabbing his finger at Tenthil. "I'm the only thi—"

Tenthil slammed his forearm into the tralix's with enough force to completely divert the big being's momentum. The tralix staggered to the side, his own weight upsetting his balance enough to send him crashing to the ground with a startled grunt.

Tenthil's gaze darted to the space that had been blocked from his view by the tralix, the spot where Abella should have been—knocked down, undoubtedly, but hopefully unhurt.

His mind could not, therefore, reconcile what his eyes perceived. There was nothing there apart from the dirty street and a few startled onlookers. There was no sign of Abella.

No Abella.

Impossible, paralyzing cold filled Tenthil's veins, and everything around him—the tralix, the crowd, the lights, buildings, and sounds—was swallowed for a few moments by impenetrable blackness. Everything but the empty spot on the street where she should've been.

In his heart, he knew what this was.

The touch of the Void.

Hand of the Master.

Awareness rushed back to him. Tenthil's body tingled with prickling points of heat in the wake of the receding cold. He raised his eyes and swept his gaze across the crowd, desperate for some sign of Abella, for *any* sign of her, but there were only leering alien faces—the infinite eyes of infinite enemies. All that remained of Abella was a wisp of her scent, weak and assailed by a thousand other smells.

Each rapid beat of Tenthil's heart was like an explosion inside his chest, resonating in his ribcage, and despite his quick, ragged breaths, he couldn't get enough air in his lungs. The heat on his skin intensified.

No Abella.

"Easiest credits I ever made," said the tralix.

Tenthil glanced over his shoulder to see the tralix push himself onto his feet. The huge being tilted his head to the side —its range of movement limited by his massive shoulder and short, thick neck—producing a low crack.

The tralix turned to face Tenthil, a smirk lifting the corner of his mouth. He flicked his wrist dismissively. "Walk along. They ain't paying me extra to hurt you."

They...

No. Him.

Dashing forward, Tenthil caught the tralix's extended wrist with both hands. He twisted the limb as he continued past the tralix, throwing his full weight and strength into the maneuver. When he slid to a stop, he was behind his foe, with the tralix's huge arm bent at an awkward, backward angle.

The tralix cried out, and his muscles flexed. If given the opportunity to regain his composure, the tralix potentially possessed the strength to break Tenthil's hold.

Tenthil leaned forward and bit down on the tralix's arm. His fangs punched through his foe's tough hide. Bitter, stinging venom flowed from Tenthil's fangs, pumping into the puncture wounds.

He held the position, forcing more venom out of his throbbing glands, ignoring the tralix's cries of protest and pain. Only when his victim crashed to his knees did Tenthil withdraw his fangs and release his hold. A few alarmed shouts rose from the surrounding crowd as the tralix fell face down on the street.

When Tenthil turned, the nearest onlookers scrambled back from him. Their reactions made no difference to him; they would either move out of his way or be removed. None of their lives mattered.

With a deep inhalation, Tenthil sought Abella's scent. Once he found a trace of it, he broke into a run, following the trail. He shoved past anyone who didn't stand aside. Their protests fell on uncaring ears. He no longer saw living beings in his path but obstacles to be surmounted by any means.

No Abella.

Fire and ice warred within him—fury and fear, passion and pain, resentment and retribution. A torrent of emotion raged beneath his thoughts, above them, through them, obscuring everything in a crimson haze.

The scent led him to a wide alley. He skidded to a halt at the entrance; the alley, strewn with trash and debris, came to a dead end only fifteen meters ahead.

Movement at the top edge of his vision called his attention upward. A figure stood on the roof of the building at the alley's dead end, clad in black battle armor and a cloak with a raised hood. Darkness shrouded the figure's face—darkness that stared down at Tenthil, that stared into him.

Touch of the Void.

He drew his blaster and fired, but the figure dropped back onto the roof, exiting Tenthil's line of sight. The low thrum of an antigrav drive pulsed in the air overhead. A hoverbike darted from the rooftop upon which the figure had stood a moment before, cutting hard across the alley.

Tenthil fired again, but the bolt only struck the flowing cape trailing behind the hoverbike. Then the vehicle was gone.

Clenching his teeth, Tenthil holstered his blaster and

stalked forward, his thundering heartbeat becoming the only sound in his awareness. Abella's scent—so weak, so small—lingered in the air, though the stench of rotting refuse was overpowering it.

There were other scents, from other living beings, and he knew the underlying odor that linked some of them together.

The distinct smell of the temple's seemingly ancient recycled air.

Snarling, he dropped his attention to the ground. The front half of the alley was blanketed in bits of debris, but in the back, all the lighter pieces, along with the dirt, had been blown outward to gather along the walls. A vehicle had taken off from here—likely more than one.

No Abella.

Only the Void...

The message was apparent. The Master had taken her, and he wanted Tenthil to know it.

A bestial roar erupted from Tenthil's chest, burning his throat like acid. He slammed a fist into the nearby wall. The metal buckled under the force of the blow, and a panel broke off to fall to the ground with a resonating clang.

This isn't the end. She's not dead.

Abella had become the bait for the Master's trap, and there was no need for secrecy now. The Master knew Tenthil would come, knew the obviousness of the trap would be no deterrent.

Tenthil curled his hands into fists.

I will have her. She is mine, and I will have her.

Warm droplets of blood welled at the points where his claws pierced his skin.

"You will wish the Void had taken your name before I am through with you," Tenthil vowed.

TWENTY-ONE

When Abella drifted up to consciousness, she was in a place so dark that she wondered, for a few terrified moments, if she hadn't woken at all. She flinched and cried out for Tenthil, but her lips were sealed, reducing her voice to a muffled moan. Awareness swept over her like a tidal wave crashing against the shore—she was in a tight, enclosed space, hands tied behind her back, and the occasional swaying of the floor suggested she was in a moving vehicle. The sensation was reminiscent of riding in the cage on the back of Cullion's hovercar.

She remembered the tralix plowing into her and Tenthil, remembered breaking away from Tenthil's hold, remembered falling and landing on her ass hard enough to rattle her teeth. She'd been stunned for a moment; if she hadn't known any better, she might've thought she'd been hit by a truck.

Then there'd been hands on her arms—strong hands. She'd known they weren't Tenthil's by the indifference in their iron grasps. But before she could struggle against their hold, before she could even call Tenthil's name, there'd been a prick on her neck and then...

Nothing.

Abella drew in a deep, shuddering breath and attempted to ease her trembling, but she couldn't get enough air into her lungs. She didn't know where Tenthil was, didn't know where she was, only that they weren't together and that this situation was too much like the night she'd been taken from Earth—bound and gagged, alone in a dark place with no idea what was happening.

She clenched her fists; her palms were clammy, and her fingers tingled uncomfortably thanks to her circulation being restricted by her bindings.

Just breathe. Just breathe.

She closed her eyes—which made no difference in the level of darkness—and exhaled, flaring her nostrils. Her next inhalation was a bit more measured, a bit more controlled.

Freaking out isn't going to get me out of this.

She focused on her breathing, counting the length of each breath until they were slow and steady. At least a hundred questions swirled through her mind, but one was louder than the rest, repeating endlessly.

Where is Tenthil?

Eventually, the vehicle drew to a stop, momentarily forcing her weight against the front wall. Doors opened and closed, their sound muted and distant. A moment later, the ceiling of her cramped compartment lifted away.

Abella squinted against the light. Shadowy figures grabbed her arms and hauled her up. She twisted and kicked, but her captors had the advantage of strength and numbers. Their fingers dug into her flesh as one of them pulled a black cloth sack over her head.

She screamed impotently against her sealed lips.

Her feet had barely touched the ground before she kicked at her captors again. None of them loosened their hold even slightly. Her shoulders burned as though her arms were going to rip out of their sockets, but she refused to give in, refused to make it easy.

They didn't strike her, didn't tighten their grasps, they simply carried her onward. Her continued struggles only tired Abella. Her captors seemed totally unfazed, and they didn't make a single sound as they moved; even their footsteps were somehow silent.

Abella suddenly knew where she was. Knew *who* had her.

She struggled to keep her breathing steady as her panic soared.

They finally came to a stop and released their hold on her. Abella fell, hitting the ground hard on her shoulder. Someone grabbed her wrist bindings, yanking them back, and she cried out against the strain on her aching joints. The pressure ceased when the bindings came loose and were pulled away. Her hands fell to the stone floor, numb and useless, as feeling slowly returned to her limbs on waves of painful prickles.

The cloth sack was torn off suddenly, taking a few strands of her hair with it.

The light momentarily blinded her, and she flinched away from it, squeezing her eyes shut. A sting pulsed across her scalp. Hesitantly, she opened her eyes again, blinking rapidly as they adjusted to the new light. She pushed herself up on her hands and took in her new surroundings through gaps in the hair that had fallen into her face.

She was in a circular room—or at least in what *appeared* to be a room. A cone of light from above illuminated the stone floor, but the walls and ceiling were obscured by thick shadow. Overhead, faint points of light and blotches of understated color swirled through the darkness, creating the sense that Abella was looking at a fathomless, ever-changing universe through a tinted window.

The only furnishing in the room was a lone wooden chair at the center that would've been at home in an Earth museum dedicated to life in centuries past.

Abella turned her head to face her captors, but they were gone—only that wall of impenetrable shadow loomed behind her, as though she'd materialized inside this room rather than having been dragged through a door. She lifted a hand to her mouth, and her probing fingers found a hardened, gel-like substance over the seam of her lips; she dug her nails beneath it and tore it off.

She opened her mouth and gasped at the burning sting.

Tossing the gel aside, she dragged a hand through her hair to pull it out of her face and slowly stood up.

A voice sounded from all around her, flowing out the darkness itself. "Have a seat."

The blood in her veins froze. She knew that voice, had heard it once before.

The Master.

Abella turned in place, scanning the seemingly empty room. "I'd rather not."

"I offer for your comfort," the Master replied, his deep voice underlaid by a raspy, echoing whisper. "Once we begin, you may find it preferable to sit."

"For some reason, I doubt you care about my comfort." Abella narrowed her eyes, but she still couldn't find him. "And begin what? What are you talking about?"

She halted her gaze on a patch of shadow along the wall blacker than the rest, and she stepped back as it coalesced into a figure.

He was taller than Tenthil, dressed in long black robes that obscured his body shape, and his face was hidden by hood and mask. This was the only being who seemed to instill any sort of fear in Tenthil. The one who'd shaped him, the one who'd controlled him.

"The most straightforward term is *interrogation*," the Master replied. He lifted a gloved hand, palm facing up, and gestured toward the chair with long, thin fingers. "But it doesn't need to be unpleasant."

Abella backed up several more steps. "I won't tell you anything about Tenthil."

The Master advanced smoothly, keeping up with her retreat, and lowered his arm. "You need not say a word. I will have the information I desire one way or another. Your resistance will only make it harder on *you*."

She turned and ran; only a few strides brought her into the shadow-shrouded wall. She slid her hands over its surface, searching for a door, a seam, a button, anything to indicate an exit.

There was nothing.

That was when she felt it—the brush of a cold finger through her mind, sifting her thoughts and leaving her momentarily bewildered. A shiver raced down her spine.

"Sit and relax, and this will be over quickly," said the Master.

Panic flaring, Abella spun around to find the Master directly in front of her. She stopped herself just before colliding with him and tilted her head back. His mask swirled with darkness so deep that it suggested light was merely an illusion, a figment of her imagination, and she felt that darkness staring at her, staring into her.

"No," she said, pressing back against the wall. She eased along it slowly, her arm outstretched, continuing her search for a means of escape.

"Tell me about your relationship with Tenthil."

Abella glared up at him and pressed her lips together. She'd given so much of herself to Cullion, had caved to so many of his demands, but she refused to give in now. She would never betray Tenthil.

Though the Master stood unmoving, his presence in Abella's mind strengthened; it felt like his hands, with their cold, spindly fingers, had plunged into her head to sort through her memories like he was browsing a collection of books in search of something interesting.

She squeezed her eyes shut and clenched her teeth, straining against the invasion. A dull throbbing resonated inside her skull. Despite her struggles, despite her expenditure of willpower, her thoughts drifted toward Tenthil. Her memories of their time together played in her mind as though she were watching a movie. Their first dance, their conversations, their caresses, their kisses, and every detail of their lovemaking —it was all there, laid bare.

I feel it inside. I recognize it in your scent. You are my mate.

"His *mate?*" the Master asked. "I knew you were important to my misguided disciple, but I underestimated his connection to you. Two animals maddened by one another's scent. It almost makes me regret what I must do."

"What the *fuck* are you?" Abella grated. The pain in her head sharpened with each second of his continued intrusion. She lifted her hands, pressing them over her temples. "Get out of my head!"

"I thought you were a symptom of his behavioral issues," the Master said.

The pressure increased, threatening to split her skull open. She dropped to her knees with an agonized cry.

"I thought I had forced those bestial instincts out of him, that I had created a being above the influence of such primal urges," he continued, "but they were lying dormant all along.

He may have hidden them for a time, but *nothing* remains hidden to me forever."

"Leave him alone," Abella rasped, glaring up at the being before her. Another wave of pain doubled her over. She dropped her hands, catching herself before she could strike the floor face first.

The Master's icy touch receded slightly from her mind. "A spirited creature. I wonder—"

Abella leapt to her feet and swung her arm, slamming her fist against his mask.

His head snapped to the side, and the mask clattered to the stone floor. Before she could recover from her attack, he backhanded her across the face, sending her reeling. Fire crackled across her cheek, and her back slammed against the wall. A metallic taste spread over her tongue. But she kept on her feet. She'd suffered worse in Cullion's *discipline room*.

Abella tilted her chin up and looked into the bared face of the being who wanted to kill her and her mate. She inhaled sharply.

The Master's skin was white, and strands of straight, black hair hung over his angular cheekbones. His lips, nearly as dark as his hair, were pressed into a tight line, and his hairless brows were angled downward. He *almost* looked human, almost looked handsome—were it not for his eyes.

His sclerae were jet black, his irises blood red, and three extra pairs of eyes, each a little smaller than the last, stared at her from his forehead.

They were the eyes of a hungry spider.

"It has been a long while since anyone saw my face," he said, his cold expression unchanging, "and longer still since anyone has surprised me. You are a fascinating creature. I will have to look more closely at your kind after you are gone. You might have made a talented acolyte."

Moving with a casualness that belied the situation, he walked to his mask, bent forward, and plucked it off the floor.

Abella remained in place, chest heaving with anxious, terrified breaths. She was afraid, but she wouldn't show it—she'd spent the last four years afraid, and it had never stopped her from seeking freedom. She understood this situation.

To Cullion, she'd been an animal in need of discipline. An exotic pet in a gilded cage. Favored by her owner but not exempt from his sadistic punishments. But here...here, she wasn't even an animal. She was the bait meant to lure an animal into a trap. She was meant to lead the man she loved to his death.

The Master straightened and held the mask aloft on his palm, regarding it. "Perhaps I will gift him with this final secret when he comes. Let him gaze upon the face of the one who made him."

"He's going to kill you," Abella said.

The Master turned his head toward her, his expression suddenly disinterested. "His name has already been whispered to the Void. His fate is sealed. But there are secrets in your mind that have not yet been offered, little human. Shall we search them out together? Shall I begin learning about your people while we await your beloved?"

Abella steeled herself, tried to block out his assault, but he broke through her mental barriers as though they were made of tissue paper. He clawed through her mind for what felt like an eternity, leaving nothing untouched. He took everything. She realized at some point that the sound in her ears was that of her own ragged screaming, but blackness claimed her a moment after, delivering her from the agony in her mind.

TWENTY-TWO

When he'd gone to liberate Abella from Cullion's manor, Tenthil had known returning to the temple would mean death —his own death. But so much had happened in the time since. So much had changed. To Tenthil the individual, the temple was doom, a final plunge into oblivion, the cold embrace of the Void. Tenthil the individual would have fought, driven by his survival instinct, and he would have died with a weapon in hand, unsurprised by the flow of his own blood over the uncaring stone floor.

But for Tenthil the mate of Abella, death was neither inevitable nor acceptable. His fight was not solely for survival. He wasn't seeking justice for the wrongs done to him, wasn't seeking payment for the choices stolen from him. Though bitterness, rebelliousness, and hatred fueled him as they always had, they were no longer his primary motivations. Not anymore. Even his anger, which burned with an intensity he'd never experienced, was not his main drive.

For the first time in his life, he was motivated by *love*.

Something he'd never been shown before Abella.

He understood now its breadth and complexity. Love was not a single idea, a single emotion—it was all ideas; it was all emotions; it was *everything*. In his love for Abella, Tenthil would face his own death.

And he would defy death to have her at his side again.

The Master had laid his trap, but his arrogance would lead him to an ultimately fatal mistake—he would wait at the center of his trap to spring it himself. To personally destroy his greatest creation...his greatest disappointment.

Tenthil eased the throttle, slowing the hoverbike. Its lights shed their glow on stained concrete, on graffiti and refuse, on a tunnel that served as a pathway to the temple of secrets—a temple buried deep in the filthy, stinking guts of a city a hundred thousand times too large for its own good. The shallow, murky runoff at the base of the tunnel rippled beneath the bike's pulsing antigrav drives.

He guided the hoverbike close to the tunnel wall, stopped, and pressed the concealed button on a nearby support beam. The hidden door opened as smoothly and silently as ever. He planted a boot against the wall, manipulated the bike's controls, and shoved off, swinging the bike's rear out to angle its front end into the tunnel opening. He switched off the lights.

Tenthil took a mental inventory of his gear as he piloted the vehicle along the tunnel; high-end combat armor, a pair of blasters on his hips, several knives and energy blades, explosives and stun charges secured in an armored belt case, and an auto-blaster slung over his shoulder. He'd obtained most of it in Nyssa Vye with Cullion's ill-earned credits.

It was more than he'd normally carry, but the Order was expecting him; stealth would avail him little, not against the Master's vigilance. Even if Tenthil hid himself from the surveillance recorders, the Master kept all possible points of entry monitored, and knew full well what to watch for. A door opening by itself was all the confirmation the Master would require of Tenthil's arrival.

The tunnel's lights activated one section at a time ahead of Tenthil's hoverbike. He clenched his jaw and forced most of his thoughts aside save the most important of them.

For Abella. For my mate.

Up ahead, the tunnel's gentle curve afforded him his first glimpse of the garage door. He swung the auto-blaster's grip into his right hand, planted its stock against his shoulder, and settled the barrel between the handlebars.

He'd spent most of his life training with Order acolytes under the Master's watch and tutelage. Despite the countless secrets the Master kept, Tenthil knew how his mysterious former leader thought. He knew how the Master utilized the Order's resources—acolytes included. And he knew there was no such thing as a perfect trap.

With his left thumb, Tenthil deactivated the energy field projected by the bike to block the wind. He cranked the throttle. The bike lurched forward with a sudden burst of speed.

The garage door began its smooth ascent.

Clamping his thighs against the sides of the bike, Tenthil piloted the vehicle up the curved wall of the tunnel and tensed his muscles as the vehicle flipped upside down. Gravity pulled against him, but he clung to the bike, keeping his eyes on the garage.

The opening door revealed the chamber beyond in small increments; the concrete entryway, painted with cautionary lines, the lower portions of the vehicles parked closest to the door, and finally, what Tenthil had anticipated—the feet and legs of at least half a dozen acolytes gathered in wait.

The first ambush.

Angling the blaster toward the acolytes, he depressed the trigger and swept the weapon from left to right. The blaster released whining thumps as it spewed bolts of plasma in rapid succession, filling the air with their pale blue glow. Many of the shots missed their marks, leaving smoldering holes in the floor and the vehicles, but enough struck true to send most of the acolytes down to the floor. Tenthil swung the weapon back in the opposite direction, still holding the trigger, before any of the acolytes could so much as writhe in pain due to their wounds. Their armor didn't long protect them from the stream of super-heated plasma.

Heaving with his legs, Tenthil swung the hoverbike right-side up just as the door opened wide enough for the remaining acolytes—positioned in the cover of the parked vehicles—to return fire. Tenthil cut the bike's antigrav for an instant, dropping it back to the floor of the tunnel. The rear end struck the ground with a grating, metallic scrape before he flicked the antigrav back on. The vehicle bounced back up to its minimum cruising height of half a meter.

The crackling white orbs the acolytes had fired from their shock staves struck the ceiling and dissipated.

If they were using shock staves, which could be adjusted to fire immobilizing projectiles or strike in melee range with the same paralyzing energy, they meant to take him alive.

Perhaps they didn't understand the stakes of this battle.

He maxed the hoverbike's throttle and fired another spray of bolts at the acolytes before they could unleash a second volley. They ducked behind their cover; whether he'd hit any of them or not didn't matter, only that he was afforded a moment to breathe.

As the hoverbike darted through the garage door, he angled it toward one of the hovercars sheltering an acolyte, braced himself, and leapt off the bike. The hoverbike smashed into the parked vehicle with a deafening crash. Bent metal and shattered parts burst outward from the point of impact, and the hovercar slammed into the next vehicle in line to produce another huge crash.

Tenthil hit the ground hard on his shoulder and rolled, his momentum stopping only when his body struck another stationary vehicle. He shook off the pain. His armor had absorbed the worst of the impact, and he could not allow himself to be slow. Not until he was holding Abella again. He shoved to his feet, letting the auto-blaster fall away and hang by its shoulder strap, and drew one of his blasters and an arc grenade.

The footsteps of the advancing acolytes were almost silent —but *almost* was not enough to save them.

He activated the arc grenade and tossed it toward the approaching acolytes before ducking around the backside of the vehicle he'd landed against. A frenzy of hurried movement preceded the detonation. The garage was lit up for a fraction of a second by an intense white flash accompanied by the sound of crackling, buzzing electricity.

Tenthil drew a second blaster and stepped out from behind his cover to advance deeper into the garage.

Two acolytes writhed on the floor beneath a thin cloud of smoke. Three of their comrades lay nearby, their contorted, unmoving bodies covered in electric burns from which curled fresh wisps of smoke. The sizzling of their flesh was audible. Tenthil swung his attention away from them, turning toward the movement at the edge of his vision. He fired before allowing himself conscious thought. His shots ricocheted off the armor-reinforced hood of one of the vehicles across the garage, catching the acolyte hiding behind it in the face, but his other shots were too high to strike his secondary target.

Several shock-orbs darted toward Tenthil. He ducked under them—their electric thrum lifted his hair with static as they darted overhead—and hurried along the wall, directing his blasters at the rows between the stationary vehicles.

The two nearest acolytes, kneeling behind separate vehicles on opposite ends of one of the rows, seemed unprepared for Tenthil's aggressiveness. He fired a torrent of bolts at them with both blasters, enough to overwhelm their armor and ensure they wouldn't survive the resulting wounds.

These assassins had been taught that planning and patience were the best means of achieving the cleanest possible kill, of reaching maximum efficiency, of guarding the Order's secrets. Perhaps that was what they'd expected from Tenthil—clear-headedness and calm in the face of danger; a cold, methodical approach; maximum efficiency.

They'd likely expected him to creep into the temple like a shadow.

But he was no longer a shadow. He was a fiery harbinger of vengeance. He was the antithesis of the Void.

He continued his advance, swaying aside to avoid another acolyte's shot before squeezing off five plasma bolts in quick succession; three struck his target's armor, dissipating harmlessly, while the final two hit the acolyte in the face.

Tenthil swung his arms to the right, toward the movement in his peripheral vision. A pair of acolytes charged toward him along the wall; they fired their shock staves just as he fired his blasters.

He had only enough time to heave his weight away from the wall and release the blasters—if his body seized, he'd risk shooting himself—before the shock orbs struck him in the chest. Electricity arced through his body, locking his muscles. He hit the ground hard, fingers clenching, back arching, and head tilting back against the concrete.

Growling, he forced his arms down, flattened his palms on the floor, and pushed himself up. Physical pain was meaningless to him. Nothing they could do would compare to the anguish of losing Abella. Just the thought of never again seeing her, never again speaking with her, holding her, or touching her, was more than he could bear. He wouldn't accept it.

The first of the advancing acolytes rounded the vehicle behind which Tenthil had thrown himself, holding his shock staff as a melee weapon—a pulsing beam of energy ran along its shaft from one end to the other, several centimeters away from the grip.

Tenthil slammed the heel of his boot into the side of the acolyte's knee.

The acolyte lost his balance, his upper body tipping in the opposite direction of his buckling knee, and planted the butt of his weapon on the floor in an attempt to right himself. Scrambling to his feet, Tenthil grasped a handful of hair at the base of the acolyte's skull. He kicked the bottom of the shock staff, avoiding its energy beam by a finger's width.

With his only support knocked away, the acolyte fell forward, and Tenthil shoved hard to help him along. The acolyte's face smashed into the next hovercar hard enough to leave a large dent on the door.

The second acolyte leapt over his collapsing companion and thrust his shock staff toward Tenthil, likely hoping to capitalize upon the relatively narrow space and catch his foe unable to maneuver away.

Tenthil grunted and twisted aside. The shock staff zipped through the air a hair's breadth from his face. He swung a hand up and wrapped his fingers around the shaft, ignoring the thrumming of the energy beam near his fingers and nose, and pulled.

Off-balance after his attack, the acolyte stumbled forward. Tenthil thrust his free hand out and caught the acolyte by the throat, digging his claws into flesh. He squeezed.

The acolyte let out a gurgling choke, released the shock staff from his nerveless fingers, and crumpled to the floor. Tenthil tore his hand away and flicked his wrist, splattering blood and a few tattered chunks of flesh onto the concrete. He tossed the shock staff aside with his other hand.

Without hesitation, Tenthil crouched and collected his discarded blasters. He dropped one into its holster and opened the other's breach, dumping the partially depleted power cell and replacing it with another from his belt. Once the breach was closed, he continued along the wall toward the garage's interior door. The remaining acolytes fired at him from the opposite side of the garage; they were clustered around one of the larger vehicles, using its bulk for cover.

Tenthil extended his right arm and squeezed off a few shots, forcing the acolytes to duck behind the vehicle, while he dropped his left hand to his explosives case. He withdrew a fusion charge and threw it across the garage. It bounced once and slid to a stop under the large vehicle. He lowered the barrel of his blaster and fired one more bolt—this time at the charge.

Tenthil dove behind the nearest hovercar as a pair of explosions boomed and sent heated air and melted, smoking debris outward from their point of origin. The red light of the detonating charge mingled with the blue of an exploding antigrav engine to briefly color the wall. Keeping his attention on the door leading into the temple, he drew and reloaded his secondary blaster one-handed. Pieces of the vehicle from across the garage clattered to the floor around him and thudded atop the hovercar at his back.

When the explosions' echoes finally faded, only the sounds of crackling flames and the muffled, pained moans of the wounded remained.

Tenthil rose and proceeded toward the temple door. He encountered no other acolytes along the way.

The door was unlocked, and the dark hallway beyond it was deserted. He holstered his blasters and swung the auto-blaster to his front, taking it in both hands and steadying it against his shoulder. His heart pounded as he stalked the silent corridor; this battlefield was very different than the garage. Within the temple's relatively tight quarters, amongst its abundant shadows, claiming the element of surprise became a matter of caution rather than aggression. The entire Order knew he was here now, without a doubt. The outcomes of his encounters within these walls would be decided by who detected their foe first—and who acted quickest.

The vestibule was also empty, and the double doors to the courtyard stood open. Tenthil kept against the wall on which the doorway was positioned as he approached the opening. He leaned to the side to check the corners in the cloister before stepping through.

Silence reigned in the courtyard. The dark, false sky loomed above, bearing no trace of its usual stars and galaxies. Tenthil walked forward. His skin itched with the sensation of being watched, of being too exposed, but he wouldn't stop. Not until he had Abella.

Though he continued scanning his surroundings, he slowed his pace as he passed the Well of Secrets. Leaning closer to its inky contents, he whispered, "The one who calls himself the Master, in any and all of his names."

Tenthil turned his eyes toward the doors leading into the knave; it was the most direct route to reach the Master's chamber, but the massive room had little practical cover. In such an open space, Tenthil's anger and hatred could not shield him from being overrun.

Hold on, Abella. I am coming.

Opting for an alternate pathway through one of the side wings, he exited the courtyard and moved quickly and silently through the halls. In the back of his mind, he tracked his steps, counting down the distance between himself and the Master.

Beneath the fury and instinct raging through him flowed a strange sense of predetermination; part of him had always known he'd one day stand against the Master, that one of them had always been the other's eventual doom, but he could never have guessed how high the stakes would be during their inevitable confrontation. Tenthil had never valued anything above his own life—which even he had seen as ultimately expendable.

But now Tenthil had Abella. She'd changed everything.

A scent lingered on the air; though it was little more than a ghostly suggestion, it was undeniably *hers*. She'd passed through these halls recently.

The soft slide of a boot over the floor brought Tenthil to an abrupt halt. The sound had come from an intersecting corridor a few paces ahead. He glanced over his shoulder to confirm the hallway was clear behind him before resuming his slow advance. He heard another sound when he drew within a meter of the intersection—quiet breathing.

Releasing the auto-blaster's fore grip, he dropped his left hand to the explosives case on his belt and pressed the release on its lid. The latch opened with a tiny click that resonated up and down the otherwise silent hallway.

Black-clad acolytes leapt around the corner and into Tenthil's hallway—a large borian, a horned groalthuun, and a pair of lanky, violet-and-white-eyed daevahs with identical-but-mirrored white stripes on their cerulean skin. Tenthil squeezed the auto-blaster's trigger, firing a burst of plasma bolts into the borian's chest armor.

Before the blaster fire could penetrate the armor, the groalthuun lunged and swung his shock staff in a downward arc, striking the auto-blaster near the end of its barrel. The force of the blow knocked the weapon from Tenthil's grasp. Tenthil sidestepped a kick from the borian, whose breastplate glowed with heat from the plasma buildup, and shrugged off the auto-blaster's shoulder strap. The auto-blaster clattered on the stone floor as the groalthuun swung the staff again.

Tenthil ducked under the blow, narrowly avoiding the crackling electric beam, and only barely raised his left arm in time to deflect a heavy punch from the borian. Dropping lower, he swept out his right leg, knocking the groalthuun's feet out from beneath him, and rolled backward. He drew the hilt of an energy blade as he sprang to his feet. Green light bathed the nearby walls when he activated the weapon, cast by the broad, flat, thrumming plasma blade it had formed.

The borian produced his own energy blade and stepped past the groalthuun, who regained his feet a moment later. The narrowness of the hallway forced the daevahs to hang back while the borian and the groalthuun advanced.

No more obstacles.

Before his foes could attack, Tenthil charged at them, swinging his blade in flowing, continuous arcs. The blade's motion left no opening for counterattack from the acolytes; the borian and the groalthuun backpedaled, parrying furiously with their own weapons. Flashes of heat and light punctuated every bit of contact between the blades and the staff.

As Tenthil swung his blade down, the groalthuun spread his arms wide and blocked the blow with the center of his staff. The electric beam spanning the staff's length hummed and hissed, binding the energy blade.

With a growl, Tenthil forced his blade down. The electric band sputtered, wavered, and broke. An instant later, the energy blade sliced clean through the other weapon's shaft.

The groalthuun's stance crumbled as his weapon split in half. He swayed backward to avoid the tip of Tenthil's blade, which caught the groalthuun's armor and cut a sizzling trail down the breastplate. The groalthuun stumbled into the borian behind him.

Tenthil grasped his secondary blaster with his left hand, flicked the power to maximum with his thumb as he drew it, and angled the barrel toward the off-balance groalthuun. He pulled the trigger. The weapon emitted a high-pitched whine, and Tenthil felt its building heat through his glove.

The groalthuun's eyes rounded.

A massive burst of plasma erupted from the blaster's barrel, engulfing the groalthuun's upper body.

When the blast ended, the groalthuun had been reduced to nothing more than a pair of legs held together by a smoldering pelvis. The left half of the borian's torso was missing, leaving only charred flesh and glowing embers around the edge of the immense wound. The plasma's path continued through the bodies, having left a massive, semi-circular hole in the corner of the intersection and an even larger one in the wall across from it. The borian and groalthuun's remains collapsed.

The daevahs—who'd managed to flatten themselves on the floor just before the blast—stood up in unison. Each raised an energy blade, taking two-handed grips on the weapons, and narrowed their eyes. Their long, thin tails swayed side to side in sync with one another.

Tenthil knew little about these specific daevahs, but he knew enough about their species to recognize the threat they posed—male daevahs were always born as twins, linked through a psychic connection.

He tossed the smoking blaster aside. The air stank of burned flesh, shorted electronics, and melting stone, but beneath it all, Abella's faint-yet-unmistakable scent lingered.

She was alive. She had to be. And she needed Tenthil.

He lunged forward and attacked just as the daevahs made their moves.

The narrow corridor became a blur of slashing energy blades, which left temporarily glowing scars on the walls as the combatants flowed through the steps of their deadly dance. Tenthil soon found himself on the defensive; though neither daevah could match his individual speed or skill, their coordinated attacks left no gaps in their collective defense and forced Tenthil to create vulnerabilities in his guard to protect himself —parrying one of their blades often meant leaving himself open to the other.

His frustration mounted as the twin daevahs advanced. He would not accept defeat, would not tolerate delay. Shifting his stance so his body was perpendicular to the acolytes, he extended his right arm to parry their attacks. The change hid his left hand from them for long enough to pluck a stun charge from his belt. He activated the device's on-impact detonator.

Tenthil growled and unleashed a quick series of wild counterattacks, briefly creating a wall of whirring plasma between himself and his foes. The daevahs took the most sensible action —they retreated just beyond the range of his swings. He hopped back and snapped his left hand forward, releasing the stun charge, and closed his eyes.

The bright flash of the device's detonation was visible even through his eyelids, and the boom—amplified by the stone walls, floor, and ceiling—deafened him, leaving a loud, insistent ringing in his ears. He slitted his eyes; the daevahs had their forearms over their eyes, energy blades held vertically in a blind, uncertain defense.

Heartbeat thumping in his head, Tenthil dove forward.

The daevahs lashed out with their weapons simultaneously. The energy blades sliced through the air over Tenthil's back as he dropped low and rolled between his foes, catching himself on one knee behind them. With one foot, he spun himself around, pivoting on his knee, and swung his weapon backhanded. The blade traced a wide arc from one wall to the other, cleaving through both daevahs at their waists.

With eyes wide and unseeing, the daevahs turned their faces toward one another.

Tenthil stood up as the twins fell, their torsos separating from their legs on the way down.

Apart from the bodies, the hallway was empty, and silence reasserted itself as the ringing in Tenthil's ears subsided. He deactivated the blade, tossed the hilt into his left hand, and drew the blaster from his right hip before continuing onward. The corridors were increasingly dark and devoid of life. Tenthil felt as though he were tumbling ever deeper into space, into emptiness, and the only possible destination was the Void itself. He was charging head-first into the darkness that terrified so many people.

But Tenthil harbored no fear; wherever his mate was, he would go to her. He would follow her beyond the universe's edge.

A right turn led him to the stairs, which he climbed quickly and cautiously, keeping his blaster at the ready. But the stairs were clear, as was the hallway into which they let out. His suspicions peaked as he moved through the corridors leading to the main hall, where only the cold, faceless statues in the alcoves along its length greeted him.

Tenthil had never liked those statues.

As he stalked toward the ominous door at the hallway's end, checking every alcove and side-corridor, his rage blazed anew. He had no idea how many acolytes dwelled in this temple—no one did save the Master and, perhaps, his second-in-command—but Tenthil knew he hadn't killed them all. Not even close.

When Tenthil was within ten paces of the Master's chamber, a black-clad figure stepped out from the righthand alcove nearest the door. He knew her before she reached up and pulled back her hood. The resentment in her stance was unmistakable.

Corelthi's eyes were blazing as they met Tenthil's. "He wouldn't let me hunt you."

Tenthil stopped and resisted the instinct to shoot the volturian acolyte; he *knew* Abella was somewhere behind that door, and there was too great a risk of the bolt penetrating into the room and harming her.

"Even after all this, he's still going easy on you." Corelthi sneered and stepped forward, offering Tenthil a glimpse of the blaster in her right hand. "You've killed what, twenty-five of our brothers and sisters now? Thirty? His judgment is clouded when it comes to you, wretch. No more lives will be sacrificed to capture you."

She raised her blaster. "*I* am going to do what should've been done long ago."

Tenthil leapt aside as she fired. He rolled into the cover of the nearest alcove, plasma bolts zipping through the air behind him. Several shots sizzled through the wall over his head, dropping globs of molten stone onto his clothing.

He ducked as low as he could, ignoring the searing sting of the debris. She'd change the angle of her fire soon, and when she did, his cover would count for little. It was all a matter of luck; if she struck his armor, he'd have a chance, but if she hit his head...

The blaster fire ceased, and Tenthil's sensitive ears picked up a faint clicking—the sound of a blaster's power output being adjusted.

Tenthil sprang out of the alcove. Corelthi tracked him with the blaster, squeezing its trigger; the weapon produced a familiar high-pitched whine as it charged. Before he landed on the floor, Tenthil activated the energy blade in his left hand and threw it.

Corelthi's eyes widened.

The whirling energy blade struck her weapon before it could fire its supercharged blast.

Tenthil slid behind one of the statues as Corelthi's blaster exploded. Intense heat swept past him, and the dark hallway was momentarily illuminated by near-blinding light. He gritted his teeth and slitted his eyes.

The heat and light faded quickly. Releasing a ragged breath, Tenthil stood up to survey the damage.

An almost spherical, three-meter-wide chunk of the hallway—floor, walls, and ceiling—had been blasted away, parts of it still glowing orange with heat. Dark scorch marks extended beyond the sphere, and the floor was littered with flakes of ash and blackened rubble. Nothing remained of Corelthi.

Tenthil drew his spare energy blade as he strode past the destruction, avoiding the patches of molten stone. When he finally reached the door to the Master's chamber, he didn't slow; he grasped the handle and tugged it open hard enough for it slam against the wall.

He stepped through the doorway, and his heart skipped a beat.

Abella sat on the chair in the center of the circular room. Her head was tilted to the side, cheek resting on her shoulder. The sheen of sweat on her face glittered under the overhead light, her skin was paler than ever, and there were bags under her eyes.

Her chest expanded and relaxed with a slow breath that disturbed the strands hair hanging in her face. The dark bruise on her cheek and the trail of dried blood leading down from her nose were sure evidence of the Master having interrogated her.

As his anger flared to new heights, Tenthil was torn. Though his instincts demanded he go to her, they also insisted that doing so would be his end. Lowering his guard for even an instant would grant the Master more than enough time to strike.

The door slammed shut behind Tenthil, and he was suddenly aware of a familiar presence.

"Finally returned to us," the Master said, his voice flowing from the thick shadows ringing the room, "and all because of this weak, soft creature."

A chill crept up Tenthil's spine. He clenched his teeth as the sensation solidified and pressed into his skull.

"I warned you, Tenthil. Warned you of the consequences," the Master continued. "You made your choices knowing full well what I would have to do. I am disappointed. Despite your flaws, you were my best."

The Master's words projected from everywhere and nowhere, curling around Tenthil like wisps of smoke clinging to his clothing—intangible, persistent, and unavoidable. Normally, his hearing could pinpoint the source of even soft sounds, but it couldn't be trusted here. Couldn't be trusted against this foe.

For Abella. Must overcome him for her.

The icy touch in his mind slithered deeper.

"For *her*?" the Master asked. "Everything I gave you—every enhancement, every advantage—you've thrown away to chase a female like an animal maddened by mating season heat. I suppose I expected better of your inevitable betrayal. Better than *this*."

Tenthil inhaled through his nostrils. This room had always possessed a unique aroma that was slightly separated from the Master's, which itself had a faint spice to it unlike anything else Tenthil had smelled in the Infinite City.

It was that slighty spicy scent upon which Tenthil focused.

Though it was diffused throughout the air, it was most strongly concentrated at one particular point amidst the shadows.

No more games, he thought.

"Indeed," the Master purred.

Snapping his torso toward the Master's scent, Tenthil fired three quick shots into the shadows. The glowing plasma bolts were swallowed by the darkness, hissing as they impacted something unseen within it.

"Clever beast," the Master said, darting out of the shadows to the right of Tenthil's shots.

Tenthil swung his weapon toward his foe, but the Master caught his wrist in his long-fingered right hand. The strength in that grip rivaled Tenthil's. He could feel the Master's smile even through the concealment of that featureless black mask.

For Abella.

Tenthil lifted his foot off the floor and kicked at the Master's leg. Before he was halfway through the action, the Master tugged him forward and slammed his left fist into Tenthil's cheek.

The force of the blow snapped Tenthil's head to the side and blasted a wave of pain across his face. A tang of blood joined the venom-induced bitterness on his tongue. The Master twisted Tenthil's wrist, breaking his hold on the blaster, which clattered to the floor. Tenthil flicked on the energy blade in his left hand and thrust its point over his right arm, aiming for the Master's face.

The Master swayed out of the blade's path and forced Tenthil's right arm up. The edge of the blade seared through Tenthil's armor and bit into the flesh of his forearm, sending an agonized, stinging jolt along the entire limb.

Growling, Tenthil raised the blade slightly and swung its tip toward the Master's head with a flick of his wrist.

The Master's black robes fluttered as he leaned backward, avoiding the energy blade, and lifted a bent leg. He released Tenthil's wrist and straightened the leg suddenly, his boot striking Tenthil in the ribs. Even through his armor, Tenthil felt the blow, and he was launched away, stopping only when his left shoulder and the side of his head slammed into a shadow-masked wall. He hurriedly disengaged the energy blade before it cut him again.

For Abella, Tenthil repeated in his head. He had to succeed for her. Had to overcome this final obstacle so he could give her the life she deserved, the life she wanted.

He had to win so she could *live.*

"Your little human cannot help you," the Master said. He made no move to advance on Tenthil again. "Such base, animalistic drives are what brought you to this point. Though I must confess, her fiery spirit has inspired me to offer you one final gift before I end you. A last secret you may carry to the Void."

Tenthil pushed himself off the wall and swayed as his legs reluctantly took his weight. For a moment, his vision blurred. If he'd been forced to choose between taking another of the Master's kicks and getting run over by a tralix, he would've picked the tralix without hesitation.

The Master raised his hands, grasping his mask with one and his hood with the other. He pulled back the hood and slid off the mask simultaneously.

Over his years in the Order, Tenthil had speculated as to the Master's species many times, though he'd never come up with any solid guesses. There'd been too few clues to pierce the cloud of mystery the Master had kept around himself.

He would never have guessed the truth.

The Master was a kal'zik—a member of one of the ancient species who'd founded the Consortium and built Arthos. A member of one of the species who lorded over the Infinite City and a huge swath of the universe beyond.

A member of one of the most powerful races in existence.

The Master stared at Tenthil with four pairs of red eyes, and his dark lips quirked up at one corner. He tossed his mask aside, grasped the inside hem of his robes, and pulled them apart, shrugging the garment off. The dark robes fell to the floor, revealing a lean but solidly built body clad in a form-fitting combat suit and a second set of arms.

Stretching those extra arms, the Master turned and walked to the side, preserving the distance between himself and Tenthil. "This is my gift to you. My final boon. Look upon the face of your Master before the Void takes you."

Tenthil shook his head, forcing away his lingering dizziness.

He held no illusions as to whether he deserved a quiet, happy life, but he would not give up his chance at one. He would not lose a single thing more to the Master.

The Master stood between Tenthil and Abella. That made him another obstacle to be eliminated. *Nothing* would keep Tenthil from his mate.

Tenthil grasped the hilt of the energy blade in both hands and reactivated it. He held the Master's gaze; the blade's glow gave the Master's white skin a green sheen.

"If nothing else, I will always recall your tenacity with fondness," the Master said.

The chill presence in Tenthil's mind slithered over his conscious thoughts. He growled and shoved it aside, charging at his enemy.

Tenthil attacked with speed and precision, seeking out any possible gaps in the Master's defenses, anything of which he could take advantage. The flashing blade traced green arcs through the air.

But the Master was just a little faster, keeping one step ahead of Tenthil. He didn't draw a weapon of his own, he simply sidestepped, swayed, and dodged, avoiding each of Tenthil's attacks, occasionally throwing a punch or a kick that struck with enough force to throw Tenthil off-balance.

Each time he was knocked away, Tenthil threw himself back into the fight with increased ferocity, but he remained cognizant of their positioning—steering the battle as far from Abella as possible.

His eyes darted to her for an instant. She looked so small and frail here, so worn, so *spent.*

The Master caught Tenthil's hands in all four of his own and squeezed. The energy blade's hilt creaked and groaned beneath the viselike pressure.

"She is a distraction," the Master said, leaning closer to Tenthil. The energy blade crackled between them, its reflection blazing in the Master's eyes. "A distraction for an ungrateful beast."

Something popped in Tenthil's left hand as his weapon's hilt buckled and collapsed. The pulsing blade flickered off.

Tenthil grunted against the pain and tensed his leg, meaning to kick the Master; before he could even move, the Master stomped on his foot and leaned his weight forward, pinning it painfully in place.

"I made you," the Master said. "I *own* you. I am inside your head. There is nothing you can do that I will not foresee."

Heat flared in Tenthil's chest as he struggled against the Master's hold. The cords on his neck stood out, his breath caught in his throat, and his arms trembled with the exertion. The Master swayed slightly as Tenthil poured more strength into his struggle. The energy blade's grip crumbled further, and pieces of it dropped to the floor with metallic *pings.*

For Abella...for...

The Master grinned, revealing a mouthful of pointed teeth. "Once you are resting in the Void's embrace, I will send her to join you. You may spend eternity searching the darkness for one another in vain. Two animals chasing each other's tails through nothingness."

Tenthil's eyes flicked aside; he could see Abella's head and shoulders just past the master's black hair. She remained in that slumped position.

She'd suffered so much already—because of the people who tore her away from her home against her will, because of Cullion and his cronies, because of Tenthil's rash decisions. Because of the Master.

Tenthil knew the agony of the Master's mental intrusions. He knew what it felt like to have his secrets ripped out like underripe fruit torn from a tree, knew the pain of being totally vulnerable and utterly exposed to a hostile being.

The Master had caused her current suffering. The Master had threatened her life, and Tenthil knew the Master made no idle threats.

As Tenthil stared at his mate, the heat in his body intensified, creating an immense pressure more painful than any injury the Master had yet inflicted.

Abella was *his*. His to hold, his to protect, his to love. That was the truth in his mind, in his heart, and in the deepest, most primal parts of his soul.

Rage, possessiveness, and love smashed together and erupted from his chest in a deep, powerful roar.

Tenthil released control, released his years of training, released conscious thought. Instinct swept in, dark and bestial. A red haze fell over his vision as his muscles swelled.

Protect.

Destroy.

The Master's grin faltered.

Tenthil snapped his head forward, slamming his forehead into the Master's nose. There was a wet crack, and the Master reeled backward, but he did not release his hold. Tenthil tugged him back into another headbutt.

Snarling, the Master abruptly released Tenthil and staggered away. Black blood oozed from his nostrils. Its scent deepened Tenthil's crimson haze; he needed to smell more, to see more, to feel that blood coating his claws.

Red eyes burning with fury, the Master stepped forward, swinging two of his arms.

Tenthil leapt at him head-on. The blows struck him in the abdomen and chest, but were stopped by his armor. Tenthil's shoulder hit the kal'zik's chest. The momentum knocked them back several paces, but the Master held his footing. Tenthil threw his arms around the Master's middle and buried his claws into the Master's sides.

Releasing a pained cry, the Master rained blows onto Tenthil's back and head. The pain registered distantly for Tenthil; it wasn't a concern.

Kill.

Planting his feet on the floor, Tenthil sank his claws deeper and lifted the Master up, heaving him overhead. He arched his back to bridge the throw. The Master hit the floor on his back with a grunt, and Tenthil dropped his weight atop him.

Tenthil rolled aside, but one of the Master's hands snagged a fistful of his hair. The Master threw two quick punches, hitting Tenthil's nose and mouth; on his third strike, Tenthil opened his jaw wide and caught the Master's fist between his teeth. He bit down hard, sinking his fangs through tendons and muscle, feeling them scrape against bone. Bitter blood mingled with the venom he forced out of his glands.

The Master snarled. "I will not succumb to your poison, you—"

Tenthil caught two of the kal'zik's wrists, shredding the combat suit and the flesh beneath with his claws. The Master punched Tenthil on the ear with his free hand.

Numb to the pain and unfazed by the ringing in his ear, Tenthil scrambled atop the Master. He planted a knee on the kal'zik's abdomen and leaned on it. The Master strained against Tenthil's hold, sinking Tenthil's claws deeper and causing more damage to his flesh. Two more rapid blows struck Tenthil's cheek, breaking the hold of his teeth on the Master's hand. He felt a gush of warmth along the seam of his right scar. His red blood splattered onto the kal'zik's face.

The Master writhed beneath Tenthil, craning his neck back and exposing his throat.

Tenthil tore his claws free and thrust his fingers to the underside of the Master's chin. Baring his sharp teeth, the Master clenched Tenthil's wrists just as the claws pierced his skin, halting their progress. Black ichor welled beneath Tenthil's fingertips.

Venom dripped from Tenthil's fangs and onto the Master's face as he leaned over his prone enemy, forcing more and more weight and strength behind his hands. The Master punched and clawed with his free hands, but the power of his blows was waning, and Tenthil's bunched shoulders shrugged off the attacks.

Tenthil's nostrils flared at the aroma of the kal'zik's bitter blood. Staring into those eight red eyes, he roared and shoved down. His claws sank deep into the Master's flesh. Something crunched beneath Tenthil's fingers, and the Master's hold weakened further.

Hatred contorted the Master's face as he dug his fingertips into Tenthil's forearms and released a wet, choking cry. Blood bubbled from between his lips.

Icy, alien tendrils slithered through Tenthil's mind, but

there was nothing for them to latch onto, nothing for them to extract.

Dropping his face close to the Master's, Tenthil roared again, spraying blood and venom on his enemy's face as he pressed his thumbs into the Master's throat.

"For Abella!" Tenthil squeezed with all his might.

The Master's neck crunched, and a fresh blood burst from his lips with the release of his final, gurgling breath. His hands fell away one-by-one, splaying around him amidst a growing pool of black.

Tenthil tugged a hand free, curled it into a fist, and hammered it down on the Master's face repeatedly, snarling as he did so, releasing all his hatred, bitterness, and rage until the red eyes and white skin were an unrecognizable mass of glistening, ruined flesh.

He shoved himself up from the corpse and onto his feet, grabbed the Master by the ankles, and dragged him as far to the edge of the room, as far away from Abella as possible. He drew a knife and stabbed it into the Master's stomach, cutting open a slit. He dropped his left hand, still dripping with black blood, into his explosives pouch and withdrew a fusion charge. After activating the charge's timer, he stuffed the explosive into the slit and hurried to shield Abella with his body.

The slightly muffled explosion was punctuated by the sound of wet chunks of flesh splattering on the walls and floor, several of which struck the back of Tenthil's armor.

Ensure your target is dead. It was one of the Order's core tenets.

Tenthil knelt in front of Abella and looked her over for injuries before collecting the Master's robes from the floor. He used the garment to wipe away as much of the blood and gore clinging to his clothes and skin as he could. It was only as he did so that his injuries made themselves known. The dull aches suddenly permeating his body were nothing compared to the sharp, pulsing stings at the corner of his mouth and on his right forearm.

He forced himself to take a moment to ease a self-sealing bandage over his cheek and retrieve his fallen blaster, dropping it into its holster before he returned to Abella. He knelt again and slipped one arm behind her knees and the other behind her back.

Her soft, warm breath brushed over the skin of his neck as he lifted her against his chest. She seemed so slight, so delicate.

Tenthil bowed his head to place a kiss atop her hair. For a moment, he remained on one knee, lips pressed to her hair, and inhaled her scent, fighting a strange stinging in his eyes. His exhalations were shaky. The pressure in his chest hadn't subsided, though its source had changed; this wasn't rage and hatred, this was relief and love, this was a gratefulness so over-whelming that words could never encompass it.

He shifted his head, pressing his chin to her hair, and squeezed his eyes shut as tears flowed from them. His throat burned, but it had nothing to do with his mutilated vocal cords. In that moment, he felt more than he'd ever felt before, and he knew the darkness would never claim him, knew the Void held no sway over him. Abella was his beacon, a shining light against which the Void could never hope to stand.

Blinking the moisture from his eyes, he forced himself to his feet. "Just a little farther."

He didn't cast a single glance toward the Master's remains as he carried Abella out of the room.

The wide hallway was as silent and deserted. He walked at a steady pace, his aches more insistent with every step, and took her back along the path by which he'd come.

A few meters beyond the blast-damaged portion of the hall-way, Abella jerked awake, eyes flashing open. Her gaze was glassy with confusion. Her muscles tensed as she screamed and struggled against Tenthil's hold.

Tenthil stopped walking and lowered his head again. He clutched her close to him. "Shh. I have you, Abella."

She stilled and finally met his gaze. Her chest heaved with ragged breaths. "Tenthil?"

He rested his cheek against her forehead. "I have you," was all he could manage to say before his throat constricted.

She burst into tears and threw her arms around his neck, clinging to him as she shook with her sobs. "He was *inside* my head. I couldn't stop him, couldn't keep him out. He took *everything*. I thought he'd take you too."

"He's gone. One with his precious Void." Tenthil brushed his lips over her hair. "He could never take me from you. Nothing can."

She sniffled and pulled back. Her watery, red eyes found his again. Lowering one of her arms, she cupped his face, brushing her thumb over his cheek. Without another word, she kissed him. It was a desperate kiss, nearly broken by another sob, but she didn't stop; she only held him tighter.

Tenthil's aches and pains fell away while their lips were together. He'd have endured tenfold more suffering for that single kiss, would've fought the world for it. When she finally drew away from him to take in a shuddering breath, he licked her taste from his lips. Despite everything, he wanted her, then and there.

But they weren't safe. Though the Master was dead, they were still in his house.

"Little farther to go," he said as he resumed walking, turning onto the staircase that led down to the main floor. "We can rest soon."

Her grip on him strengthened briefly. "I can walk."

He frowned. He didn't want to let her go, didn't want to

have even the slightest distance between them, but he could better protect her if she was walking—at least then he could use his weapons freely and shield her with his body.

When they reached the bottom of the stairs, he gently set Abella on her feet, keeping one arm around her back. She put an arm around his waist and leaned against him for a few moments, swaying slightly. Once she'd found her balance, Tenthil drew his blaster and walked on with her tucked against his side, angling himself to remain ahead of her.

Neither of them spoke when they passed the scene of his battle with the borian, groalthuun, and daevahs. They encountered no living beings in those halls—not until they entered the courtyard.

Eight acolytes stood in front of the closed double doors that led into the vestibule and the garage beyond, armed with blasters, energy blades, and shock staves. Tension crackled through the air; though the acolytes kept their faces serious, their expressions hard, several of them fidgeted and repeatedly flicked their gazes toward their comrades as though uncertain of themselves.

Tenthil guided Abella behind him as he swept his gaze over his foes.

"Tenthil," Abella whispered fearfully.

He felt the gentle pressure of her hands against his back armor and found strength—found comfort—in her touch. He walked toward the Well of Secrets slowly, keeping his eyes on the acolytes, who made no move to attack despite their number advantage. Abella kept close on his heels as he mounted the broad steps to the edge of the well.

"I reclaim our names," he called. "Tenthil and Isabella Diane Mitchell. The Void no longer holds claim to us."

Several of the acolytes exchanged startled glances.

Tenthil released a slow breath. He'd have, at best, a second to act if things went wrong. It wasn't enough, not against so many. "Our contracts are closed. Do any of you object?"

The acolytes' eyes were fixed on him, and the weight of their gazes was heavier than the silence that settled over the courtyard.

One of the acolytes—the same female sedhi Tenthil had seen in the garage on the night he met Abella—took a single step forward. She bowed her head and crouched, deactivating her energy blade as she laid it on the ground. Without looking at Tenthil again, she rose, turned, and walked toward one of the side doors around the courtyard's edge.

One by one, the other acolytes followed her lead, laying down their weapons and departing, none making eye contact with Tenthil as they did so. Within a minute, Tenthil and Abella were alone.

Abella returned to his side and released a shaky breath as she put her arm around him. He settled his arm over her shoulders, and they stepped down from the well together. The false sky overhead didn't seem quite so dark while they crossed the courtyard.

When they reached the double doors, he shoved one open and crossed into the vestibule with Abella, pausing only long enough to turn and kick the door closed again. The echo of it slamming shut held a satisfying note of finality.

The Order of the Void was no longer his concern.

TWENTY-THREE

They returned to the safehouse in the Bowels after Tenthil abandoned the vehicle they'd taken from the temple garage and procured another hovercar. Neither of them had spoken as they traveled. Tenthil had kept a hand on Abella's thigh, thumb brushing absently over her pants, and she'd held her hand atop his. That simple contact had been enough to ground her, to chase away her sense of impossible, overwhelming vulnerability, to tell her he was real, alive, and with her.

As soon as they were inside the safehouse with the door closed, Abella threw herself against Tenthil, wrapping her arms around him. He stumbled backward into the door as he caught her in his embrace, and her hands hit the metal behind him, but she didn't register the pain, didn't care. She rested her cheek against his chest.

They had escaped the darkness and were together again. That was all that mattered.

She inhaled deeply, relishing his familiar scent despite it being layered with the smells of blood, smoke, and sweat. "Is it really over?"

He smoothed a palm down her hair. "Yes."

"They won't come after us anymore?"

"They won't. The Master and his second are gone, and we have reclaimed our lives."

"What was he, Tenthil? It was...it was like he was inside me. I couldn't stop him, couldn't push him out. He knew my past, my thoughts, my desires, everything about us." A shudder wracked her as a phantom of the Master's icy presence passed through her mind. Even the memory of his intrusion was almost too much to bear; it felt like insects clawing around in her skull.

"He was a kal'zik," he replied, voice weakening as he spoke, "one of the Consortium races. They are ancient and powerful. I know little beyond that."

Abella tilted her head back and looked up at him. Tenthil's pale gray skin was splattered with blood of various hues, but one color stood out from the rest—the crimson of his own blood. She lifted a hand to brush her fingertips beneath the scar on his right cheek, part of which looked like it had been freshly sealed.

She'd seen the remains of the assassins Tenthil had fought in the temple, had seen the odds he'd defied to rescue her. The sight had numbed her; when the need arose, he was more a force of nature than a man, unstoppable and merciless. Nothing standing between him and his goal would escape unscathed.

Now, without any doubts, she understood just how strong he was, just how dangerous...and just how vulnerable.

I could have lost him.

Stepping back, Abella took his hands and led him farther into the room. She stopped him beside the bed and removed his gun belt and weapons, carefully setting them on the nearby table, before setting to work on his armor. She let the blood-splattered plates fall to floor. Her gaze rose to his as she unfastened his shirt, pushed it down his shoulders, and slid it gently off his arms.

Tears welled in her eyes as she took in the damage wrought to his body.

Dark bruises mottled his skin in several places, the worst of them on his side and shoulders, and there was a blackened wound on his right forearm like the one he'd received fighting the acolytes in the alleyway several days before. His face showed more signs of bruising, and, now that she was looking closely, she *knew* he'd hastily bandaged his cheek scar, which had clearly split open recently.

"Oh, Tenthil," she whispered, lightly running her fingers over the bruises on his chest. She didn't know what he would have looked like had he not been wearing armor during the fighting—she didn't even want to imagine. Hot tears spilled down her cheeks.

He moved a hand to her face and wiped away the moisture with the back of his finger; something in his hand cracked as he moved his wrist.

She grabbed his forearm. "Stop. Please stop. Just...tell me what to do to help you."

The left corner of his mouth lifted in a small, lopsided smile. "Love me."

Abella stared up at him, jaw hanging open, for several seconds. "But you're *hurt!* You can't really want to...to..."

He chuckled and shook his head, mirth dancing in his silver eyes like she'd never seen. "Need a few hours to heal before *that*. Just need your love now. And a shower."

Her cheeks heated, and—despite their situation, despite all they'd just gone through—arousal bloomed within her core. Something about the look in his eyes and the sound of his laughter deeply affected her. She returned the smile. "I can do that."

After guiding him to sit on the bed, she knelt on the floor, tugged off his boots, and set them aside. She helped him remove his remaining clothing; his nakedness only revealed more of the damage he'd suffered. Her heart ached.

The light touch of his knuckles against her cheek brought Abella's attention back to his face.

"You had the worst of it," he said softly.

"How could you possibly think what I had ·was worse? Look at you, Tenthil. You're covered in cuts, bruises, and blood."

"Most of the blood isn't mine."

"That doesn't change anything!"

Tenthil cupped her face, brushing loose strands of her hair back behind her ears. "My body will heal. Already is. But what he did to you..." He frowned and gently tapped the pad of his finger against her temple. "This doesn't heal as easily. I have carried those scars for years. They are the worst of them all."

Abella covered his hands with hers, briefly turned her face to kiss his palm, and closed her eyes as she leaned into his touch. His presence was a balm to her soul; she knew, in time, her scars from the Master would fade.

She looked back up at him. "I have you here with me now. That's all that matters."

He stared into her eyes before he slipped his hands beneath her arms and drew her body against his, slanting his mouth over hers. His kiss was as deep, as intense, and as passionate as his stare had been, and it sent a thrill through Abella from head to toe. Her only regret at that moment was that she still had her clothes on.

She slid her hands over his shoulders and down his back, careful of his wounds. She needed to touch him, to *feel* him, to lose herself in his embrace. Pressing her mouth harder against his, she parted her lips. She moaned at the first taste of his sweet venom and flicked her tongue over the tip of his fang, seeking more.

Tenthil's hands dropped to her ass. His fingers curled around each cheek, and he pulled her more firmly against him. His hard cock pressed along her belly.

Abella gasped, put her hands on his shoulders, and pushed back from him, breaking the kiss. "Tenthil, your wounds!"

"They can wait," he growled. "Need you *now*."

He turned, laid her atop the bed, and quickly divested her of her boots. Her breath hitched when he grasped the waistline of her pants and yanked them down her hips and legs. Excitement surged through her. He tossed them over his shoulder, spread her knees, and dropped his mouth to where she craved him most.

Abella cried out, propping herself up one elbow as she moved her other hand to his head. She caught his hair in her fingers, and it took everything in her not to tug on those silver locks as his tongue stroked her folds, dipped into her sex, and teased her clit. Pleasure coursed through her—so strong, so intense, so overwhelming that she attempted to close her legs to alleviate it. Tenthil only strengthened his grip on her thighs and spread them farther, opening her wider.

She moaned, unable to tear her eyes away from him as he greedily lapped at her. The sight of his face between her thighs sent a fresh wave of heat through Abella.

He met her gaze. His eyes were dark, sensual, gleaming with hunger and need.

All she wanted was him. She needed *him*.

"Now, Tenthil. Please," she begged. "I want you inside me. I need to feel you. All of you."

She felt Tenthil's fingers flex just before he surged up and over her. He caught her shirt with his hands and shredded it with his claws. He tore the tattered fabric from her body and lowered himself, settling his chest atop hers and dipping his head to claim her mouth.

Abella wrapped her arms around him and returned the kiss. The taste of his venom mixed with the flavor of her slick, which lingered on his lips. She relished the warmth of his bare skin against hers. It didn't matter that the blood of their enemies clung to him; she had her beast, her mate, her love. He was alive. *Alive.*

He wedged his hips between her thighs. A moment later, the head of his cock pressed against the opening of her sex. Abella moaned and undulated her hips.

"Now," she breathed. "Now, Tenthil."

Growling through bared teeth, he thrust his hips forward and sheathed his cock inside her.

Abella gasped, tightening her arms around him. He held himself still; his shaft stretched her, filled her, burned her, and she wanted *more.*

He placed his hands on the bed to brace himself over her, and Abella wrapped her legs around his hips, digging her heels into the backs of his thighs to pull him deeper. His mouth hovered above hers; they shared breaths as they stared into each other's eyes.

The fire in his gaze changed—his intensity eased without losing heat, his desperation abated without losing the glimmer of longing. Though his eyes remained fully black, a tender light shone within them. He rocked his hips, setting a slow rhythm, pressing farther into her with each undulation. Every stroke heightened her pleasure and her desire just a little more.

Leaning his face down, he kissed her again and again, over and over—on her lips, her cheeks, her chin and along her jaw, on her neck, shoulder, and collarbone. He leaned on one elbow and trailed his hand over her body from thigh to hip, from side to chest, and teased her budded nipple. She shivered in delight as he covered her breast with his palm.

On and on Tenthil rocked his hips without altering his pace. She clung to him while their breathy sighs and moans filled the room and their coupling brought them ever closer to the pinnacle of ecstasy. As much as she craved that final release, this slow-building sensation was a taste of paradise. There was no rush—they had time, time to be *together*, and she wanted to spend as many moments of her life as possible savoring her mate.

Abella's core tightened an instant before she was swept away on a wave of pleasure. She cried out his name and chanted her love for him as she rode torrential currents of bliss. Digging her nails into his shoulders, she tilted her head back and bared her throat, silently begging for her mate's intoxicating bite.

Tenthil groaned and moved his mouth up past her collarbone. His warm breath tickled the skin between her neck and shoulder for a moment before his fangs sank into her flesh. The brief prick of pain, followed by two rushes of exhilarating heat —venom flowing from his fangs and his seed pumping into her —launched her climax to new heights.

Muscles tensing, Tenthil growled against her shoulder. He tightened his hold on her and quickened his hips, pistoning back and forth until he and Abella, shuddering with the overwhelming power of their pleasure, collapsed onto the bed.

Abella ran her hands over Tenthil's back as they lay wrapped in each other's embraces. Each of the little tremors that flowed through him sparked a thrill in her. Turning her head, she brushed her lips over his temple and held him tighter.

Tenthil's chest rumbled, and he rasped her name against her neck before lifting his head and looking into her eyes. His brow softened as he brushed the backs of his fingers over her cheek.

"Never letting go again," he whispered.

She'd been angry that he'd withheld information from her, that he'd refused to bring her to the human embassy, that he'd claimed her as his without her say, but she would endure all of it again and again so long as it brought her back to this moment. Back to these feelings; she was protected, cherished, *loved*.

She would endure a hundred times as much so long as it brought her back to him.

Abella smiled and slid her hand to the nape of his neck. "Never."

TWENTY-FOUR

Abella glanced down at the tiny red mark on her wrist for what must've been the thousandth time and brushed a fingertip over it. In another day or two, it would fade away, but its significance would remain with her forever.

Alkorin had kept to his word. In four days, he'd created two ID chips with complete background information and integrated them into the Consortium systems. His delivery of the chips as promised had been enough to finally earn Tenthil's trust. They'd theorized together that Tenthil and Abella had been sold out to the Order by one of the informants who'd originally directed them to the forger. Alkorin had vowed to rectify the matter.

But none of that could bother Abella now; she and Tenthil were registered citizens of Arthos. They were free to go wherever they wanted.

Smiling, she looked at Tenthil as he maneuvered the hovercar into an upward-slanted express tunnel. He hadn't been exaggerating when he'd mentioned he healed fast—no evidence remained of the injuries he'd suffered at the temple. Abella, on the other hand, still sported some faint green and yellow bruising on her cheek.

Leaning toward Tenthil, Abella pressed her lips to the scar on his cheek.

He smiled the sort of easy, carefree smile she never would've expected him capable of when they first met. "Look outside."

"Why? All these tunnels look the same to me. I much prefer looking at you."

"Trust me."

With a chuckle, she turned her head to look out the window.

The lights, other vehicles, and signs flitted by in an almost hypnotic blur. It reminded her a little of the antigrav trains she'd taken to visit her family after she'd moved away for dance school, many of which had traveled at high speeds through long, subterranean tunnels.

The quality of the light changed gradually, growing brighter and somehow purer. She faced forward to see a wide opening ahead.

When they exited the tunnel, she had to lift a hand and squint to shield her eyes from the intense light. It took a few seconds for her eyes to adjust, and a few seconds more to realize it was *natural* light. She hadn't seen natural light in years.

The hovercar climbed at a sharp angle, moving through several free-floating rectangular frames that must've been there to guide traffic. Abella found herself staring up at a sky tinted pink, orange, and gold, dotted with soft clouds stained the same colors. She blinked away the tears suddenly misting her eyes.

When the hovercar finally leveled out, Abella's breath caught in her throat. A massive city sprawled out before her, stretching beyond the limits of her vision. Buildings of wildly varying size, shape, and architecture stood all around, many of them towering over the hovercar, which itself had to be hundreds of meters off the ground. Streets and walkways spanned gaps above and below in numerous tiers, reminding her a little of the Undercity—but this place was open to the air.

Plants in colors and varieties she couldn't have imagined in her wildest dreams adorned many of the buildings and pathways, and there were fountains, statues, and waterfalls everywhere. Sparkling canals of pure, cerulean water wound through the city, culminating in a massive lake. More buildings stood along the lake's far shore. Countless vehicles darted between and above the buildings, following the rectangular frameworks in seemingly endless streams, and tens of thousands—if not *millions*—of aliens wandered the streets and walkways.

Several clusters of buildings stood out from the rest, taller, more majestic, each group unified in its own unique style and coloration. They shone like beacons amongst the somewhat disjointed but no less beautiful structures surrounding them. She'd heard just enough about the city above the surface to guess that those clusters were the sanctums—the sanctums of the races comprising the Consortium.

But it was the city's backdrop that awed her more than anything else. The source of that bright, natural light wasn't a star like she'd expected—the sky was red near the horizon, colored by what looked like a huge, swirling cloud that was brightest near its center. A beam of light pierced its middle, fading somewhere high above. Though the sanctums were dim compared to that column of light, they all seamed to glow with just a hint of its impressive luminosity.

"What is that?" she asked.

"A quasar," Tenthil replied. "The Consortium draws energy from it to power this city."

"I've never seen anything like it. I mean, I vaguely recall hearing about them, and I think I've seen a picture or two, but Earth has nothing like this."

"It doesn't."

Something in Tenthil's tone pried her attention away from the beautiful, alien sky.

Abella turned her head to find him staring intently at her. Her face warmed under the intensity of his gaze, and she smiled. "There are plenty of others like me on Earth. Everywhere you look, there's another human."

Tenthil shifted his gaze back to the airspace in front of them. "No."

"What do you mean, *no?*"

"There's no one like you anywhere but right here."

Abella's heart quickened, and her belly fluttered with excitement. She clasped her hands together to stop herself from reaching for him. For someone who didn't speak often, he sure as hell knew the right words to say.

She ran her eyes over him, seriously contemplating climbing into his lap. "Are we almost there?"

He didn't look at her, but his nostrils flared, and his widening smile displayed his fangs. "A few more minutes. Will you last?"

Abella's gaze stopped on his mouth. She squeezed her thighs together; she knew *exactly* what that mouth could do. "I don't know."

He inhaled deeply and closed his eyes for a moment. His tongue slipped out and glided over his lips. "You tempt me, female."

Abella chuckled and leaned back in her seat, brushing her

finger over his forearm. It was as much touching as she could trust herself with while he was driving. "*After.*"

His smile faded. "Yes. After."

Her own smile fell at the sudden change in his demeanor. Before she could ask what was wrong, he broke the hovercar away from the flow of traffic and angled it down. They descended toward one of the smaller buildings. While much of the city looked alien in architecture and design, there was something familiar about this structure—beyond the patches of emerald grass and neatly trimmed shrubbery dominating the open space around it.

This building would've fit well in any city back on Earth.

Realization dawned on Abella when her eyes drifted to the building's entrance. Wide, gently sloping steps led to the doors, with a large fountain situated near their base. At least a dozen flagpoles stood around the fountain, flying flags representative of all the regions of Earth and the space colonies. The United Terran Federation flag was largest of all, positioned at the center.

"Is this...is this the human embassy?" Abella asked.

She saw Tenthil nod from the corner of her eye. Without speaking, he piloted the hovercar around the back of the embassy and down to a lower level, where they entered a parking area beneath the building. He directed the car into the first open space.

Tenthil disengaged the engine and settled his hands on the controls.

"I should not have taken this from you," he said, his voice so low and rough that Abella almost couldn't make out his words. "I should've given you the choice. A true choice."

Abella stared at him, brows low. The pleasure she'd felt only moments before was replaced with an almost nauseating dread. "What are you saying, Tenthil?"

"You have a home. A family."

"Yeah, I do."

"And you are *free*."

Abella searched his face. His pupils dilated and receded, as though he were struggling to maintain control, and palpable tension radiated from him.

"So, what? You're just going to drop me off here so we can go our separate ways?" Abella asked, glaring at him through tear-filled eyes as her hurt gave way to anger. She turned, opened the hovercar door, and climbed out, slamming the door behind her. She started walking; it didn't matter which direction she was going, as long as it was away.

She just...just needed time to think. To calm down.

Abella had only managed a few steps when a strong hand caught her arm. Tenthil spun her around to face him. When she turned her head away, he took hold of her chin and forced her to look at him.

"You have had your choices stolen from you for years," he said, his pupils swallowing his eyes. "And I was one of the people who took those choices from you."

"Shouldn't it already be clear the choice I made?" Abella jerked her chin away and smacked his arm, taking a step back. "After all this time with you saying *you're mine, I'm never letting you go*, and now you're just dropping me off? I chose you, Tenthil! You should have known that the moment I said I loved you!"

"And what have I ever known of love before you?" he demanded, moving forward to close the gap between them. "What choice did I ever give you but *me*? I want you, Abella, I *love* you, and that means I want you to choose the future that will make you the happiest. I want you to have what you want, not what I want."

Tears streamed down Abella's cheeks, and her throat constricted. "I want you to *keep* me, Tenthil."

Tenthil's eyes flared. The muscles of his jaw ticked, but he remained unmoving and silent. A million words roiled behind his gaze, but he seemed unable to get them out.

She raised her hands to cup his face. "I love my family, I miss them, but if I had to choose between you or them, I choose you, Tenthil. *You* make me the happiest, and I know we'll only be happier once we take our chance to live." She brushed her thumbs over his cheeks, gently tracing the raised scar tissue. "But I don't have to choose one or the other, I can have both. Come with me. To Earth. Meet my family...because you're already part of it. But if you'd prefer to go back to your home, I will go with you. I'll go anywhere with you, Tenthil, because my home is *with* you."

He took gentle hold of her wrists and rubbed his thumbs over the backs of her hands. "My only home is with you, Abella. I've never known another. But can I follow you there? Will they have me?"

"There's only one way to find out. *Together*. But no matter what, *I* will have you. *I* want you. Just don't abandon me."

"I didn't kill half the Order to abandon you, female," he said, voice ragged.

He slipped his arms around her, drew her body against his, and took her mouth in a passionate kiss. Abella slid her hands up his chest and clutched at his shirt, tilting her head to the side to allow him to deepen the kiss.

For a moment, she'd thought he had abandoned her, that he'd simply given her up despite all they'd gone through. That moment was all it had taken for her to *know*. Returning to Earth—to her family—alone would have destroyed her. Earth was not home without Tenthil. She loved him with every fiber of her being, and she belonged at his side. He was her mate, as she was his.

Soulmates.

Abella smiled and pulled her head back, breaking the kiss. She grinned as she looked up into his eyes. "Guess that says it all, doesn't it?"

"I'll show you more, Abella." Tenthil's grin revealed his wicked fangs, and his dark eyes glittered with promise. "*After.*"

EPILOGUE

California, Earth
Terran Year 2111

TENTHIL EASED the hovercar into its usual parking place beside Abella's, killed the engine, and climbed out of the vehicle. The wind sighed through the trees around their dwelling, rustling the foliage and spreading the sweet scent of living plants and aromatic wood. He paid little mind to the black hovercar behind Abella's; the company was expected.

Even after his years with Abella on Earth, it was still felt strange for him to be at ease, to let his guard down.

Mostly down, anyway.

His old life had taught him every shadow held a new danger, but he was learning how to relax, build relationships, and trust. Though shaking off his old habits was a slow process, he was making progress.

He filled his lungs with the fragrant air as he followed the path to the front door.

He entered the home—his home, *their* home—and glanced across the open living space, which was lit by streams of sunlight pouring through windows on the roof. The living room led directly to the kitchen, where Abella's father, Richard, stood fussing over something on the counter that served as the border between the two rooms.

Tenthil closed the door. Richard glanced up from his work and smiled, displaying those flat, white human teeth that had become so normal to Tenthil.

"Hey Tenthil," Richard said. "Abella said you wouldn't be home until later. Get off early?"

Tenthil nodded and walked across the living room, stopping across the counter from Richard. The human was only about ten centimeters shorter than Tenthil, but he was thin, and the lines around his eyes and mouth showed his age. But his eyes themselves—the same green as Abella's—were bright, intelligent, and usually full of joy. His short, dark hair was heavily streaked with gray.

Richard returned his attention to the tray in front of him. "Figured I'd pitch in and throw these together for dinner. I know Abella and Hannah have a lot going on with the festival tomorrow, so I wanted to give them one less thing to worry about."

Dozens of little sandwiches were arranged atop the tray, comprised of a variety of meats, cheeses, and garnishes. Tenthil had grown fond of sandwiches, especially the ones with peanut butter and jelly. Abella teased him about it sometimes, but always stole bites of those sandwiches when he made them.

"How's everything been going down at the base?" Richard asked.

"Same as always. They bring me soldiers. I train them." Tenthil reached across the counter for one of the sandwiches.

Richard pulled the tray out of Tenthil's reach and clucked

his tongue. "These are for dinner. You can have one when everyone else gets one too."

"I am not a child, Richard."

Richard's smile widened, and something twinkled in his eye—the same spark of joy Tenthil so often saw in Abella's gaze. He slid the tray closer. "*One*. But don't tell anyone, or I'll get swarmed, and everyone will be hungry again by the time we're supposed to eat."

Tenthil smirked and plucked up the sandwich that appeared to have the most meat, finishing it in two bites.

"How long do you have left on your contract?" Richard asked as he settled a clear plastic lid over the tray and carried it to the refrigerator.

"A year. But they already offered a renewal."

"They must love you down there."

"Don't know why."

The background Alkorin had fabricated for Tenthil's identification chip had included extensive experience in private security with a specialization in covert operations. Though it seemed a fitting cover—and one not far from the truth—it had caused him some trouble during the immigration process. The United Terran Federation had scrutinized his background thoroughly, suspecting him of malicious intent, but it had eventually led to opportunity; he possessed skills valuable to the terran defense forces, who were still new to matters of intergalactic security, technology, and tactics.

Though he'd not been told the details of the operations, he knew that the training he'd provided had led to terran special forces managing to track down and break at least one of the trafficking rings responsible for kidnapping humans and selling them in places like Nyssa Vye back in Arthos.

Richard laughed and turned on the sink, rinsing his hands.

"I'm proud of you, son. You're making the best of where you came from, and it's doing good in the universe."

That word—*son*—always threw Tenthil off-guard when Richard used it.

Despite the challenges and dangers he'd faced over his life, despite the number of times he'd faced death without so much as a flutter in his stomach, Tenthil had been more anxious than ever about meeting Abella's parents when he'd finally been cleared to return to Earth with her those years ago.

There'd initially been some justified skepticism on Richard's behalf, but he and Abella's mother, Hannah, had been so supportive and accepting that Tenthil had barely been able to process it. He understood now that their acceptance had been so readily offered in large part because he'd brought home their daughter, their baby girl, after she'd been missing for four years. The local authorities had presumed Abella dead.

Tenthil would never have the words to express his appreciation for these people. He would never be able to tell them how much it meant to him to have a family—not only Abella, but a whole group of people who'd banded around him like a tribe.

Richard dried his hands, walked back to the counter, and leaned his hands atop it. He smiled at Tenthil.

Tenthil's brow furrowed slightly. Richard was a man who seemed to put most people at ease—likely a valuable trait when he sometimes described his job as *head torturer*—but conversation had never been Tenthil's forte.

What had Abella's advice been?

Ask people about themselves, but don't press. Keep it *casual.*

"How's...the office?" Tenthil asked.

"Oh, same as always. They bring me broken teeth, I fix them," Richard replied with a chuckle. "Think it's almost time though. Another year, maybe two, and I'm going to hang up my gloves and drill for good."

Tenthil wasn't sure how to reply. His experience with leaving his prior *career* had been somewhat complicated, and he had no desire to reflect upon it. "Sandwich was good."

"You don't have to stand around and make small talk with me, Tenthil. Abella's out back with the kids. Go on." Richard waved Tenthil toward the back door, his smile never faltering.

Tenthil readily accepted the offered escape route; he walked around the counter, crossed the kitchen, and pressed the button beside the glass door on the rear wall. The door slid open silently, granting him another taste of the fresh air.

He stepped out onto the porch. There was something satisfying about the sound of boots on wood that he'd never experienced with Arthos's concrete and tristeel, something primal.

For a moment, he looked out over the field behind the house and watched the long grass sway in the breeze. This wasn't his home planet, but this was his home. The place he and Abella had chosen *together*.

Their forever home, as Abella called it.

Abella and Hannah stood on the trimmed part of the grass with their backs to Tenthil as Abella posed and demonstrated a few dance steps to their five-year-old daughter, Zena. Lucian, their two-year-old son, leapt up with a little growl to chase a passing butterfly.

Tenthil walked down the steps to the grass as Zena mimicked Abella's dance moves. Though the girl lacked her mother's precision and discipline, she had natural grace and agility—neither of which saved her when her brother, attention fixed on the butterfly overhead, ran into her back.

The children tumbled to the ground.

"You ruined it, Luca!" Zena whined.

Lucian rolled over and sat up. He looked at his sister questioningly and then shifted his attention to the escaping butter-fly; he let out a distressed cry.

Hannah and Abella laughed.

Zena turned to her mother, sticking out her lower lip in a pout. "*Mommy*! He messed me up."

Abella caught her bottom lip between her teeth to hide her grin as she walked to Lucian. She knelt and picked the youngling up. "It was an accident, Zena. But you were doing so well!"

Lucian wrapped his arms around Abella's neck and lifted his silver eyes to meet Tenthil's. "Daddy!"

Tenthil closed the distance between himself and his family, smiling. He extended an arm and ruffled Lucian's black hair.

"Daddy! Daddy! Did you see me?" Zena asked as she ran toward him. "Did you see me dance like Mommy?"

He crouched and caught Zena in a hug as she leapt at him, smoothing back her silver hair. "I saw, little one."

Abella stood up and turned toward Tenthil, smiling softly. "You're home early."

Still holding Zena, Tenthil rose and met his mate's gaze, returning the smile. He shifted his daughter to the side, leaned forward, and kissed Abella. "Not early enough."

Desire sparked in Abella's eyes as Tenthil straightened, subtly altering the tone of her smile.

Zena giggled. "Daddy kissed Mommy."

Hannah laughed. "That's because your daddy loves your mommy very much." She placed a hand on Tenthil's shoulder and gave it a gentle squeeze. She was a slender woman, a little shorter than her daughter, and had clearly passed her physical grace to Abella. "It's nice to see you, Tenthil."

He nodded. During his old life, *it's nice to see you* was more likely to have been the preamble to a threat rather than a genuine greeting, but he trusted its sincerity from Hannah.

His eyes returned to Abella's. To that fire burning in her gaze.

"Looks like it's almost time to head to town," Hannah said. "Do you kiddos want to come with grandma and grandpa to pick up uncle Josh from the train station?"

"Yes!" Zena wiggled until Tenthil set her down on her feet. "Is uncle David coming, too, with our cousins?"

"They'll be here in the morning, dear."

"Yay!"

Hannah kissed Abella's cheek before taking Lucian from her. "We can pick up a treat on the way home too. We'll be sure to take our time." She winked at Tenthil.

"Be careful, Mom," Abella said. "It's going to be busy down there for the holiday."

Though Tenthil had never celebrated a holiday before coming to Earth, he'd grown to appreciate many of the celebrations, especially because they made Abella and the kids happy, but tomorrow's—United Galaxy Day—held special importance to him. He still thought the name was vague and a bit ridiculous, but Abella had explained it was a celebration of the treaties that had integrated her people with the rest of the universe and opened the United Terran Federation to trade and immigration with alien civilizations.

Those treaties had made their shared life on Earth possible.

"We'll be fine, and the kids will love seeing the Galaxy Day decorations that are being set up." Hannah held her hand out to Zena. "You two enjoy the quiet. It won't be long before you have your hands even fuller."

Tenthil's gaze dropped to Abella's stomach. She was only just beginning to show; they had months before the baby arrived, before their family grew a little larger. He slipped his arms around her middle from behind and drew her close, leaning his chin over her shoulder. He spread his fingers and trailed his palm over her belly.

He couldn't wait to meet their coming child, to witness the beauty of what their love had created once again. They hadn't realized they could reproduce with one another until their final medical exams during the relocation process; the scanner tech had casually asked about Abella's baby, shocking both of them into stunned silence.

The mutative compound the Consortium used to make people's bodies adapt to new environments had caused more changes in Tenthil and Abella than seemed possible—their bodies had adapted to one another. They'd become compatible in a way for which they'd never dared hope, in a way they would never have imagined.

"Come on, Zena," Hannah said softly. "Let's get grandpa out of the kitchen before he starts munching."

"Bye, Daddy! Bye, Mommy!" Zena waved. As she walked away, she looked up at Hannah. "Is uncle Josh bringing his girlfriend?"

Hannah chuckled. "I believe he is."

Lucian looked at Tenthil and Abella over Hannah's shoulder and waggled his little fingers in a wave.

Once Hannah and the kids were out of sight, Abella covered Tenthil's hand with her own and turned her face toward him, brushing her lips across his cheek.

"Hi," she said.

"Hi," he echoed, holding her a little tighter. "Missed you."

Abella tipped her head against his. "I missed you too."

They stood together, silent, relishing one another's presence as they basked in the clear, warm sunshine. The whispers of rustling leaves and grass flowed around them on the breeze.

"Are you happy, Tenthil?" Abella asked after a while.

He frowned and guided her to turn toward him, searching her face. "Do you need to ask?"

She lowered her eyes and shrugged. "I just need to know... is this the life you would've chosen for yourself?"

"No."

She looked up at him and frowned. "No?"

Tenthil slipped an arm behind her, pressed his forearm along her spine, and cupped the back of her head, fingers twining in her hair. He swept her into a low dip. She gasped and grabbed fistfuls of his shirt. He dropped his other hand to her ass as he pressed his lips over hers. He slid his tongue—already coated in sweet venom—into her mouth and breathed her in, letting Abella wash over his senses. His eyelids fluttered shut.

Abella moaned, clutching him closer as she lifted her leg and hooked it around his hip, kissing him fervently in return.

When he finally pulled back, he stared down into his mate's beautiful, half-lidded eyes and smiled. "It's infinitely better."

AUTHOR'S NOTE

Thank you so much for taking a chance with us on this new journey and checking out our new series, The Infinite City! We really hope you enjoyed *Silent Lucidity*.

We had such a blast writing this book, in part because the characters, Tenthil and Abella (while a little different from their original iterations), are characters Rob and I used to role-play years ago in a text-based fantasy RPG. They've always been favorites of ours, and we hoped to some day write their story, and we finally did! We never imagined they'd be written in this type of setting, but it fit so perfectly for them, and they most definitely won't be the last characters we bring over.

It was a little sad to come to the end of Tenthil and Abella's story, but we're so excited to delve more into this setting. We had so much fun building this world—a mixture of science fiction and fantasy with a dash of cyberpunk—in large part because it is so different from our Kraken Series. It was refreshing to explore something new.

And if you haven't already guessed, the next book, titled *Shielded Heart*, will be featuring our sexy, three-eyed sedhi forger, 'Alkorin'!

And if you really enjoyed *Silent Lucidity* and have a moment to spare, please consider leaving us a review. They are also much appreciated!

Be to follow us on Facebook and/or join our Facebook

Reader Group to see all the extras including updates, artwork, fanart, snippets, and cover reveals. Also subscribe to our newsletter for a direct way to see what is going on with us monthly—sales, new releases, and more.

ALSO BY TIFFANY ROBERTS

THE INFINITE CITY

Entwined Fates

Silent Lucidity

Shielded Heart

Vengeful Heart

Untamed Hunger

Savage Desire

Tethered Souls

THE KRAKEN

Treasure of the Abyss

Jewel of the Sea

Hunter of the Tide

Heart of the Deep

Rising from the Depths

Fallen from the Stars

Lover from the Waves

THE SPIDER'S MATE TRILOGY

Ensnared

Enthralled

Bound

THE VRIX

The Weaver

The Delver

The Hunter

<u>THE CURSED ONES</u>

<u>His Darkest Craving</u>

<u>His Darkest Desire</u>

<u>ALIENS AMONG US</u>

<u>Taken by the Alien Next Door</u>

<u>Stalked by the Alien Assassin</u>

<u>Claimed by the Alien Bodyguard</u>

Saved by the Alien Crime Boss

<u>STANDALONE TITLES</u>

<u>Claimed by an Alien Warrior</u>

<u>Dustwalker</u>

<u>Escaping Wonderland</u>

<u>Yearning For Her</u>

<u>The Warlock's Kiss</u>

<u>Ice Bound: Short Story</u>

<u>ISLE OF THE FORGOTTEN</u>

<u>Make Me Burn</u>

<u>Make Me Hunger</u>

<u>Make Me Whole</u>

<u>Make Me Yours</u>

<u>VALOS OF SONHADRA COLLABORATION</u>

Tiffany Roberts - Undying

Tiffany Roberts - Unleashed

<u>VENYS NEEDS MEN COLLABORATION</u>

Tiffany Roberts - To Tame a Dragon

Tiffany Roberts – To Love a Dragon

ABOUT THE AUTHOR

Tiffany Roberts is the pseudonym for Tiffany and Robert Freund, a husband and wife writing duo. The two have always shared a passion for reading and writing, and it was their dream to combine their mighty powers to create the sorts of books they want to read. They write character driven sci-fi and fantasy romance, creating happily-ever-afters for the alien and unknown.

Sign up for our Newsletter!
Check out our social media sites and more!
http://www.authortiffanyroberts.com